THE TEXAN'S CONTRACT MARRIAGE

BY
SARA ORWIG

Published in Great Britain 2013
by Mills & Boon, an imprint of Harlequin (UK) Limited,
Eton House, 18-24 Paradise Road, Richmond, Surrey TW9 1SR

© Sara Orwig 2013

ISBN: 978 0 263 90479 6
ebook ISBN: 978 1 472 00618 9

51-0713

Harlequin (UK) policy is to use papers that are natural, renewable and
recyclable products and made from wood grown in sustainable forests. The
logging and manufacturing processes conform to the legal environmental
regulations of the country of origin.

Printed and bound in Spain
by Blackprint CPI, Barcelona

Sara Orwig lives in Oklahoma. She has a patient husband who will take her on research trips anywhere from big cities to old forts. She is an avid collector of Western history books. With a master's degree in English, Sara has written historical romance, mainstream fiction and contemporary romance. Books are beloved treasures that take Sara to magical worlds, and she loves both reading and writing them.

To David with love

One

Marek Rangel glanced at his watch and pushed aside the papers in front of him. It was the morning of the second day of April, a sunny, spring day. Two minutes until his appointment with the opera singer. He had no idea why Camille Avanole had requested to meet with him or even how she had gotten through to his private line. He didn't attend the opera and it wasn't on the list of charities of his family's foundation. He had been tempted to refuse to see her, but, out of courtesy, he had decided he would meet her briefly.

He gazed around his corner office on the twenty-second floor in the building that was headquarters for his company, Rangel Energy, Inc. His secretary was to interrupt them if Ms. Avanole ran over the allotted thirty minutes he had agreed upon.

A light knock on the door brought him to his feet.

His secretary thrust her head into the room. "Camille Avanole is here."

"Tell her to come in," he said, stepping away from his oversize antique mahogany desk.

A vivacious black-haired woman approached him with her hand extended. A smile revealed white, perfect teeth; she had a sparkle in her enormous, thickly lashed blue eyes. The plain black dress she wore with a black scarf wrapped casually below her neck was striking. She had an inviting presence, as if she were about to share a delightful surprise. Suddenly, Marek's interest stirred.

"Mr. Rangel," she said. "I'm Camille Avanole."

Her warm hand was soft, yet her handshake was firm. At the moment of contact, he was jolted by an electric response, an intense awareness that he had not felt with any woman since he had lost his fiancée. Realizing he was staring, he released her hand.

"Please have a seat."

Marek focused on her interesting walk. As she crossed the room, he noticed her tiny waist. Her beauty had to be an asset to her career.

"Just call me Marek," he said, certain this meeting would be brief and he would never see her again.

Two antique velvet wingback chairs stood in front of the mahogany desk. Marek sat down facing her. She crossed long, shapely legs that had to be the best-looking legs on the opera circuit.

"Are you in Dallas for a performance or is this your home?" he asked politely, noticing she had the largest eyes he had ever seen. Striking, spellbinding eyes.

"I'm back in Dallas this spring for a performance I'll have soon."

He had the feeling of being studied as intently as a bug under a microscope.

"So what is the mysterious reason you wanted to see me that we couldn't discuss on the phone?"

Her smile vanished and she straightened. He could add the word *compelling* to his description of her. He couldn't imagine her playing any part on stage except the star; she would steal the show even in the background. Even while sitting still, she exuded energy.

"You lost your brother and your fiancée a year ago this March. I'm sorry for your loss," she said.

"Thank you," he replied stiffly, waiting and wondering why she had brought that up.

"I knew your brother," she said quietly.

Surprised, he focused on her. "How's that?"

"We met at a New Year's Eve party. You had a very charming brother."

"Yes, Kern was charismatic, fun," Marek said, his mind racing. Had she and Kern secretly married? He dismissed that notion immediately. Kern would have told him. "Let's cut to the chase here. What does your knowing my brother have to do with your asking for an appointment to talk to me?"

"I'm going to give you a shock and I'm trying to lead into it instead of just hitting you with it all at once."

"At this point, I'm ready for you to hit me with it," he said, unable to fathom what she might be about to tell him.

She pulled out a picture to show him. He looked at a baby boy with big dark eyes who was smiling. Marek's breath left him as if he had received a blow to his midsection. The picture looked like dozens he had seen at his parents' home. The baby had big brown eyes like his brother, tangled black hair, the same color his brother's had been, the same color as his own. Marek looked up. "Who is he?"

"I think you already know," Camille answered quietly. "He's my son. Your brother was his father."

Even though that was what he had already guessed, it was another hard blow to his midsection to hear her declare it.

"I can see a resemblance, but Kern would have told me. I'm sorry, I find this difficult to believe. It could be a coincidence he looks like my brother. How old is this child?"

"He's six months old now. Noah was born October 4, last year."

"Six months old," Marek repeated, dazed. He stared at the picture in disbelief, an icy chill setting in as he wondered if this was a play for money. "Kern never said a word about knowing you. He would have said something to me."

"We met at a New Year's Eve party over a year ago," she said in her silky soprano voice. "Kern charmed me. We had mutual friends, so I felt safe leaving with him. It was an exception in my very structured life—two nights of passion that I'd never had before and never since. We used protection, but I still got pregnant. I've managed to keep the publicity low-key. It hasn't been difficult to keep the baby out of the spotlight. An opera performer—at least at my current level—is not the same as a movie star. I have only recently had more success and more fame."

"I find it difficult to believe this baby really is Kern's."

"He is. You can have a paternity test. The DNA should give you an answer."

Marek could not stop looking at the picture of the baby. "What's his name?"

"Noah Avanole."

"I'm still amazed Kern didn't tell me."

"He said he was going to tell you, but he probably never had the chance."

"You're right." Unable to sit still, Marek stood and walked to the window to stare at the picture while questions raced through his thoughts. "Kern had a baby. How long before the flight did he know?" Marek asked.

"The evening before he left I told Kern I was pregnant, so he didn't know until the day before the plane crash."

Marek drew a deep breath. "Was this on his mind when he flew to Denver?"

"I'm sure it was," she answered.

Marek felt as if he had had another blow. A year ago in March, his brother had had a flight to a horse sale in Kansas City. Marek had intended to fly to Denver to pick up his fiancée, who had been there for a wedding. Instead, Kern had offered to pick her up after leaving Kansas City. On the way home they had been caught in an unexpected storm. When the plane had crashed, both had been killed. Now he wondered how much his brother's thoughts and attention had been distracted by the news from Camille. Marek continued staring at the baby's picture. He remembered Camille and turned to find her sitting quietly.

"Thank you for telling me," Marek said, crossing the room. "I'll think about the paternity test. Since you're telling me now, I assume you want me to do something. We might as well get to the point of this meeting."

"I've had time to think about this. I can support Noah. What I want is for Noah to know the Rangels. Kern was such a cowboy. I want Noah to have an appreciation for ranching, so he will understand his father better. I think he should know his father's family."

Marek had received one surprise after another. If she really didn't want money, he would be shocked. He figured this was a ploy to get him to let down his guard.

"I'll have to think about this and talk to my attorney."

She smiled. "I hope you don't need an attorney. I felt you should know, and there was no good way to tell you on the phone or by email. Even in person, it's a shock. But what's done is done."

"The crash was a year ago last month. Why did you wait until now to tell me?"

"I was busy caring for Noah and undecided what to do.

I was away from Dallas, and I wanted to tell you in person. I knew I would be back. Also, it's given me time to really think this through. You could help by being a father figure for your nephew, too."

Marek drew a deep breath at the thought of the responsibility she wanted him to take. Yet if this baby was Kern's, a part of Kern, Marek wanted to know him and watch him grow up. A part of Kern—the thought twisted his insides. He looked at the picture again. Why hadn't Kern told him? He probably had planned to when he returned from the flight.

"Kern never knew this baby. You'll take good care of him. Maybe it would be better if I just stepped back out of the way," Marek said stiffly. He still harbored a kernel of doubt that this was Kern's baby and expected her to make an effort to pull him back into being part of the baby's life.

"I hope you'll come see him. Of course, what you do now is your choice. And I'll take the best care of him I possibly can. If you ever want to see him, you'll be able to contact me."

"That's good to hear. Do you have parents who are living?"

"Yes. My parents live in Saint Louis." She smiled, remaining poised. "Your brother told me how different the two of you were. I supposed I'd hoped you would react the way Kern did, but you're not Kern."

She reached into her purse to withdraw a piece of paper. She held it out to him. "Your brother sent me an email, and I printed it out. This is a copy of it. I've made an effort to preserve it for Noah."

For the first time, Marek began to believe what she had told him. He was reluctant to read the email. He was certain his life was about to take another unexpected turn. Drawing a deep breath, Marek quickly scanned the message.

Camille:

When I return from Denver, we'll go to dinner. I want to be with you when Noah is born. Perfect name. I can't get used to the fact that I'm going to be a dad. Super-mega-duper! I'm overwhelmed, overjoyed. I want to be a big part of his life. Already love him. I want to be with you. My deepest gratitude for telling me. I'll call tomorrow night. We didn't plan this. Miracles happen. I'm overjoyed.

Kern

Marek felt weak in the knees. This was Kern's message. Marek looked up at Camille, who gazed back steadily. He was certain now that she had given birth to Kern's baby. There was another Rangel in the world. Until this moment, Marek hadn't fully believed the baby was Kern's. Now he couldn't doubt it.

Marek felt another tight squeeze to his chest, this time as if his heart had been grabbed by a giant fist. He missed Kern terribly, and this brought back all the incredible pain of his loss. With thoughts of Kern came remembrance of Jillian. He hated the knot in his throat. Making an effort, he struggled to get his emotions under control before he looked up or spoke. Finally, he raised his head and handed back the letter.

"That definitely sounds like my brother. Super-mega-duper—one of his favorite expressions. Thank you for showing me the message."

"That's fine. That's a copy. If you want it, keep it."

"Thanks," he said, dropping the paper on his desk. "I'll take it to show my sister. I would like a paternity test just to settle any questions that would ever arise. This is Kern's baby. That message is Kern talking. There's no mistake."

Smiling, looking happier, she nodded. "We can do a paternity test. I expected you to request one."

"This has been almost as big a shock as if you told me I

have a son. My brother and I were close. I assume you haven't contacted my sister because I would have heard from her."

"No, I didn't because in what little time we were together, your brother talked far more about you."

"She's seven years older than I am. Kern and I were closer, but she'll want to know about Noah."

"If you and your sister decide you want to see him, we can arrange that."

He nodded. He felt as if his breath had been knocked out of him. He needed to think about the baby and make decisions about what he wanted to do.

"You won't always live in Dallas, will you?" he asked.

"I've only been in Texas three times in my life. I'll leave here the end of June. I'll be singing in New Mexico in August, so I'll stay there."

"And you'll take the baby with you."

"Yes, of course, but I still hope that he can get to know you and your family as he grows. If he does, you would be a good father figure for him, I'm sure. Kern would have been a wonderful one."

"You could have gone on with your life and never told me," Marek said, looking into her wide crystal-blue eyes. "There's no way I would have found out. Now you'll have to share Noah."

She studied him intently. "It wouldn't have been right. I couldn't do it. I thought about doing that because it would have been infinitely easier, but I love Noah and want what's best for him. The day will come when he'll want to know his father. Since he can't do that, he will want to know his father's family. I truly think you'll be a good influence. The ranching aspect has to be good for a growing boy. If he gets to know you and know ranching, I'll feel as if he knows part of his father."

"I agree with that, and I'm glad you made that decision,"

Marek said in a tight voice, trying to control his emotional reaction to her statement. "Will you be in town if I want to get in touch with you?"

"Yes. In June I perform here in Dallas. Then in July I'll go to Santa Fe for my August performance. After that I'll go home to Saint Louis through September so I can be with my family. I have a voice teacher here in Dallas that I like very much, so I may be in Texas more often than I have been in the past."

"You have a busy schedule. Thank you for calling me. You didn't have to share with us at all," he said again, still amazed she had done so.

"At first I was shocked by the news of my pregnancy. I thought it would end my career, and I was torn up over trying to figure out what to do. I felt uncertain about telling him. We only knew each other that one weekend. But the more I thought about it, the more I wanted Kern and the Rangels to be part of my baby's life."

As she walked to the door, Marek accompanied her. When she paused, he turned to face her, once again briefly caught in the blue of her eyes. She was a beautiful woman, and he understood why his brother had been attracted to her. "I'll talk to my sister. Also, I'll let my parents know. Thank you again for telling me," Marek said.

"I'm sorry for both your losses, your brother and your fiancée."

"Thank you," he replied stiffly. "I'll be in touch after I've talked to my sister."

She nodded. "I'm glad to have finally met you and glad you know about Noah. I'm sure I'll hear from you."

He watched her walk away and turned to go back into his office with his thoughts swirling. How much had Kern had his mind on the fact that he was going to be a father instead of concentrating on his flying? Had that news been a factor in Kern's crash?

And another baby in the family, and this time not only a little boy, but Kern's baby. He thought how delightful his two little nieces were. Now they would have the girls and Kern's little boy.

Marek canceled his appointments and called his pilot to fly back to the ranch to talk to the person he had been close to all his life.

Two hours later, Marek stood in the barn while his ranch foreman repaired a stall. Jess Grayson had pushed his battered, wide-brimmed brown hat back on his head and had his sleeves rolled high. While Jess drove in a nail, Marek held a board in place. "You can have a paternity test even with Kern gone."

"I know I can and I will, but I don't need to. That message is Kern's. It sounds like him. The baby looks like him. I've asked for a paternity test just to be sure."

"Good. So what are you going to do? Have you told Ginny?"

"Not yet. Wanted to talk to you first," he said, looking at Jess's weathered skin, which was the color of cowhide except for a pale band below his hairline where his hat shaded his skin from the sun.

"Ginny's family. I'm not."

"You might as well be. Your opinion still counts. I was all set to walk out of there and never look back when she pulled out Kern's message. I want you to read it when you finish nailing this board."

As soon as the board was in place, Marek fished the paper out of his pocket, unfolded it and handed it to Jess.

After a moment Jess looked up to meet Marek's gaze.

"Super-mega-duper," Jess repeated. "That's Kern." He shook his head as he returned the paper. "An opera star."

"A rising one. I don't know if she's a star yet. At this point, I don't know anything about her. Except I'm sure she's telling the truth about the baby."

"You really think she's not after money?" Jess asked, picking up another board and setting it in place below the first one. Marek stepped closer to help.

"She doesn't act like she is. Doesn't matter, really. Since I know this is Kern's baby, I can't walk away. He wouldn't if this were my baby, and I can't with Kern's."

"Even if he didn't love the lady?"

"Even if. Besides, you read that message. I would bet the ranch Kern was running through his mind how he could get her to marry him."

"Might be right. So you want this baby in the family?"

Watching Jess hammer, Marek thought a long time. "Yes, I do. Suppose he's a lot like Kern or even a little like Kern? It would drive me nuts to think a little boy was out there, Kern's son, who looked and acted like Kern and we didn't know him and didn't care. I can't do that. She wants us in his life. She wants him to have an appreciation for ranching. I can't argue against either of those."

"Then you've made your decision. Tell Ginny."

"I guess I have to."

"Frankly, I'd kind of like to see the little fellow myself."

"I'll call Ginny and then I'll call Camille and see if I can arrange to see her again, which will be easy to do. Per Kern's usual taste, she's a beauty," he said, remembering his first impression of her. "Also, she said she'd like me to be a father figure for Noah."

"That may be difficult if she doesn't live around here."

"True. She's leaving Dallas in July and going to Santa

Fe. She has a busy schedule. Until then, I'd like to know this child."

"Have you called your parents?"

Marek nodded. "I'm going to call to tell them. I want this baby to know the Rangels and us to know him. I'll go call Ginny. Thanks, Jess."

"You might get a little bit of Kern back," Jess said somberly.

"I'd like that, Jess, but I'm scared that's too much to hope for. I'll let you know what she says." Marek jogged to the house and inside, letting the door swing shut behind him.

While he called his sister, he remembered Camille—her vivid looks, her energetic presence. Good genes with Kern's genes. Should be a good combination. He talked for ten minutes, chatting briefly with each of his little nieces before his sister returned to the phone.

"Ginny, I have some news that will shock you. I can come back to Dallas to tell you or I can tell you on the phone, but you're in for a giant shock."

"You have to tell me now, Marek. Good grief, after that I can't wait for you to get to Dallas. What is it?"

"Do you know who Camille Avanole is?"

There was a moment's silence. "I don't think so. I can't think of a single Camille I know."

"Do you recognize the name?"

"If you don't tell me what you're getting at, Marek, I'm going to reach through this phone and grab you."

"Ginny, she called me and said she wanted to talk to me," he said, recalling the sparks he'd felt when they had touched while shaking hands—something he hadn't felt with a woman since the loss of Jillian. "She knew Kern," he continued. "Camille and Kern went out on a weekend over a year and a half ago. She got pregnant with Kern's baby."

"Kern had a baby?" Ginny's voice sounded faint and breathless.

"Yes, he did. He found out she was pregnant the day before he flew to Denver."

"Oh, my word. Do you suppose that's why he lost control and crashed? Was he thinking about the baby? Is it really Kern's? Maybe it's not and this is one of those women who try to take advantage—"

"Ginny," Marek stated firmly. "Listen to me. She has a note Kern sent her right before the flight. It's Kern's message. It sounds like him. She gave me a copy of it, and I'll show it to you."

"Marek, I do need to sit. This is a shock. A baby."

"A little boy named Noah. He's six months old. I have dinner with Camille tomorrow night to talk about the future," he said, realizing he was looking forward to seeing her again. Another first since losing Jillian. Maybe the numbness was wearing away. Or maybe it was Camille's beauty and captivating presence that had stirred his reactions. "I can't turn my back on that baby. I know he's Kern's son. She had a picture, and he looks like Kern."

"We have to know this little boy. Will she let us? Is she famous? You asked if I know her."

"She's in opera. I've looked her up. She's young. Only twenty-five. Her résumé is impressive to me," he said, thinking her looks were just as impressive.

"Opera? How did she get with Kern?"

"A New Year's Eve party where they had mutual friends."

"No wonder I didn't recognize the name. I'm country. What are you going to do?"

"I don't know. I'm thinking about options. I'll let you know."

"We have to keep this baby in our lives. If he's Kern's baby, we can't cut him out. Does she live in Texas?"

"No. She'll leave in July and take him with her."

"Have you told Jess?"

"Yes. He'd like to see the baby, too. I guess we're all hoping for a bit of Kern in our lives again."

"Wouldn't that be wonderful? You've given me a shock. You better break it gently to Mom and Dad."

"I will. I'll call Camille and see what I can set up to see him. I'll let you know. We'll both see him, I promise you."

He told her goodbye and called his parents, spending the next half hour breaking the news to them and catching up on their news.

Finished with family calls, he phoned Camille. In minutes he had plans to pick Camille up the next day and take her to Houston for dinner.

"You're not going out with him," Stephanie Avanole said, glaring at her sister.

"Yes, I am. I've given this a lot of thought. We've talked about it. He's Noah's relative," Camille replied, wiping her forehead and the back of her neck as she walked away from the treadmill. "I know you don't feel the way I do about this, but I think the Rangels have a right to see their nephew."

"They'll want to take him from you or tell you what to do with him. They're not going to ignore him. These are wealthy, powerful people, accustomed to getting their way. You said Kern said his older brother ran the family after he was grown. That he was much more serious than Kern."

"Tomorrow night Marek Rangel can talk and I'll listen. Stephanie, he's had a terrible loss and this is a shock."

"I still say you'll be sorry. You should never have told them about Noah, much less have agreed to go out with Marek Rangel tomorrow night. He's a tough cowboy and tougher businessman. I've heard a few people talk. He's had big losses—his fiancée as well as his only brother. He doesn't sound like the lighthearted, I-don't-care type."

"I had to tell him."

"I'm warning you," Stephanie said, frowning and placing her hands on her hips, "you'll regret this day. Marek Rangel will want to be part of Noah's life."

"I think he's entitled to be. I don't think he's any threat to me at all."

"You'll never convince me that this is good."

"Then you have a closed mind about it. He's not an ogre," Camille replied, remembering a handsome man with troubled brown eyes, a man who appeared hard, closed in a shell, inscrutable and preoccupied. A man who was nothing like his charming, devil-may-care brother.

Late afternoon Wednesday she dressed carefully in a deep blue dress with a vee neckline and long sleeves. Hoping to look successful, attractive and poised, she twisted and combed her hair to one side of her head, fastening it with a blue scarf. She had butterflies in the pit of her stomach and she didn't know why, unless deep down, she was more worried about what Marek might want than she had told her sister.

The moment he arrived at her house, dressed in a navy suit, a white Stetson and boots, he looked like the successful Texas rancher that he was. He also appeared powerful, commanding and threatening to her future. Stephanie's warnings haunted her.

In spite of the veiled look on his face, he was handsome enough to cause a jump in her pulse. For a fleeting moment she had a jittery dance of nerves and wanted to reach up to pat her hair. With a deep breath, her confidence returned.

"Come in," she invited, stepping back, feeling as if she had stepped into a new world where her life would never be the same. "Noah is still awake."

Two

As he entered a hallway his boot heels scraped on the polished oak floor. To his right through a wide-open archway, he glimpsed a piano in the corner of a large room with a hardwood floor and a brown leather sofa. To one side stood a large wooden desk. Marek drew a deep breath. An uncustomary nervousness plagued him, and he hoped he hid it. "I would like to see Noah," he answered in a voice that deepened and sounded strange to his ears.

She closed the door and motioned with a wave of her hand. "Come with me to the nursery. Both my sisters are here."

As he walked beside her, his pulse quickened while uncertainty grew with each step. "My nieces aren't babies any longer. I've forgotten how to deal with a baby. I don't remember much about them."

She laughed, a soft, delightful sound that made him relax slightly. "I'll admit, I had moments before he was born when

I felt terrified and overwhelmed. I've found out that you learn very fast when you have a baby to care for."

He placed a hand on her arm. "I'm sorry you were alone when he was born. I'm sorry Kern didn't live to be there. He would have been a huge support for you. I'll try to do what I think Kern would have wanted, but I can't take his place. Kern was unique."

"I hope you will, and it'll be wonderful if you do," she said.

He followed her into a playroom in shades of blue with paintings of animals hanging on the walls. Two other attractive women faced him. One was a pretty brunette in a red sweater and matching slacks, who stood looking at him with curious blue-green eyes. "Ashley, meet Marek Rangel, Noah's uncle. Marek, this is my sister Ashley Avanole." Camille turned slightly to another woman, who bore little resemblance to Camille or Ashley.

He was momentarily startled by the hostility in her cold gaze and assumed she didn't want him involved in Noah's life. "Stephanie, meet Marek Rangel. Marek, this is my sister Stephanie."

Marek greeted her, lost in thinking about being an uncle. His gaze shifted to the baby in a tire-shaped cushion on the floor.

Camille swept the baby up and held him, smiling and speaking softly to him. "Marek, meet your nephew, Noah Avanole." Noah waved his arms, blowing bubbles. She held him out to Marek, who took him carefully. He pulled the baby close, cradling him in his arms and looking down into twinkling, wide brown eyes that were filled with mischief as Noah blew bubbles and drooled. Marek felt weak-kneed as he had a moment of déjà vu. It was as if he were looking into Kern's eyes after he had played a joke on Marek. How could a little baby look like a grown man? If Marek had had a doubt before who had fathered this baby, it vanished now.

"He's Kern," he whispered without realizing he was speaking aloud. For a moment, he had a flash of the future, thinking this child and Ginny's girls would be the children in his life. Since the loss of Jillian, he never expected to marry or have a family. His arm tightened slightly around Noah. He felt a warmth toward the baby while they looked into each other's eyes; it was as if a tangible bond formed, which Marek knew was foolishness. From the first glance there was no way he could keep from loving this baby.

"He does seem to have a resemblance, but I'm going from memory and I thought maybe it was my imagination," Camille replied.

"There's more than a physical resemblance. He's like Kern. Is he always this happy?"

"Yes, he is," Camille answered, smiling and stepping closer to look at her son with Marek. "He's a wonderful baby."

Babbling unintelligible sounds, Noah blew more bubbles and Marek's smile broadened. "He's so tiny."

"He'll grow. He's gained weight and gotten much bigger since his birth." She gave him a moment longer. "If you're ready, I'll take him and we can go."

Marek handed Noah to her, brushing her arms and catching a whiff of an enticing jasmine scent. He hated to turn loose Noah, whose brown eyes gazed intently at him.

"And you're his nanny?" he asked Ashley, glancing at her and trying to politely include her.

"Yes. When he was born, I had to learn fast. Camille hired a nurse for the first month, so she taught me quite a bit. Being his nanny right now is a good job to have."

"And I help manage my sister's career," Stephanie interjected. "We love Noah very much."

Her tone was polite, but Marek's caution returned. Her glacial dark blue eyes held a warning, which reemphasized what he guessed was worry about his claims on Noah. For the first time, it occurred to Marek he might not ever have easy access to his nephew.

It was obvious the sisters were not in agreement about sharing Noah with his paternal relatives.

"It was nice to meet you," Ashley stated. Stephanie merely nodded perfunctorily, and Marek was certain about her feelings toward him. At the door he couldn't resist turning to glance back at Noah, who was playing with a rattle, kicking his legs and enjoying himself.

Marek's glance rested only briefly on Stephanie, who glared at him. Her mouth was set in a hard line. Marek followed Camille into the hall.

"I take it your sister Stephanie doesn't share your feelings about allowing Noah to know the paternal side of the family. I couldn't get a reading on what Ashley felt."

"Don't worry about Stephanie. Noah is my child, and I want you to know him. I told you, I want him to know the Rangels and ranching. I want you as an influence in his life. Ashley is all right with letting you see Noah."

"I'm glad," he said, "because we all want to know him. It's startling to me to look at him. There's something about him that really resembles Kern."

As they walked toward the front, he caught another whiff of the perfume she wore. When they passed the room with the piano, he glanced inside. "Is this where you practice your voice lessons?"

"Yes. It's an office of sorts, too. Stephanie wanted an office this spring to work on taxes. Noah disturbs her sometimes, so this room is the farthest from the nursery. I study languages every day, trying to improve my grasp of Italian, French and German. Wherever we go, I take my own furniture, so that's why we have such a minimal amount. I like having my own bed. But I rent the piano. I can't practice in a hotel."

"Good idea. I don't blame you. It sounds like it works out well," Marek said, thinking she must not have much time in her life for Noah.

In minutes they were in his black limousine, headed toward the airport. He sat facing her. "I feel as if my life is changing and I don't have control over the changes," he said. "That's unusual. I'd like to work out something before you leave Texas. Something that's permanent as far as seeing him periodically," he added. He'd like to see more of her. She interested him and seemed different from other women he had known.

"We may have to have those lawyers yet," she replied.

"Let's try to work it out between us," he urged, thinking she had a flair for the dramatic in her manner and her dress. Once again, she stood out with her midnight hair secured with a blue scarf and her deep blue dress that emphasized her lush curves and narrow waist. Her startling pale blue eyes were a vivid contrast to her thick, black lashes.

He had never associated with women in show business, much less in opera. She was an unknown in many ways. His gaze rested on her full, enticing lips. What would it be like to kiss her? His question startled him. He hadn't noticed any women in a personal way since losing Jillian, but Camille was bringing him back into the world without any effort to do so. She had been forthright, businesslike about Noah. Yet his physical response to her was becoming more personal. "I have a lot of resources. I have a plane available at all times. Most of the time I can come and go as I please. We should be able to adjust schedules," he said.

"We'll try. I might be out of the United States some of the time."

"Let's take it as it comes," he suggested, wondering whether they could ever work out an acceptable plan for sharing Noah. "Tell me about your life," he said, his curiosity about her growing. "I'm sorry I don't already know about you, but I haven't been into opera."

She smiled at him. "Then I believe you are in for a treat, but that's because I love it. You will either love it or not care for it at all. To me it's the most beautiful music possible."

Her enthusiasm made him smile. "So you've always dreamed of this career?"

"Yes, actually. I started singing early and began voice lessons when I was young. Now, looking back, it seems like forever."

He listened while she talked about growing up in Saint Louis and singing, and he wondered about her past. When she paused in her talk, he leaned closer.

"Have you ever been in love?"

"Not really. I thought I was in college, but it was never that serious. I really haven't had much time for a social life since."

"Maybe you should take some time."

She laughed. "With a baby now? I don't think this is the time. There's no room for romance in my life. A baby plus an opera career—those would send anyone running."

"Maybe running with you, but not from you—take another look in your mirror."

"Thank you," she said, smiling at him. "Seriously, I haven't given a lot of thought to what I'll do in the future. I need to start looking into schools for Noah."

Marek smiled. "You have time."

"It flies past, and I may pick a school where he has to go on a waiting list."

Marek's thoughts shifted to Noah. He had to think of a way to keep the baby in the family. He couldn't sit by while she went to France or Germany or Italy for a year and took Noah with her.

He took Camille to a quiet, elegant dinner club in Houston. The decor was dark blue, with dark walnut paneling and dimmed crystal chandeliers. It was a place he had gone often, and he felt they would not be disturbed by fans or his friends, but he had forgotten about the dancing. There was a small dance floor; out of courtesy he felt he needed to ask her to dance. He remembered holding Jillian in his arms, laughing at something she had said. He didn't want to dance with this woman who was so alive and who made him feel so alive.

He realized he had ceased talking during dinner.

"You're thinking about your fiancée," Camille remarked. "Again, I'm sorry for your loss. It's understandable for you to think about her. My guess is that you both came here to eat occasionally."

"You're right. Sorry if I got distracted. That's past, but there are moments it comes rushing back. Would you like to dance?"

"You don't have to dance," she said, smiling. "This is fine."

Relieved, appreciating her understanding, he wanted to accept her reply and forget dancing, but he had to pick up the pieces and go on with life. He stood. "C'mon. It'll do me good to get out there and move around."

It was the first time he had danced since he had been with Jillian. He took a deep breath and focused on Camille, smiling at her.

"You really don't have to dance if you'd rather not," she said gently, startling him.

"It shows that much?" he asked, focusing on her more intently.

"Maybe a little. I can also imagine," she added gently.

"Do you like to dance?" he asked, leading her to the dance floor.

"Yes, but if you want to stop, I'll understand why."

He took her lightly into his arms. "You're sensitive to other people," he said, studying her large, thickly lashed eyes. "You look beautiful tonight," he added, and she smiled.

"Thank you."

"I mean it." As he danced the first few steps, he had another moment when pain stabbed him. He missed Jillian, her slender body, her laughter. He focused on Camille and the moment passed. "I just know how I would feel if I were in your position."

"You never saw Kern any other time?"

"No. The weekend I met your brother was the only time I was with him. While I had a wonderful time with him, we really weren't that close."

"Kern was the embodiment of charm and fun." He realized she was as easy to dance with as she was to talk to. Her perfume was enticing, and the low vee of her neckline revealed the beginning of full, soft curves.

"Do you want a bigger family—a husband, maybe a sibling for Noah?"

"Yes, at some distant future point in my life. But right now I have a career to pursue, and it's on the rise. I have a baby to take care of and he's most important."

A fast number began, and, in seconds, he was dancing with enthusiasm. It felt good to move, and he liked to watch her. She was an energetic, sensual dancer. While he moved, cares and heartaches dropped away and burdens lifted from his shoulders.

A samba followed and they continued dancing. He shrugged off his suit jacket and draped it over an empty chair at the edge of the dance floor. He looked at Camille's mass of black hair and wished she had left it loose. She was enticing, melting away some of his hurt and numbness. As the dance ended, he pulled her close to lean over in a dip.

When he gazed into her blue eyes, desire stirred, feelings that had ceased after his loss. Startled he swung Camille up, smiling at her.

The realization that he was beginning to get over his loss shocked him.

When a slow ballad started, he drew Camille into his arms to dance. "I have to admit, the dancing is fun. I haven't done this in a while. Maybe it's therapeutic."

"Actually, it probably is," she said. "Dancing is definitely good for me. It's relaxing, and you're extremely good at it."

"Thanks. You've made it easy for me," he said. Once again, he had a flash of awareness of her. He held her in his arms, and they gazed into each other's eyes. The moment changed, became personal. Feelings that had been dormant in him for over a year stirred again, stronger this time. He looked at her full, sensuous, curving lips.

The number ended, and they returned to the linen-covered table. By the time he sat facing her, his thoughts were partially on the baby again.

"Do you know your schedule for the rest of the year?"

"Yes. After Dallas, Santa Fe and Saint Louis, I leave for Budapest in October, and I will be there until December. Next March I will be in New York at the Met, where I'm not the lead but thrilled to perform."

"Budapest, New York—hell of a long way from Texas."

"I'm sorry, but that's my life at this point."

"I understand. We'll work on it as long as you want us to be part of his life. In the meantime, can we arrange a meeting where my sister can see Noah?"

Before Camille could answer, white china plates with greens were placed in front of them. When they were alone again, Camille set down her water goblet. "I'm sure we can work out a time for your sister to see Noah. Actually, the weekend is coming up. Saturday morning would be a good time for us. Mornings are better because Noah will be awake. He'll nap in the afternoon. I'll have my voice practice, and I schedule time regularly for exercise, but I won't stay with you anyway, so that won't matter."

"I'll let you know about Saturday morning. I need to run that past my sister because she has a family. I'd like to bring someone else with me, if I may. My ranch foreman has been with us all my life. He's like a member of the family to me, and he was to Kern. I'd like him to see Noah."

"Of course," she said, smiling warmly. "You're not exactly like I thought you'd be," she added, studying him. "You're not like Kern, either."

"Definitely not like Kern," he said. "So what did you expect?" Marek asked, amused and curious. When her cheeks turned pink, his curiosity grew. "You're blushing. Your opinion must have been not so great. Now I'm curious."

"You're more friendly than I thought you'd be," she said, her cheeks growing even more red. "I thought you would be like you were the first few minutes at your office."

He smiled. "I'll have to improve my image. I'll have to admit, I wasn't friendly at my office. I thought you wanted a donation for something to do with the opera."

She laughed, a light, inviting sound, making him want to cause her to laugh often.

Conversation shifted to other topics. For the next hour over dinner, he enjoyed her company and enjoyed being out for the evening with a beautiful woman again.

Later, when they returned to the dance floor, he found it was easier. He still thought of Jillian, still missed her badly, but he had better control of his emotions and he was happier about dancing. "I really would like to see Noah again before

Saturday. Is there anytime that would be convenient for me to drop by when he's awake?"

"Of course. Just call ahead. Come tomorrow when you want. I'll be home. I have a voice lesson, a workout and a French lesson, but I can break away briefly. We'll be happy to see you."

"When do you have free time?"

"I have some to be with Noah. There are moments my life is like everyone else's. We're all busy."

"Very well. I'll come in the morning if that's all right."

"It's fine. It might give Ashley a bit of a break. Stephanie will vanish with errands, so you won't cross paths with her."

"She feels that strongly about me," he said, shaking his head.

"She's just scared."

"She doesn't need to be afraid I'm taking your baby. I would never do that. No judge would let me anyway."

"Oh, one might. I think you have a lot of influence in this state."

"How I wish. Where was Noah born?"

"Oddly enough, I had a special performance here and he was born in Texas. I had excellent care. I was in a Dallas hospital."

Marek smiled. "So we have another Rangel who's a Texan. That would please Kern."

"I think it pleases you."

"Yes, it does," he said.

"I don't think I've mentioned it, but I named him Noah Kern Avanole. I hope you don't object."

"I'm glad you did. Did you tell Kern what you planned to name him?"

"Of course, and he was delighted."

"I'll bet he was. I'm still amazed he didn't call me. Usually Kern didn't keep things to himself. Noah Kern Avanole. Good name."

"Thank you. I thought so. Right now is a good time for everyone to see him. When I'm performing, I won't be as free."

"That's what I figured," Marek said, thinking she had a face and figure to have gone into movies instead of opera. They danced until she mentioned the time and said she had to get home.

They talked all the way during the flight back to Dallas and by the time he brought her to her condo door, he realized he had enjoyed the evening. Impulsively, he took her hand.

"I've enjoyed getting to know you. I still can't tell you how much I appreciate you sharing Noah with us. There aren't words for that."

"I'm glad you're happy about him and interested in him."

"I hope your sister stops worrying. I'll never try to take Noah from you."

"Stephanie will be all right. She's just scared right now because you can do more for him than we can. I don't think she understands how I feel as a mother, wanting him to know his father's family, to know ranching. That's important to me."

"I'm glad," he said lightly, leaning forward to brush a kiss on her cheek, catching the scent of her perfume again. Her skin was soft and smooth, and he was grateful to her for making the evening enjoyable. "I'll see you in the morning. I'll call before I come by."

"Fine," she said, smiling at him. She stepped inside and closed the door.

On the drive to the ranch, he had time to consider the evening. The vision of Camille dancing around him remained indelibly etched in memory. He thought about Noah and holding him in his arms. Camille would be in Santa Fe this summer, Budapest in the fall. How could he keep Noah in their lives in Texas when he would be far away with his mother? Noah was too tiny now to take him away from her for a long visit.

Saturday morning Camille showered and dressed in blue slacks and a matching shirt. As she pinned up her hair, Ashley stood watching her. "You've gone out with him three nights this week, and he's been here to see Noah every day. He's crazy about Noah."

"He'll be a good father figure for Noah," Camille remarked.

"I'm beginning to wonder whether Steph is right. Is Marek going to want to have custody of Noah? Or is there any chance part of it is he's coming to see you, too?"

Camille laughed. "No. He's interested in Noah." Her smile faded. "He's still having difficulty about losing his fiancée, although he seemed to get a grip on those feelings when we were dancing." She pulled a brush through more long strands of hair before pinning them up. "As far as Noah is concerned, Marek has told me repeatedly that he won't ever try to take Noah from me. I know he wants to be part of Noah's life, and I think he should be. I want Noah to be part of the Rangel family. He needs to know them. Marek can show him a cowboy's life."

"Some cowboy," Ashley said, laughing. "He's a billionaire."

"Ashley, he's a good guy. He truly likes the baby, and he's promised me he won't try to take him. We'll work out something everyone can live with."

"Let me have Noah before you have to change again," Ashley said, taking Noah from Camille. He went willingly, happy to be carried. Camille brushed a kiss on his cheek.

"I won't let anyone take him from us," Camille said quietly, feeling fairly certain Marek meant what he said. What little Kern had said about his brother indicated that he was a man of his word, yet that might have been the man Kern knew.

Thursday when Marek had come to see his nephew, she had watched him hold the baby and talk to him. All the hesitation and uncertainty Marek had shown that first time he had held Noah had disappeared. She left them alone for a time, and, when she returned, Marek was seated on the floor, holding Noah and talking to him about a large, brightly colored ball and rolling it around for him.

Marek had glanced at her and smiled, his attention quickly returning to Noah. She was constantly reminded of Marek's loss because he seemed cool and distant in many ways. She suspected he rarely saw her as anything more than Noah's mom, which, under the circumstances, was just as well.

"Camille, you haven't heard a word I've said to you," Ashley said as she finished changing Noah.

"Sorry, Ash, I was lost in thought about Marek."

"I can see why. He's a good-looking man. Even more so than his brother. I never really saw his brother in person, just pictures, so maybe that's not fair."

"He's more handsome, but he has none of the laid-back charm his younger brother did. He's far more serious."

"You each have serious issues to deal with—how Noah will be raised, plus the personal issues. Can you trust Marek and will he ever get over his loss? Maybe he's charming when there's nothing at stake."

"You're probably right. His fiancée was stunning, constantly in society pages, and I'm sure photographers loved to take her picture. No woman can be as beautiful as she was."

"I have to agree with you. Her pictures look like she was a movie star or top model."

"He's still grieving for her, but now Noah is a distraction from his loss."

"The crash was dreadful. His grief is understandable. I'll

have Noah ready when they come. I want to get him fed now before I try to clean him up or dress him."

"I can feed him," Camille said, reaching for her baby.

"Not if you don't want to have to change again. You're dressed and ready. Let me run the risk of him blowing breakfast or spitting up."

Laughing, Camille shrugged. "He's yours. I'm nervous about meeting Marek's sister."

"Why on earth would you be nervous?"

Camille shrugged. "I suppose since she's the mother of two. I feel like she knows more about babies. I'm still a novice at this."

"Don't be ridiculous. Besides, Marek is nice. A little fierce-looking sometimes. And a heartbreaker. I pity anyone who falls in love with him. Since he's still grieving over his fiancée and brother, he isn't going to want to lose Noah, too. I still think Steph may be right on this one."

"Time will tell, but I don't think so," Camille replied, feeling a tiny knot of worry surface. In spite of his reassurances and his brother's good opinion of him, the nagging fear wouldn't go away.

Two hours later, after introductions had been made and she and Marek had talked briefly, she gathered her sisters and left Marek and his sister and foreman with Noah.

At the end of their visit with Noah, Marek flew back to the ranch with Jess and worked beside him the rest of the day, finding release for pent-up feelings in sheer physical labor. He did the same on Sunday, mulling over his options regarding Noah. Sunday evening he saw Jess in the corral riding a new horse.

Marek grabbed his Stetson and went out, stretching out his legs as he walked to the corral. He perched on the fence to watch Jess work with the quarter horse. Jess turned, riding close and swinging down out of the saddle. "This is a fine horse."

"You've got him as gentle as a lamb."

"That's what I mean. He's a good one. You made an excellent purchase. Want to ride him for a minute?"

"Sure," Marek replied, jumping down from the fence and climbing into the saddle. He circled the corral, urging the horse to a trot. When he finished, he returned to Jess to dismount.

"Here he is, as good as you said." He handed the reins to Jess and walked beside him as he led the horse into the stable. In the cool shadows Marek leaned against a post to watch Jess unsaddle the horse.

"I've been thinking what I can do about little Noah. Whatever we do, we can't take him from Camille. Her sisters are crazy about him, too. I don't want to hurt anyone, but we have to be part of his life and be able to watch him grow. He's a tie to Kern that I want in our lives."

"I can't see any simple solution, but I'm not thinking on it too much because that's your worry," Jess said, lifting the saddle off the horse.

"It's worrying Ginny, and I can't sleep nights for trying to come up with a workable answer. I can't imagine Camille letting me have Noah for any significant amount of time."

"I agree with you."

"Ginny reminded me of how take-charge she thinks I am and how she thinks I've spent my life getting everyone to do what I want. I don't quite see it that way, but she's told me this time I won't be able to do that."

"Sometimes we just have to adjust to what life hands us."

"Jess, I don't go into things expecting to fail. I've looked at this every way I can think of. There's no easy answer, but I may have something workable if I can persuade Camille to cooperate."

"All you can do is try. And if she says no, try something else," Jess stated shortly, beginning to groom the sorrel.

"I don't think you'll like it."

"All right. Tell me. How do you plan to get her to agree?" Jess asked, frowning slightly as he studied Marek.

The following Friday night, a spring evening with the sun slanting in the sky, Camille sat across from Marek. They were on his patio at his Dallas home. Steaks had just been put on the grill. She was sipping her glass of wine while Marek had a barely touched martini. She had dressed with care in a red cotton sundress with high-heeled sandals and her hair was up on her head. She suspected she could have worn a gunnysack and Marek would not have noticed. She still didn't think he ever saw her as a woman, which was just as well because she didn't want to get into a relationship with any man at this point in her life.

Tonight, it seemed he was taking his time because he had not brought up the subject of what arrangements he hoped to make with her regarding Noah, which he had said was the purpose of asking her to dinner. She had no intention of rushing him, either. She had mulled it over constantly and the most workable plan she and Ashley could devise was for her to always get a home large enough for the Rangels to come visit when they wanted. They would be welcome wherever she lived, either here or abroad. If she could get a wing where they could stay off to themselves, she thought they might be happier. She couldn't imagine leaving Noah behind in Texas. She and Ashley had agreed on that one and she had constantly reassured Stephanie she would stick to that decision.

Taking a deep breath, Camille hoped to calm her nerves. A steady uneasiness plagued her because she had big doubts that he would agree to what she intended to offer.

She watched him stand over the steaks, which were sending a spiral of gray smoke into the air. When he had arrived at her house to pick her up in a limousine, he had looked as commanding and successful as ever. Wearing a charcoal suit and red tie, he looked ready for an evening out. Had the suit been meant to be a reminder of his wealth and power? Enticing smells of the grilling meat would usually tempt her, but her stomach churned. Marek seemed strong willed, a man totally accustomed to getting his way. His fortune held a possible threat like a twister spinning on her horizon.

Marek picked up his drink and returned to sit near her. "Steaks will be done soon. I hope you have an appetite."

"I'll admit I'm nervous, and that's killing my appetite. I'm far more anxious over this than going onstage."

"Don't be disturbed," he said quietly. "We'll work something out, hopefully to the satisfaction of all and in Noah's best interests as well. He can't participate in this, but he has the biggest stake."

"That's true," she said, feeling better that Marek sounded as if he would put Noah first.

Marek leaned forward to take her hand lightly in his. His compelling dark eyes made her breath catch. Why was she having this reaction to him?

"Relax, Camille," he said in a gentle tone. "We'll try to find a solution that will be in *everyone's* best interest."

"I hope so. That's what I've prayed for," she replied, aware of the jump in her pulse. She was certain it was a very one-sided attraction that she shouldn't have to him. And she couldn't guess what he was going to ask her to do regarding Noah.

"Relax, have some wine, eat some steak. Let's have dinner and then we'll talk about Noah."

She nodded, unable to speak. Smiling, he patted her hand

and sat back to raise his drink. "Here's to a happy solution and to you and Kern having a beautiful, adorable son."

She had to return his smile as she touched his glass lightly. "I'll have to drink to that," she said, taking a tiny sip.

"And I have to say, my brother always had great taste in his female friends," he added with an uncustomary smile as he raised his glass to her.

It was the closest he had come to flirting. "Thank you. I'm not sure about great taste. Perhaps we were thrown together on a festive occasion and everything clicked."

"You have a great little boy. Thank you for letting me know about him."

"I've told you why. I'm pleased that you're responding in a positive way."

He smiled and sipped his drink before glancing at the cooker. "I'll get the steaks."

They ate outside at a glass-topped table with dinner served by his staff. After dinner they moved back to the lawn chairs overlooking the pool and yard. The staff quietly cleared the table, and, when they were left alone, Marek turned his chair to face her.

"Tell me what you propose," he said. He listened as she talked about getting a place wherever she went that would be large enough for all of them and how he and his family could visit whenever and however long they chose.

Marek simply listened and nodded, and her heart raced as she talked. Her palms had grown damp.

After she finished, he sat quietly, sipping a tall glass of iced tea. She waited in silence, letting him take his time. It seemed eons before he set down his drink and spoke.

"That's a feasible plan," he said, and she let out her breath. She couldn't relax completely because she was certain he had something else in mind.

"I have another idea. All I ask is for you to listen to what

I propose. Don't give me an answer tonight—we can talk about it. I want you to think it over before you answer."

"That sounds reasonable but scary."

He smiled again, a smile that softened his features and made him slightly less intimidating. "Good. You are totally tied up in your career and Noah, right?"

"Yes. You know that."

"I lost my fiancée, and I'm not interested in a deep commitment. Jillian had my heart. I enjoy women and the day will come when I won't be so numb with grief, but I can't imagine ever loving again. What I'm getting at is both of us have set loving one special person on hold, more or less."

"You're right," she said, her curiosity soaring.

"Camille, will you marry me? A marriage of convenience would help both of us and should be so much better for Noah."

Stunned, she dropped her glass of tea, barely aware of it shattering on the patio.

Three

"Please don't answer me now because I want you to think about it. Any answer you give me immediately will be a knee-jerk reaction. Marry me—it'll be a marriage of convenience in the fullest sense," he repeated. "At some point I would expect us to have a physical relationship. I think it would be unrealistic to expect otherwise."

His voice sounded as if it came from far away, and she felt light-headed. Marry him! "Sorry, I think I'm going to faint."

He stopped talking instantly and stood. "Put your head down for a moment." She did as he said and soon felt a cold wet cloth being placed gently on the back of her neck. His warm fingers on her nape were disturbing in a far different way than his proposal had been.

As her head cleared, she sat up.

"Take a deep breath or two and just relax."

"I broke your glass," she said, glancing at the sparkling shards at her feet.

"Forget that. Just relax a moment. The proposal is a surprise, and that's why I want you to think about it. When you
feel clear and are ready to hear them, I can give you reasons
I came up with this solution."

"I suppose I'm ready."

He studied her, and she gazed back, trying to calm down
enough to listen to him. She wanted to blurt out a refusal
now. Why would she have to think it over? How could he
have ever expected her to accept?

"Marriage will give Noah the Rangel name. If we're mar-
ried, I think you'll feel better about leaving him with me.
We'll work out times you can live with. I'll be a dad for him.
I would like to adopt him."

"I'll lose him," she whispered. "He'll be your son in every
way except one. You'll have far more claim over him than
you will as his uncle."

"You won't lose him—I promise. And we will have a
prenuptial agreement, a contract that you will approve. I
will work with you on when I can be with him. I will see to
it that financially you and Noah are completely taken care
of. You'll have a private plane whenever you want. You'll
have a generous allowance. You'll be more financially free
to pursue your career. I know you're doing well, but I can
help you do better, and I can definitely do a lot for Noah."

"I don't need money."

"I know you don't, but this will make it easier. Definitely
better for him."

"I want to do well with my career."

"I expect you to," he said. He took her hand again. While
his hand held hers, his thumb brushed her knuckles lightly,
keeping her aware of his contact. *Married to him.* Even as
the proposal seemed impossible, the prospect made her pulse
race.

"I hope to be part of Noah's life," Marek continued. "I

want to be an influence in his life, to get to know him. By proposing, I feel I'm doing what Kern would have done if it had been my baby. I loved my brother. I just want to watch Noah grow up. I feel as if it gives me a tie to Kern," Marek said, his voice deepening.

Camille's eyes filled with tears.

"Camille," he said quietly. "I don't want to hurt or worry you. I want you to be happy with whatever we do."

"How can I be happy with this? You'll have Noah, and I won't be able to do anything about it?" she cried, standing and walking away in embarrassment that she couldn't control her tears.

He came up behind her to place his hands on her shoulders and turn her to face him. He framed her face with his hands and wiped away her tears with his thumbs.

"Stop crying. I promised I wouldn't hurt you," he said gently. "Causing you distress is not what I intended. If I were Kern and had just proposed—the two of you were not in love—wouldn't you consider his proposal?"

Startled by his question, she gazed up at Marek while silence stretched. What would he do if she refused to marry him? He was far more powerful and had more resources. "I suppose I would give it thought," she replied.

"I'm not Kern, but, believe me, I have his interests at heart."

Mulling over what he said, she decided she would have given some serious thought to a proposal if it had been from Kern. "You're a little more serious and forceful than Kern."

Marek's faint smile lifted one corner of his mouth, calming her slightly. "I'll try to be less 'forceful.' All I ask is for you to think about the possibilities. Now, are you ready to hear what I propose in the way of finances?"

"Another surprise," she said without thinking. "Finances are really incidental. That's not the issue here."

He released her. "I know it's not the issue, but I think we ought to look at all aspects of this. Finances, arrangements, a physical relationship. Want some more tea while we talk?"

His voice deepened, and that surprising fire he could ignite effortlessly between them sent a shiver to her toes. With the flicker in the depth of his dark eyes, she guessed he felt the same sparks, too. "Yes, thank you," she said, walking to the outdoor kitchen with him and watching while he poured another tall glass of tea for her. This handsome, wealthy Texas rancher intended to marry her. The idea was impossible.

After retrieving his tea, he directed her to a chair away from the broken glass and slid his chair close to hers.

As she sipped the icy tea, she focused on him. His eyes gave away nothing about his feelings. He could have been discussing the weather as far as his demeanor and expression were concerned.

"We will draw up papers so our arrangements are as binding as any contract. If you accept, I will pay you five million dollars."

Her shock returned full force. What were his real intentions? To offer that much money, was he working toward getting custody of Noah? "If I marry you, I get five million dollars from you," she repeated.

"That's right," he said quietly. "You'll get one million when we sign the papers and four million as soon as we are husband and wife. You will get a million each year we are married, plus a generous allowance. I will set up a trust for Noah and pay for everything for him. You can spend the money I give you as you please because there will be no strings."

Her shock mushroomed over the fortune that he was dangling as an inducement to accept what he wanted. She could only stare at him, speechless over his offer that would transform her life and the lives of every member of her family. The money was both frightening and dazzling. "Now I see why you get your way so often," she whispered without even realizing she had spoken aloud.

She had been counting on her career to help her family. With this money she wouldn't have to worry whether she made stardom or not. Life should be far easier, and yet...

"That's a huge amount of money," she said, thinking it was an even bigger power play. Marek looked relaxed, as if accustomed to bargaining with such high stakes, but these were the highest possible as far as she was concerned. This cool rancher had thought this out and come up with an offer that she might be unable to refuse.

"I can afford it and I'd want to do it. If you say yes, you'll be giving me far more because I know I will become a permanent part of Noah's life."

"You hardly know Noah. How can you feel this strongly about him?"

"It's easy," Marek replied. "I feel this strongly about my brother. This baby is a definite tie to Kern."

She nodded, touched and aware how vulnerable he was where his heart was concerned. "I can understand that." She rubbed her forehead. "Wow. You've turned my life topsy-turvy. Actually, if I accept your offer—my whole family will be topsy-turvy. That fortune will change all our lives. You'll want Noah a lot of the time. I'm sure you've thought about how much."

"You and I would live in the same place some of the time. I don't want to give up being a rancher or living on my ranch. But I don't do that all the time now, and I can give up some of the time. When Noah gets to school age, you'll have to give serious thought about how much he will travel with you."

"I know, but I can't foresee what my career will be. It's filled with uncertainties at this point."

"You'll have enough money that you can give it up completely if you want."

Momentarily, her tension lightened, and she smiled. "No, I've dreamed of this all my life, and things are beginning to open up for me. At this point, I definitely do not want to toss aside what I've gained. I want to sing. I want to be a star. I love opera. But I love Noah and I want what's best for him."

"Then I think you'll have to seriously consider my offer."

"I suppose I will," she said, gazing beyond him, watching the splashing water in the fountain in the pool. "This is a beautiful place."

"This is my Dallas home. The best place is the ranch."

"I know very little about ranches."

He reached over again to take her hand. "Camille, Kern was drawn to you, and I feel certain he would have proposed. I think you and I can have a workable arrangement that will benefit Noah. I've tried to do what will benefit you. This million a year I've offered—your monthly allowance will be enough that you shouldn't need to touch that money. You should be able to invest it and I can help you and make it grow. I want what will make you happy—as happy as I will be if you accept."

"Suppose you fall in love with someone later?"

"Divorce still exists, but I don't expect to fall in love again in my life. I gave my heart to Jillian." He looked away, and she instantly regretted bringing up a subject that would open his wounds.

This time she reached out to touch his arm, placing her hand on him. "Marek, I didn't mean to cause you hurt."

He inhaled deeply. "Sometimes it just comes out of the blue, and I feel weak in the knees. Don't apologize. You had no way of knowing."

"You talked about a physical relationship. I won't have a lot of time, and I'm not about to jump into one when we're strangers," she said. "I did that once in my life, and I won't do it again. Your brother charmed and captivated me that night. Now, a physical relationship will have to come later, maybe much later."

"I keep busy at the ranch and try to do the hard, physical jobs. That's helped. Remember, we'll be married. You're a beautiful woman, Camille. You're getting shortchanged here, but you've told me you don't have time for a man in your life and I won't be in the way or demand your time. A physical relationship will have to be mutual."

His answer reassured her. She smiled. "You'll probably hope I'll disappear for months on end."

One corner of his mouth lifted in a crooked grin that she realized was about the best he would do for a smile most of the time. "I won't be hoping any such thing," he said. "We can work out a schedule. You think about what you'd like for a schedule."

"I can't even imagine. What about when I'm in New Mexico this summer?"

"You decide what you want, and I'll look at it and we'll go from there."

She thought about all he had said to her as they sat in silence. "How different this might have been if Kern had lived," she remarked, going from memories about Kern to thinking the two brothers were so different in looks, personalities, in nearly every way. The only similarity was their blood tie and their shared love of ranching.

"I still think he would have proposed and done something to convince you to marry him. He wouldn't have wanted to leave Texas, either, any more than I do."

She studied Marek's handsome features. Mrs. Marek Rangel. The idea took her breath away and seemed totally impossible. Millions would be hers. She thought of all the things she could do for Noah and for her family. Marek would do so much for Noah that she wouldn't have to factor in what she could do. It was staggering to try to deal with his proposal. But this was about so much more than money. It would give her a father figure for Noah. It would make him close with the Rangel family, and he would know ranching and a cowboy's life. These were all things she wanted and the reason she had contacted Marek in the first place.

She had to think about his offer, discuss it with her sisters and with her family. Silence stretched between them. He sat watching the fountain, sipping his iced tea. How much had his solitary life contributed to this proposal? To lose his brother and his fiancée—the two people he was closest to and loved—that would be devastating for anyone. She could see why he had latched on to Noah so swiftly.

She studied his profile, his full black hair and thickly lashed eyes. What if she married him and fell in love with him? She didn't want that distraction to her career. Even worse, Marek wouldn't return her love, and that would be devastating. There were no doubts he would be agreeable to a physical relationship, but anything more? She believed what he said, that he would never love again. The pictures of Jillian had been breathtakingly beautiful.

"I guess I should go home and think about this. We've discussed it tonight, and I'm at least getting adjusted to thinking about your offer."

"Good," he said, giving her a bigger smile. "You'll have to give up Noah sometimes, but you'll be busy. You would have to anyway because of your career."

She nodded and stood. "I think I really should go."

He stood to take her arm. His slight touch caused another jump in her pulse. "I'll see you home. Take as long as you need to consider my proposal and to talk to your family about it. When would you like to go out again?"

"Tomorrow I want to be with family. This is Friday. I'd

prefer to wait until Tuesday to see you," she said, thinking this would also give her time to talk to her attorney. "This will send my sisters into orbit. If I accept your proposal, our lives will have major changes."

"Not anything you can't live with, I hope. I tried to find something that would benefit all of us."

Marek climbed into the limousine with her. As the limo pulled away, her gaze roamed over the colonial house with massive Corinthian columns along the front porch. This would be her home, too, if she married him. Dazed, she couldn't envision that ever happening.

"Your parents will be all right with our marriage if I accept?" she asked as the limo drove through the tall iron gates.

"I'm a grown man. Yes, I expect them to be all right with it. They've made a life for themselves in California and are busy all the time with social and charitable activities. Dad plays golf and recently fell and broke his ankle, so he's on crutches right now, which will slow him down about traveling to Texas. My mom hates to fly and they usually drive, but that's out until Dad's ankle heals."

"I'm sorry about that."

"You'll definitely pass inspection. Although they loved Jillian. They were heartbroken over the crash besides being so hurt over the loss of Kern."

"That's understandable."

"I've thought this proposal over. You're beautiful, and you're a rising opera star. They sounded impressed."

"This is their first grandson. Is that correct? Your sister has two girls."

"That's right. My parents are not into grandchildren as much as a lot of parents or they wouldn't live over a thousand miles away."

"So your sister is the person you'll be concerned about. I assume she's happy with this."

"She doesn't know about it yet. I wanted to talk to you first."

"Have you told Mr. Grayson?"

"Yes, I discussed it with him. Jess approves."

"That surprises me. You're very close to him, aren't you?"

"Sometimes I think he's more my dad than my own father. He taught me a lot about the ranch. He's been around as far back as I can remember. I'm closer to him than I am to my parents. They were always busy, but Jess had time for me and Kern. Actually, for Ginny, too, but she didn't hang out with him when she became a teenager. I did a lot. Now Jess is a best friend, maybe sometimes still a dad."

"You can't beat that combination," she said, smiling at him. "I'm glad you have someone like that even though no one can take away your grief or replace your brother. But your sister may not be happy to see you marry without love."

"Ginny will adjust. She knows I'm doing what I want. I take it you're close to your sisters."

"I'm closest to Ashley," Camille replied. She lapsed into silence for a time. "My head is spinning with all this. I can't believe this is happening."

"My offer is real, and I hope you accept. I know you didn't have it in your plans to share Noah a lot of the time, but I think when we do this, it will work out where both of us are happy. I hope you'd rather have him with Jess and me out on the ranch some of the time than backstage going from pillar to post."

"Backstage is exciting to me, but backstage will not begin to hold the draw for him that your ranch will."

"If you accept, the Circle R will be his ranch, too," Marek replied. Startled, she stared at him, thinking about all the changes in their lives. If she married Marek, Noah would become Marek's heir.

She shook her head. "The whole thing is staggering.

You're a very wealthy, powerful man. I forget about that when I'm with you, but then moments come when I'm reminded about your status. Is this a command instead of an offer?"

"Of course not. We'll negotiate, but I've tried to be generous."

"You've been generous far beyond my imagination. When I met Kern, I didn't know how wealthy your family is. I'm not from Texas and at that time had never heard of the Rangels. Your brother was so down-to-earth and unpretentious. He was filled with fun and he was sort of happy-go-lucky. I didn't dream he had this fortune. I didn't know that until after the weekend."

"That was Kern absolutely. Money meant little to him. We were born into wealth, and I've increased it. Kern worked for me and he helped. I've been lucky, but after a point where you're comfortable and fed and have necessities, the wealth is not what makes you happy."

"Whatever it was, your brother was a happy man."

"If Kern had lived, you would have been Mrs. Kern Rangel. He would have charmed you into accepting. Kern wouldn't have given up."

They both became silent for the rest of the ride. At her door he took her hands. "Listen to me. Don't worry. I want you to be happy. You're Noah's mother, and Kern would have done anything he could to make you happy. The last thing I want to do is hurt you. We'll work out something here. This is a start, but I thought a marriage, even though it is definitely a marriage of convenience, would be the best solution for all. Especially for Noah."

She nodded, aware of him standing close, holding her hands, trying his best to be nice to her while trying to persuade her to accept his offer. If they married, could she avoid losing her heart to him? Or letting the marriage destroy her career?

"I'm a little overwhelmed. Actually, a lot overwhelmed. I'll talk to my sisters and my family and try to get accustomed to the idea. Start thinking about a few more details regarding when Noah would be with you and when he would be with me," she said, realizing before the words were out of her mouth that he had probably already planned what they would do.

"You tell me what you want on that," he said, surprising her.

"He's too little to leave with you."

"One more thing to think about—when I have him, will Ashley stay? I'll need a nanny."

Startled, Camille stared at him. "I hadn't thought about that, but she would stay with Noah. I'd want her to continue as his nanny. I'll have to ask because she may not want to do so. Staying on your Texas ranch would be entirely different for her than traveling with both of her sisters."

"That's right. But if she'll do it, I'd prefer her to remain his nanny. I think everyone will be happier, including Noah."

"If she stays, it'll completely change her life."

He gave that faint crooked smile again. "I hope it's not that big a change. We have a great ranch and I'm usually working from sunup to sundown, so I won't be underfoot. I'll pay her salary. Whatever it is, you can promise her a raise."

"You're generous."

"If you let me have Noah part of the time, you'll be the most generous."

Once again he framed her face with his hands. "Camille, I'll try my best to make you happy. I just want to be part of his life and so does Ginny."

"I understand. I want you to be in his life. That's why I contacted you in the first place."

She gazed into his earnest dark eyes and wondered about their future. She had tied her life to his and there was no turning back now. He was unbelievably handsome, and her heart drummed. He leaned forward to brush a light kiss on her forehead, and then he stepped away. "I'll call you about Tuesday."

He turned and headed to his limo in long strides.

Dazed, Camille stepped inside, locked the door and leaned against it. Ashley stood waiting farther down the darkened hallway.

"I didn't think you were ever coming inside. I know you weren't smooching out there, so what was going on?"

"I have to talk to you. I assume Noah is asleep. Where is Stephanie?"

"Stephanie is out with the latest guy. Noah is asleep. You're later than I thought you'd be. We can go anywhere to talk. The baby monitors are on."

"Let's go to my room. Let me see Noah for just a second. I promise I won't wake him."

"Sure. What did you do tonight?" Ashley asked.

"We went to his Dallas home and he cooked steaks. He had a staff to do everything else."

"I can't even imagine. What's the home like?"

"Not as fancy and elegant as I expected. Upper scale, nice, but not knock-your-socks-off elegance. Very comfortable with everything you could want. Pool, patio, outdoor living area and kitchen," she replied as they paused in front of the nursery. "I'll only be a minute."

"I'll be in your room," Ashley said, walking ahead.

In the rosy glow of a small night-light Camille tiptoed across the nursery to the high-sided white crib and looked down at her sleeping son. Her heart felt squeezed, and she longed to hold Noah close. Tears stung her eyes. No matter what they did, she would lose Noah some of the time. He would have Marek's influence now. He would spend part of his life with Marek. Stephanie had been right. Momentarily, bitter regret enveloped her, and she wished she could go back and undo telling him about Noah. She reached out to touch his hand lightly, feeling the smooth, warm skin that was so soft. She had never loved anyone the way she loved Noah. Even though it would be difficult to live with, deep down she felt she had done what was right by revealing his existence to Marek.

Hopefully, Marek would be a good influence for her baby. And the Rangels deserved time with Noah just as Noah deserved a dad and his ranching heritage. She wiped her tears and took a deep breath. "I love you, sweetie," she whispered, touching a wispy lock of his hair. She wiped more tears and turned away, glancing back once at the sleeping baby.

She paused in the empty playroom, picking up a stuffed pink pig that Noah loved. Camille ran her hands over the pig while she tried to get her emotions under control. She didn't want to go to Ashley in tears. Her sisters loved Noah, too. Stephanie would be furious, but the money might calm her. Stephanie had a profound appreciation for money.

After taking a deep breath and trying to think about something else for a few minutes, she went to the master bedroom.

Ashley was curled up on the sofa, quietly waiting.

"Let me change quickly and I'll join you," Camille said. "Do you want anything to drink before we start talking? We may be here awhile."

"Now I'm getting really curious. I'll go get us both something. How about lemonade?"

"Sure. I'll be right back."

When she returned in a turquoise T-shirt and plaid pajama pants, Ashley was waiting with two tall glasses of lemonade on the table near the sofa. A plate of cookies rested between them.

"Let's hear what's up."

"Get ready for a shock. I'm talking a really big shock," she said. Ashley nodded. "He's proposed a marriage of convenience."

"No!" Ashley's brow furrowed while her eyes widened. "You turned him down, didn't you? You can't do that—"

"Ashley, listen to me. Remember, I contacted him in the first place because I wanted Noah to know his paternal family. I wanted Marek to be a father figure to Noah. I haven't given him any answer. He asked me to think it over, and I told him I would get back with him next Tuesday after talking to my family."

"You can't even give his proposal a moment's consideration. You don't have any reason to agree and you have every reason to say no."

"Do you want to hear everything or not?"

"I want to hear. Marriage is impossible. He would have far more legal claim on Noah. You'd be tied into a loveless union. Even though he is handsome, wealthy and sexy. I'll give him that much. You'd have to share Noah. Big-time. Marek wouldn't love you. He would interfere with you in every way. You can't even consider it."

"Do you want to hear his proposal or not?" Camille went through all Marek had offered. When she relayed how much money he would give them, all the color drained from Ashley's face and her mouth dropped open.

Camille grasped Ashley's hand, which was cold as ice. "Ashley. Are you all right?"

"Five million now and a million a year plus an allowance?" Ashley repeated breathlessly, sounding dazed.

"That's right. I'm trying to avoid thinking about the money, but it's impossible. With funds like that I can send you to school. I can give Mom and Dad financial help in taking care of Grandma. I can pursue my career without feeling I have to make it to be able to survive and help my family. Ashley, that money would lift a huge burden off my shoulders."

"I knew he had money, but I didn't know he had that much," she said, still sounding dazed as she stared beyond Camille.

"It will change your life and mine, for sure. It will change Noah's. He'll have a trust fund set up for him, and I'm sure it will be generous. Marek will be a father to him. We'll lose him some of the time, but definitely not all of the time. And Marek asked if you would stay as Noah's nanny. That's what he wants, and he said he would pay your salary, which, I'm certain, would be larger than what you're getting now."

"My word. I can't imagine all this, Camille. Mom will faint. She doesn't do well with surprises."

"I know. I'll break it to her slowly."

"When you started, I figured Stephanie would be furious with you for revealing Noah to Marek. Now, I don't think she will be if you tell her about the money at the same time you tell her about the proposal. You know Stephanie and money. That's the driving force in her world. How much is he going to want Noah?"

"We haven't gotten to that, but Marek keeps telling me that he wants me to be happy and he doesn't want to hurt me in any way."

"You'll be a millionaire."

"Ashley, get around the money. It's a plus and you can't ignore it, but that isn't what's critical here. I think Marek should be in Noah's life. I also think a marriage of convenience might work and benefit Noah, which is the paramount criterion."

"True, but I cannot stop thinking about the possibilities the money would give us."

Camille listened to Ashley talk while part of her thoughts

were on Marek and his proposal. Was he happy with the prospects? How much of the time would he want Noah at the ranch with him? Could Ashley live in the isolation of a ranch on the Texas plains?

She didn't have answers to those questions, and she tried to focus on Ashley, who was still chattering about Marek's offer. Camille couldn't see how she could have any answer except one.

The next morning Marek sat over coffee with Jess, who had hung his hat on a hook at the door in the back entrance. Jess studied him as he sipped steaming black coffee. "What did Ginny say?"

"You can guess. She's totally opposed, thinks I'll regret getting locked into a loveless marriage. She's certain I have a lot to lose. As you can imagine, she was wild."

Jess merely nodded. When Marek's phone rang, he glanced at the number. "Here she is again. I'll have to listen to all her arguments this morning."

"Hi, Ginny," he said. He nodded. After a moment, he ended the call. "She's on the drive coming in. The whole Dalton family came with her so the girls can ride while Ginny talks to me. Frank will stay with the girls. She wants to talk to me in person. For her to drive all the way out here from Dallas is even more serious."

Jess drank the last of his coffee and stood. "That's my cue to get the horses ready. I'll see about Frank and the girls. You can deal with Ginny. She'll come around, but you'll have to listen to her vent about it. She's just looking out for you and your best interests."

"I know." Marek walked out with Jess and watched Ginny and her family spill out of their van. Jess greeted Ginny, and they talked a moment with Ginny waving her hands before she walked toward the house. Jess shook hands with Ginny's husband while the girls stood waiting for his greeting.

Frank Dalton, Ginny's husband, was a no-nonsense accountant with his own business. Marek liked him and thought he was a good match for his sister. Jess hunkered down to say hello to the little girls, and they all headed toward the barn. Ginny sailed through the back gate, her short, shaggy black hair blowing in the wind.

Marek told himself to hang on to his patience with her.

She swept into the kitchen, her face almost as red as her shirt. "Marek, have you lost your senses? You can't marry someone you don't love."

"Hi there, sis. You look a little hot and bothered. Want a cool drink?"

"No, I don't. We drove all the way out here so I can talk some sense into you. Pray she turns you down."

"Ginny, I'll have the cool drink. And I hope she accepts. I think this is the solution to the problem. I don't think it will create a bigger problem."

"And when you fall in love again?"

"There is still something called divorce if this marriage becomes a burden. But I do not expect to fall in love again. Sometimes someone falls in love for a lifetime. He loves that one person and that is the only love of his life on this earth. You don't believe that happens?"

"Maybe sometimes, but I don't think that will be the case with you. You hurt now, but you're strong and young and you'll love again."

"Is your crystal ball out in the car? You think you know me better than I know myself?"

"I don't want you locked into something where you get hurt."

He smiled at her. "Relax, Ginny. I appreciate your concern. I've thought about this and I think it's a workable solution," he said, retrieving a cold beer and opening the bottle. "Want to sit where it's comfortable?" he asked, motioning toward the living area adjoining the kitchen. "You can see the girls riding around in the corral from there."

"They brought their swimsuits because they'll be hot after they ride. They were overjoyed to get to see the horses. Marek, please do not do this. I know you will be unhappy."

"Stop worrying. I've looked at this every which way and I still think this is the best solution. I'll have some control. We'll have Noah with us far more. She'll be in Budapest this fall. If I don't do something, she'll take him to Budapest and we won't even see him all the time they're gone. I don't want to lose him. Or even be merely a tiny part of his life. He's too important to me. I think he is to you, too."

"He is, but so are you," she said, frowning. "I don't want you hurt."

"Ginny, stop worrying. I've gotten myself into this. If it doesn't work, I'll get myself out. This is an ambitious, busy woman who doesn't have time for a private life. She sings at the Metropolitan in New York next spring. Her career is rising, and she'll need help with Noah."

"She has help. Her sister is her nanny." Ginny sat staring at him, rubbing her forehead. She shook her head. "I pray you're right and you know what you're doing. She's trying to carve out a career for herself and she's been somewhat successful so far. What happens if you fall in love with her? You'll get hurt. She isn't going to settle down and give up that career."

"I would never ask her to, and I'm not going to fall in love."

"You're still suffering over your loss, but eventually you'll heal and move on. You'll hurt yourself. She will let you see Noah some without you marrying her. Please don't do this."

"I want more than brief visits with him several times a year."

"Since when did you want to become a dad?"

"You know how I love your girls."

"Yes, but you're their uncle, not their dad, which is much more demanding. It's a demanding, full-time job and you'll love that baby like you can't believe. Then, if you and Camille split, you'll really be torn. Have you thought about that?"

"Yes, but life is fraught with hazards and you just have to take some risks when you love someone whether it's a child or an adult."

She turned away to watch her girls. "You don't know what love is until a child comes into your life. Frank's life and mine revolve around the girls. You take that baby to raise part of the time and you'll love him more than you can possibly imagine. Maybe you already love him just because he's Kern's."

"Ginny, stop worrying. I want to take the chance. I want him in our lives."

Silence stretched while they studied each other. He waited patiently, certain of what he planned.

"Okay, Marek, I'll try to stop worrying and I'll stop arguing with you," she said finally. "I'm going on record though. I think you're making an enormous mistake."

"If this were turned around and Kern was in the spot I'm in and it was my baby, I think Kern would want me to do the best thing for Noah. I've mulled it over, and this seems the best solution to keep Noah in our lives."

"You might be right. When will she give you an answer?"

"Tuesday night we'll get together again. I think I'll know then, and I'll call you as soon as I do. She's talking to her sisters now."

"I can't imagine you doing this. I can't imagine her doing

it, either. Both of you have switched off your common sense. Maybe her sisters will talk her out of it."

"Stephanie will try. I'll call you Wednesday morning."

"You call me Tuesday night. I'll be a wreck. In the meantime, I'll try to think up another plan."

He smiled. "Thanks, Ginny. Tuesday night we'll know whether I'll marry Camille or not."

Tuesday night, he had butterflies in his stomach. He had made multimillion-dollar deals without a qualm, but tonight he suffered uncustomary nerves. For once in his life he didn't have a backup plan. This was it, and he could only pray she accepted. Stepping into the entrance of her condo, he experienced the same reaction as the first day he had met her, an awareness of how striking she was and the sense of energy surrounding her even as she stood still. Her hair was a midnight cascade, falling below her shoulders. Her sleeveless black dress with a scooped neckline revealed lush curves. A thin gold chain with a diamond pendant circled her throat.

"Hi," she said, smiling at him. "Come in."

"You look gorgeous," he said.

Marek could not discern any indication of her decision from her expression. He realized she was an actress as well as a singer and she hid her feelings well. She would do well in a boardroom in a high-stakes negotiation. "You asked to see Noah before we leave for the evening," she said, leading him into the living area and motioning toward the leather couch. "Have a seat, and I'll go get Noah. I won't be gone long."

"So Noah is awake and happy?" Marek suspected that with one look at her sisters he would know Camille's answer to his proposal.

"He's awake and bubbly. Stephanie has gone out for the evening, and Ashley is on the phone." She hurried out of the room to the nursery, where Ashley waited with Noah.

"Thanks, Ashley. I'll bring him back to you. Sure you don't want to come say hi?"

"No, I might start crying," she said, pushing up the sleeves to her gray sweatshirt.

"We've talked about this. The money should be some consolation."

"I worry about you. I worry about how badly you'll miss having Noah with you."

"I'll be fine. I have my career. Marek said he can change the schedule if we want to see Noah more."

"I hope he holds to that."

Camille took her son and hurried back to the front room. Marek stood by the piano, looking at sheet music. His navy suit and tie were a quiet understatement of his power and wealth. A tall, handsome and appealing man, always commanding. Was he ever at a loss or uncertain? He turned to cross the room.

"Ah, the happy baby," he said, reaching for Noah, who kicked and held out his arms.

"Do you really want to take him? Your shirt looks fresh and it's white as snow."

"I'm not fragile and my shirt washes," Marek said, taking off his coat and tossing it to the sofa. He turned to Noah.

"I think he remembers you."

"Hey, that's great. I hope so. I suspect he's happy to see everyone. So far, I haven't seen him unhappy."

"He has his moments, but most of the time, he's happy."

Marek walked away, talking to Noah, carrying him to the window to show him the outside. Then he sat on the floor with him and handed him some toys. It amazed her to watch him, the wealthy, powerful rancher dressed in his immaculate suit, tailor-made white shirt and his hand-tooled boots that could have been custom-made, while he sat on the floor playing and making goofy noises for Noah. Noah laughed, a hearty sound that made him shake all over, and she couldn't keep from laughing with him.

"Why will grown people do anything to get a baby to laugh?"

"Got me, but it's fun. You can't keep from laughing in return," Marek said, making another silly sound and laughing with Noah. Her heart squeezed while her pulse jumped. Marek's appeal soared when he laughed. Creases bracketed his mouth and his even white teeth flashed. Her heart was definitely in for a bumpy ride.

Finally, he stood. "I'll give him to you. Another night we'll play longer."

"I'll take him back to Ashley. Just a minute and we can go."

She hurried out of the room, holding Noah tightly in her arms, wondering whether she was making the right decision or not. After tonight, there wouldn't be any turning back.

Just as before, they went in a limo to his Dallas home, where they sat outside with drinks. He removed his navy suit jacket and tie as he had the last time. While she watched him, it occurred to her to wonder about his handsome appeal. Was she in any danger of falling in love? He sat close, facing her. He set both drinks on a glass table.

"I've waited long enough, and we're alone now," Marek said. "What's your answer? Will you marry me?"

Four

Her insides roiled and her palms became damp even though her hands felt icy as she gazed into his brown eyes.

Taking a deep breath, she nodded. "Yes, I will."

He closed his eyes briefly, then opened them. He pulled her up and gave her a light hug. "Thank you," he said in a voice that sounded choked with emotion.

He smelled of citrus and sandalwood and the fresh cottony scent of his immaculate dress shirt. He was warm and tall, and his arms around her felt reassuring. He leaned away a fraction to look down at her and her only thought at that moment was how handsome he was. "We'll make this work, Camille," he said in a husky voice. A pang racked her because his emotional reaction was not due to her, but to her baby.

"I don't want to fall in love," she whispered, biting back the words that if she did, he would break her heart.

His dark eyes widened and then narrowed as he gazed at her, a look that became more intense. She felt as if he was seeing her as a woman for the first time. He inhaled deeply, and a hard look came to his features while a muscle worked in his jaw.

"Forget what I said," she said, stepping out of his embrace, walking away from him to put distance between them and to keep him from seeing the flush of embarrassment in her cheeks. "My heart is in my career and Noah, and, right now, I can't imagine us being together a lot of the time." Her words spilled out, sounding rushed to her, and she felt foolish. Trying to get a grip and be less emotional, she finally faced him.

"Thank you, Camille," he said, looking composed again. "We can start working out details, put down what we want in a prenuptial agreement that we can turn over to our lawyers to finalize. How's that?"

"Sounds fine." She returned to get her glass of wine and sit in a green-cushioned teak lawn chair. He sat facing her and sipped his drink. "I'll get a tablet to make notes as we talk about what we want." He left to get papers from a cabinet and returned to hand a tablet to her. She looked down at proposed schedules.

"I have schedules worked out, but you know your bookings and shows. This is just something to start from. Also, as soon as we sign the papers, I'll have money transferred to you."

"That's sort of staggering," she said, unable to imagine that she would soon become a millionaire. Her gaze ran over him, his broad shoulders, his capable, well-shaped hands.

"We'll be married, Camille. As far as I'm concerned, your money is yours to do with as you please. I'll pay your expenses and your housing, all that sort of thing. Just get Stephanie to keep accurate records."

"That's very generous considering how much money you're giving me. I earn a good living so far."

"I'll treat you the same as I would a wife in the fullest

sense of the word as far as finances and that sort of thing are concerned. How are your sisters and your parents with this arrangement?"

"Ashley is worried about Noah. The money means a lot because she's saved and scraped together for her education. Stephanie is practical enough to accept this. She does not like sharing Noah, but she is going to like the money immensely. She sees the possibility of having her own business, perhaps picking up more clients than she has now."

"Good. What about Ashley staying on as nanny?"

"Ashley will be nanny at first. Later, if you can find a good nanny, she would like to go to college full-time and finish her education."

"Sure. Tell her to let me know when to start looking for a new nanny."

"I haven't told my parents yet about the money. I'd rather they meet you first and feel this is a marriage of two people in love. Otherwise, they may not get past the money and may never be able to see the reasons I want this for Noah as a tie to his father."

Stretching out his legs, he looked relaxed, as if they were discussing the latest movie or electronic breakthrough. Watching him, no one would guess he was making life-changing decisions. The evening had become surreal. She couldn't imagine the changes, yet they were happening. Even more impossible to imagine—she would soon marry a man she didn't love and barely knew. She let her gaze roam down the length of him, and her pulse raced. He appealed to her, and she hadn't really had a man in her life in a long time. To her regret, she had a strong physical response to him. Already, if he came close or if there was physical contact with him, her pulse jumped. With her life focused on her career, she didn't want complications by becoming emotionally entangled with Marek.

"Well, what we've both avoided and what we have to work out is how will we share Noah? I've thought about all sorts of ways to divide the time. I've come up with something that's a start. We can change it completely so that each of us finds it workable."

"Right now, this part is difficult to imagine," she admitted, fighting back tears because she felt as if she stood on the verge of losing Noah. For a panicky moment, she wanted to change her mind, but there was no turning back time and events. "The first thing I'll do when I get home tonight is go see him. I miss him when I'm away from him for just hours," she said, struggling to hang on to her emotions. "Days are impossible to think about."

"The first little bit will be the hardest, and we won't jump into a schedule the minute we marry," he promised, taking her hand. "Stop worrying so much, Camille. I'll work with you on this and maybe we can't do a lot at first while he's tiny. Besides, some of the time, you and I will be under the same roof and you'll have him as much as ever. The difference will be I'll be living with you, too."

A shiver spiraled through her as his words echoed in her thoughts. How vastly her life would change. Locked into a loveless union, she would spend part of her time on his ranch. She couldn't imagine that. His thumb lightly rubbed the back of her hand while his brown eyes hid his feelings. Yet why should he be emotional over this proposition—it was his idea and what he wanted desperately. Her acceptance of his proposal was worth millions to him, so all he hid was his desire to convince her to cooperate.

"Let's face it, Camille," he said in a softer tone. "We have a positive physical response to each other now. That's a plus any way you look at it."

Her heartbeat increased a notch. "I didn't know you noticed."

"I've more than noticed since the first day I met you," he said. "We'll get along," he added in a huskier tone that surprised her, a tone that made his words sound as if he referred to a physical relationship. "We'll just do a day here and a day there so you get more accustomed to this and see if it's workable," he said, getting back to the matter at hand. "When we're in the same town, we'll be in the same living quarters so there will be no problem. At some point, I'd like him a week out of each month. You will get him the other three weeks. That's not even half the time. How does that sound to you?" he asked. He leaned forward, his elbows on his knees. Marek once again sounded businesslike, in control of the situation.

Trying to avoid thinking about Noah, she picked up the calendar. "I'll be in Budapest in the fall, so you will have him two weeks out of those months."

"I said at some point. For now, he should stay with you while he's under a year old."

She stared at him, feeling as if a huge weight had lifted. Her pulse began to race with rising joy. "Do you really mean that?"

"Of course. When you're in New Mexico, you'll have him all of the time because we're just starting and he's too little to be away from you. We'll ease into this. As he grows, the schedule will change anyway."

She felt as if sunshine had just spilled over her. "You didn't say that before. I'm so relieved. I've been trying to imagine him in Texas when I'm in Santa Fe and I can't even bear to think about it. That is a wonderful wedding gift. Marek, I'm overjoyed," she said, giving him a squeeze.

He laughed in one of his rare moments with a flash of white teeth. "I think you are far happier over this news about Noah than over your ring or the money or any material gain."

"Of course, I am. You should understand why."

"I should have come to this conclusion from the start," he said, still smiling, and her happiness rose. "I want Noah to be a Rangel, and I hope he loves the ranch. Kern loved ranching."

"In our weekend together, I got that much from him, so I feel I'm giving Noah part of his dad by our marriage and seeing that he grows up knowing the ranch life. It's a relief to know he won't start living there without me when he's so tiny. If I find any of what we do difficult to live with, you'll hear from me about it."

"I'd want to. I want something we can both live with."

"Right now, even when he's older, I can't imagine him gone for almost a month."

"We'll work into long stays gradually. You can come visit anytime you want, and if that's bad, I can bring him to see you or we can try to work something else out."

He loosened his tie and pulled it off, unbuttoning the top button of his shirt. Her mouth went dry watching him. He was way too appealing. She looked away, reminding herself to guard her heart carefully. There was no room in her life for love right now, and Marek was definitely not the man to be the object of her affections. Not until he could love again—if that time ever came.

"We need to pay off your lease and move you to my Dallas home before the wedding. You, Noah, your sisters, everything. I want you to look tomorrow at my house and begin to decide which rooms to make over for you and your family, a nursery, a music room—the whole thing."

"That's monumental."

"Not at all. We'll get it done," he said with supreme confidence. "If the redecorating isn't finished when you move in, it won't matter."

"I feel as if I'm caught in a whirlwind."

He smiled. "You're caught in a marriage of convenience

that I think will make us both happy. I've been sort of caught in a whirlwind since you entered my life," he said, and she laughed.

"No way. You're insulated."

"You're beginning to bring me back to life, whether I want it or not." He picked up the calendar to hand it to her. "I'd like to marry as soon as you feel you can. We can have a big church wedding or something small or something somewhere in between. I want the wedding to be whatever you would like and make it as much a real wedding as possible because we might stay together."

"We might stay together," she repeated, shaking her head. "This is a dream and I think I'll wake up from it. I can't imagine so much of this. Staying together? That seems totally impossible. I think one of us will fall in love with someone else and that will be that."

"No matter what we plan, you can't foresee the future. You never expected this to happen, and neither did I. That first day I was in total shock. That morning I had a list of other things I had planned for my day, my week and my month. When you left my office, my life had changed forever."

"Actually, there we had the same experience. My life changed just as drastically. For me, though, it was for the second time. The first big change was when I met your brother."

"Kern and I were so damn close. I still miss him every day," Marek said, looking away, his voice changing, becoming harsh and cold. He spoke as if talking to himself, and she wondered if he had forgotten her presence and withdrawn into his shell again.

He turned to her. "Let's get back to thinking about a wedding."

"I haven't given any thought to a wedding. I've been so busy thinking about Noah." She studied the calendar. "Under the circumstances, I prefer a small wedding with our families and very closest friends."

"Whatever you want," he replied. "Big or small, I'll pay all the expenses and we can pull the event together quickly. I'd like it as soon as possible because it would be better if we can get settled somewhat before you take off for New Mexico. I'll lease or buy a place in Santa Fe this summer. You can select it and then I can come when I want to."

For the first time, she realized he might be in her life far more than she had expected. "You don't mind leaving your ranch?"

"I'd rather be on the ranch, but I do have others who'll keep it running smoothly. I can rely on Jess as much as I can on myself." Marek sipped his drink and set down his glass.

"Do you care for more wine?"

"No, thank you. My head is spinning enough over all the changes from your proposal."

He sat back and studied her. "We're going too fast for you. Want to stop and think about what we've said for a couple of days and then go back to planning?"

"I'm tempted," she said, relieved he wasn't pushing this on her too much. "We might as well go ahead. If the plans get to be too much for me, I'll tell you. These are monumental changes coming one right after another, like a series of wrecks all in one day."

His eyes narrowed. "I hope it isn't as harsh as a series of wrecks. I hope you can gain more than just money out of this."

"Noah will gain more—he'll get a dad who, hopefully, will love him."

"I already love him. All I have to do is look at him and think about his dad. He's a happy baby, so that makes him doubly lovable."

She looked away, having another moment when her emotions threatened to overwhelm her. "I can maintain better control on a stage than I can here."

"That's different. You can walk away from that without it tearing up your life."

Startled that he understood, she turned back to look at him. "You're perceptive, thank heavens," she admitted. "That makes me feel a tiny bit better."

"Good," he said gently. He placed his hand on her cheek lightly. "Camille, we'll get through this. Just always tell me and I'll tell you if something isn't working."

Again he surprised her and also made her feel better. "Thank you," she whispered, looking into his dark eyes and wondering about the future.

Picking up the calendar, he studied it. "A small wedding should be easy. How about the last Saturday in April?"

"Two weeks and a few days?" She laughed, her worry transformed to amusement over his ridiculous expectations. She shook her head. "That seems impossible, even for a small wedding. I'm free right now from any performances, so I agree it should be before I perform in Dallas and definitely before I go to New Mexico, but two weeks? It can't be done. I'm sure I can't even book the church with that short of notice."

"If necessary, we can marry at my ranch. There are plenty of places. Remember, don't worry about expenses. I'm paying and I can get people moving," he said in a determined tone.

"I'm sure you can," she replied, looking at the calendar he was holding. He had well-shaped hands, strong wrists. His French cuffs had gold links that flashed when he moved. Returning her attention to the calendar, she studied it. "It's April. How about the second Saturday in May? That is really fast for a wedding."

"How about the first Saturday in May?" he asked. "I

promise, we can pull this together. I'll give you all the help you want."

She stared at the date and finally nodded. "If you think that's possible, I guess that will be all right."

"I know it's possible."

She glanced up at him. "You're supremely confident, but I imagine you get what you want the majority of the time."

"No. I didn't with Jillian and Kern. But some things are doable if you have the resources."

"Or the determination," she added quietly.

"We're doing well together, Camille. This is a good sign," he said. He patted her hand. "See, it's working."

Again, his slightest, casual touch, a touch that was meaningless to him, stirred unwanted responses in her. Was she getting herself into a situation that would hurt deeply later? This change with Noah was unwanted, foisted on her. Falling in love would be equally as unwanted and complicated. Realizing that he was saying something to her, she tried to get her mind back on their discussion.

"I'll need to get the church, let my sisters be bridesmaids, even though I want to keep this small. I need to take you home to meet my family."

"It's fine with me however you want to handle it. They're your family. Except you didn't tell them everything, so they had no part in the decision you made."

"Correct. I think they would see all this differently. And they don't fully understand the job or career that I have, either. They like my singing and are proud of me, but I know they wish I had a regular job where I lived in Saint Louis or one particular place and went to an office each day."

"They'll get used to your career as it grows. So we go meet Mom and Dad."

"And brother and grandmother. What about your parents? You said they're not very involved now with you and your sister."

"They've said they will be here as soon as they can. Mom hates flying, but she'll do so. They'll be here for the wedding, I'm sure."

"You're still hurting over your loss. We barely know each other. Frankly, I prefer to put a physical relationship on hold. If we stay together the time will come when we might want to have one, but at this point, there are a lot of uncertainties and we're not in love."

"Whatever you want. We should make decisions about a honeymoon."

"A honeymoon seems foolish under the circumstances. We have a business arrangement."

"One, for distant relatives and friends, it will be simpler because everything will appear normal. Also, we can take three or four days off and get to know each other. We can take Noah if you want. As far as I'm concerned, that would be fun. Or if you'd like just a few days away from the baby, your lessons and your practice, we can be the only ones. Actually, it might be wise for us to get to know each other a little better. We won't be able to as much if we have Noah."

"I'll think about being away from him. Three days is definitely the longest I want to be gone."

"That's fine. What would you enjoy doing for a few days together?" he asked.

"If we're going to do what I want, it would be magical to take just a couple of days, just a weekend, and go to some tropical place, perhaps the Caribbean. Somewhere that has palm trees and an ocean. If we go with Noah along, I'll be willing to stay longer. Without Noah, I don't want to be gone more than a day or two there plus a day going and a day to return."

"That's easy enough."

"Frankly, I've been to Europe and will be going again. I've been to Russia and various cities in the U.S. I've never been to the tropics."

"The lady is not only beautiful, but easy to please. The tropics it is. If the weather is good, and it should be, a villa on Grand Cayman in the Caribbean might be the perfect place. Do you want just us or everyone?"

She laughed. "Since we're not telling the world that this will be a marriage of convenience, I suggest we go alone," she replied. "Just two days in the tropics with a beach and I'll be happy and store it in my memories forever."

"We'll take four days. Get married on Saturday, head for the tropics, stay two days, fly back to Texas." He sat forward. "We'll be going to an island where we can choose from several things to do the night we get there. We can go dancing, attend a show."

"You just mentioned a villa. Let's just stay there. It's all new to me, and I'll be happy just to sit and relax."

"You're easy to please, Camille," he said again. She was a beautiful woman and she did turn heads anytime they were in public. He thought of Noah and, as always, his nerves calmed. This was the right thing to do and the only thing to get Noah really into the lives of the Rangels. "Let's go to dinner now some place where we can dance. We'll let off steam and celebrate working this out." Without waiting for an answer, he stood and pulled a cell phone out of his pocket to make a call and get reservations for two.

Dynamic was another trait she could add to his description. He had taken charge and barreled through everything quickly, efficiently in a lot of ways. Would she have charge of her life from now on, or would Marek Rangel constantly influence it?

Within the hour they were seated in a private club overlooking the city with glass windows giving a floor-to-ceiling view. Steaks had been ordered, and Marek stood. "Let's dance," he said. On the dance floor he took her into his arms, holding her lightly. She was more aware of each contact with him, of her hand in his. The fact that she would soon be his wife was as impossible a prospect as the realization she would soon be a millionaire.

"I'm pleased by the prospects of marrying, seeing Noah grow up and being part of his life. I hope you are."

"I have mixed feelings, and my sisters do, too. We're all scared how we'll feel the first time we're away from Noah."

"That's natural. When we start, we'll keep those times very brief."

"Thank you. I feel much better knowing separation won't be so long. So, Jess and your sister think this is a good plan?"

"Jess does. I told you that. Ginny is not so enthusiastic. Actually, Ginny is worried about me, which is ridiculous, but she's my big sister and sometimes that pops out. She calmed down some after we talked and is a little better about accepting our marriage."

"Our marriage. I won't believe it's happening even after we've walked down the aisle."

"Camille, if you ever do fall in love with someone, come tell me."

As they danced to an old ballad, she gazed into his eyes, seeing the earnest look, realizing he didn't have any expectations that they would fall in love. "I will tell you if I think you need to know," she answered.

He shook his head. "Tell me whether you think I need to know or not. I don't want to hold you to something if you're unhappy. Promise me you'll tell me."

"No. You won't win this one. If I think you need to know, I'll tell you."

He frowned slightly, looking over her head in the dis-

tance as if watching something far away. "I'm not happy
with that answer."

"Put it out of your mind. Tonight there's no need in worrying about something that might happen."

Her gaze was held by his as he gave her a searching look.
"Just remember, I tried to get you to promise to tell me."

"I will remember," she said, knowing she always would.
How much time would they spend together? Questions constantly ran through her thoughts about her future. Could she
avoid falling in love? Would he ever really notice her or get
over his grief and come back into the world?

The next number was fast and it felt good to dance with
him, a silly tune that made everyone on the dance floor
smile, let go and enjoy themselves. Her gaze was locked with
Marek's, and he looked happy, but why wouldn't he, when
he had her promise to give him everything he wanted? He
had let go, dancing with zest, making sexy moves.

She danced around him. At the end, he caught her hand,
spun her around and dipped her low, holding her. She clung
to him because she was off balance as he leaned down so
her hair touched the floor. Both of them laughed when he
swung her up.

"You're beautiful, Camille," he said lightly, smiling at her
with his even white teeth showing. His rare smiles always
heightened his appeal.

"Thank you. I didn't know you've ever really noticed me,"
she replied.

"I've noticed you," he answered. "Ready to go back to
the table?"

As they were seated the waiter appeared to open a bottle
of champagne, an expensive brand she had only had once
before in her life.

"We're celebrating your acceptance of my proposal."

"Congratulations," the waiter said to Marek, then turned to smile at her. "Best wishes, miss."

"Thank you," she replied, laughing as he walked away and Marek raised his glass.

"Here's to a successful union for both of us. May it fulfill needs and bless everyone involved."

They touched glasses with a faint ringing sound of crystal.

"Marek, there are only two people involved in a marriage," she pointed out drily.

He shook his head. "There are a lot of people involved. It will change other lives. Noah's, Ashley's, Stephanie's, your family, my family. This wedding definitely will touch more lives. And this is a celebration because I hope, for one and all, the effects will be great."

"I agree to that one."

"May your joy be full, Camille, and your career soar."

They touched glasses again, and she took another tiny sip of bubbly champagne.

She held up her glass. "May your joy be full, too, Marek, and may joy replace grief and give you peace," she said, touching his glass lightly, watching him over the rim of her glass as she sipped. Her heart drummed. She couldn't keep from glancing at his mouth, wondering about his kisses, wondering whether he would ever really kiss her. She looked up to find him watching her, but he still had that faint crooked smile and she suspected he had not noticed her studying his mouth, much less seen anything in her expression when she had looked up.

He leaned across the linen-covered table, moving a vase of roses out of his way. "I'm beginning to look forward to our tropical getaway, to being alone with you and getting to know you," he said softly, stirring more tingles.

"You're almost flirting, Marek," she said lightly.

"We might as well have a little fun," he answered. "And you'll be my bride soon."

"Sounds impossible. I hope your plans work as you expect. Such upheaval and monumental changes are scary," she replied, thinking about having to part with Noah sometimes, as well as about Marek's promise to keep her happy. He would try in every way except one. His heart was deeply guarded, locked away. Would he ever let go and love again?

He pulled a card out of his shirt pocket and held it out to her. "I'll go with you tomorrow to this jeweler. I can put a limo at your disposal, so after the jewelry store you can shop for a wedding dress. If you prefer, I can fly you to New York to select your dress."

"I'll find a dress in Dallas," she said, thinking this would never be as important as it would have been had she been in love.

"This jeweler is good. You can work with him on the engagement and wedding ring you'd like to have. Do not worry about the price. That's why I'm going. I want to make sure you spend at least a certain amount, but you might as well select your ring."

"I don't need some fabulous ring."

"I want you to have a 'fabulous' ring for marrying me and bringing Noah into my life. Kern would definitely want you to have a spectacular ring. We might as well discuss this now instead of in the jewelry store. Don't hold back. I want you to get what you want. I mean that. I want you to have at least an eight-carat diamond. You can go from there."

"Marek, that is an enormous diamond that isn't necessary or logical. It doesn't represent our love."

"It represents my gratitude," he said. Continuing to hold her hand, he sat close and she looked at the slight curl of his thick, dark lashes that framed his eyes and added to his handsome looks. "If we were deeply in love, I would select your ring and surprise you with it. Under the circumstances, I thought you might as well get what you want. I want it to be nice. I want it extravagant, a constant reminder of my gratitude to you. You can select a design working with this jeweler. He's excellent."

"Thank you," she replied, feeling touched that he had made such a huge effort to convey how grateful he was. A tiny twinge of guilt fluttered because she knew if she could go back and undo telling him about Noah, she might do so.

The day would have come when Noah would ask about his father, and she would have to tell him, but not while he was a baby. She might have waited the first formative years until he was in school and she was separated from him anyway. At the same time, her guilt would have been greater because this way, she felt she was doing the right thing for Noah. He should benefit all his life from this union.

They sat back down when their steaks had been served, but Camille had no appetite. The monumental changes she faced were all she could think about. To her relief, they both lapsed into silence and Marek didn't seem compelled to talk or try to entertain her.

"You're worried, aren't you?" he said finally.

"I can't keep from thinking about all of the plans we've made. I've been accustomed to goals and schedules. Suddenly I'm facing a whole new way of living."

"You're not eating. I didn't want all this to upset you."

"It's just different. You're not exactly wolfing down your dinner, either," she said and received a faint smile.

"Want to dance again? Would you rather go home?"

Relieved, she nodded. "I would rather go home. This has been quite a night."

In a short time they were in the limo headed to her condo. "Can you go at ten in the morning to look at rings?"

"Yes," she said.

He half turned toward her and folded her hand in his. "If you want to call me during the night, I don't care what hour, go ahead. If you have questions, worries, let me know."

"Thanks. I have a million questions. Will this work out? How will I get through giving up Noah? Will he be happy?"

"Ashley will still be with him."

"Right now, I'd rather be his nanny and have her be the singer."

"Do either of your sisters sing?"

"No. Stephanie, absolutely not. Ashley has a nice voice but not a strong one, and she doesn't have the drive to want this. She loves children, wants to be a teacher. We're all rather different."

"As different, I guess, as Kern, Ginny and I are. I wish I could take away your worry, but I can't. The money was supposed to help. This goes way beyond money, which becomes insignificant."

She had to smile. "Millions do not become insignificant," she said. "Well, maybe the thrill of the money does diminish next to the rest," she admitted.

"I know it does. It shows in every way. If I told you I'd changed my mind and didn't care and was going to stay out of your life and take my money, your only feeling would be relief. I don't have to ask if I'm right."

She looked outside at the busy thoroughfare and again had to fight tears. He was right. The millions meant nothing next to letting him have so much of Noah.

They rode the rest of the way to her condo in silence. On her porch, he placed his hands on her shoulders. "Camille, I'll repeat—I'm thrilled beyond measure over your acceptance of my proposal. I promise to try to keep you and your sisters happy. I'm thrilled and excited over the prospects and we'll get along in this quasi marriage."

"I hope so," she said. "I pray this is good for Noah. That's the one thing I really cling to. The money will benefit me and my family in several ways, but it's the thought that you'll be good for Noah that really makes this acceptable. It's what I wanted in the first place."

"I'll do everything in my power to make it good for him." Marek's brown eyes were unfathomable as he studied her. "When we wed, we'll kiss in church. I don't want that to be our first kiss," he said, his dark gaze focusing on her mouth. Her heart drummed so violently she hoped he couldn't hear it. His announcement that he intended to kiss her caused every nerve to come alive. Why was it so enormously unsettling? His kiss should be meaningless.

As his arm circled her waist, she could barely get her breath. He drew her closer, and she rested her hands lightly against his upper arms.

When he leaned down, she closed her eyes, tilting her face up to his. His mouth covered hers lightly, then pressing more firmly, warm, sexy, tempting. Her lips parted and then his did while his tongue slipped into her mouth. The first stroke changed their relationship for her forever. No more was he a new acquaintance becoming closely involved with her. He was an appealing, sexy man she would be entering into an intimate relationship with. Slowly, with deliberation, he kissed her while he drew her up against him. Feeling the bulge of hard biceps beneath her hands, she stood quietly. Leaning over her, he tightened his arm around her.

She kissed him in return, tumbling into an abyss that made her stomach flip and her heart pound faster. Without thinking about what she was doing, she slipped her arm around his neck, and then she realized how she had responded. She leaned away and gasped for breath.

"Now we've kissed," she whispered, feeling stunned because his kiss had been sexy, possessive—a hot kiss that conveyed he cared while that wasn't actually the situation.

He gave her another inscrutable look and said nothing.
"Good night, Marek."

"I'll see you for dinner tomorrow night and we can firm
up plans, call parents and whoever we need to tell while
we're together. I'm happy, Camille," he said, smiling at her.

He turned away to get into the waiting limo while she
went inside, her heart pounding. His kiss had melted her,
shaken her and set her on fire. Could she live with this? How
long would it be a marriage of convenience only?

She would lose Noah part of the time. Now another threat
loomed that she might fall in love with Marek and complicate her life in every way possible. She had known that was
a risk, but it had seemed slight. His kiss had smashed that
opinion to bits. Her lips tingled, and she shook her head.

"I can't fall in love with him," she whispered. Yet her
heartbeat still raced from his kiss and she would remember
forever the look in his eyes afterward, a heated, possessive
look, a look that clearly expressed that he saw her as a desirable woman.

"I thought I heard you," Ashley said, coming into the hall
from the family room. She was in turquoise pajamas and a
matching robe.

"I'm going to marry him," Camille announced as if trying to convince herself. "I accepted. You know that's what
we decided."

Ashley shook her head. "I hope you know what you're
doing. I'll be with Noah, but you won't be."

"I'm going to be with him more than I thought at first."

"All that money, Camille. I can't even imagine our lives."

"I think you'll want to go to school before long. Maybe
by next fall. We'll find a nanny. There's bound to be another
good one in the world."

"Let's just take this a little bit at a time. This will change
the lives of everyone in the family."

"Where's Stephanie?"

"I'm here," she said from the shadows, coming into the hallway. "I heard you accepted."

"I'll go out with him tomorrow night and we'll call our parents to make the official announcement."

Ashley walked to Camille to hug her lightly. "I'll pray this works out."

"It has to be good for everyone. We're not losing Noah and he's gaining a dad and we're all improving financially."

"That's an understatement," Stephanie said. "I think sleep has gone for tonight for all three of us. While you go change, Ashley and I will get some hot chocolate. We can hear your plans and maybe help you with some."

"Thanks, Steph," Camille said, smiling at her sister and thankful that Stephanie was beginning to accept Marek and the situation. "I'll need help with plans. We're aiming for a wedding in about three weeks. He'll pay for everything, he said. I think our whole family will be all for this. If they aren't, Marek will win them over."

"I think you're right. That first night I didn't think I ever wanted to see him again. Now I can't help but feel like this may benefit Noah and everyone else. Hurry and change so we can talk," Stephanie said.

"Sure," Camille replied and left the room. As she changed, all she could think about was his kiss that had set her heart pounding. It had been sexy, hot and had made her want more. Had Marek felt anything?

At home Marek shed his coat and tie and unbuttoned his shirt as he went to the desk in his bedroom. He thought about Noah, remembering holding him and looking into his lively eyes. He already loved the baby, and he could imagine how Camille must feel.

He remembered holding her in his arms tonight when they

kissed. He dropped his pen and leaned back to think about her. Her kiss had shaken him because it had stirred him. For the first time since his loss, he had stopped feeling numb. Numbness had been replaced by desire, lust really. That had given him a shock. Because of her kiss, he had no doubt that they could have a successful physical relationship. Would this marriage work? He had been so positive with her, but deep down he now had as many unanswered questions as she did.

The question startled him because up until tonight he had thought about going into this marriage only as something that would revolve around Noah. After their kiss tonight, that expectation had flown away. There would be a physical relationship between them. He was sure of it, and he already wanted it.

Would he fall in love with her? He shook his head even though he wasn't talking to anyone. He wouldn't love again. He was as certain of that as ever. But lust was another thing. Could she handle that? As swiftly as the question rose in his mind, the knowledge that she could reassured him. She was tied to only two things: Noah and her career. Since she didn't want to fall in love, she would be guarding against it as much as he.

He had thought he was in no hurry to rush into an intimate relationship, but her kiss had changed that. Desire was palpable, strong, a torment. With a deep breath, he picked up his pen and began to list what he needed to do in the next few days.

In minutes he again was thinking back to kissing her tonight. For a few moments he was lost in a fantasy about making love to her, holding her close. With an effort he tried to get back to things he needed to do.

He would be with her tomorrow night to make plans together and to tell their families. They could get on Skype and it would be almost like being together. His gaze fell on his brother's picture, and he picked up the snapshot. Kern had his cocky grin and stood beside his favorite horse.

"Brother, I wish you could see your son. He's a great little kid. He's happy all the time and a good baby, but he has a little look in his eyes like you had plenty of times. He's going to be like you," Marek said quietly, getting a knot in his throat and wishing Kern had lived to see Noah. "At least you knew about him. I imagine you were planning to marry Camille and you probably had absolutely no doubt whatsoever that you could talk her into it. Kern, I'm sorry for the way things turned out, but I'll do my best with Noah."

Marek wiped his eyes. He missed his brother so often. Such a waste! He pulled off his shirt, feeling restless, wishing he had someone to talk to for a while. He wondered what time Camille went to bed. The thought of her stretched out in bed set his pulse racing. She wanted to wait on a physical relationship, but he suspected neither of them would wait long. If he had his preference, they would not wait at all. Just the thought set his pulse racing faster. He knew nothing about her except the facts of her background that he had gleaned from what she'd told him and the little on the web about her. She wasn't heavily into social media and neither was he, so he hadn't learned much there.

In slightly over three weeks he would be a married man—married to a woman he barely knew. The idea astounded him.

Two weeks later Marek's cell phone jingled and he answered to listen to his sister.

"Mom and Dad are so worried about you and what you're doing."

"Don't let them get to you. The paternity test indicated Noah is Kern's baby. I'm doing what I want. I think it will work out."

They were both tense about the upcoming evening. "I'll

see you at the party tonight," he said, thinking about the engagement party that was being held by his parents' dinner club and oldest friends.

"Okay, little brother. I just want you happy. Noah is a cute little fellow and he does look like Kern."

"Whether he looks like Kern or not, Noah is Kern's, Ginny. Could you let him go now?"

"No. You win. See you tonight."

"Ahh, that's my sis." He ended the call and left for the corral, thinking about the wedding. He still did not expect to love again. To love was to risk your heart, and he would never go through the kind of hurt he had experienced after losing Jillian. That was vastly different from lusting after someone. Camille knew this, and she knew what to expect from him. She was completely aware that love would never be part of the equation. Still, he wanted to make love to her. He wanted her in his arms, in his bed. He wanted her as his wife in the fullest sense. Thinking about her aroused him, and he glanced at his watch, counting the hours until he would see her.

Walking into the barn, he found Jess with his head under the hood of a truck.

"What's wrong with the pickup?"

"Nothing I can't fix," Jess said. He straightened. "They giving you a hard time?"

"Yes. Mom and Dad are worried about me rushing into a marriage. They're interested in Noah, but feel I can work out a better arrangement. I've had a call from Ginny about their opinion."

"Do *you* think you are making a mistake?"

"No. No matter how I look at it, I don't. You've seen Noah, and we all know he's Kern's baby. I can't just see him a few times a year."

"Kern's little boy, growing up here—I don't see how you can go wrong with him growing up as part of the family."

"Both Camille and I want him to have this ranching legacy."

"Amen to that. 'Course, you're tying your life to hers and hers to you, but that should work out."

"I think it will. Can I help with this?" Marek asked, leaning over the truck.

"It's a dirty job," Jess said.

"I take that as a yes. Give me the wrench, and you take a break."

"Won't argue with that one," Jess said, handing Marek his wrench and stepping away to sit on bales of hay.

Marek was soon absorbed in the truck, glad to find something that occupied his thoughts, thinking it would be a long day until he could pick up Camille for the party.

"Wedding will be here before you know it, so you better be sure," Jess said.

"The sooner the better," Marek replied. "I want to get this over with and put an end to the arguments. As soon as my tux is done, I'm ready for a wedding. I hope Camille is, too."

Five

Dressed in a tailored white silk dress with a skirt that ended below her knees, Camille stood poised to walk up the aisle in a small chapel in the Saint Louis church she had attended all her life. Her arm was looped through her father's, and he smiled at her. "You look beautiful. I hope you're happy."

"I will be, Dad," she said, watching Ashley walk up the aisle.

"This isn't what we'd hoped for you when Mom and I talked about all of you growing up and marrying, but if you're all right with it, we will be, too. As long as you're sure you're not doing it for the money."

"Absolutely not. The money is a plus, but I've tried to keep that from influencing my decision. This is about Noah."

"I hope you mean that. Camille, if this marriage doesn't work, then get out of it," Anthony Avanole said solemnly. "You'll have enough money to invest it and never touch it.

Use the interest from it and what you have if the amount grows. It'll be there to give back to Marek if you need to."

"I know, Dad," she said, looking at the tall, handsome man who stood waiting at the altar and within moments would be her husband. "Marek and I think this marriage will work. Time and again, I've been over all the reasons."

"The money is a blessing for you and for all of us. It will change our lives, but I don't want it at the cost of your happiness."

She shook her head. "It won't be. I won't stay in the relationship if it's unhappy or not the best for Noah, for all of us." The marriage still dazed her as much as the ring on her finger. She glanced down at her hand as she held the large bouquet of white orchids, lilies and white roses. Her eight-carat diamond with sapphires and diamonds along the gold band sparkled on her finger. The contradictions in her wedding were as numerous as in Marek's personality. A small wedding, an enormous bouquet and a huge, dazzling diamond. A honeymoon for two people who were almost strangers. She looked again at Marek, feeling her pulse racing. Jess was best man because Pete Rangel, Marek's father, had asked Marek to let someone stand in for him because of his crutches. His dad had been happy that Marek had asked him, even when he could not accept.

When Camille had asked Marek about it earlier, he had made it clear to her that he was happy to have Jess as his best man.

"It's time," the wedding planner said, and Camille and her dad started the walk up the aisle. As she neared Marek, she saw the somber look on his face, a look she recognized. He was fighting his emotions, and she could imagine he was thinking about his fiancée and the wedding he had expected to have.

She hurt for him, wishing she could erase his ache, knowing no one could. He stepped to her side to take her hand, his dark eyes unreadable. He smiled, but it was perfunctory.

She went through the ceremony, repeating her vows, too aware she was taking an enormous risk as well as aware of Marek's pain.

The moment the minister said, "You may kiss the bride," warmth returned to Marek's eyes as he focused on her. His kiss was light, but the look he gave her was reassuring.

When they turned to face the guests and their minister introduced them as Mr. and Mrs. Marek Rangel, her parents smiled at her and her mother dabbed her eyes. Marek's parents smiled, even though Marek's mother also had tears.

Marek took her arm to walk up the aisle, and she smiled with relief that the ceremony had ended.

They had pictures with both of their families. Even though it was a small wedding, there were more guests than she had originally thought they would have. They constantly talked to guests, and it wasn't until Marek began the first dance with her that she was alone with him. He held her lightly, smiling at her, but it was a strained smile. A muscle worked in his jaw and she hurt for him, certain he was thinking of his fiancée.

"You look beautiful today," he said. His voice sounded labored, and she would be thankful when the reception was over and they could get away.

"Thank you. You look handsome, and your pain doesn't show very much," she said, wishing she could do something to help him.

"I'm all right." He glanced beyond her, looking around the large ballroom. "Our security is tight and I don't think there are any unwanted people looking for pictures or a story."

"The security is the best ever."

"You're as calm as a summer morning. But then you're accustomed to going on stage and hiding what you feel."

"I've made my decision, and I'm hoping for the best. Noah

has been on his best behavior all day as if he senses something special is happening." Marek's slight smile looked real this time, and she relaxed a little. "Perhaps someday we'll dance and you'll be delighted that I'm the person in your arms."

"I am happy over this, Camille. In more ways than you can guess. You've brought me out of the grief I had sunk into. I think this union is going to be great for all of us."

"That's what I'm counting on, too."

"We'll do all right together, because we each have our own lives and we're really not going to be together that much," he said, sounding as if he were preoccupied. "The arrangement we have is a trial—remember that. As much as we can, we'll live together under the same roof when you're not performing, and for now you'll call the ranch home. As soon as possible, we'll all go to the ranch."

"That will be a totally new experience for me and my sisters. Noah won't know the difference," she said, enjoying dancing with Marek as she always did. He looked incredibly handsome, and for a fleeting second she wished life had been different. The longing was gone as swiftly as it had come.

"You can get whatever decorator you want," Marek said. "We've already made changes at our Dallas house."

"*Our* house—it will take a while to become accustomed to thinking that way. I'm still astounded at how fast you got the changes in I wanted."

"It's our house from this day forward, until we make a legal change."

"That sounds permanent. The ranch is another thing I'm trying to become accustomed to. Horses, cattle, ranches—I know nothing about them."

"Ranch life is pretty plain. It's hard work, but just taking care of cattle, horses, land, fences, a million things strung out over lots of land. It won't mean much to you, and when you're there, you won't even know it's going on."

"My ring is beautiful. Thank you again."

"I'm glad you like it. Let's get through this and out of here when we can. I'm ready to be alone with you. You look gorgeous today."

"Thank you," she said, smiling at him. "You're nice. You look supremely handsome."

He smiled. "Mutual admiration. That's good. There's so much that's good. I'm happy, Camille."

They circled the dance floor in silence.

"I like dancing with you, but we can do that on our honeymoon," Marek said finally. "After this dance, we probably should circulate and talk to guests so we can get out of here sooner. I want you to myself," he repeated.

"Marek, just a reminder, I can't rush into anything physical."

"We've agreed on that subject, and I promised it would be mutual." He leaned close to her ear. "I'll tell you now. I'm going to seduce you, Camille. I want to make love to you. You're a desirable woman," he whispered, making her tingle, although she suspected he was trying to smooth over the lack of deep feelings between them.

"I could be a little green woman from Mars and you wouldn't notice," she said.

"Not true. I know I'm with a beautiful, desirable woman," he said in a warm voice, looking down at her in one of the rare moments when it seemed as if he really saw her as a woman.

The ballad ended and another began. Her father appeared to ask her to dance, and Marek left to ask his mother.

By early afternoon she saw Marek give her a look and then glance toward the door. She sat at a table with her family. "I think we're leaving now," she said. She gave each one a hug and stopped longer with Ashley. Noah had fallen asleep beside her in his carrier. "Don't hesitate to text about anything. Keep in touch."

"You'll hear from me often. Don't worry. He'll be fine. We'll all take care of him."

"Take care, Ashley, and call if there's anything. Marek can have us flown right back here."

"I know he can. See you in a few days. Enjoy the water and palm trees. And your handsome husband."

Camille laughed and hugged her sister briefly. "I will."

Joining her, Marek took her hand to rush to the waiting limo that took them to the airport and a Rangel plane.

As they headed east over Texas, Marek gazed out the window. Noah would be part of his life now. He already had an attorney working on the adoption. In spite of wanting this marriage and being overjoyed that Camille had accepted, he had hurt earlier today. The morning had distressed him, bringing back too many memories of Jillian.

The marriage ceremony had opened old wounds. Camille had been aware of his pain. Her kindness and understanding and, later, her happy expectations and quiet cheer, had lifted him out of the hurt. She was a beautiful, intelligent, talented woman. For that afternoon, at least, he had forgotten and set aside the past, something that was happening more and more since she had come into his life. Now he reached out to take her hand, then impulsively tugged her closer and leaned forward to kiss her. It was a brief kiss because anything longer would set him on fire.

When he sat back, he smiled at her, and she smiled in return. "It's been a good day," she said. He nodded.

She had been convincing in assuring him that a marriage of convenience was all right. He knew people who felt that way and then fell in love and marriage was the thing they wanted most. She had made her choices, and both Camille and her family seemed happy.

Their wedding night would be a letdown for most, but they had had a frank talk about their plans for this honeymoon and both had agreed to set aside a physical relationship at this point in their lives. He would let their relationship develop at whatever pace worked out, but he wanted to make love to her. It would please him if they could have a real wedding night.

He thought about the day's events. His parents had seemed wary of Camille and Noah. They always had great interest in Ginny's girls when they were with them. Once they returned to California, they seemed to retreat back into their own world. Perhaps they'd come around to welcoming Camille and Noah.

Shifting his attention to Camille again, he wished her long hair was down. She looked sophisticated, composed, satisfied. Her expression and demeanor hid the stormy emotions he was sure she battled.

"You look beautiful. You have all day," he said, meaning what he told her.

"Thank you. And you look breathtakingly handsome in your new tux and your fancy new boots."

He wiggled his foot. "Thank you. I don't know about fancy, but they are new, clean and comfortable."

"The boots made the men in the wedding look like the cowboys they are."

"Frank didn't have on boots. Just Jess and I did. My dad wore them. He's continued wearing them even after leaving the ranch."

"I'm excited about our destination. I know this may be old to you, but it's a marvel I haven't experienced before."

"Enjoy yourself. Just don't swim alone except in our pool."

"*Our* pool. You've made the transition quickly."

"I'm trying to. This is what I wanted and I'll go as far

as I can to make it work. In every way, Camille," he added, thinking about the physical side. Her cheeks flushed, so he knew she understood his reference and reacted to it.

She turned to look outside, and he glanced down at the band on his finger. It seemed unreal in so many ways. Marek touched the band, which was wide and plain gold. Jillian's face floated in front of him, her cascade of white-blond hair, her large blue-green eyes, her smile that always made him smile in return. He took a deep breath. He missed her so and she was supposed to be sitting beside him as he headed off for his honeymoon. Instead, he was traveling with a black-haired beauty he barely knew.

"You're thinking about Jillian, aren't you?" Camille asked gently, touching his hand.

"Yes. It's the wedding that's triggered a lot of memories. They'll fade out of my thoughts. Sorry."

"Don't be ridiculous," she said. "I understand."

"I'm surprised, because you've never lost anyone extremely close."

She shook her head. "No, but I've played characters who have, and I have given a lot of thought to feelings and reactions."

"Maybe that's part of your success," he said, speculating about her and realizing he should hear her perform. "I wonder if Noah will sing. Kern could whistle. That was his musical ability." He grinned. "My brother didn't sing. If he did, the dogs started howling."

She laughed, and his insides heated. She was not only beautiful, but desirable. Her laughter was an enticing, contagious sound.

"You should have had more laughter today," he said.

"I'm doing all right. I never thought about Noah singing. Right now, I think more about him talking. Do you think your family will ever accept Noah or me?" she asked.

"If we stay together, probably more than they do now. They've surprised me. I didn't expect the reaction I got from them at all. Frankly, I think my mother is afraid to let go and love him. She loved Kern. When we were growing up, I always thought she favored him. Ginny and I both did. Kern was probably more lovable than we were. He could charm anyone. I think she's scared of getting hurt again if she gets too close to Noah. If she lets go and loves him, she wouldn't want to go back to California. My dad could be feeling the same. Don't let it worry you. They'll go back to California before we return and you won't see them for a long time."

"I'm just sorry they didn't welcome Noah. He's a sweetheart. They know you did a paternity test, don't they?"

"Yes, they do," Marek said, unable to understand how his parents could so easily reject Kern's baby when they knew he was their grandson. "Don't worry about it. They shouldn't be that important to you. I think they tried to avoid seeing Noah, just so they wouldn't become attached. We'll be together sometime when Ginny's girls are around and they'll have to get to know him. If they do, I expect them to change. How can they resist him?"

She smiled. "I quite agree. He's the most adorable baby in the whole world," she said, and Marek smiled with her. "Ahh, I made you smile. That's good. A real smile." She patted his hand, a light, warm touch that heightened his awareness of her.

"Well, at least my family has accepted you. Actually, they're grateful for all you've done for us."

Marek reached over to take a pin out of her hair. "I like your hair down. The wedding is over and it's just us."

She smiled at him as her long, raven locks fell.

"Giving away money is the easiest part of this. Making the changes in our lives—that's the hard part. You can't always predict the outcome of your actions," he said, concentrating on taking down her hair. When it fell freely, she shook her head. His pulse quickened. The midnight cascade fell over her shoulders, framing her face and giving her a more earthy appearance. With her lush curves and flowing hair, she looked hot-blooded and passionate. He could remember kissing her in total detail because it had been a sizzling kiss.

"Were you and Kern always close?"

"Yes. He just tagged along after me and I accepted that. Sometimes I thought he was a pest and would shake him, but most of the time I let him come with me or do what I was doing. By the time we were out of high school, we were becoming close, a closeness that grew as we did things together. As adults, the age difference didn't matter. I miss him every day. I could count on him for a lot."

"That's sort of a description of my relationship with Ashley. Not so much Stephanie, who is older. A lot of the time she did her own thing. She has a deep regard for money, so you couldn't have picked a better way to win her over."

"Works with most people," he replied, even though he knew it was a cynical attitude.

"If I hadn't thought this would be good for Noah, I wouldn't have agreed for any amount," she said quietly, and he gazed into her blue eyes that held him as if she had immobilized him.

"I don't think you would have," he replied and they lapsed into silence.

"I can't wait to get there."

"We'll get there in time for a swim, and then we can have a long, leisurely dinner overlooking the water. And there are palm trees around the veranda. I made sure of that before I leased this place."

She smiled. "I want to wish the plane there now. It sounds like paradise."

He didn't want to point out that paradise would be doing

this with a person she loved. She seemed happy, and he wasn't trying to shoot down her joy because it was a difficult situation. A strained honeymoon with a stranger, both of them locked into a paper marriage of convenience. He had never expected to find himself in any such thing. And he would not have been if Jillian had lived. He would have been married to her by now, perhaps starting his own family, and he would have had to let Noah go and only see the child from time to time. Taking a deep breath, he dropped his thoughts of Jillian and any "what-ifs." With Camille to keep his mind elsewhere, he was finding it easier to focus on the present, and that's what he needed to do—try to be the best husband and dad he could be.

When they finally flew over the Caribbean, Camille hovered by the window, fascinated as a child by the bright blue water below. "Marek, it's beautiful! It's what I've imagined."

"Camille, you've been south and have seen sights like this—Houston, San Diego, Miami."

"Only Houston—I haven't gone to Galveston or along the coast. I've been on northern coasts and in Europe, but I haven't been to Miami or San Diego."

"I'm surprised." He smiled slightly again, watching her turn back to look, glad she was enjoying herself because he thought this so-called honeymoon in Grand Cayman was cheating her in too many ways.

They landed, and all her attention was on their surroundings as they drove to the villa he had leased. It was within high walls with a gatekeeper. The security wasn't obvious, but Marek had already hired a company and knew it was in place. When they stepped out of the limo he took her hand to go inside.

"I love this," she said, inhaling deeply, her gaze roaming over the sprawling villa. "I see we'll have security here."

"We will and a full staff who will stay out of our way.

Under the circumstances I didn't see any point in dismissing the staff," he remarked.

"This is a magic place and maybe magic will happen."

"You've been performing in make-believe stories too long," he said, still amused by her enthusiasm. "Don't count on magic. I know you have been places far more exotic and beautiful than this."

"It's what captures your fancy that becomes so special. And this does mine more than castles and mountains and bustling cities."

He swept her into his arms, and her eyes flew wide. For the first time since they had flown away from the U.S., he had her full attention. "I'll follow an old tradition even though it's ridiculous for us. This may be the only marriage for either one of us, so I intend to do what I can to make it work and to keep you happy."

She smiled broadly and wrapped her arms around his neck, her blue eyes ensnaring him in that manner she had. "Watch out, my husband, or you'll cause me to fall in love with you. Neither of us can cope with that."

"I don't think there's much danger, but if you do, we're married."

"If I do, then I will do everything in my power to make you fall in love with me," she whispered, suddenly looking solemn. "That's a promise," she said, tapping his chest with her forefinger while he carried her over the threshold and inside.

He looked at her intently, desire stirring as it had the night he had kissed her. It had surprised him then and it did now. With their gazes locked, he set her on her feet. She still had her arms around his neck and she gazed up at him, fires in the depths of blue, a sultry invitation that made his heart beat faster.

He forgot the past and was lost in the moment. His gaze

lowered to her mouth and he remembered her steamy kiss, a kiss that had jolted him and pulled him solidly into the present. He leaned down, placing his lips on hers while her arm tightened around his neck.

She pressed her soft curves against him. She was tall, warm and enticing. The moment his mouth touched hers, thoughts shut down, desire flickered to life. He tightened his arm around her narrow waist, pulling her closer against him. Long-dormant feelings stirred. His body came to life, heart pounding, fire consuming him while she kissed him passionately in return.

Her kisses were fiery and demanding. That energy and zest for life that she exhibited channeled into passion and melted him. His body responded fully. Desire rocked him. She surprised him when she leaned away. "Marek, wait," she gasped. "Let's not complicate our lives more. I'm not ready for a purely physical relationship in spite of saying marriage vows today. We've both agreed on that."

Raising his head, he tried to get his breath. His body needed to cool. He desired her and suspected it would take little to crumble her argument and seduce her.

"I want to wait, and our kisses are leading to lovemaking," she added. "This isn't what either of us planned."

Six

Camille tried to catch her breath. Her heart pounded, and every nerve was alive. She wanted Marek, but she had meant her argument. What she hadn't told him was that she was not going to fall into his arms and into his bed at the first few kisses because it would be totally meaningless to him.

Sooner or later he would overcome his grief and he would want her physically, but it was lust and nothing else. If she succumbed, it was not going to be the first afternoon they were husband and wife, when they had nothing between them except working out this paper marriage and Noah's care.

She intended to stick to what she had said, even though her body clamored for more. She wanted his kisses, wanted his lovemaking, but common sense said at this point that was the road to disaster. If she went to bed with him, she wanted him to be aware of her as a desirable woman, to remember she was his wife, to truly want her and know her way better than he did at the moment.

His brown eyes had darkened to midnight, and he was breathing heavily. He looked as if he could devour her. She didn't know whether he was weighing her argument or trying to get desire under control as he stood staring at her.

Walking away from him, she viewed the open living area in front of her.

"This is fantastic," she declared, trying to focus on something besides Marek and her own desire for more kisses. "It's perfect and more than I dreamed." The entrance opened into an airy, large living area with columns dividing the room from an adjoining dining area. Floor-to-ceiling glass doors opened to a veranda that ran the length of the house. Beyond it was the pool with fountains and gardens that overlooked the white beach and clear blue water. Tall palms ran along one side of the veranda, and there were palms scattered between the white beach and the water.

Camille walked outside, inhaling deeply and holding out her arms. "It's gorgeous." She spun around to tell him. He stood only a few feet behind her, watching her with such cool speculation in his eyes that her pulse jumped. Was he thinking about their marriage and what it might mean?

"This is perfect, Marek. I'm so happy with it. I won't want to leave."

"Yes, you will. You'll miss Noah. You'll feel guilty about missing your voice practice and language studies."

"I plan to do those here."

"Because of Noah, you'll be ready to leave, but I'm glad you like it. For now we can change and swim or we can just sit out here, have drinks and then dinner."

"A swim. I have to get into that water. I'll beat you there," she said, rushing past him, and he smiled again.

He was ready first, waiting when she came out. She wore a pink T-shirt that came to mid-thigh and hid her curves. She was aware of his scrutiny, far more aware of him. He wore plaid trunks. His muscled chest was bare; his broad shoulders and arms were hard muscles, probably from the ranch work he did. He had a smattering of dark chest curls and his legs were long. Realizing she was staring, she dropped her things and pulled off her T-shirt, hotly aware that he watched her.

She turned, flipping her head, causing her hair to swing back over her shoulders.

"I'll race you in," she said, dashing past him. In seconds he passed her and ran in the water ahead of her, splashing out until it was deep enough to swim. After a few strokes he turned to watch her as she caught up.

"You're a good swimmer," he said.

"You're better. You beat me."

"I used to compete in swimming a long time ago."

"Then I won't challenge you again."

"You challenge me on a regular basis," he said in a husky voice. He was flirting with her. A subtle change in their relationship.

"I didn't think you noticed."

"I'm not completely numb."

"Did you say 'numb' or 'dumb'?" she asked sweetly, teasing him. He laughed and splashed her with a wave of water. She shrieked and swam away. In a flash he caught up and swam beside her. He grasped her upper arm lightly while he treaded water.

"See that buoy?" he said, pointing at an orange buoy that bobbed gently in the small waves. "They told me that is the farthest out we should swim. It's much deeper and tides are stronger."

Glancing back at the beach, she was surprised how far they had come. "This water is beautiful."

"It's prettier when you snorkel. I have all-new equipment on the beach."

"Then, Mr. Expert Swimmer, I'll race you back to it," she

said, starting to swim as vigorously as possible. For a few seconds, he let her lead and then he passed her. When she walked out of the water, he waited, and she could feel his gaze drifting slowly over her in a long, leisurely look that became almost a caress. She tingled from head to toe. Desire ignited, a flame deep inside. Her awareness heightened of the skimpiness of her two-piece red suit.

"Where's the snorkel equipment?"

"Maybe we should just stay out here and enjoy the scenery," he drawled, still studying her.

"I think that's the way to complications. We discussed this earlier," she said without moving. She tried to keep her gaze on his face, to keep from looking him over as he was her. He was breathtaking, masculine, sexy.

"Marek, where did you put the equipment?"

"Camille, the best equipment on this beach is what I'm looking at," he said, walking to her. "You're gorgeous. I can't stop looking," he added.

"Yes, you can," she said, her words sounding distant to her. "Snorkel equipment or I go inside and dress."

He walked up to place his hands on her shoulders and she was riveted, her threat of leaving impossible to carry out. His light touch burned as if it had been a brand. Aware of him only inches away, she tingled. Could he hear her pounding heart?

His arm slipped around her waist. "You're bringing me back to life. I didn't think it was possible."

"For that, I'm glad," she said, meaning it, but barely able to focus on conversation. His hands were on her, his body only inches away and both of them wore very little. All her cool reserve had shattered, and the look in his eyes was something new in their relationship, yet age-old, blatantly sexy. She was breathless, too aware of his body, his arm around her and his mouth so close. She looked up into dark eyes with fire in their depths.

"For the first time in over a year I feel alive," he whispered. He drew her closer and leaned down to kiss her. His mouth was on hers, his tongue stroking her with slow deliberation that made her pounding heart race.

She slid her hands over his smooth back, pressed against him and felt his arousal. Her arms tightened as she returned his kiss eagerly, unable to resist, knowing they both had just crossed a line.

There would be no going back from this fiery kiss to an occasional peck on the cheek. She closed her eyes tightly, relishing the feel of his hard muscles, his strength, the deepening passion in his kisses.

His hands ran over her back and bottom, down along her bare thighs.

She finally ended the kisses. "Slow down, Marek. This changes everything far too fast. Let's cool down before our lives take another turn and complications beset us."

Breathing hard, he gazed at her with longing in his expression. With a pounding heart, she tried to cling to the sensible speech she had just made, but that wasn't what her heart wanted. She stepped back. "We should swim," she whispered. She passed him, heading to the water to cool down and to put some distance between them. Their lives had just taken another major turn. Was it already out of her control?

He showed her how to wear her goggles. His casual touches were even more disturbing than before. She had always had a reaction to him, but not as intense as it had now become. Desire was a constant, a hot, running need that she hoped to control.

In minutes, the fascinating sea creatures swimming around her captured her attention. Finally, Marek tugged on her arm and motioned to get out.

As they surfaced, she took off the breathing tube. Marek was beside her. Tall, muscular, appealing—how could she return to being casual, unaffected? Close to shore, they could easily stand in water that was only a little over four feet deep.

"It's later than you think. Let's have a drink and then dinner so I can release the staff for this evening."

"Certainly. That was fascinating. I want to come back in the morning," she said, thinking Marek was far more fascinating.

He looked amused. "You can snorkel all day if you'd like. The fish won't mind."

"When was the first time you came here?"

"I've never been to this particular villa, but the Caymans, probably when I was five or six. I don't even remember."

"You've done it all. No wonder nothing excites you."

"Oh, yes, there are things that excite me," he replied, his voice changing as he flirted again.

"I'm not asking what."

"Who, not what. You already know the answer."

Pulling on her T-shirt, she wriggled it down over her hips, glancing around to see him watching her.

She picked up all her things. "I'll change and be back."

"Sure," he said, flipping a towel over his shoulder as he headed inside with her.

After a shower, she dressed in a deep blue cotton sundress and sandals and dried her hair, letting it fall loosely over her shoulders. When she went outside, he was waiting at the table. He looked relaxed in chinos and a navy knit shirt. A chilled bottle of champagne was on ice and he had already partially filled two flutes. He handed one to her and picked up the other.

"Here's to a happy union that blesses all concerned, especially Noah."

"I'll drink to that," she said, touching his glass lightly,

watching bubbles rise in the pale golden champagne. She sipped her drink and looked out to sea.

"Sit here, Camille. We'll have our drinks before dinner."

She sat in a lawn chair, and he sat in another close beside her. "This is truly beautiful, Marek, and I'm having a wonderful time."

"I'm glad," he said, gazing at the water. She was beginning to be able to tell when he was thinking of his fiancée and grief was present because his voice and expression were both remote.

"This is the hardest time of day. Sundown. Somehow it seems a time of loss. The sunshine is gone, the night isn't here. This is when I've had a bad time. You'd think it would be late at night, which sometimes it is, but this time of day really gets me." He talked, but she thought he had almost forgotten her. He was looking toward the horizon. To the west the sun was a ball of orange fire only half-visible above the horizon.

She couldn't think of anything to say that would help him. He was wrapped in his own world, and his hurt was understandable, but at least today, he had had moments when his pain had lifted and she had glimpsed the lively man he was before the crash.

She gazed out to sea, still shocked that she was locked into a marriage of convenience with a man who might always love another woman. Would he break her heart if she fell in love with him? She would do exactly as her father had suggested—keep the money tucked away so she could return it if this arrangement did not work out to everyone's satisfaction.

"Marek, what do you want from life? You've already been enormously successful in business. You have the ranch you love."

"I want to be a dad for Noah. I hope our marriage and this arrangement work out."

"Aside from Noah, what do you hope to achieve? You have an enormous fortune, so it's not that. What is it?"

"Still make money. Also to help others. I have certain charities and, of those, there are a few I'm particularly interested in. I've established a ranch for homeless kids. It's not far out of Fort Worth. Some kids are there on a temporary basis, some permanent. I've gone through our church."

"That's great," she said, surprised by his answer.

"Don't sound so startled that I would help someone."

"I'm just surprised at the particular project."

"I only put up the money and helped them get established, but I've liked working with them occasionally. For my own pleasure I've done calf roping in rodeos this past year—and won, amazingly enough. That takes my mind off everything else. Do you like rodeos?"

"I know as much about them as you do opera."

"Maybe a rodeo is like an opera—you either love it or you don't like it at all."

Smiling, she shook her head. "Rodeos and opera—I don't think you can quite lump them together even in that way."

"I'll take you to a rodeo sometime soon. There'll be one in New Mexico."

They talked, drifting from one subject to another until dinner was served, delicious blackened grouper.

Over dinner, conversation became more impersonal and she felt better about him. The staff was discreet, keeping out of sight most of the time.

After dinner the dishes were cleared away while they moved to another area on the veranda. Marek spoke briefly to the staff and then joined her again. It was almost dark, and various veranda lights and torches on the beach had come on or been lighted.

"I suppose Jess runs the ranch when you're not there."

"Jess runs the ranch when I'm there and when I'm not there."

"He's sort of closed off from the world. Or maybe just quiet. Is he married?"

"No. Jess is closed off from the world to a degree. Jess had a wife and son. They were killed in a car wreck years ago. If anyone understands what I've felt, it's Jess. He never married again. He has a solitary life, but he gets along. We understand each other, and I can count on him."

"That's dreadful. Both of you with such similar losses."

"He's never had to say anything. He's just been there for me, which helped. After the plane crash sometimes he'd come up to the house in the evening and bring cold beer. We'd sit, drink and maybe not say three words all evening, just sit on the porch and sip beer. It helped just to know he understood and he was there."

"I'm glad you had somebody."

"Jess is all for this marriage and bringing Noah into our lives."

"You just never know what problems other people carry around," she said quietly. "I've been fortunate."

"When we get back, we'll get your things, Ashley's and Noah's moved to the ranch."

"Noah growing up a little cowboy—that seems impossible."

"It's possible. I'll get a horse for you. You can ride with me early in the mornings if you'd like. This time of year it's beautiful out."

She laughed. "I don't know one thing about horses, but I would love to learn. That sounds fun, Marek."

"Life's a blast for you, isn't it?"

"A lot of the time. It's a lot of work and sometimes scary, too."

Finally, she said she would turn in.

"Before you do, let's walk on the beach. The moon is out and I think you'll like a stroll. You can't do that at home."

With his arm draped casually across her shoulders, they walked along the sandy beach, where flickering torches cast yellow-and-orange reflections over the dark waters and high-lighted whitecaps. When he walked with her to her bedroom door, she turned to face him.

"This is a weird wedding night, Camille. You're getting shortchanged here."

"No, I'm not. I'm getting a lot from this marriage. I expect a lot."

One dark eyebrow arched. "How's that? Don't expect me to fall in love. I'm coming out of my grief, I'll admit, but I'll never be in—" She placed her finger on his mouth.

"That wasn't what I was talking about, but that, too. You don't know what lies ahead. I expect you to be a father for Noah. A good father. You've given us a fortune. Because of this marriage, I'm wealthy and my family has options and can do things they could not have done otherwise."

"You see the world through rose-colored glasses."

"Maybe, but that makes for a pretty world," she said, smiling at him. She stood on tiptoe, wrapped her arm around his neck and kissed him on the mouth. She wanted to shake him out of his insulated world. Marek's arm circled her waist and he returned her kiss, holding her tightly while he wound his other hand in her hair. Her pulse roared in her ears and her heartbeat raced as she kissed him, pouring herself into the kiss, wanting to break through the barriers around his heart. She had started the kiss, but then Marek dominated, burning away caution, causing wild responses from her.

When he picked her up to carry her into her bedroom, she realized they were headed for a real wedding night. "Wait, Marek—" she whispered.

"You started this," he said in a voice that was as deep as

a growl. Giving her a searching look, he set her on her feet. Her heart pounded, part desire, part exhilaration that she had shaken him out of his remote numbness as she had intended.

"We stop now," she said. "Weird wedding night or not, it's been more than either of us expected. Far more than I ever expected. I still don't want to rush complications."

"I think complications are barreling down on us," he said. "You have to take some of the blame. You're filled with a zest for life that's irresistible. I believe you started this tonight."

"I don't have any regrets," she whispered and saw a flicker in the depths of his dark eyes. "I've had a wonderful wedding day. It's not what either of us would have if we could have whatever we want, but under the circumstances, for a paper marriage, it was a great day."

"I agree. I wondered how I would get through it. Thanks. You got me through this one and it's been good."

"Will you be all right tonight?"

"I don't know," he replied. "Want to come hold my hand and make sure I am?" he replied, a faint smile hovering on his mouth.

She laughed. "Good try, but not this night. You'll be okay. Let's have a sunrise swim."

"Sure. Want me to come get you out of bed?"

"Another good try, but, no, I don't. I'll be up early. And I'm sure, as a rancher, you get up early every morning. If not, I'll go on without you."

"And me miss the sight of you in your swimsuit? I think not. I'll be there."

She laughed. "Good night, Marek." He caught her up, holding her tightly to kiss her hard. Just as abruptly he released her.

"Some night, Camille, you won't tell me to wait."

"Just make sure that's what you want," she whispered as her heart raced.

"I can give you the same warning." He left, closing the door behind him.

Staring at the door, she gave herself over to memories of the whole evening. Whether it would complicate her life horribly or not, she was going to fall in love with her husband. Or maybe she was already in love with him.

When she was ready for bed, she stepped onto the veranda outside her bedroom. Moonlight spilled across the water in one long, white beam. She was married to a Rangel now. Mrs. Marek Rangel. This was never how she had dreamed she would have her wedding night. It could have been different tonight. Was she ready for that big a change?

"It will work out," she told herself, thinking how Marek seemed now compared to the day she had walked into his office. She thought about their kisses, escalating in intensity. She combed her hair back from her face with her fingers, thinking about being in Marek's arms today, dancing with him, the moment he had swept her up to carry her over the threshold. Just when she thought she had him figured out, he surprised her. She finally fell asleep in a chair, dozing and then waking to crawl into bed to sleep.

The next two days they spent swimming, eating, dancing and getting to know each other better, yet all the while, she felt sparks and tension growing between them.

The last night they went into town to a show and afterward they went to a popular bar. The steamy bar was raucous, the dancing frenzied, strobe lights flashing. Marek unbuttoned his short sleeve island shirt, letting go after the past month filled with tension and a strained wedding filled with painful memories.

Relaxed, he enjoyed dancing. Afterward, when the floor was cleared for limbo, they watched as a few patrons tried it. The crowd got into it, cheering on the dancers.

Marek had his arm around her shoulder, but he stepped

out to participate. The music was deafening, and he concentrated on trying to get down. After the first easy try, they lowered the bar. Again, he made it to cheers and clapping. He grinned at Camille. They lowered the bar and he tried once again to louder cheers. He laughed as Camille gave him a thumbs-up.

Feeling sweat pour off himself, he motioned for another try, getting lower than any of the amateurs so far until he felt his balance going. He put down his hand to wiggle under the bar and bounced to his feet to cheers and applause as he bowed.

Laughing, he caught her around her waist.

"I didn't know you were so talented," she yelled over the noise of the crowd. He led her back to the bar and the bartender gave him a cold beer and congratulations.

"Hey, man, beer's on the house," he said, grinning.

As Marek took a long drink, Camille laughed. They walked back into the crowd to watch the dancers until the professional dancer returned to outdo everyone else.

When they stopped the limbo, a samba began, and Marek took her hand to dance. He already knew she was an excellent dancer. As she followed his moves across the dance floor, he realized they were in perfect step. Her red dress with a halter top had a skirt that was fitted over her hips and then flared fully below. With every turn her legs were revealed, drawing an audience quickly.

With his gaze locked with hers they danced in unison as if they had practiced for weeks. The fast, sexy dance sent his heart racing. Every move felt even more exhilarating. He watched her twist her hips while dancing in perfect step with him. She was taunting and sexy, and he wanted her. Desire burned hotly, more than the scorching air in the bar. He wished he had her alone, far away from a crowd.

The growing audience began to circle and watch, cheering them on, whistling and clapping until the end when they got resounding cheers. Exhilarated, filled with energy, he laughed as he pulled her to him. "Let's give them a thrill," he said and kissed her, dipping with her so she had to put her arms around his neck. Dimly, above his roaring pulse, he heard the crowd go wild with yells.

Wanting to take her home and to bed now, he swung her up to audience applause. "Take your bow. You're a great dancer. How you did that and stayed as cool as you look, I don't know." They bowed and walked away while the band took a break. Marek wiped his sweat-covered forehead and pushed back tangled locks of his black hair.

Camille caught her long hair to braid it swiftly. "I need a clip or rubber band for this hair."

He took her hand and they crossed to the bar to get one. As soon as she fastened her braid, he held her arm and they went outside, where welcome cool air hit her. He spun her around. Her eyes widened and she placed her hands against his chest.

While Camille's heart pounded, he pulled her to him to kiss her possessively. She wrapped her arms around him to kiss him in return. His body was hot, damp from the dance, flat planes and hard muscles. His hand ran down her back and over her bottom and she was thankful they were at the bar and not at the villa with privacy and bedrooms. She still didn't want to get into an intimate relationship and complicate their lives and do something that he would take as lightly as he had the dancing tonight.

His kisses stirred passion to a storm that buffeted her. In spite of her caution, she wanted him. She ran her hands over his back, wanting to tug his shirt out of his chinos but resisting.

His tongue went deep, a demanding kiss that shook her.

He was not steeped in grief tonight. Far from it. He had been losing the past swiftly, and tonight his body was hot with desire.

Relishing their kisses, she didn't want to stop, either, aware their location would eventually end their lovemaking before it went too far. Momentarily letting go of her caution, she kissed him eagerly, sliding her hands over his chest to feel the solid muscles. He was aroused, sexy. Knowing she shouldn't, she couldn't keep from wanting him. In spite of knowing he was a threat to her career, she wanted him, but she wanted more of him than just his body. Even when she shouldn't, she wanted his heart.

His hand went to her throat and then slipped lower, over her breast, and she gasped with pleasure as he caressed her. She closed her hand around his wrist.

"Marek, we're in a very public place."

"There's no one paying any attention to us. They're all inside. You're a fabulous dancer," he replied in a muffled voice as he continued to shower kisses on her throat, moving lower. He shoved the neck of her dress lower to kiss her. She wriggled and stepped back, straightening her dress.

"We can go back and dance or go to the villa, but we need to stop the lovemaking out here in public."

He gave her a long steady look before he finally nodded. "Which is it? What do you want to do? Dance more or go back?"

"Go back and walk on the beach. It's our last night."

"The last night of our honeymoon. We could make it real, Camille," he said in a husky voice.

"You mean we could make love. It would not be real love between us, and you know that. You said you didn't mind having a relationship without sex for now."

"I didn't think I wanted one. You're making me want things I didn't think I would. This past week—maybe even before—for the first time since I lost Jillian and Kern, I feel like life is good again."

"Frankly, I'm glad. I want some kind of caring between us if we have a physical relationship. You agreed to that."

"So I did," he said. "We'll have some kind of caring, Camille. I already do care," he said, his dark eyes holding her spellbound. He leaned close to kiss her, his mouth firm, demanding on hers until three men burst outside, noisily spilling past them.

Marek leaned away and smiled at her. "All right, we'll go back to the villa. I'll get the car," he said, sending a text message.

"It was fun to dance. We did well together," she said when he finished sending the text.

"Amazingly well. I'll bet people who watched thought we had danced a samba together dozens of times. Frankly, it surprised me."

"I had years of dance lessons when I was growing up. Someday we'll come back maybe and try and see if it happens again."

"That sounds good—someday we'll come back. This is a good marriage."

"I think you've had too much to drink tonight."

He shook his head. "Hardly. I had two beers all evening long. I didn't finish the last one, so it wasn't even two. For a paper marriage it's a good marriage."

"There. That description is far more accurate. Let's go."

As soon as they reached the villa, they went outside for the walk along the beach that she had wanted. Kicking off her shoes, she listened to waves lap against the shore.

"I've finally cooled off. The bar was hot, dancing even hotter," she said.

"Kissing you was the hottest of all," he added, and she smiled.

"I could have added that but didn't. This has been wonderful. Thank you for finding this place and the villa—it has fulfilled a dream I've had for a long time."

"I'm glad you're pleased. I'm glad you're here for the first time with me. Tomorrow we'll return home, and next week we'll go to the ranch and plan the changes you want to make."

"I need to get back the following week. It's getting closer to performance time, and I have to practice. My time will be more deeply involved with my profession."

"I understand. I may stay at the ranch some of the time and keep out of your way."

She nodded, wondering how well they would work out their time and if he would accept the demands of her career. She suspected he was unaccustomed to having to give up anything he wanted in daily living.

"Stephanie is not interested in ranch life. Right now, she's delighted to be going back to Saint Louis. I think she'll open an office and work from there. She'll do my accounting, but I'm going to hire another manager because she wants to go home and settle down. Remember, Ashley is going to Saint Louis for the week when we return to Dallas. They'll both be gone and I'll take care of Noah."

"That's when you'll need to let me or Ginny help take care of him."

"At this point, I feel better about Ginny. She's accustomed to caring for a baby. You're not."

He smiled, and her heartbeat quickened. Her response to him was increasing instead of diminishing with familiarity.

After they walked along the beach, they sat on the veranda, sipping iced tea and talking until she realized the time. "Do you know how early we've planned to leave? It's three in the morning."

"With a phone call I can change tomorrow's flight."

Thinking about the week ahead, she shook her head. "We

should get back. We have plans made and everyone will be expecting us."

They walked to her bedroom door, where they stopped as they had each night. "It's been good, Marek," she said, aware of his disheveled state, his shirt unbuttoned, revealing his muscled chest, his tangled hair falling partially on his forehead. His shirttail was out of his chinos. He looked sexy, ready for love.

"Thanks to you, this trip has been a good one. Tonight was a blast and a relief to just let go in every way."

She smiled at him. "I'm glad. Good night," she said, reaching up to put her hand on his shoulder and kiss him lightly. The kiss changed into a passionate one that had them both gasping for breath when they stopped.

"Sometime, Camille, you won't say no."

"I imagine you're right," she whispered. She stepped into her room and closed the door, her heart pounding. "I didn't want to tonight," she whispered, touching her tingling lips lightly with the back of her fingers. She looked at the ring on her hand, watching the diamond sparkle. "Mrs. Marek Rangel. I want it all. I want your love, and then this ring will hold meaning," she whispered, wondering whether he could ever let go and love again. She mulled over his remark earlier—*I already do care.* How much did he care? Tiny changes had happened, and maybe they were making a difference in him. Would he ever fall in love or forever be holding a memory in his heart?

And what if he did fall in love? Would she wreck her life and the career she had guarded and given all her effort to for her lifetime? She couldn't imagine living in isolation on his ranch. Voice and language lessons would be an impossibility. If he ever fell in love, was she willing to sacrifice what she had achieved?

Seven

The trip to Dallas seemed short, and she felt a rush of joy as Noah held out his arms and kicked his legs at the sight of her. She scooped him up to hug him, looking over his head at Ashley, who smiled happily.

Marek stood beside her and she handed Noah to him. "Thank you, Ashley."

"Ma-ma," Noah said. Startled, Camille looked at him and then at Ashley, who laughed and shrugged.

"He's beginning to talk. He has a two-word vocabulary—ma-ma and bah for bottle."

"I missed his first word," Camille said, shaking her head.

"I did videotape it for you. I wanted to surprise you when you returned and heard him. Also, I'm going shortly if that's all right with you," Ashley replied. "I'll stay with my friend Patty Collins tonight and be back early because I'm going to Saint Louis tomorrow."

"Of course, run along. We're fine, and we'll see you in the morning."

"Great to have you back," she said. "I'll see you later, Camille. Bye, Marek."

"Goodbye, Ashley," he replied, making noises at Noah that made the baby laugh.

Sitting on the floor, Marek played with Noah while Camille left to unpack. Later, she showered and changed to blue shorts and a T-shirt. She returned to find Marek holding Noah in a rocking chair and reading a story to him.

"He doesn't know a word you're saying," she said, laughing.

"Look at him. He likes this. He's happy and listening."

"He must be on the verge of falling asleep."

"You just can't admit that he's precocious and likes being read to."

"No, I can't," she said. "And neither can you. Try that in the morning when he gets up."

Noah wiggled and hit the book with his hand. "See," Marek said, glancing at her. "He wants me to read."

"You just go ahead and read. When you're ready, I'll put him in bed."

Marek read softly to Noah without bothering to answer her. She stared at them, amazed Noah would sit still as if he were hanging on each word.

Marek turned a page. "I just have the magic touch."

She laughed and shook her head. "What you have is an exhausted baby. I'll bet he's asleep in ten minutes."

"Bet a few kisses and I'll take you up on it."

"I'll win. What do I get if I win?" she asked, placing her hand on her hip to wait.

"What do you want?" he asked.

She tilted her head. "Live dangerously—be surprised. I'll tell you when I win."

"Deal," he replied, his gaze raking over her before he returned to reading. Glancing at her watch to make note of the time, she left to write thank-you notes for wedding gifts. It astounded her how fast Marek had rooms remodeled and changes made. She had come by often to look at the progress or answer questions, but they had the house ready and the move was made three days before the wedding. Now she just had to become accustomed to a new home and the most luxurious house she had ever lived in. In ten minutes she returned and Marek looked up. "I win," he said.

To her surprise, Noah still sat quietly in Marek's arms. "You do have a magic touch. Although his eyelids are getting droopy."

"Doesn't matter. I win."

"Then you'll just have to come collect your prize later when he's tucked in bed."

"You can count on it," Marek replied and returned to reading in a softer voice. Noah blinked and closed his eyes.

"That hardly counts because you just barely won," she said. "He's fallen asleep."

"There's no such thing as barely winning. A win is a win whether barely or by a mile. I definitely won and soon I expect to claim my prize."

"I still don't know how you held his attention for that long," she said, looking at her sleeping child.

"You come sit on my lap and I'll get your attention for just as long. I can do things that will make you sleep like a baby. Later."

She smiled. "Although that's a tempting offer, for now, I'll pass."

"You're missing out on a great deal of—" he paused a moment "—of something you won't forget and you'll enjoy immensely. I promise."

She fanned herself with her hand. "I do believe I've married a very sexy man," she said in a sultry voice. "Your self-assurance is about to overwhelm me," she added in a normal tone. "I'll take Noah to bed."

"It's just like you said you wanted." Marek stood easily. "I'll take him. You can come with us."

The sleeping baby snuggled against Marek's shoulder as he carried him to the nursery, which was near the master bedroom suite and adjoined the bedroom suite where Camille stayed. Marek glanced at her. "See, we can be a family for him. This is good, Camille. This is very good for him."

"I know it is, and that's why I agreed," she answered solemnly.

"Don't sound so unhappy about it."

"I've had him all to myself. There are moments this whole change seems overwhelming. The fear passes swiftly, and then I feel better about what we're doing."

"I'm glad. Also, guess what—he can say da-da."

She stopped to stare at Noah. "No kidding. You've taught him to say da-da," she said, laughing softly.

"Might have."

Marek put Noah into his crib gently, turning to place his arm around Camille as she stood close beside him. They both looked at the sleeping baby. "I suppose every mother thinks her baby is the most beautiful baby in the whole world. I love him with all my heart," she said.

"That's the thing about love—there's always room for more. I already love him, but he constantly reminds me of Kern and I know that's part of the reason. A delightful part," Marek added.

"I'm glad." She smoothed wispy hair on Noah's head, then turned and left the room. Her pulse was more erratic as they returned to the family area.

Marek faced her, encircling her waist with his arm. "I collect my winnings. I've been waiting and looking forward to claiming my prize."

Her heart skipped a beat as she gazed up at him. His attention was on her mouth, and he leaned closer. She inhaled, her heart pounding, and then his mouth covered hers, opened hers, and she lost awareness of everything else.

Wrapping her arms around his neck, she returned his kiss. As his kiss became more passionate, his arms tightened around her.

In a light, sizzling caress, his hand roamed over her bottom and along her leg, sliding beneath her shorts to caress her bare thigh. In seconds his hand slipped beneath her T-shirt, warm on her skin, his callused palm slightly rough as he unfastened the front snap of her bra and then cupped her breast.

Wanting to touch him, she moaned softly in pleasure. She was overwhelmed by caresses, hot kisses, touches, his fingers delving, intimacy enveloping them. Whether he realized it or not, each contact brought them closer. Loving caused sensations to bombard her, and she wanted to stir the same responses in him. Sliding her hands beneath his shirt, she felt the slight mat of chest hair that tickled her palm. Trailing both hands lightly over him, she tugged his shirt. He paused to raise his head and yank it off.

Watching her intently with desire blazing in the depths of his eyes, he pulled away her T-shirt and tossed it aside. He cupped her breasts, circling each lightly as she gasped and closed her eyes.

The slightest touch heightened desire, but the closeness, opening herself to him, carried with it a bonding that she couldn't continue to fight. Love had blossomed, and every physical stroke increased desire but also locked her heart more securely in his possession. There was no turning back from this now. They were legally wed, husband and wife.

His closeness with Noah tonight had captured her heart more than ever before.

She moaned softly, partly in pleasure, partly in frustration for a love that was totally one-sided.

As he unfastened her shorts she closed her fingers around his wrists and made an effort to stop kissing him. "Marek, wait a minute."

He watched her through hooded eyes and slowly raised his head, breathing deeply as if he had run a marathon.

"I know we're married and we can go to bed as husband and wife, but that's meaningless in matters of the heart. I have to go slowly into this or I'll hurt badly."

"Whenever you say no, I'll honor it, Camille. I promised I never wanted to hurt you. I mean that, and I intend to hold to it as much as humanly possible."

She closed her eyes, rocking on her heels, thinking his words just made her fall a bit more in love with him while nothing she did could even cause a tiny crack in the wall of ice that enveloped his heart.

He held her lightly and showered her with feathery kisses. "Don't worry. We're doing better together than I had expected. Our marriage is working far more than I dreamed possible. You're becoming a friend, helping me with the rough moments."

"Thank you and I'm glad," she said, thinking his statements heightened how much she liked him. "I know you've had some really bad moments because none of this, this bargain marriage, the relationship—you never expected or dreamed you would have anything like this in your life."

"Damn straight, there," he said, letting out a long breath. She was pulling herself together, and she stepped out of his arms to grab up her bra and T-shirt, pulling them on swiftly with her back turned to him.

Turning around she found him watching her intently. He

had made no effort to pull on his T-shirt, and she couldn't keep from surveying his chest, which made her breath catch and started her pulse pounding again. When she glanced up, his gaze had narrowed slightly.

"Knowing you and having this paper marriage has been good and that's partly because of you. Noah is the other factor in making this workable. He's an adorable baby."

"I have to agree with that. He likes you."

"He should. I love him already," Marek said softly.

"Don't make me fall in love with you," she whispered, knowing it was far too late for that request.

He stepped close again to slip his arms lightly around her waist. "I don't think you will. You're vulnerable and so am I, because neither of us have had a physical relationship in a long time. When you get back to being onstage, you'll forget me a good part of the time. I don't think there's any danger of either one of us falling in love. That will never be part of the equation, and we both can be open about it, which is also refreshing."

His words stung, and she hoped he never realized her growing feelings because he obviously did not return such emotions and didn't think he ever would. Unfortunately, her heart responded whether there was reciprocation or not.

Trying to lighten the situation, she smiled. "I think we were headed somewhere when we started this."

"We'll sit and talk if you want." He draped his arm casually across her shoulders and walked to the sofa to sit close, turning to face her. "I want all of you to live on the ranch when your schedule allows it. You might as well get accustomed to the ranch. I love it. I'm a rancher, a cowboy. Living that far from town will be different for you."

"It'll be a monumental difference since we've always lived in a city," Camille replied. "It's going to be a huge change for my sister."

"She'll be paid well," he remarked drily. "Sometimes that helps ease the change. Does Ashley want to go back for this fall semester?"

"Because of all the changes in our lives, she's agreed to wait until the January semester starts. Remember, tomorrow one of your jets is flying her home to Saint Louis for the rest of this week."

His gaze traveled over her features slowly. She reacted to the sensual study that held almost as much impact as physical contact. She forgot their conversation and was lost in his dark eyes.

He leaned closer and she could no more resist than if she had been hypnotized as she bent toward him. When his lips brushed hers, she closed her eyes, circling his neck with her arm. She paused only briefly. "We weren't going to do this."

"We haven't for a while," he whispered back.

He lifted her to his lap to embrace her. His arousal was hard against her hip, a throbbing reminder of his heated desire.

"Marek," she whispered, and his mouth on hers stopped her from talking. After a few minutes she pushed against him and gazed at him.

He pulled his head back slightly to look into her eyes. "You'll be mine soon, Camille," he whispered, and her heart thudded.

"Be careful, Marek. I'm going to melt that ice that encompasses your heart. You possess my heart, but you're making yours vulnerable to the fires we generate," she warned. "I want you to want me with all your being," she whispered, barely aware of what she said, uncertain that he even heard her, much less gave any thought to what she was telling him.

He kissed her hard, his tongue playing over hers and going deep, possessively, as he pulled her tightly against him.

Winding her fingers in his hair, she kissed him in return.

Finally, she slipped off his lap and walked away. "I should call it a night."

"Not at all. Sit and talk. It's early. We don't have a full day tomorrow. I'll send Ashley in the limo to the plane. Ginny and the girls will come to get Noah. We'll do what we want."

"You're right," she said, sitting slightly farther from him on the sofa.

"How did you decide on the name Noah?" he asked, his dark eyes holding passion.

"That was my grandfather's name. He's named for my grandfather and for his own father," Camille answered while trying to calm and wishing her voice wasn't as breathless.

"Does your dad mind being skipped over?"

"No, one of the granddaughters is named for him. Chelsea Taylor Avanole."

"Nice name. I'm glad you gave Noah Kern's name. I remember your text from Kern. The name made Kern happy. When he's old enough, I'll get a small, gentle horse for Noah. Long before that he can ride with me."

"I can't imagine my baby on a horse," she said. "You and I know little about each other's worlds."

"That makes life interesting," Marek said, smiling at her and moving closer. "And you're too far away," he said, slipping his hand lightly on her nape. "I'll take you to a rodeo and we'll also go dancing sometime and you can learn the two-step if you don't already know it. When you see the ranch house, just remember that we can remodel and redecorate any way you want. This is my house that I had built, and it's not old and filled with sentimental memories."

She listened and watched him while he talked, only half hearing what he told her, remembering their kisses and fighting the urge to reach out and touch him. If she did, she would be in his arms again.

In her wildest imaginings, she had never expected to have

a marriage of convenience, a honeymoon without making love, a husband who didn't love her. Yet they were getting to know each other and there was a physical attraction that neither one of them could resist.

It was two o'clock when she stood. "Now I do have to go to bed. I'm sleepy," she said, picking up an empty glass to take to the kitchen.

He went with her, and as they walked to her new bedroom that adjoined his with closed double doors between them, he draped his arm across her shoulders to draw her against him.

"You're not staying in here tonight," she whispered.

"I know I'm not," he replied. He gazed down at her. "Guard your heart well, Camille. Mine is frozen, and, make no mistake, it won't thaw."

"I've got your warning," she whispered. "I'll take care of myself."

He kissed her lightly and left.

Marek walked to his room, his thoughts on Camille. He would never fall in love and already she had a starry-cyed look and was telling him this would mean more to her with each kiss. He should leave her alone, but that was impossible. She was a desirable, beautiful woman, now his wife, as legally binding as any marriage.

Startled, he realized he was coming back to life fully. It still surprised him how much and how fast she had brought him out of his grief. How huge the transformation since the day Camille had walked into his office! The diminishing of his heartache had been subtle, gradual, but he was less steeped in heartbreak, each week more lusty. Camille was filled with life, her passion for living spilling over onto all around her, including him. He rubbed the back of his neck and wondered where they would be in this relationship a year from now.

Images and memories of Camille returned full force: of Camille in his arms, of kissing her, of her soft lips, of her body, dancing the samba with her and her seductive moves. The memories set his pulse racing and sent his temperature soaring. Maybe someday he would fall in love with her—something that seemed impossible now, but she had brought about changes he would have thought impossible three months ago.

It shocked him how much he wanted her. A month ago, he was completely oblivious to women. But from the moment Camille had slipped into his life, hot, passionate, she had stirred responses from him he hadn't known he could possibly give again. On their honeymoon he'd wanted her. If she had cooperated they would have consummated their marriage. Even now, he was certain it was only a matter of time before he seduced her. She was a passionate, hot-blooded woman and they were just getting to know each other. He thought her reluctance would melt away because she was responsive to his slightest touch, flirting with him, physically aware of him.

Noah had contributed, too, in bringing him back into the world fully. The baby was adorable, and Marek would do anything to get a laugh out of his tiny nephew, soon-to-be-adopted son. Already he loved the baby as much as if he were his own. If only Kern could have known Noah—how much Kern would have loved the little fellow.

Marek prayed Camille accepted all of their arrangements and let him have a lot of time with Noah. "Kern, you have a fine son," he said to no one. "I'll do my best for him."

Marek showered, climbed into bed and lay in the dark still thinking about the monumental changes in his life, thinking about holding Camille and making love to her.

He slept only a few hours and rose to dress, pulling on fresh jeans and a navy knit shirt. When he entered the kitchen he gave a swift appraisal of Camille in jeans and a red T-shirt. Her hair was caught behind her head in a red ribbon. She smiled and returned to feeding Noah and talking to Ashley, who was already back from visiting her friend. Her bags for her trip to Saint Louis were packed, ready by the door.

Half an hour after Ashley left for the airport, Ginny and her girls arrived to pick up Noah. She got instructions from Camille while Marek loaded the car with Noah's things. The girls hovered over Noah, who seemed happy with their attention.

As they drove away, Marek stood on the porch with his arm around Camille's shoulders. As Ginny and the girls waved, Marek and Camille waved in return.

"Thanks for letting them take him." Marek looked down at her. "Don't worry about him. He'll have everyone's undivided attention, and Ginny is an experienced mom. The girls have found a real live doll to play with. The whole family will hover over him like he's suddenly been crowned king of the world. They're only a thirty-minute drive away here in Dallas if you just can't stand being parted from him."

Camille smiled nervously as they walked back into the house together. "I won't worry. I felt ridiculous giving your sister instructions. She's had two girls and knows more about parenting than I do."

"You're used to Noah. All little kids are different."

"Says the man who told me he knew nothing about babies."

"You remember that? That was the first week we met."

"I remember everything about you."

"Do you really?" Marek turned her to face him. "Have you noticed?"

"Noticed what?" she asked, wondering what she had missed. "You have a new haircut?"

"No. We're home alone. A moment I've been looking forward to for some time. Guess why?" His heartbeat raced in anticipation that had built all morning. He looked into her compelling blue eyes.

"I believe the look in your eyes gives away your answer, but I'll ask. Why?"

"So I can do this," he said, drawing her into his embrace.

She tilted her head to give him access to her mouth. He leaned closer, brushing her lips with his, a teasing stroke that caused her lips to part.

"I want you, Camille," he whispered before his mouth came down on hers.

Eight

His tongue toyed with hers, fanning fires deep within her, making her want more of him. Her faint moan was barely audible in her own ears because of her roaring pulse.

They were alone, husband and wife. He had said he could never love again, and she was fully aware this was lust and went no deeper emotionally for him, but they were married. How much had he changed since their first night out? How much would he continue to change?

She framed his face with her hands and opened her eyes to look at him. His breathing was heavy and his eyes half-lidded with a sensual look that conveyed his intentions more than ever. His brow furrowed slightly. "What?"

"You've been up front with your warnings, Marek," she whispered. "I'll give you one. Guard your heart. If we continue, you may fall in love."

A harsh, shuttered look changed his expression. "There's no chance of that—"

She covered his mouth with hers, pressing her lips slowly on his, catching his lower lip lightly in her teeth to stroke slowly with her tongue. He inhaled, gave a conflicted moan as he tightened his arm around her and pulled her hard against him.

His thick erection reinforced his scorching gaze. She slid against him, lowering herself from tiptoe to flat-footed, sliding slowly, sensually along his hard body. Desire pounded in her, a heated longing for total commitment from him. "Marek, I've been to a doctor. I'm on the pill."

He kissed away further conversation. Yanking off his shirt, he tossed it away. While he kissed her, her fingers drifted lightly over him, tracing his sculpted chest muscles, bulging biceps, his hipbones. In feathery caresses her fingers trailed along his upper thighs in her fascination with his body, in her need to be as intimate as possible.

His raspy breathing deepened while his tongue was erotic, heightening her need.

Twisting her hips slowly, inching them over him so he would become aware of all of her, she let one hand drift toward the inside of his thigh and then trail higher.

He leaned away. His midnight eyes flamed with desire, a promise in just a look. Her heartbeat raced while he slipped his fingers beneath her shirt, moving with a tantalizing slowness that made her want to grasp his hands and place them on her tingling breasts as he watched her.

"Marek," she whispered, wanting to relay her feelings for him, to declare the love that built each day, but she held back, biting back words while she let her care flow into her kisses.

His fingers teased, heightening her desire as his hands caressed her full breasts, circling each and avoiding her taut peaks. Craving his touch, she leaned away to remove her shirt.

Inhaling deeply, he held her to look at her, slowly letting

his gaze consume each inch, making her quiver and ache with desire. With deliberation he pulled away the ribbon holding her hair, caressing her nape as he released the ribbon.

"You're beautiful."

"Marek," she said, tugging his shoulders to bring him closer, but he still held her away. He leaned down, his tongue trailing lightly on her throat, down between her breasts, circling underneath as his fingers had. Warm, wet, his tongue heightened her quivering need. Her nipples throbbed, and she grasped his wrists to hold his hands, looking down at him.

With lips swollen from passion and his eyes black from desire, his gaze consumed her while his hands persisted in fiery torment. Desire overwhelmed her, burning, pouring over every inch.

"Touch me," she whispered.

"I want you to really want my hands, my mouth on you," he whispered, showering kisses on her throat and lower.

She framed his head in her hands, tangling her fingers in his thick hair to draw him closer, to place his mouth, his kisses, where she wanted.

"Marek," she cried out in pleasure, gasping and throwing her head back as she clung to him and was immersed in sensation. Desire centered low in her. She thrust her hips against him and caressed him, her fingers shaking as she tried to yank his belt free and shove away the last clothing between them.

He stepped back to do the task himself, still watching her with hooded eyes, a blatant look that made her want to draw him close against her.

With deliberation she unfastened her slacks and let them fall, stepping out of them to kick away her sandals. His chest expanded as he drew a long breath, his gaze roaming slowly over her.

She hooked her fingers in the bikini panties, drawing them

slowly down, spreading her legs slightly as she stepped out of the bit of lace.

With a groan that conveyed both need and urgency, he drew her to him. His fingers were everywhere, following the course of his scrutiny and then moving where his gaze could not go between her thighs.

His mouth covered hers again, his tongue sliding over hers with tantalizing deliberation while his fingers toyed with her intimately. Writhing with pleasure, she clung to his broad shoulders, a sensuous thrust of her hips against his hand as she opened her legs farther to give him more access.

While he kissed her, his hands worked magic, making her want him more than she ever had, more than she would have dreamed possible.

"Marek, wait," she whispered, breaking away with an effort, giving him an intense look before she went down to take his thick rod to caress and kiss him. As his fingers combed through her long hair again, he shuddered, closing his eyes to let her love him with slow deliberation.

She wanted him to burn with need, to be totally aware of her and want her with every fiber of his being. If she could never have his love, she could have his body.

He leaned down slightly to put his hands beneath her arms and pull her up to gaze into her eyes. "Someday I'll have your heart," she whispered.

"You've been warned," he whispered in return before he kissed away any reply she might have wanted to make.

So have you, she mused as he kissed away rational thought. She held him tightly while he pulled her bottom up even more against him as they kissed. Passionate kisses increased desire until she wanted to hold him tightly, wrap her arms around him and urge him to fill her, to make love with her.

He swept her into his arms, walked to the bedroom and

placed her on the bed. As he eased beside her, he continued caressing and kissing her. She wanted him with all her being. Their lovemaking had driven her swiftly over the edge. Running her hands over him, she caressed him, trying to drive him to as great a need as she felt.

So many things had been life altering between them—just meeting and informing him about Noah, then marrying him—something in her wildest dreams she had never expected. Now their lovemaking was taking them to a new level—a change from which there would be no going back.

He moved over her, trailing his tongue and kisses down, circling each nipple and then taking each taut peak into his mouth to taste and kiss.

When he shifted lower, his hand slipped over her thighs. While he showered kisses over her belly, she writhed in pleasure beneath him. His tongue toyed with her lush breasts, his fingers creating intimate pleasure, teasing, heightening her need until her pulse pounded and she clung to him, crying out for him in urgency.

"Marek, come here."

"I'm here, and you're fantastic," he said, moving between her legs to trail more kisses along the inside of her thighs.

She cried out eagerly, her fingers winding in his hair while her hips arched to meet him as if seeking more of him.

"I want you," she gasped, knowing he could never guess the extent of what she felt.

He placed her legs over his shoulders, leaning down to tease the honeyed place, stirring up a wilder storm of passion. Pausing to watch her intently, he kissed the inside of her thigh. "I'm loving you until you're screaming for me," he whispered before he dipped between her legs and his tongue ended any rational thought.

"Love me now! I don't want to wait."

"I want you to want me more than you ever thought possible," he said.

"I want you with all my being," she whispered, arching her back, absorbed by desire. She gasped for breath. "Marek."

Her eyes flew open and she met his gaze, saw his intent and closed her eyes, wanting him and unable to wait longer. He eased partially into her, slowly filling her, a hot, hard torment more erotic than all else. Then he slipped away in a sensuous move that increased her need. She arched to meet him, and he entered her again.

She arched beneath him, crying out in longing and pleasure as they rocked together until urgency overwhelmed her.

Certain he held back to pleasure her, she thrust her hips faster until she felt his control shatter. His hips rocked with hers, tension reaching the ultimate peak. She cried out as rapture enveloped her and she soared with pleasure.

He followed, thrusting in a wild release that wracked him with spasms. His weight came down heavy, masculine, welcome. She held him tightly, feeling their hearts pound together.

"You're mine, my husband," she whispered, certain he wouldn't hear her.

"Ah, Camille, my love, this is good. I never thought this possible. You've taken me to paradise."

Flowery words, precious, intimate moments. She meant everything she said and she could only wish that he did, too. She ran her fingers through his hair, watching black locks spring away. "You're a handsome man, Marek Rangel. And an incredibly sexy one."

He smiled, showering light kisses on her face and throat. "You win that prize. I want to keep you in my arms all night long."

"If you do, you know what will follow."

"I have no idea. Let's try it and see what happens," he said, teasing her.

She smiled at him while she ran her fingers over his jaw, feeling the stubble that was beginning to show. "You're a handsome devil, Marek Rangel."

"And you're stunning," he said. He rolled to his side, taking her with him, and they faced each other while he smiled with satisfaction.

"This is a good marriage, Camille. We'll be good for Noah."

She laughed. "You say that only days since our wedding. It hasn't been a month yet. You can't tell whether this is good or bad."

"Of course I can. You don't think it's good?"

"It's wonderful," she replied. "Noah is happy, and now he has a daddy, which I think is a fine thing for him. He'll have grandparents because Jess will be another grandfather, I suspect. He has aunts who love him, now more cousins."

"Ginny and her family are already crazy about him. In his quiet way, Jess is, too."

"I'm glad. I've told you in June I will perform *La Traviata* here in Dallas. I will sing Violetta's part. I want you to come for opening night."

"I'd be delighted," he said.

"If you don't care for opera after you've been to a performance, tell me. I know not everyone does. I won't burden you with attending again if you don't like it."

"I'm going to love watching you," he said and she smiled, shaking her head.

"You have no idea whether you will or not. Save the flowery declarations until you can say them truthfully."

He grinned. "I think I will love it. Afterward, will you come home?"

"Of course. There may be a party, but eventually I'll come home. You'll be with me, whatever I do."

"Then I'll be happy. I told you earlier, I've waited eons to be alone with you. It seemed this time would never arrive."

"You wasted no time when they all left," she remarked drily.

"If you knew how much I've thought about making love to you, you'd know why I wasted no time." He propped his head on his hand. "Want to shower or sit in a hot tub and relax?"

"When you put it that way, the hot tub wins."

Standing, he picked her up and she wound her arm around his neck. "You're a feather."

She laughed. "Hardly. It takes a body to have the voice I have. No feather here."

"A gorgeous, lush, to-die-for beauty," he said, carrying her to his sunken tub. She watched as he began to fill the tub and shortly they both sat with her in front of him, between his legs, while he caressed her lightly, toyed with long strands of her hair and talked about growing up spending a lot of his life on his grandfather's ranch.

He carried her back to bed and made love to her again, loving her through the night. Afterward she stayed in his embrace, still talking about their lives before they had met each other. He asked about her career, and she could feel a closer bonding with him. Did he feel the same or was this a casual conversation that he would forget swiftly?

He rolled on his side, holding her close with one arm while he propped his head on his other hand. "Camille, we're married. Share a bedroom with me."

Startled, she gazed into his inscrutable dark eyes. "I'm surprised you want that," she said, giving herself time to think, but also admitting the first thought that came to mind. This was not something she had expected, and her heart leaped. Could this mean that he cared more for her?

"I've given it thought. Our sex life is fantastic," he declared in a husky voice, brushing a kiss on her lips. "I like having you in my arms and in my bed. I would like that on a regular basis. We're husband and wife—why not? We are making love and it's good. I like being with you. It's that simple."

A mixture of feelings gripped her. His declaration and invitation to sharing a bedroom meant a big shift in their relationship. She loved him, and her deepest reaction was joy. Along with it was awareness of all she had worked to achieve. What would a closer relationship, her growing love for him, do to her career?

Was her relationship with Marek a threat to her career? She might be reading more into his actions than she should, but this was a wonderful change in so many ways. The more she could be intimate with him, the more they were simply together and enjoyed each other's company, the more likely he was to lose that barrier around his heart. There was a far better chance of his falling in love if they lived together as husband and wife.

But if he did, could she cope with Marek's demands and the demands of her career?

She had to follow her heart.

She shifted slightly to wrap her arm around him. "Yes, I will move in with you."

Pleasure flared in his expression, and he kissed her long and deeply. In seconds, caressing began and the conversation was temporarily over.

When they were finally back in bed, in each other's arms, Marek faced her and brushed long strands of hair away from her face. "When do you want to move to my bedroom? Tonight?"

She laughed. "I think I am 'in.' Perhaps it will be easier when I move to the ranch."

"Fine with me," he said, looking contented. "I like this. It'll be better. You'll see."

"I don't believe you heard any argument from me," she said, amused by his remarks.

He looked startled and then smiled faintly. "That's good. We're in agreement. Noah will like it, too."

She laughed. "Noah wouldn't care if we camped out at separate ends of your ranch."

Marek had to grin. "Maybe not, but he will have fun being with both of us at the same time."

"I'll agree with you there, too."

"This is good, Camille. Very good."

"Don't sound so surprised," she said, finger combing his dark hair away from his face.

"I am surprised. I never expected to find happiness in this marriage, much less to have it happen so swiftly."

Her heart skipped a beat again, and more pleasure filled her. "I'm glad. Some of it has surprised me. We took some risks."

He gave her a piercing look and then his expression changed as his gaze shifted to her mouth. He leaned down to kiss her and pull her closer.

It was dawn when she lay in his arms with her head against his shoulder and their bodies pressed close. She looked at him and saw the steady rise and fall of his chest. For the first time in her life she was in love. She was more deeply in love with him each day. In so many ways, he captured her love, her heart, her respect, giving her joy and excitement. She expected him to be a wonderful dad for Noah.

Where was she headed with him? She hadn't been able to prevent falling in love. How much could she steal his affec-

tions and bind his heart to hers? If she did, could she cope
with the love of a man shared with pursuit of a career?

Through the days while they were alone at the house, they
made love often with neither of them leaving the house for
anything. When Ginny called, Camille longed to have Noah
home again. Since Ginny and the girls sounded so overjoyed
to have him, she would not do anything to cut his visit short.
Once when they finished the call, Marek turned to her.

"You've given them the most blessed gift. They love Noah,
and you can hear how happy they are to have him visit. I
know it's hard for you because you're not accustomed to
being separated. Thank you," he said with so much sincerity, she was touched.

"I'm glad they love him. It's good for him to get to know
his new family. I want him loved by all his family."

His gaze lowered to her mouth and he leaned closer. His
kiss ended their conversation.

Late the next morning, Marek stepped out of bed. "Don't
go away. We need to talk business and I'll be right back."

Mystified, she sat up and pulled a sheet beneath her arms.

Shortly he returned with papers under his arm and a tray
with glasses of orange juice and cups of coffee.

She laughed. "Marek, it's almost noon and you're bringing breakfast in bed."

"Not a complete breakfast, but a partial one." He handed
her the tray. "Hold everything while I get back beside you."
He sat and took a cup of coffee and a glass of orange juice
to place on a bedside table. "You can put yours next to your
side of the bed."

"Thank you," she said, sipping the orange juice after she
had placed the steaming coffee on the table. "What on earth
do we have to do?"

"We have to childproof my ranch house fast."

She laughed. "He isn't walking yet."

"I want to be ready when he does. I want you to look at some designs and you can help pick one out. We need gates on some of the doors and where there are steps. I want a play area for Noah with a slide and swings."

She laughed. "Marek, wait until he walks. He can get something like that for Christmas."

"I might want to swing him. Babies like to swing."

"In little baby swings. Let's look at the brochures."

For the next hour they pored over plans and brochures and talked about decorators and builders. Finally Marek took all the pamphlets and notes and dropped them over the side of the bed to the floor.

"Good. We'll pick something out and I can have it installed so it'll be in place when we get there. "I want to get the ranch house so it's safe and comfortable for you and Noah because I want you to love it the way I do."

She looked at him and he turned to study her. "What?" he asked.

"You're turning into a great daddy. I'm amazed."

"What did you think I was, some kind of ogre?"

"Of course not, but you knew nothing about kids and he's not your baby actually—"

Placing one finger on her lips, Marek silenced her.

"He's my baby now, Camille. I love him already. I want to start the adoption procedure as soon as we possibly can, and my attorney has been getting it lined up. I'll be Noah's dad and I want his last name legally changed to Rangel." He put his arm around her shoulders. "We'll be a real family."

"That's fine with me," she answered. "That's what I expected from what you have already said."

They gazed into each other's eyes, and her heart began to beat faster as the air thickened and desire blazed again.

He placed his hand lightly on one side of her face. "This is so damn good. I never dreamed it would be like this," he whispered, before his mouth crushed hers and she forgot about fences and swings.

Monday they flew to the ranch on one of Marek's jets. As she looked below, Camille marveled at the changes in her life. She was more in love than ever with Marek, a love that grew daily, and he didn't have a clue. He sat beside her, dressed in a Western long-sleeve cotton shirt, tight jeans, a hand-tooled leather belt and Western boots, looking every inch the handsome, rugged cowboy. It was as foreign to her way of life as someone from another planet. Even so, right now, she longed to reach out and touch him, to hold his hand or even just flirt with him, but they weren't alone.

She had chased stardom all her life. Now she pursued a man's love. Marek had so much to give—and she wanted to give to him. His hurts would heal if he would open his heart and let in love.

She looked at her sleeping baby in his carrier, which was buckled securely. Noah wore a pale blue jumper and white shirt and she thought he looked adorable and angelic. Noah was blissfully unaware of where he was going or how his life had changed. He definitely had taken to Marek, and it was mutual. She had been astounded to discover how much Marek cared for Noah.

Wrapped in her own world, Ashley sat reading college brochures. Camille was happy for her whole family as they changed their lives and began to do what they wanted. Her mother would retire from teaching after the coming year and then she could spend more time with Noah. Now her brother could afford college easily. When they had last talked, Stephanie had bought a condo in Saint Louis and was acquiring new furniture.

Camille glanced out the window, looking at the sprawling land below. Her future was difficult to imagine in so many ways. Her attention returned to Marek. He was changing, but to what extent? He turned to look at her and arched one dark eyebrow.

"What?" he asked.

"Just wondering what you're thinking?"

"Thinking about you mostly, but I've been going over ranch finances," he said, putting away the papers in his lap. "Looks as if Ashley's getting prepared to enroll. I'm not going to have to change my schedule on looking for a new nanny, am I?"

"No, we won't. You won't be getting one on your own, either. She's trying to work out a way to take classes online and then go for those short, intense classes so she can continue as nanny until Noah gets older."

He glanced at Ashley, who was concentrating on her reading. "I'm sure you'd feel better if she stayed on longer."

"I would. I'm trying to stay out of it and let her make her own decision without any pressure from me. She came up with this plan on her own. Of course, I'm delighted because he's so little. When he's gets bigger and can talk, I'll feel better about hiring a nanny and letting her go. My parents wish they could spend more time with Noah, but they both work full-time."

"That will change for your mom. You'll be able to afford to help them."

"We have so many changes in our lives."

"I hope you like the ranch and life there. To me, it's the best place on earth."

"I won't know until I try," she said, but it was difficult to imagine the life awaiting her.

"I told Zeb to fly over the ranch so you can see it from the air."

"I'll tell Ashley. That will be fun to see," she said, turning to her sister.

When Marek finally told her they were flying over the ranch, she and Ashley both turned to the windows. Marek leaned close, his shoulder touching hers. "I think you can tell the main house where I live."

"There's a town below."

"No, that's the ranch."

"Ashley, Marek said the ranch is below," Camille said, unable to take her eyes off the structures spread below. "You have a palace. It's huge, and there's an enormous swimming pool. Why all the homes near your house?"

"For staff. Jess has one."

"This isn't what I imagined at all," Camille said, astounded at everything she saw below. "You have your own small town."

"Not quite," he said, laughing. "It's home and I love it. I'm going to love having you in it."

She smiled at him, happy about his statement.

The plane headed south and she sat back, astonished by what she had seen.

"All of that belongs to you?" Ashley asked, looking dismayed.

"Yes, it does. You'll like it, Ashley. You'll see."

They landed in town and then climbed into a waiting limo for the drive to the ranch, which took almost as long as the flight had taken.

They sped along a deserted gray ribbon of highway, passing land covered with feathery mesquite bent from the prevailing south winds. Green cacti sprouted across the land beneath the mesquite.

The moment the ranch house loomed in sight, Camille's breath stopped and she gazed out the window. Stunned, she looked at a one-story palatial home that looked far bigger from the ground than it had from the air. "My heavens," she gasped softly, turning to look again at the powerful rancher she had married.

Nine

The ranch house and other structures spread in all directions with wings built on the mansion. The ranch revealed Marek's power and wealth far more than the Dallas home, which had been lavish, comfortable and well-appointed. This was a town with an enormous home at the center.

When she glanced at Marek, he looked back at her with his eyebrows arching. "What?" he asked.

"More than ever, your ranch is an indication of your immense wealth," she said. She didn't add power, but she shuddered slightly, reminded again how easily he could take her to court now to get custody of Noah. By marrying Marek, she had given him far more control over her baby.

Smiling at her, he reached over to take her hand. "Stop looking at me as if I'd just grown fangs. I'm the same person and, basically, a cowboy. All the buildings serve ranch purposes or are homes for my staff and the cowboys who work for me."

"It's an enormous compound."

"It seems large because you're unaccustomed to it. The first thing I'd like to show you is our bedroom," he said, desire plain in the depths of his dark eyes.

"That may have to wait until later," she answered, a breathlessness coming into her voice along with eager anticipation. His innuendo was plain. He was beginning to flirt more, making more innuendos. Subtle changes in him were surfacing and she wondered about their significance. Were his feelings shifting, too?

He held her hand and she glanced down, looking at their entwined fingers. More and more he casually hugged her, held her hand, touched her. He spent time with her when he was home. How important was she in his life? And there was also the persistent worry: if he ever fell in love, could she cope with a commitment that would complicate her career? It was a small problem next to how much she wanted his love. She was confident if there was mutual love, she could work through the complications.

They went through another tall iron gate, this one closed with a code to punch to open the gate. In minutes the limo rolled through and shortly they approached the main house, a sprawling stucco structure with north and south wings.

The yard had a tall, ornate iron fence surrounding well-kept grounds with tall shade trees and beds of colorful spring flowers. Red, pink and purple crepe myrtle bushes flanked the front porch that ran the length of the house. In front of the house was a pond with three fountains.

They circled the house, driving around and passing a corral with a large barn. Beyond it were rows of stables and another corral. Buildings and houses could be seen farther to the north. Beyond the well-kept yard the land returned to the wild mesquite and cacti she had seen on the drive from the airport.

When she had told Ashley she would move into his bedroom, her sister had arched her eyebrows. "Is that what you want?"

"Yes, it is," Camille answered.

"You're in love with him," Ashley said.

"How'd you know?" Camille asked her, surprised. "Does it show?"

"I know because I'm your sister. I don't think it's obvious otherwise. I don't think Stephanie ever noticed."

"Stephanie hasn't been around as much as you have."

"No, but I've known for a while. Since you came back from your honeymoon."

"I think before that," Camille admitted.

"I don't blame you. He's a great guy, Camille, and I hope he doesn't break your heart because he was so deeply in love with his late fiancée."

"I know. You can't control the feelings in your heart for someone."

"Try to take care of yourself."

"I have Noah to love—that keeps me from hurting too badly over anything else. I have my career. That will always take my thoughts off my private life," Camille answered, doubting if her career would be enough.

"I just pray you aren't hurt. He seems to have his heart completely locked away."

"I can't undo what I feel at this point."

"Well, as I said, just take care of yourself."

Camille gazed out the limo window. Would Marek cause her heartbreak?

When they parked to go inside, Ashley carried Noah. At the door, Marek picked up Camille. "Welcome home, Camille," he said in a husky voice. Her heart thudded. If only he meant what he said! She held him and gazed into dark eyes as he smiled at her and then carried her over the threshold into an entryway. It was filled with hooks holding rain slickers, two tall hat racks holding broad-brimmed Western hats, boots lined neatly on the floor. He set her down.

"Come meet the staff, namely, my great cook and the man who manages this place. I doubt if the others are around at this hour."

Marek took Noah from Ashley, and they entered a large kitchen that held stainless steel appliances and had an adjoining sitting room and an informal dining area with a brick fireplace filling one corner.

A black-haired man in a white apron smiled at them. "Ladies, I want you to meet Hector Galban," Marek said. "Hector, meet my wife, Mrs. Rangel, her sister, Miss Avanole. This is Noah," Marek said, turning the baby to show him to the cook.

Camille smiled and said hello to a compact man who looked more like he should be working with cattle on the ranch than in the kitchen cooking for a living. Barrel-chested with thick black curls, Hector greeted each one of them. They chatted a moment and then entered a wide hallway with a polished plank floor. Another man in black trousers and white shirt appeared.

"This is Cletus Byrne, who is my house manager and butler when I need one," Marek said, making introductions.

Camille greeted another man who looked as if he should work out on the ranch instead of in Marek's house. He was broad-shouldered and tall with sandy hair and a quiet manner.

"Cletus will get your things. We have a temporary nursery set up in a large bedroom where Ashley can stay with Noah. Let's get settled and then I'll give you a tour of the house," Marek said, carrying Noah as they walked toward the front and down the wide hallway filled with oil paintings of Western art. In the wide entrance, a brass candelabra caught the afternoon sunlight streaming through tall windows that flanked the front door.

"Marek, this is a beautiful home," Camille said. "Not exactly what I expected."

"I can imagine," he replied with amusement in his voice.

He took them to the temporary rooms for Ashley and Noah. "The master bedroom is at the end of the hallway, so you won't be far away. When we take the complete tour of the house, both of you can look at bedrooms and select where you want Noah's room. There will be a nursery with an adjoining playroom and a suite for Ashley."

They walked into a bedroom and sitting room filled with afternoon sunshine. Camille wandered through it, looking at the white furniture and the adjoining bathroom, which was enormous.

"This is beautiful," Camille said. "You've already got it ready for Noah. Maybe I should cancel the decorator."

"Not at all. I want a place fixed with Noah in mind. This already existed and it's not a nursery, not even a bedroom for a young boy. You've been planning and you and Ashley have talked about what you want with the decorator. We'll have him out here this week and get this moving."

"This is a wonderful place for Noah," Ashley said, circling the room that had been turned into a temporary playroom.

"Good. It'll have to do for the time being. I'll show you where we'll be," he said, taking Camille's arm.

Ashley turned. "You two go ahead. I'm going to change Noah and then I'll join you," she said.

Camille turned to go with Marek. When they were alone in his suite, she turned to him. "I think Ashley wanted to give us a moment to ourselves."

"That's fine with me," Marek replied. "I'd prefer the rest of the day and tonight," he said, placing his hands on her waist.

She smiled. "You'll have to wait."

"You can't imagine how reluctantly," he said, giving her another hot look that made her sizzle.

"If you wait, you'll appreciate me more," she added in a sultry voice, stepping away from him.

He inhaled deeply. "If I 'appreciate' you more, I'll go up in flames. You keep that up and I'm going to lose my self-control."

"Maybe I'm trying to keep 'that' up."

"Camille," he said in a husky voice, reaching for her again.

She smiled and walked away. "Ashley will join us soon. Now show me your bedroom."

He stared at her a moment in silence, desire burning in his gaze. "Our room," he said as if reminding himself. "You can also get the decorator and change our rooms however you like," he said. "All I ask on that is let me see the changes. I have an office of sorts in one corner and some things I still want to keep in there."

"Of course. I'm not changing anything in your room at this point. I won't without telling you, either."

When she stepped into the large sitting room, he pulled her to one side of the door. "Ashley hasn't come and you started this. We have a minute and we're married anyway," he said, embracing her and leaning down to kiss her. While her heartbeat jumped, she held him to kiss him in return.

"Welcome home, Mrs. Rangel," Marek whispered, framing her face with his hands. "Camille, you and Noah are the best possible things that could have happened. This marriage is great. Far more than I expected."

"I agree," she whispered, her heart racing over his declaration. How easy it would be to tell him she loved him, but she wouldn't, not until he made a declaration, if that ever happened. He was far from falling in love yet, but she had hope as long as they were happy together and he wanted to be with her and make love with her.

"Marek, Ashley really will join us in a minute," Camille said, stepping away from him but wanting to close the door and stay in the bedroom with him the rest of the night, which was impossible.

She looked around the rooms where she would now live. Like everything else, Marek's suite was appealing. The floors gleamed with polish and thick area rugs were centered in the sitting room and adjoining bedroom. The furniture was covered in navy leather with fruitwood and she saw his corner office held a rolltop desk that looked antique. One wall was filled with shelves of books, pictures, trophies, a collection of memorabilia. She crossed the room to pick up a picture of Marek and Kern. Both had Western hats pushed to the backs of their heads. Both were in boots, jeans and Western shirts. They casually had arms around each other's shoulders. A horse stood behind them, its head by Kern's shoulder.

"This is a good picture," she said.

Marek crossed the room and smiled. "Kern had just won that horse from me in a bet and he was delighted. It was worth losing to see him so ridiculously happy. He loved that roan and wanted it from the day I got it." Marek laughed and shook his head. "That was a fun time. One of the good memories."

He glanced at the shelf as she replaced the picture next to one of Jillian.

He picked up the picture to fold the back and lay it flat on the shelf. "I'll put away Jillian's pictures."

"You don't need to," Camille said, turning to him. "I truly don't mind. You loved her and you were going to marry her. I'll feel better because I imagine you like to see them."

"That's past and gone. I don't need the pictures to remember her and I can look at them if I want. I'll put them away. It'll probably help me to move on."

She didn't think he would have done any such thing before their wedding and honeymoon. He was changing, coming out of the shell, but how much would he open his heart in the future?

She walked around the room and roamed into the masculine bedroom, with a bed that had an old-fashioned high headboard and navy-and-white pillows and comforter.

"This room looks like you."

"You can change this however you want as long it isn't pink or purple. I can't do purple or pink."

She grinned. "Aw, shucks, imagine that," she said, teasing him, unable to imagine Marek sprawled in a pink bed.

They heard Ashley and went out to find her in the sitting room. She held out Noah and Camille took him.

"Give him to me and we'll have a quick tour," Marek said.

Marek showed them the gym, with an indoor pool of pale blue tiles with white Corinthian columns on each side. Next they went to the entertainment room. "Both of you—this is your home, too, now. Ashley, you and Camille both feel free to use these rooms, the gym, the entertainment center, the kitchen, the pool, anything you want whenever you want, middle of the night or whatever. This is your home now," he repeated, gazing at Camille.

"Thank you," Camille said.

"Come on, we'll continue this tour," he said. By the time they stepped outside on a patio that was as big as the central part of the house, Camille wondered if she would ever find her way around. She stopped and looked around at the outdoor living area stocked with what looked like indoor furniture with a well-equipped kitchen. Beyond the chairs and furniture and outdoor rooms was a fenced area with a cabana, a dazzling pool that had slides and fountains and beds of flowers and palm trees.

To one side of the yard was another waterfall, as well as a fish and lily pond that was equally gorgeous.

There was a play area with a portable fence already set up for Noah. It was large enough for adults so Ashley took Noah from Marek. Holding the baby she stepped into it with him and set him down, giving him his toys. She sat near him, playing with him.

Marek declared happy hour and served everyone the drink of her choice. When they all had drinks, Ashley lifted her daiquiri. She sat in the fenced area on a blanket with Noah beside her and toys spread in front of him. Rising to her feet, she said, "Here's to the best brother-in-law ever, besides being the only one I have," she added, smiling at Marek. "Thank you for coming into our lives. Noah will thank you a few years from now."

Marek stood and crossed to her, leaning over the plastic fence to touch his glass to hers. "I'll drink to that," he said, turning back to Camille to toast her glass as well. She sipped, looking over the rim of her glass at him and wanting to be alone with him. His dark eyes held her gaze, conveying a sensual promise for later that night.

Marek's cell phone rang, and he excused himself to answer it.

When he was out of earshot, Camille smiled at her sister. "That was a nice toast, Ashley."

"I meant it, Camille. He's been incredible."

"I think so," Camille answered.

"Don't let him break your heart," Ashley whispered, looking at Marek, whose back was turned.

"I just hope for the best, but he's being very good to us."

"Amen to that."

Marek returned with phone in hand. "Ginny's on the

phone. The girls want to have Noah back. Any chance of them keeping him again anytime soon? And feel free to say no."

"It's fine with me." Camille looked at Ashley, who glanced at Noah.

"If you two don't mind, I'll fly home to Saint Louis again this weekend. I could leave on Friday and get back Sunday night if that would be all right."

"My plane will take you. Actually, we can go to Dallas and spend the weekend there. Ashley will fly home and Ginny and the girls can take Noah. How's that?"

Camille laughed. "All of us flying to Dallas so two little girls—"

"And one big one," Marek interrupted.

"So they can play with Noah for a couple of days. I don't care. I'd like to spend the weekend in Dallas."

Marek raised his phone. "Ginny, we're not doing this every weekend, but we'll come back to Dallas. Ashley is going home to Saint Louis. We'll come early Friday and you can have him from Friday around noon until Sunday afternoon. How's that?" He held the phone away as squeals erupted.

Shaking his head, he said, "Tell the girls to calm down. They'll see a lot of him. Okay. See you Friday. I'll tell them."

He put away his cell phone and looked at Camille and Ashley. "Profuse thanks, ladies, for sharing Noah. I'm sure you could hear the girls' screams of joy that he's coming for the weekend." Marek glanced at Noah. "He's oblivious to all this hoopla. I may have to have a talk with my sister and tell her to get those girls new dolls or, better yet, get another baby in the family. Maybe you can pick out new dolls for them," he said to Camille.

Camille laughed. "The girls seemed totally fascinated with him and he likes them, but then, Noah likes everyone."

"He's Kern's son," Marek remarked. "Thanks again, hon," he said to Camille.

"He'll be happy," she replied, thinking of Marek's casual endearment. The *hon* was so lightly stated, yet the term was a warm, fuzzy blanket wrapping around her heart, making her feel that he cared about her.

Friday, Camille saw the Rangel jet take off with Ashley on board, headed to Saint Louis. In the next hour, she watched Ginny and the girls come by Marek's Dallas house to pick up Noah. Finally, Camille turned to look at Marek as he closed and locked the door behind his sister and her brood.

"We're alone," he said when he faced her. "Come here, Camille."

Monday when they returned to the ranch, Marek held Camille's hand on the plane. The weekend had been fabulous. The more he made love to her, the more he wanted her. That amazed him. In so many ways, from that first day he had met her, she had constantly surprised him.

June approached, when she would be locked into performing for two weeks, and he knew he would see almost nothing of her in that time. He didn't like the thought. When had she become important to him? It was as if he couldn't get through a day without her in his life.

He shifted to look at her. Camille was dressed in red slacks and a matching red silk blouse. A red scarf encircled her hair at the back of her neck. He wondered whether she was wearing red or black underwear, vowing to buy her something sexy soon. Very personal, very sexy. His blood heated at the thought. He glanced out the window without seeing anything. Was he falling in love with his wife? The question startled him. He had constantly credited his feelings for Camille to pure lust, but did it go beyond that? Had she replaced the void left in his heart? He would always love Jillian, but there was only a memory and a heartache over her loss. Camille was here, filled with zest and life.

Could he have already fallen in love with his wife without realizing it? He turned again to look at her. How he wished they were alone. He would like to take that red scarf off her hair and let the mass of midnight hair fall freely over her shoulders. He wanted to bury himself in her heat and softness. *Am I in love?* The question nagged at him as he stared at her. She turned to look at him. "You look deep in thought."

"I'm thinking about the changes we need to make at the ranch. We'll need a nursery that can easily be transformed into a suite for a little boy. You'll need a music room. We can do that."

"That I do want," she said, a somber note in her voice.

"Anything worrying you?"

She smiled. "Not at all. Just curiosity, and maybe I'm a little overwhelmed. My life is changing swiftly. You came into it like a bolt of lightning and absolutely fried my old life instantly."

He leaned closer to her. "I believe I can say the same thing. Mine is better now, Camille."

"That's the nicest possible thing you could say," she whispered.

"I mean it." He wished he could be alone with her because he wanted to say more, but this wasn't the time. He glanced away. Across the aisle, Ashley was buried in her brochures and books and Noah slept, unaware his life changed by the day now.

Marek ran his thumb lightly across Camille's knuckles, placing her hand on his thigh and putting his hand over hers as he sat back and gazed out the window. "We'll be there soon."

She had brought about the impossible in his life, something he thought he would never again experience. He wanted to scoop her up now and kiss her and it took all his control to sit and try to think clearly about when he could possibly first be alone with her.

That night Camille and Marek got Noah bathed and in his pajamas and Camille took him back to the family room to rock him to sleep.

Still marveling how much his life had changed, Marek sat watching them while the women talked softly. Camille's hair spread over one shoulder with the sleeping baby on the other. She was beautiful, and she had filled a void in his heart.

He studied her solemnly. Already, his relationship with her had gone where he never thought it would. He had never even considered the possibility that he would care for her to the extent his heart would be touched. She wasn't the woman to get involved with. Her heart was taken by her career. Would it be possible to get her to give up her career for a full, family-centered life? Already, he was deeply involved with her, and he wanted to be.

She stood and cradled the sleeping baby in her arms. Ashley jumped up. "I'll take him to bed. I'm turning in, anyway," she said, taking Noah as Marek stood. Camille brushed a kiss on the top of his head.

"'Night, Marek, 'night, Camille," Ashley said, leaving with Noah sleeping against her shoulder.

"So you've seen the ranch and spent a few days here now," Marek said, sitting close to Camille as she sat again on the sofa. "What would you like to remodel? Redecorate? Change?"

"I'm checking into the names of decorators you gave me about the nursery. I definitely want to change that whole suite so it looks as if it belongs to a little boy. I also need a music room. Other than that, I'm fine for now. I don't want to come in and change everything."

"The way you've changed me," he said, moving closer to her where he could wind his fingers in her hair. "I'm not the same person I was when I met you. I'm happy, Camille. So happy with you."

She leaned forward to brush his lips lightly with hers. His hand tangled in her hair, and he kissed her hard.

When she leaned away, she gasped for breath. "Maybe we should go back to discussing redecorating."

"Do what you want. End of discussion. This is much more interesting," he said, moving closer to slip his arm around her waist and kiss her.

She leaned forward to kiss him in return.

He released her. "Ashley's gone to bed. We can talk in our room. Let's go," he said, standing and holding out his hand. She took his hand to stroll through the house with him while he switched off indoor lights.

"I told you my schedule involved going to Saint Louis in September to see my family after I finish performing in August in Santa Fe. I'll amend that slightly. I'll come back here for two weeks and then go to Saint Louis for one."

"I can't argue with that," Marek replied.

When they stepped into his bedroom suite and he closed the door, he reached out to draw her against his chest. "I've wanted you in my arms all evening," he said in a husky voice, leaning closer to kiss her, thoughts of the future gone.

The following week they returned to Dallas and she threw herself into practice and lessons the majority of her waking hours to get ready for her upcoming performance of *La Traviata*.

Marek stayed in Dallas, dismayed by the amount of work she put into her practice. He heard her sing scales and exercises, but he left early to go to his office and returned in the evening to stay out of the way. He wouldn't have realized the full extent of her efforts except he phoned her during the day, avoiding the hours he knew she spent in rehearsal. Sometimes he would only to talk to her briefly, and then she would return to practice her voice lesson, or go over her lesson in getting her Italian correct for the performance. She also worked out each day and they began to work out at 6:00 a.m. together, just so he could see her during her waking hours. After seven in the evening was the only time she let go and played with Noah. Finally after everyone else had gone to bed, she would go with Marek to their bedroom. They made love for hours into the night the first two nights, but by the third, after making love, she fell into an exhausted sleep and he knew he should not wake her again, but let her have the rest she needed. By Thursday, he went back to the ranch to stay out of her way and not be a distraction because each day she poured herself more into her work.

As he twisted wire, working on mending a fence, he realized he was standing, staring into the distance, his thoughts totally focused on Camille. His heart thudded and he found it difficult to breathe. He was in love with Camille when he had been certain such a thing could never happen. He had lusted after her, admired her, seduced her, laughed with her, shared Noah with her, but he hadn't expected to fall in love with her.

From what she had told him, she was getting back to a normal routine, which meant she would not have as much time for him as she had been giving him through the wedding and right after. Had he gotten himself into a situation where he would only experience more hurt? He couldn't ask her to give up her career and be a rancher's wife. He couldn't give up the ranch and go back to city life and work in an office on a daily routine. They had agreed that sometimes he would travel with her, which would be good, but he couldn't do that all the time. He couldn't imagine spending his life following her from town to town. And he hated the separations. He missed her anytime that he was away from her now. How had she so ingrained herself in his heart?

Thinking about being with her, he had to admit it was love he felt. He didn't even know how long he had been in love with his wife. Maybe since their honeymoon. That's when she had broken through the barriers around his heart. He just hadn't realized how thoroughly she had. He hadn't recognized or stopped to think about his own feelings. Maybe it had even been before their honeymoon, a gradual thing that he hadn't recognized as it had been happening. A miracle for him.

He loved her. Totally, completely. And if he loved her, he wanted her in his life, not this piecemeal seeing each other between her voice lessons and, soon, her performances and trips home to her family. He wanted her in his life just as he had wanted Noah in his life. Each night he had missed her more than ever. Now, he sat thinking about how he could ask her to give up her career. He hated the absences, but he hated hurting her more. How could he ask her to give up what she'd worked so hard to achieve?

He had lost one love. Had he set himself up for another devastating heartbreak?

On the weekend he returned to Dallas. Ashley had flown home again, and Camille had agreed to let Ginny keep Noah Friday and Saturday nights and have him home with Marek Sunday night before Marek returned to the ranch.

Between Camille's full schedule in Dallas and their separation when he was at the ranch, he wondered about their future. As she succeeded in her career, she would probably be busier than she was now. Could he deal with that?

Monday, the last week of May, he stayed in Dallas and

told Camille he was going to his office. As soon as the stores opened, he called his jeweler and talked briefly before leaving for the jewelry store.

It was after six when Camille finished her daily routine and showered, dressing for dinner in black silk slacks and a matching sleeveless top.

Marek played with Noah in the room that had become a temporary nursery until the redecorating was finished. Seated cross-legged on the floor, Marek talked to Noah while playing patty-cake with him. Noah laughed and clapped his hands in imitation.

"Having fun?" she asked and Marek rose to his feet, scooping up Noah to hold him. When the baby held his arms out to Camille, she took him.

"Ashley left for the evening. Told us to not wait up. I told her we wouldn't," Marek said in a husky tone. "I have plans for you."

"I can't wait. But I do have to feed this fellow or no one will do anything else and he'll still be awake when we go to bed."

"When we go to bed," Marek repeated. "I can't wait. Let's feed the hungry boy."

"I agree."

It was nine o'clock when they were in their room and finally alone. Marek drew Camille into his embrace. One look in his dark eyes and her heart began to race. "I've waited all day for this moment," he whispered and kissed away her answer.

Her heart thudded. Each time they made love, he became more important to her. In the throes of passion, she had whispered her declaration of love, but he had never heard her and she intended to keep it that way until she heard words of love cross his lips.

She poured out her passion as they made love far into the night. Holding him tightly, she ran one hand down his bare back as he lowered himself between her legs and slowly filled her, taking time to heighten tension, making her want him desperately as she arched beneath him and then rocked with him. "I love you," she cried, unable to hold back, certain he hadn't heard her as it had always been.

She held him as his control vanished and he thrust swiftly, taking her over an edge. "Marek," she cried, grasping his solid body as if he were the only anchor in her life.

"Camille," he ground out her name while he shuddered in his climax. "I love you."

Her eyes flew open. Moving with him, she held him. Had she imagined his declaration? She had dreamed of it too many times to count. Passion drove away her questions and she rocked with him, united physically, her heart belonging to him totally.

When he finally held her in his arms as legs were entwined and her black hair spilled over his shoulder, he showered her with light kisses. "I love you, Camille."

She gazed into his dark eyes while her heart missed beats. "You really mean that?" she whispered.

"Yes," he said gruffly, gazing at her solemnly. He brushed long strands of her hair away from her face. "Love may complicate our life."

"Never. This is better. I love you and I've loved you since before we said wedding vows."

He stared at her intently. "Why didn't you tell me?"

She shook her head. "You weren't ready."

He stared at her again in silence, and she wondered what he was thinking. "I'm ready now," he whispered and kissed her hard, holding her against his heart while joy filled her.

"Wait," he said, turning to open a drawer in the bedside table. "This is for you."

Surprised, she glanced from the package to him, and then she took it to untie a blue ribbon and tear away the wrapper. She opened the box to take out a black velvet box. When she opened it, she gasped as the sapphire and diamond necklace caught the light.

"This is magnificent. It's stunning," she said, sitting up and pulling the sheet beneath her arms.

"Here's what is stunning," he said, sitting up to fasten it around her neck.

"Marek, thank you. This is the most beautiful jewelry I've ever owned except my wedding ring, which is gorgeous."

"I love you, Camille," he said again and kissed her.

Her heart pounded wildly, more from his declaration of love than the necklace which had taken her breath at first sight.

He paused. "We can make this a complete, real marriage. If we both love each other. Have you thought about the possibility of scaling back your career?"

Startled, she frowned. "No, I haven't. My career doesn't diminish my love for you or Noah. I don't want to scale back or give it up. I can't do that. I feel I can achieve so much more, and I love opera. I live and breathe opera. But it doesn't take away from the love I feel for you."

They stared at each other and she hurt, with a knot tightening inside. A muscle worked in his jaw as he stared intently at her. She had no idea what he was thinking.

"I don't know about our future. I do know about now," he said gruffly, reaching for her to pull her into his embrace.

She wrapped her arms around him and let her love for him pour into her lovemaking.

They loved far into the night again and early the next morning he left for the ranch to get out of her way and return to his own work. As she showered and dressed, she thought about his impossible request, his declaration of love that obviously had a stipulation. She didn't know if that would cause him to end this marriage of convenience or give it less time and attention. Whatever happened, she couldn't turn her back on her career now.

Saturday Marek had to stay at the ranch because of a crisis on a neighboring ranch where the barn caught on fire and two trucks burned. Marek loaned a truck to the neighbor and tried to help any way he could, but by the time he returned to his ranch and had cleaned up, Camille said she was exhausted and going to bed early, so he decided to fly to Dallas on Sunday.

She had a rehearsal on Sunday and a costume fitting that had been unexpected. Once again, it was late when she was finally free and they ate a cold dinner at ten.

The weekend was too short. The next week Marek mulled over the prospects of their married life. He hated being away from her. He loved her, and, as time went by, he knew that love would grow until it was as strong as the oaks that grew at his ranch.

What could he do to keep them together?

The phone rang, interrupting his thoughts, and he answered to hear his sister. "I was calling to tell you we are all excited about Camille's performance. The girls are deliriously happy to be going and this will definitely be their first opera. It's my first and Frank's and I suspect it's yours."

"I've seen bits and pieces, at an event years ago."

"No doubt some beautiful woman talked you into it. We're thrilled to get to keep Noah opening night so Ashley can attend with her family."

"It's good for him to spend time with your family and Ashley is happy to be going with her family."

"You don't sound happy. Is everything all right?" Before

he could answer, she continued, "You're in love with her, aren't you?"

"Ginny, stop being big sis for a few minutes."

"Impossible," she replied. "I'm sorry. Take care of yourself."

"At least you didn't say, 'I told you so.' I thank you for that."

"I won't say any more on the subject, but I'm here if you want to talk."

"Thanks."

"I'll call Camille about Noah."

He heard the click and she was gone. He felt torn between the heartache of loving Camille and living this way or ending this paper marriage or trying to get her to give up her career. Of all his choices, ending the marriage was not tolerable. He loved her even if he was going to get hurt again as much as he had been hurt over losing Jillian. Why was love such a risk?

He would go to opening night and then for two weeks, he would see almost nothing of her. What kind of incentive could he offer to get her to cut back a little?

For her opening night performance, he had no intention of doing anything to take away the glory of that moment from her.

Ten

The following night Marek sat in the box Camille had arranged. He was with the Avanoles. Her parents, her brother and both sisters were present. Marek thought he should have gone sooner to hear her sing. He had heard her sing scales and practice exercises, but nothing else.

When the conductor appeared and the orchestra commenced playing, Marek's mind was on Camille and when he would be alone with her, something he didn't expect to happen until this opera ended its last performance. And then Camille came onstage and his attention went to her. She had told him the story, which sounded sad and gloomy with death for her character at the end.

As she sang, Marek was mesmerized. He had heard her practice, but he had never been in the room with her. Now the full richness of her voice filled the opera house.

Chills ran down his spine. He knew nothing about opera. He had seen singers on television performing bits, but never a whole opera, never in person. Camille's voice soared, filling the opera house with purest sound.

He was transfixed, steeped in the crystal sounds of her voice. She stopped and in minutes the music started again and then her golden voice with its astonishing range.

Her acting was lively and vivacious as he had expected, while her singing captured his heart. He would remember this night the rest of his life.

She was meant to sing. She had a true talent and his heart felt as if it were breaking into a million pieces. Even though he knew nothing about opera, there was no mistaking that she had incredible talent. This went beyond their two lives. This was a talent that should be shared.

All this time he had had no idea how gifted she was.

Press releases and media could be filled with exaggerated hype, fed by agents, luck, friendships and the views of the reporter. Her voice flew beyond all those things. No one could question her tone, range or ability.

In a moment of clarity, he saw he could never take her from the stage. Her voice was meant for the famous opera, meant for the world to hear.

She belonged to her talent and she needed to give herself to the public because her gift was awesome.

He stopped thinking and listened to her clear soprano as she sang. He hurt with an incredible pain. How could he have done this to himself again? He couldn't ask her to compromise, so perhaps he was going to have to, in order for them to have a bearable marriage.

Music filled the room, like sunshine surrounding him, while at the same time he felt as if he were tumbling into the darkness of another lost love, of pain and separation because he loved her. She had captured his heart and he had enabled her to do so.

He wondered at the perverseness of humans as he shifted

restlessly, because for the first time in his life, he had met a woman he couldn't love on his own terms.

Dazed, hurting while at the same time spellbound by her singing, he sat through the opera, applauding, calling "Brava" with others and knowing she was lost to him. He could never try to win her away from the life she had been destined to live.

He went through the motions, talking to her family.

Camille had an opening night party for the cast. Families were invited. Backstage, he stood to one side to let others surround her to talk to her. She was radiant, smiling constantly, and she looked more gorgeous than ever.

His pain increased as he watched her and saw what he was losing. There was absolutely no possibility of his having more than a fraction of her life. He thought of the new ring he had bought for her, to give her as a token of his love for her. He loved her, but he would not take her from her career and he would not give her that ring.

Her family was staying with them, so he wasn't alone with her until one in the morning when they finally closed the bedroom door. Her black hair was partially braided and fastened on her head. The remaining locks fell freely across her back. Her makeup was thick, dramatic, emphasizing her large, expressive eyes and full mouth, making her breathtakingly beautiful. She smiled in triumph at him.

"You have a fantastic voice," he said, crossing the room to place his hands on her shoulders. "You belong onstage, Camille. I've become an opera fan."

"I'm so glad. So happy," she said, hugging him and standing on tiptoe to kiss him.

Desire consumed him. He needed her kisses, her love on this night. He knew he would lose her in the future, but tonight she was in his arms, radiant from performing and her success. He tightened his arms around her and kissed her hard, wanting to hold her, love her and make her want to stay in his arms forever. For a few hours, he would cling to a dream that had no substance, but would give him joy tonight.

Later, when she was stretched against him, she chatted and finally raised herself slightly on her elbow to look at him. "Why so quiet tonight?"

She met a dark, impenetrable gaze. "I hadn't thought that much about your voice and your singing," he answered finally. "You have a true and beautiful talent. Your voice is wonderful. You'll be a star and it will take you far from here."

"I'll always be able to come home."

"That's right. But you'll also always have to leave to go perform somewhere."

"This shouldn't interfere with you and it may actually give you more time with Noah. Besides, at this point it is sheer speculation. I have a long way to go to become that kind of star."

"I have a feeling it will come much faster than you think."

"I think you're biased, but I hope you're right. I'm overjoyed you liked the opera."

Camille's *La Traviata* performance had been a triumph and the time had flown. Now as she sat on a Rangel jet bound for Santa Fe, she glanced next to her at Marek, who was poring over Noah's baby book.

Marck's thick black lashes were dark shadows above his cheeks. A stray lock of hair curled on his forehead. He had withdrawn into a shell the past few days, and she had wondered what had triggered it. Was it something in his life or had it been the interference of her performance and the intense practice beforehand?

"What? You have the intense look of a cat ready to pounce on prey."

"How'd you know that?" she asked.

"I can tell," he answered casually, closing the baby book to hand it back to her. "Nice. You need a picture of Kern. I'll get you one."

"I'd like that."

"Now, why the intense examination?" he repeated.

She could feel heat fill her cheeks. "You've changed and I was trying to figure why. You're preoccupied."

"Business," he said. In the time she had known Marek, she had never seen him concerned about business problems or ranch problems. Jess bore the brunt of those. Marek had a shuttered look and she couldn't glean anything from his expression.

"I don't think that's really the answer," she said, letting it drop for now until they were alone. They were flying to Santa Fe to get a place to live and then she would leave Dallas. Was it the move that had him on edge?

She was amazed how fast and efficient Marek was when they arrived in Santa Fe and later when she went through the move. She had another opera performance to prepare for, and they agreed he would leave Noah with her in Santa Fe and he would return to the ranch until opening night.

When she told him goodbye at the airport in New Mexico, he held her tightly and kissed her until she was breathless, her heart racing, and she didn't want him to stop.

He released her abruptly. "Better go," he said gruffly, his gaze trailing over her features as if memorizing them. When he turned away to board the jet and she left to go back to a waiting limo Marek had arranged for her while she was in Santa Fe, she had a distinct feeling something was amiss.

Getting up before sunrise, working until dark at any physical labor he could find, Marek threw himself into work at the ranch. He hated being alone in the house, trying to keep books, because his mind would wander constantly to Camille. He missed her and he missed Noah. He talked to Camille each day and saw them on Skype and tried to keep a fragile contact, but she was busy getting ready to perform Pamina in *The Magic Flute,* and Noah couldn't converse with him. When he saw them on Skype, he hurt badly, wanting her, loving her, but hating the separation. He missed Noah's happy little face.

Instead of growing accustomed to being away from her, to seeing her on opening night and when the performance was over, he hurt more with Camille and Noah out of his life and getting only tiny glimpses and contacts with them.

The last week in August he had to be in Dallas for a Rangel Foundation meeting, and Ginny had asked him to lunch beforehand. He listened to her chatter about the girls and saw their latest pictures.

"I haven't seen them for too long, Ginny. Bring them to the ranch this weekend so they can ride."

"I will accept that invitation," she said over a crisp green salad while Marek ate only a few bites of his onion burger. "You miss Camille, don't you?"

"Camille and Noah. Yes," he said, giving her a steady look. "Want to hear you were right?"

"No, I don't. I don't want you hurt, and you've lost weight and look like you haven't slept for weeks. Maybe you should go see her more."

Marek shook his head. "I'm in the way when she practices or has lessons. She's busy when she's getting ready to perform and when she's performing."

"I can imagine, but you can't keep on like this."

"I know, Ginny," he said, looking away and she let the subject drop.

Through the meeting Marek thought about the future. He flew back to the ranch, the one haven in his life and now even the ranch seemed empty and hurtful.

That evening Jess appeared at the back door with a six-pack of cold beer. "Want company?"

Marek smiled slightly. "Hell, yes. I can use some company, Jess. Beer looks good, too. Come on in."

Jess's boot heels clicked against bare floorboards as he headed to the kitchen. In minutes they sat at the kitchen table while silence stretched between them.

"Camille was meant for opera. I can't take her from that because she has the talent to be a star."

After another stretch of silence, Marek ran his finger along the cold bottle. "Maybe I've been looking for what I had with Jillian, but Camille is different. I can't expect her to give me what I expected with Jillian. Camille has all this talent. I'm going to have to settle for being a small part of her life, something I'm not used to doing."

"If you love her and that's what it takes, that's a good decision," Jess said. "I'd give anything for a small part of my family."

"You're right, Jess. I suppose it's because I'm not used to being the one who compromises."

"I don't think you are."

"For Camille, I'm willing to try to make this marriage work."

"If you love her, that's a good solution. You'll do what you have to. So will she. You won't lose Noah. What boy wouldn't want to come to the ranch?"

"Might be a few, particularly one who's raised backstage at operas."

"You'll see," Jess said, and Marek felt a degree better. His cell rang. "That's her, Jess."

"Go ahead. I'll head home anyway. Keep the beer for next time," Jess said, standing and picking up his hat to go while Marek answered his phone. His heart missed a beat when he heard Camille's voice.

* * *

After talking for over an hour to Marek, Camille lay in bed and contemplated her future. She loved Marek and she didn't think she would ever love again. Life without him looked unbelievably empty. What did she want in her future? Would it matter to him what she wanted? One time he had asked her about scaling back her career, and she couldn't. The last time they had been together, he had seemed restrained, preoccupied, yet their lovemaking had grown better and more passionate each time they were together.

What did she want in the future for herself? As his wife, money was no longer in the equation. Did she want to sing for the thrill and enjoyment of it? For the success? It was grinding work—voice and language lessons, daily voice practice, studying operas and arias, working out. She had Noah to consider. What did she want for her future?

She wanted Marek in her life and Noah's. She wanted another baby. She also wanted to sing at La Scala and to reach a pinnacle in opera where she became a name.

Tears flowed freely and she turned, burying her face in her pillow to cry silently. She wanted it all—the best of both worlds, her love, her baby and her career. What did she want to sacrifice?

All the time Camille was in Saint Louis, she thought about her future. At night she sat up long hours, staring out the window at the familiar yard where she had grown up. What did she want most of all? Marek couldn't make that decision for her. That one she had to make herself.

Making her decision, she cut her visit home short by two days and returned to Dallas, calling Marek and telling him she knew what she wanted to do.

Eleven

When Marek met her at the airport, as arranged earlier, they took Noah to Ginny's before going to Marek's Dallas house.

Struggling to wait to hold and kiss her, Marek finally placed his hands on her waist and took another long look at her, relishing every moment of having her with him. In a clinging, low-cut black dress that ended above her knees, she looked breathtaking. Her hair was pinned up on the sides, hanging free in the back. While it was gorgeous, he longed to take it down. Take down her hair, kiss her, seduce her and spend the rest of the day and night in bed making love.

"You can't imagine how much I've missed you," he said, kissing her passionately.

Minutes later, she leaned away to frame his face with her hands. "You haven't seemed as happy lately. I didn't want to talk about it over the phone. I wanted to wait until we were together."

"I couldn't be happier now that you're in my arms," he whispered, kissing her throat.

"Marek, listen a minute." He raised his head to focus on her.

"You asked me some time ago to scale back my career, and I told you I couldn't. Things haven't been quite the same between us since."

"I've had a lot of time to think about that. You were meant to share your talent. I love you and I'll settle for the time I can have with you."

"You mean that?" she asked, her eyes growing huge.

"I mean it. Even if it's just a little of your time. I love you. I need you in my life. I need to know that I have your love."

Smiling, with a sparkle coming to her blue eyes, she kissed him passionately again. His hands wound in her hair as he kissed her in return, and then his arm circled her waist to hold her tightly.

She finally leaned away. "That thrills me, that you are willing to make such a sacrifice for me."

"You don't know how much I love you," he said, desire a smoldering fire in him.

"Marek, while we were apart, I gave thought to what I want to do. You think my life should be opera. I'm not the only singer—not even remotely. As your wife, my earnings no longer are part of this."

"That's beside the point."

"Not when my family needed my help and I had to count on my voice. I still want success in opera. Specifically, I want the lead in an opera at the Metropolitan. I want the lead at La Scala."

"You should be the lead both places," he said, his voice thickening. He could inhale the scent of her perfume, feel her narrow waist beneath his hands. They stood with only inches separating them. "I also want the love of the man I love," she said in a throaty voice as tears filled her eyes. "I want Noah to have a family. I want him to have two siblings. I want a family."

"I want you to have both," Marek whispered. "I want you to have it all. Everything possible to make you happy."

"I love you," she said, gazing solemnly at him. "Listen a moment. Here's my plan." Her voice strengthened, and she poked his chest with her forefinger as if she needed to get his attention. "Give me three years. I'm only twenty-five. For the next three years put up with the separations and the inconveniences and let me pursue my career totally. In three years, I will retire. Noah will still be in preschool, a little boy, not too old for siblings."

"In three—"

"Do not interrupt until I'm through," she said, startling him. "I will want to give it up in three years. I've thought this through carefully. I know you thought you had our marriage all mapped out and it would work and then it didn't. I'm sure that I don't want to pursue my career for years. I want my family. I want your love. I love you and I'm not giving you up just because you're shocked by my talent and think I should give up everything for my career. Occasionally in your life, you're wrong. Can you give me three years if I give you the rest?"

Stunned, he stared at her while he thought about what she proposed.

"Marek, for heaven's sake. I love you," she cried, standing on tiptoe to kiss him.

Marek's resistance to her kiss disappeared. His arms locked tightly around her and he kissed her, letting go all the longing he had bottled up since hearing her perform. As if a dam had burst, desire poured over him, making him shake with urgency. He wanted her desperately and everything else vanished.

Oblivious of her hands moving over him, he unzipped her dress. She fumbled with his shirt and he yanked it off, popping buttons and sending them flying while she shook out of her dress and let it fall.

In minutes he picked her up to love her while they kissed and her long legs were locked around him. She was soft, a flame burning away all hurt. He loved her wildly, wanting to hold her forever in his arms.

When she finally clung to him, relaxing against him, he let her slide to put her feet on the floor. She glanced up.

"I think you've already given me your answer. Right?"

That night in his bed, he held her close as he toyed with long locks of her raven hair. "We'll follow your plan, Camille," he said. "In three years, you may change—"

She placed her fingers lightly on his mouth while she shook her head. "No. I adore Noah. I want a family. I love you and want your love. With the money you have, I can continue to have voice lessons and sing in local events in Dallas or Houston or even New Mexico, maybe once a year or less. We'll see, but I'm sure I will not continue with this all-consuming career that takes everything."

"You don't have to talk me into it. For better or worse, I'm accepting your idea," he said happily.

Smiling, she rolled over to trail feather kisses on his cheek and jaw, down over his shoulder. "If I get my wish about the Met and La Scala in less than three years, we can move up that timetable."

He laughed, a deep rumbling sound that vibrated in his chest. "Wait a minute."

Turning, he opened a drawer in a bedside table. He settled back to take her right hand in his.

"Camille, you've given me my full life back. You've given me Noah. You've given me love. Your wedding ring was a token of our contract and agreement to marry for Noah. This ring is a token of my gratitude and all my love," he said in a husky voice. He dropped a small package in her lap.

She blinked and looked up at him, seeing warmth and love in his eyes. Her heart thudded over his declaration. Tearing away wrappings, she opened her gift. With a racing pulse, she raised the lid to see a dazzling diamond ring.

"Marek, it's beautiful," she said, throwing her arms around his neck. "I am overjoyed."

He smiled at her. "I'll do everything in my power to keep you happy."

"Including coming to Budapest part of the time with me, even though I'll be busy."

"Including going to Hungary part of the time," he answered, smiling with her. "Whatever I can do to keep your love, keep you happy, keep you and Noah in my life however much or little that turns out to be."

Joy shook her and tears of happiness spilled. Before he could say anything more, she kissed him, knowing his love and being a family for Noah was what she wanted more than all else.

* * * * *

"There's one more thing that we haven't covered."

"What would that be?" For the life of her, Summer couldn't imagine what there was left to be decided after their many conversations on the subject.

"We're going to start acting like we're a couple," Ryder stated.

"You mean, as if we've fallen in love?" Things just kept getting more complicated with every conversation they had.

"It's easier to go with that than it is to try and explain everything." He leaned over and briefly pressed his lips to hers. "Besides, that's what people are going to think anyway. We might as well go along with it."

"Does that mean we'll be openly affectionate toward each other?" she asked, liking the way his kiss made her feel warm all over.

"Yup. That's what people do when they're …involved."

She frowned. "Do you think we can be convincing?"

"Let's see…" he said.

A BABY
BETWEEN FRIENDS

BY
KATHIE DeNOSKY

Published in Great Britain 2013
by Mills & Boon, an imprint of Harlequin (UK) Limited,
Eton House, 18-24 Paradise Road, Richmond, Surrey TW9 1SR

© Kathie DeNosky 2013

ISBN: 978 0 263 90479 6
ebook ISBN: 978 1 472 00619 6

51-0713

Harlequin (UK) policy is to use papers that are natural, renewable and recyclable products and made from wood grown in sustainable forests. The logging and manufacturing processes conform to the legal environmental regulations of the country of origin.

Printed and bound in Spain
by Blackprint CPI, Barcelona

Kathie DeNosky lives in her native southern Illinois on the land her family settled in 1839. She writes highly sensual stories with a generous amount of humor; her books have appeared on the *USA TODAY* bestseller list and received numerous awards, including two National Readers' Choice Awards. Kathie enjoys going to rodeos, traveling to research settings for her books and listening to country music. Readers may contact her by emailing kathie@kathiedenosky.com. They can also visit her website, www.kathiedenosky.com, or find her on Facebook, www.facebook.com/Kathie-DeNosky-Author/278166445536145.

This book is dedicated to my editor Stacy Boyd
for allowing me to spread my wings and soar.

One

Ryder McClain's temper flared as he stared at the five men grinning at him like a bunch of damned fools. Having spent their teen years together on the Last Chance Ranch, a home for boys that the foster care system had labeled lost causes, he loved all of them. In all ways except by blood, they were his brothers. However, at this moment, nothing would be more satisfying than to wrap his hands around their throats and throttle every one of them.

"I'm only going to say this one more time and then I expect you all to drop it," he said through gritted teeth. "I brought Summer Patterson to the party tonight because she's a friend who didn't have any other plans. Period. There's absolutely nothing going on between us."

"Sure, if you say so, bro." Jaron Lambert's skeptical expression indicated that he didn't believe a word Ryder had just said. "And I'll bet you still believe in the Easter Bunny and the Tooth Fairy, don't ya?"

"I'll give you all a hundred-to-one odds that the lady in question has other ideas," Lane Donaldson said, rocking back on the heels of his handcrafted Caiman leather boots. A highly successful, professional poker player, Lane used his master's degree in psychology to read people like an open book. In this instance, the man was definitely reading the wrong chapter.

"Yup. I'd say she's cut you from the herd and getting ready to measure you for a saddle," Sam Rafferty added, laughing. The only married one of his foster brothers, Sam and his wife, Bria, were throwing the party to celebrate the renewal of their wedding vows, as well as Bria's pregnancy. "You might as well face it, Ryder. Your bachelor days are numbered."

"You're just hoping one of us will join you in the pool of the blissfully hitched," Ryder said, blowing out a frustrated breath. "But as far as Summer and I are concerned, that's not going to happen—now or in the future. Neither one of us have any intention of being anything more than best friends. End of discussion."

Smiling, T.J. Malloy paused with his beer bottle halfway to his mouth. "Ryder, did you get kicked in the head by a bull at the last rodeo you worked? That might explain you not being able to see what's as plain as your hand in front of your face."

"Well, now, this makes things a whole lot easier for me," Nate Rafferty said, smirking as he turned toward the dance floor where Summer stood talking to Bria and her sister, Mariah. "As long as you're not interested, I think I'll just mosey on over there and ask the little lady to dance."

Ryder knew that his brother was baiting him, but without a second thought, his hand came down like a vise-grip on Nate's shoulder. "Don't even think about it, Romeo."

"Oh, so you *have* staked your claim," Lane said smugly.

"No, I haven't." Ryder's jaw was clenched so hard that he wouldn't be surprised if it took a crowbar to pry his teeth apart. "But Summer doesn't need Nate's brand of grief." He thought the world of his foster brother, but Nate Rafferty had a love 'em and leave 'em philosophy that had left a string of broken hearts across the entire Southwest and then some. "No offense, Nate, but you're the last thing she needs."

"He's got you there, Nate," Sam said, nodding. The only two biological siblings of the group, Sam and Nate couldn't have been more different. The older of the two, Sam had never even come close to having the wild streak that his younger brother Nate had.

Nate shrugged. "I can't help it if I love the ladies."

"You take your interest in women to a whole other level," Ryder said, shaking his head in disgust. "Leave this lady alone and we'll get along just fine. Cross that line and you and I are going to have one hell of a big problem, bro."

He chose to ignore the knowing looks his brothers exchanged and, in favor of doing them all bodily harm, walked away. For one thing, he didn't want to ruin Sam and Bria's reception by getting into a knock-down, drag-out brawl. And for another, he made sure he never raised a fist in anger to anyone for any reason. He had been down that road once, when he was a teenager, and the results had damned near ruined his life. He wasn't going to risk going down it again.

"Ryder?"

Turning at the sound of the familiar female voice, he watched the pretty blond-haired woman with the bluest eyes he had ever seen walk toward him. He and Summer had been best friends for the past few years, and although any man would be lucky to call her his woman, Ryder had avoided thinking of her as anything but his friend. Anything more between them and he would feel obligated to tell her the reason he had finished growing up at the Last Chance Ranch. That was something he didn't care to share with anyone and why he didn't intend to enter into a serious relationship with any woman. Some things were just better left buried in the past. Besides, he didn't want to take the chance of losing the easygoing friendship they had forged by becoming romantically involved with her. He suspected she felt the same way.

"Is something wrong?" she asked, her expression reflecting her concern.

Letting go of his anger, Ryder shook his head as he smiled at the petite woman standing next to him. "No, I just got tired of listening to my brothers' bull."

She smiled wistfully. "You're lucky. At least you have brothers to irritate you. I've never had that problem."

Ryder felt as guilty as hell. As aggravating as his foster brothers could be at times, there wasn't a doubt in his mind they would all be there for him no matter what—the same as he would be for all of them. They meant the world to him and there wasn't a day that went by he didn't thank the good Lord above that he had them in his life.

But Summer had never had anything like that. Over the course of their friendship, he had learned she was the only child of an older couple who, during her senior year in college, had been killed in the small plane her father owned. With their deaths, she had been left with no family at all.

"Yeah, they sure can be a thorn in my side sometimes." As the last traces of his anger dissipated, he grinned. "But I guess after all these years I don't have any other choice but to keep them."

She laughed. "Good idea, cowboy. But seriously, your family is great. I know some of your brothers from seeing them compete at the rodeos we've worked, but I'd never met Sam's wife and her sister. They're very nice and I think it's wonderful that you all have stayed so close over the years."

When Ryder noticed Nate eyeing Summer like a fox sizing up an unguarded henhouse, he shot his brother a warning glare, then asked, "Have you had a chance to dance yet?"

"Only the line dances," she answered, glancing at the dance floor Sam had his hired hands construct in one of the barns for the celebration.

"I thought I saw Sam's head wrangler ask you to dance a little earlier," he said, frowning.

"I suppose he was nice enough," she replied, shrugging one slender shoulder. "But I wasn't in the mood to dance then."

"Well, if you don't mind a cowboy with two left feet and the worst sense of rhythm this side of the Mississippi, I'd be honored to stand in one spot with you and sway in time to the music," he offered.

Her eyes filled with humor. "I thought all Texas cowboys took pride in sashaying around the dance floor doing the two-step or the stroll."

"You know me better than that, darlin'." As the band started playing a slow, dreamy country tune, he shook his head in mock disgust and placing his hand to her back, guided her out onto the dance floor. "This is one Texan who doesn't sashay, prance or shimmy anywhere. Anytime. Ever."

"I beg to differ with you," she murmured, placing her hands on his biceps when he rested his at her trim waist. "I've seen you when you're dancing with a two-thousand-pound bull. You have some pretty smooth moves, cowboy."

"That's because it's my job." He shrugged and tried to ignore the warmth of her soft palms burning his skin through the fabric of his chambray shirt. "If I don't get those old bulls to dance with me, a bull rider gets run over."

"Don't you have a degree in ranch management?" she asked. "I would have thought you'd be content to stay home and run your ranch instead of traveling around the country playing chicken with a bulldozer on hooves."

"Yup, I'm a proud graduate of Texas A&M." He put himself between her and a couple enthusiastically two-stepping their way around the dance floor in an effort to keep them from bumping into her. "But I have a good, reliable foreman I pay quite well to check in with me several times a day. He gives me a full report on how things are going, I tell him what I want done and he sees that it's taken care of. That frees me up to be out on the rodeo circuit saving knuckleheaded bull riders like Nate and Jaron."

As Summer gazed up at him, she frowned. "I don't think I've ever asked, but why did you choose to be a rodeo bullfighter instead of a rider?"

"One time when our foster dad, Hank, was teaching us all to rodeo, one of the training bulls got loose and tried to mow down Jaron. I didn't have a clue what I was doing, but I jumped in the arena and put myself between the two of them to keep that from happening. It turned out that I was pretty good at distracting a bull and getting it to chase me." He shrugged. "I've been doing it ever since."

"In other words, you like being a hero," she said, smiling.

Laughing, he shook his head. "Nah. I'm in it for the adrenaline rush, darlin'." It was an easier explanation than admitting that he had always felt compelled to protect others from danger at the risk of his own safety.

When the song ended, Ryder led her off the dance floor and after finding an empty table for them, made sure she was comfortably seated before he went to get them a couple of drinks. He frowned as he made his way to the bar. His arms still tingled where she had rested her hands, and for the life of him, he couldn't figure out why. That had never happened before. Had his brothers' ribbing put ideas in his head about Summer?

As he continued to ponder the strange sensation, he looked up to see his brothers watching with no small amount of interest. They all wore the same sappy, know-it-all grin, making him want to plant his fist in all of their guts.

Ryder was extremely grateful that their foster father had instilled a strong sense of family among the boys he helped guide through their troubled teenage years. As Hank Calvert always told them, once they were grown they would appreciate having each other and a little bit of history together that they could look back on since none of them had any other family to speak of. And that's the way Ryder felt…most of the time. But at other times—like right now—having brothers could be a real pain in the ass.

As Summer waited for Ryder to return with their drinks, she absently watched the dancers form a couple of parallel lines and begin to move in unison to a lively tune. She couldn't get over how much she was enjoying herself. Normally she turned down all invitations from the men she worked with, no matter what the occasion or the circumstances. But Ryder was different. They had been best friends from the time she took the job as public relations director for the rodeo association southwestern circuit, and for reasons she couldn't explain, she trusted him. He was honest, didn't play the games that most men did, and despite his above average height and muscular build, she didn't feel at all threatened by him.

Of course, that might have something to do with the way he had run interference with some of their more aggressive male coworkers when she first started working for the rodeo association. From the day they met, Ryder had made it a point to remind all of them that she was a lady and should be treated as such. He had shown her nothing but his utmost respect, and it hadn't taken long before they had developed an easy, comfortable relationship. And not once in all the time she had known him had he indicated that he wanted anything more from her than to be her friend.

Unfortunately, she couldn't say the same for a lot of the men she knew. Most of them fell into two categories—blatant flirts who made it clear what they wanted from a woman, and the seemingly harmless type who lured a woman into a false sense of security before revealing their true hidden agenda. It was the latter group that was the most dangerous. The flirts were easy to spot and, once rebuffed, usually moved on to set their sights on another female. But the men with hidden agendas were nothing more than predators hiding behind a facade of sincerity.

As she absently stared at the dancers, a shiver slithered up her spine. Regrettably, she had learned that lesson the hard way. But it was one she never, as long as she lived, intended to forget.

"Would you mind if I join you, Summer?" Bria Rafferty asked, from behind her. "After that last dance, I need a minute or two to catch my breath."

Turning to glance over her shoulder, Summer smiled at the pretty auburn-haired woman. "Please have a seat." She looked around. "Where's the rest of the clan?"

"Sam, Nate, T.J. and Lane are in a lively debate about the differences between breeds of bucking bulls and which ones are the hardest to ride." Bria laughed as she pointed to the other side of the barn. "And Mariah and Jaron are arguing again about whether I'm going to have a boy or a girl."

"What are you and Sam hoping to have?" Summer asked, smiling when Bria lowered herself into the chair across from her.

"I don't care as long as the baby is healthy," Bria said, placing her hand protectively over her still-flat stomach.

"What about your husband?" Summer was pretty sure she already knew the answer. "What does Sam want?"

The woman's smile confirmed her suspicions. "Sam says he doesn't care, but I think he's secretly hoping for a boy."

Summer smiled. "Isn't that what most men want?"

"I think it's because men want a son to do things with, as well as carry on their family name," Bria answered.

"Not to mention the fact that females of all ages are a complete mystery to most men and they'd rather not have to deal with raising a child they can't understand," Summer added.

Grinning, Bria nodded. "Well, there is that."

While one of her guests stopped to congratulate Bria on her pregnancy, Summer couldn't help but feel envious. Nothing would please her more than to have a child of her own—a son or daughter to love and to love her in return. She had been so lonely since her parents died that she craved that sense of belonging again, that connection with a family. Having a child of her own would help restore some of those ties and if the plan she had come up with over the past six months worked, she would accomplish just that.

"When is your baby due?" she asked as the guest moved on.

"In early spring." Bria glowed with happiness and Summer knew it had to be because she had just entered her second trimester. Ryder had mentioned that almost a year ago Bria and Sam had lost a baby in the early weeks of pregnancy—a baby they had both desperately wanted.

"It won't be too much longer and you'll know for sure whether you're having a girl or a boy." She hoped one day in the very near future to experience the joys of expecting a child herself and learning if she would be having a son or daughter.

"Sam and I have decided we don't want the doctor to tell us." Bria laughed. "But the closer it gets to having the sonogram, the more I think Sam is going to change his mind."

"Why do you say that?"

"He keeps asking me if I feel like I'm carrying a boy." The woman rolled her eyes. "Like I would know."

"Men just don't have a clue." Summer marveled at the misconceptions some men had. "If there's a bigger mystery to a man than a woman it has to be pregnancy."

Grinning, Bria nodded. "Exactly."

"Would you like for me to get you something to drink, Bria?" Ryder asked, returning to the table. He handed a soft drink to Summer, then set a bottle of beer on the table in front of the empty chair beside her.

"Thank you, Ryder. But I think I'm going to go see if Sam is ready to cut that humongous cake he insisted we had to have." Bria rose to her feet. "I'm pretty sure he wanted to support the old saying that everything is bigger in Texas."

Summer glanced over at the giant, four-tiered cake in the center of the refreshment table. "The cake is beautiful, but I have to agree with you. It's definitely worthy of the axiom."

"I hope you have plenty of room in the freezer," Ryder added, chuckling as he pulled out the chair and sat down. "From the size of it, I'd say you're going to have about half of it left over."

Nodding, Bria flashed a smile. "I won't have to make a birthday cake for any of you for at least another year. I can just thaw out some of this one, put a candle on it and sing 'Happy Birthday.'"

"She makes each of us a dinner and a cake for our birthday," Ryder explained as Bria walked across the barn toward her husband. "All of us that is except for Jaron. He's crazy for her apple pie, so she makes a couple of those for him and sticks a candle in the middle of them."

"I think it's wonderful that you're all so close," Summer said wistfully.

Having spent the past several years alone on her

birthday and holidays, she coveted Ryder's family gatherings. She was sure if he had known, he would have insisted that she join them. But she hadn't let on because she didn't want that, hadn't wanted to be reminded of all that she had lost. That was the main reason she had taken the job of the on-site PR person for the rodeo association. She was constantly on the move from one town to the next coordinating the many rodeos held throughout the southwestern circuit, and she was always so busy that she didn't have time to think of how lonely her life had become. She was, however, glad that Ryder had invited her to his family's celebration tonight. It made her more certain than ever that she had made the right decision to start her own family.

"Did your foster father celebrate with you all before he passed away?" she asked, curious to hear about how they had come together and bonded as a family.

"Bria made sure to include Hank and her sister, Mariah, in all of our get-togethers," Ryder replied. "Family is everything to Bria and we all appreciate that. It helps us stay close and in touch with what's going on with each other."

Watching Ryder from the corner of her eye, she admired him and his foster brothers for the change they had made in their lives and the tight-knit bond they had formed. They might have been brought together because of their troubled youth, but with the help of a very special man, they had all learned to let go of the past and move forward. Through dedication and hard work, all six of them had become upstanding, highly successful men, and in the process, they had remained just as close, if not closer, than any biological siblings.

When Bria and Sam finished cutting the beautiful Western-themed cake, then invited their guests to have some, Ryder rose from the chair beside her. "I'll go get us a piece of cake, then if you'd like we can dance a few more times before I take you back to the hotel."

"That sounds like a pretty good plan, cowboy," she said agreeably.

He had invited her to spend the weekend at his ranch, but she had decided against it, opting to stay in a hotel room in a nearby town instead. For one thing, speculation about their friendship had already surfaced with some of the other rodeo association contract personnel on the circuit, and she didn't feel the need to supply the busybodies with more fodder for their rumor mill. And for another, she wanted to discuss her future plans with Ryder on the drive back from the party. Depending on his reaction, staying at the Blue Canyon Ranch with him could become a bit awkward.

An hour later, after congratulating the Raffertys once again on their renewed nuptials and Bria's pregnancy, Summer let Ryder help her into the passenger side of his pickup truck, then anxiously waited for him to come around and climb into the driver's seat. This was the part of the evening she had anticipated for the past two weeks—ever since making the decision to ask for his help.

"Are you cold?" he asked, sliding into the driver's seat. "I can turn on the heater."

"No, I'm fine. But thank you for asking." There was

a little nip in the evening air, signaling that autumn had arrived, but she had been too distracted to notice.

"I hope you had a good time," he said, starting the truck and steering it down the long drive toward the main road.

"I really enjoyed myself," she reassured him with a smile. "Thank you for asking me to attend the party with you."

When Ryder turned onto the highway, he set the cruise control then turned on a popular country radio station. "You'll have to come back for one of our birthday get-togethers sometime."

"I'd like that," she said, realizing she meant it.

They fell into a comfortable silence and while Ryder drove the big dual-wheeled pickup truck through the star-studded Texas night, Summer studied his shadowed profile. If she'd had any doubts about her choice before attending the party with him, watching him throughout the evening had completely eradicated them. Ryder McClain was the real deal—honest, intelligent, easygoing and loyal to a fault. And it was only recently that she'd allowed herself to notice how incredibly good-looking he was.

With dark brown hair, forest-green eyes and a nice, effortless smile, he would be considered extremely handsome by any standards. But combined with his impressive physical presence and laid-back personality, Ryder McClain was the type of man most women fantasized about. His wide shoulders and broad chest would be the perfect place for a woman to lay her head when the world dealt her more than she felt she could handle. And the latent strength in his muscular arms as he held her to him would keep her safe and secure from all harm.

"Summer, are you all right?" he asked, startling her.

Slightly embarrassed and more than a little disconcerted with her train of thought, she nodded. "I was just thinking about the evening and what a nice time I had," she lied, unsure of how to start the conversation that would either help her dream come true—or send her in search of someone else to assist her.

"I can't think of any of our get-togethers when we haven't had a lot of fun," Ryder said, beaming.

"Even when your brothers irritate you like they did tonight?" she teased.

His rich laughter made her feel warm all over. "Yeah, even when we're giving each other a wagonload of grief, we still enjoy being together."

"From what you said earlier, I take it you were the one in the hot seat this evening?"

She was pretty sure she knew the reason they had been teasing him. Due to the demands of both of their jobs there had been very few occasions she and Ryder had been seen together anywhere but at one of the many rodeos they both worked. It was only natural that his brothers would speculate about their relationship, the same as their coworkers had done when she and Ryder started hanging out regularly at the rodeos they were working.

He shrugged. "As long as they're bugging me, they're leaving each other alone." Grinning, he added, "A few months back, we were all on Sam's case about what a stubborn, prideful fool he can be."

"Was that when he and Bria were having a rough patch in their marriage?"

"Yup."

"Do you always know that much about each other?" If he agreed to help her, she wasn't certain she would be overly comfortable with his family knowing about it.

"It's hard to hide things from the people who know you better than you sometimes know yourself," he acknowledged.

"So you don't keep any secrets from each other? Ever?"

"There are some things that we don't tell each other, but not very many." Turning his head to look at her, he furrowed his brow. "Why do you ask?"

She had purposely waited until they were alone in his truck and it was dark so she wouldn't have to meet his gaze. But the time had come to make her case and ask for his assistance. Considering the state of her nerves and the gravity of her request, she only hoped that she would be able to convey how important it was to her and how much she wanted him to help her.

"I've been doing a lot of thinking lately..." she began, wishing she had rehearsed what she was about to say a bit more. "Although I've never had a sibling, I miss being part of a family."

"I know, darlin'." He reached across the console to reassuringly cover her hand with his much larger one. "But one day, I'm sure you'll find someone and settle down, then you'll not only be part of his family, you can start one of your own."

"That's not going to happen," she said, shaking her head. "I have absolutely no interest in getting married, or having a man in my life other than as a friend." Ryder looked taken aback by the finality in her tone. They had never discussed what they thought their futures might hold and she was sure her adamant statement surprised him. Making sure her words were less vehement, she added, "I'm going to choose another route to become part of the family I want. These days, it's quite common for a woman to choose single motherhood."

"Well, there are a lot of kids of all ages who need a good home," he concurred, his tone filled with understanding. "A single woman adopting a little kid nowadays doesn't have the kind of obstacles they used to have."

"I'm not talking about adopting a child," Summer said, staring out the windshield at the dark Texas landscape. "At least not yet. I'd really like to experience all aspects of motherhood if I can, and that includes being pregnant."

"The last I heard, being pregnant is kind of difficult without the benefit of a man being involved," he said with a wry smile.

"To a certain degree, a man would need to be involved." They were quickly approaching the moment of truth. "But there are other ways besides having sex to become pregnant."

"Oh, so you're going to visit a sperm bank?" He didn't sound judgmental and she took that as a positive sign.

"No." She shook her head. "I'd rather know my baby's father than to have him be a number on a vial and a list of physical characteristics."

Ryder looked confused. "Then how do you figure on making this happen if you're unwilling to wait until you meet someone and you don't want to visit a sperm bank?"

Her pulse sped up. "I have a donor in mind."

"Well, I guess if the guy's agreeable that would work," he said thoughtfully. "Anybody I know?"

"Yes." She paused for a moment to shore up her courage. Then, before she lost her nerve, she blurted, "I want you to be the father of my baby, Ryder."

Two

Never at a loss for words, Ryder could only remember a couple of times in all of his thirty-three years that he had been struck completely speechless. At the moment, he couldn't have managed to string two words together if his life depended on it. Summer asking him to help her have a baby was the last thing he'd expected.

To keep from driving off into a ditch, he steered the truck to the side of the road, shifted it into Park, then turned to gape at the woman seated in the truck beside him. How in the world was he supposed to respond to a request like that? And why the hell was his lower body suddenly indicating that it was up for the challenge?

Shocked, as well as bewildered, his first inclination had been to laugh and ask her who it was she was really considering. But as he searched her pretty face, Ryder's heart began to thump against his ribs like a bass drum in a high school marching band. He could tell from the worry lines creasing her forehead that she wasn't joking. She was dead serious and waiting for him to tell her he would father her child.

"I know this comes as a bit of a surprise," she said, nervously twisting her hands into a knot in her lap. "But—"

"No, Summer," he said, finally finding his voice. "An unexpected gift or winning a few bucks in the lottery is a surprise. This is a shock that rivals standing in ankle-deep water and grabbing hold of a wire with a few thousand volts of electricity running through it."

She slowly nodded. "I'm sure it was the last thing you expected."

"You got that right, darlin'."

Ryder took a deep breath as he tried to figure out how to proceed. He knew he should ask some questions, but he wasn't entirely sure what he wanted to know first. What made her think that she wouldn't one day meet the right guy to change her mind about getting married and having the family she wanted? Why had she decided that he was the man she wanted to help her? And how did she figure she was going to get him to go along with such a cockamamy scheme?

"We're going to have to talk about this," he said, deciding that he needed time to think. Starting the truck's engine, he steered it back onto the road. "We'll stop by the hotel long enough for you to get your things and check out of your room. Then we'll drive on down to the Blue Canyon."

"No, I think it would be better if I stay at the hotel

instead of your ranch," she said, her tone adamant. "It might look like we were—"

"Seriously?" He released a frustrated breath as he glanced over at her. "You're worried about what people might think, but yet you want me to make you pregnant?"

"That isn't what I'm asking," she said, shaking her head. "I don't want you to *make* me pregnant. I'm asking you to put a donation in a cup for a clinical procedure in a doctor's office."

Ryder grunted. "Don't you think that's splitting hairs? The bottom line is, you'd be pregnant and I'd be the daddy."

"Oh, I wouldn't expect you to support the baby or help raise him or her," she insisted. "My parents left me more than enough money so that I never have to worry about taking care of myself and a child."

He barely resisted the urge to say a word she was sure to find highly offensive. Did she know him at all? She wanted him to help her make a baby and then just walk away like it was nothing?

Not in this lifetime. Or any other for that matter.

"Summer, we're going to wait to finish this conversation until after we get to my ranch," he said firmly. He needed time for the shock of her request—and the irritation that she didn't want him to have anything to do with his kid—to wear off before he was able to think rationally.

"No, I'd rather—"

"My housekeeper, Betty Lou, will be there with us so you don't have to worry about how things are going to look," he stated, wondering why she was so concerned about gossip. It wasn't like there wouldn't be plenty of that going around if he lost what little sense he had and agreed to help her—which he had no intention of doing. But he needed to get to the bottom of what she was thinking and why she was willing to risk their friendship to make her request.

He cleared his throat. "You'll have to admit that what you're asking of me is pretty massive, and we need to talk it over—a lot. Staying at my ranch until we have to take off for the next rodeo in a couple of days will give us the privacy to do that."

She didn't look at all happy about it, but she apparently realized that going to the Blue Canyon Ranch with him was her best chance of getting what she wanted. "If that's the only way you'll consider helping me—"

"It is."

He didn't want to give her any encouragement or mislead her into thinking he was going to assist her. But he needed to talk to her and make her see that there were other alternatives to have the family she wanted besides going around asking unsuspecting men to help her become pregnant.

She took a deep breath then slowly nodded. "All right. If you won't consider helping me any other way, I'll go to your ranch with you."

They both fell silent for the rest of the drive to the hotel and by the time she gathered her things, checked out and they drove on to the Blue Canyon, it was well past midnight.

"It's late and I don't know about you, but I'm pretty

tired," he said when he turned the truck onto the lane leading up to his ranch house. "Why don't we get a good night's sleep, then we can hash this all out after breakfast tomorrow morning?"

She nodded. "I suppose that would probably be best."

Parking in the circular drive in front of the house, Ryder got out and walked around to open the passenger door for her. "I guess before we go inside I'd better warn you. You'll need to steer clear of Lucifer."

"Who's that?" she asked, looking a little apprehensive.

"Betty Lou's cat," he answered, reaching into the back of the club cab for her luggage while she gazed up at his sprawling two-story ranch house.

"Oh, I won't mind being around him," she said, turning to smile at him. "I adore animals."

Ryder shook his head. "You won't like this one. I'm convinced he's the devil incarnate."

"Why do you say that?"

"He barely tolerates people." Ryder carried her bag to the front door, then letting them into the foyer, turned to reset the security system. "He hisses and spits at everyone who crosses his path, except Betty Lou. And there are times I think she walks on eggshells around him."

"You get chased by the biggest, meanest bulls the stock contractors can offer on a regular basis...and you're afraid of a house cat?" she asked with a cheeky grin.

Relieved that the awkwardness that followed her request seemed to have been put aside for the moment, he shrugged as he led her over to the winding staircase. "I know what to expect with a ton of pissed-off beef. But that cat is a whole different breed of misery. He's attitude with a screech and sharp claws. Sometimes he likes to lurk in high places and then, making a sound that will raise the hair on the head of a bald man, he drops down on top of you as you walk by." Ryder rotated his shoulders as he thought about the last time Lucifer had launched himself at him through the balusters from the top of the stairs. "He's sunk his claws into me enough times that I'm leery of walking past anything that's taller than I am without looking up first."

"Then why do you allow your housekeeper to keep him?" she asked when they reached the top of the stairs.

He'd asked himself that same question about a hundred times over the past several years—usually right after the cat had pounced on him. "Betty Lou thinks the sun rises and sets in that gray devil. She adopted him from an animal shelter after her husband died and when she took the job as my housekeeper, I didn't think it would be a big deal for her to bring him along with her. I like animals and besides, I'm gone a lot of the time anyway, so I don't have to be around him a lot."

"That's very nice of you," she said, sounding sincere. "But it's your house. You shouldn't have to worry about being mauled by a cat."

Ryder shrugged. "I don't see any reason to be a jerk about it when Lucifer means that much to her. I just try to steer clear of him as much as possible when I do make it home for a few days." Stopping at one of the guest bedrooms, he opened the door, turned on the light for her, then set her luggage beside the dresser. "Will this be all right? If not, there are five other bedrooms you can choose from."

He watched her look around the spacious room a moment before she turned to face him. "This is very nice, Ryder. Did you decorate it?"

Her teasing smile indicated that she was awaiting a reaction to her pointed question. He didn't disappoint her.

"Yeah, right. I just look like the kind of guy who knows all about stuff like pillows and curtains." Shaking his head, he added, "No, I hired a lady from Waco after I bought the ranch to come down here and redecorate the house."

"She did a wonderful job." Summer touched the patchwork quilt covering the bed. "This is very warm and welcoming."

"Thanks." He wasn't sure why it mattered so much, but it pleased him that she liked his home. "I bought it right after I sold my interest in a start-up company my college roommate launched while we were still in school."

"It must have been quite successful," she said as she continued to look around.

He grinned. "Ever heard of The Virtual Ledger computer programs?"

"Of course. They have a program for just about every kind of record-keeping anyone could want." Her eyes widened. "You helped found that?"

He laughed out loud. "Not hardly. I know just enough about a computer to screw it up and make it completely useless. But my roommate had the idea and I had some money saved back from working rodeos during the summers. I gave it to him and he gave me 50 percent of the company. Once it really took off, I sold him my interest in the company and we both got what we wanted out of the deal." He took a breath. "He has total control of The Virtual Ledger and I have this ranch and enough money to do whatever I want, whenever I want, for the rest of my life."

"Then why do you put yourself in danger fighting rodeo bulls?" she asked, frowning.

"Everybody has to have something that gives them a sense of purpose and makes them feel useful. Besides, I have to watch out for boneheads like Nate and Jaron." When she yawned, he turned to leave. "Get a good night's sleep and if you need anything, my room is at the far end of the hall."

Her smile caused a warm feeling to spread throughout his chest. "Thank you, Ryder, but I'll be fine."

Nodding, he quickly stepped out into the hall and closed the door behind him. What the hell was wrong with him? Summer had smiled at him hundreds of times over the past few years and he had never given it so much as a second thought. So why now did it feel like his temperature had spiked several degrees?

He shook his head as he strode toward the master suite. Hell, he still hadn't figured out why his arms had tingled where she rested her hands when they danced at the party. And why did the thought of her wanting him to be her baby daddy make him feel twitchy in places that had absolutely no business twitching?

* * *

When Summer opened her eyes to the shaft of sunlight peeking through the pale yellow curtains, she looked around the beautifully decorated room and for a brief moment wondered where she was. She was used to awakening in a generic hotel room where shades of beige and tan reigned supreme and the headboard of the bed was bolted to the wall. But instead of spending the night in a hotel as she'd planned, she had agreed to accompany Ryder to his ranch.

Her breath caught as she remembered why he had insisted she come home with him. After weeks of trying to find a way to bring up the subject and ask him to be the donor for her pregnancy, she had worked up her courage and made her request. And his answer hadn't been "no." At least, not outright.

He thought they needed to talk it over and although his insistence that they stay at his ranch had made her extremely nervous, she had agreed. She needed to reassure him that she would sign whatever document was needed to ensure that she would be solely responsible for the baby and that he would be under no obligation. She was sure that once he understood that, he would be more inclined to help her.

As she threw back the covers and got out of bed to take a shower, she thought about what Ryder would want to discuss first. He would probably start off with wanting to know why she didn't feel she would ever meet a man she wanted to marry. Or he might try to convince her that, at the youthful age of twenty-five, she had plenty of time and should wait to make such a life-changing decision.

Standing beneath the refreshing spray of warm water, she smiled. She might not have practiced the way she worded her request as much as she should have, but she was armed and ready with her answers for their upcoming discussion about it. She knew Ryder well enough to know he would try to talk her out of her plans, and she had painstakingly gone over the way she would explain her reasoning and how she would frame the responses she intended to give him. Once he realized that she was completely serious, along with the promise of a legal document relieving him of any commitment to support or help raise the child, surely he would agree.

Anxious to start their conversation, she toweled herself dry, quickly got dressed and started downstairs. Halfway to the bottom of the staircase, she stopped when she came face-to-face with one of the largest gray tabby cats she had ever seen.

"You must be Lucifer," she said tentatively. From Ryder's description of the cat, she wasn't sure how he would react to encountering a stranger in his domain.

She hoped he didn't attack her as she walked past. But instead of pouncing on her as she expected he might, the cat gazed up at her for a moment, then letting out a heartfelt meow, rubbed his body along the side of her leg.

Reaching down, she cautiously stroked his soft coat. Lucifer rewarded her with a loud, albeit contented purr. "You don't seem nearly as ferocious as Ryder claimed you were," she said when he burrowed his head into her palm, then licked her fingers with a swipe of his sand-papery rough tongue.

When Summer continued on down the stairs, Lucifer trotted behind her as she followed the delicious smell of fried bacon and freshly brewed coffee. "Good morning," she said when she found Ryder seated at the kitchen table.

"Morning." He rose from his chair as she entered the room, and Lucifer immediately arched his back and hissed loudly at Ryder. "I see he's still the same happy cat he's always been," Ryder said sarcastically as he shook his head. "Would you like a cup of coffee, Summer?"

"Yes, please. It smells wonderful."

"Just a little cream?" he asked. They had met for coffee so many times over the past few years, he knew exactly how she liked it. Just as she knew he always liked his coffee black.

"Yes, thank you." She smiled. "You know, I think Lucifer likes me. He rubbed against my leg and let me pet him when we met on the stairs."

"See, I told you it's just you he has a problem with, Ryder." The woman standing at the stove chortled.

"I don't know why." He looked as if he might be a bit insulted by her comment. "Most other animals don't seem to think I'm all that bad of a guy."

"Maybe you aren't home enough for him to get used to you," Summer suggested.

"Whatever." Shrugging, he walked over to take a mug from one of the top cabinets, then poured her some coffee. "Betty Lou Harmon, I'd like for you to meet my friend, Summer Patterson."

"It's nice to meet you, Mrs. Harmon," Summer said warmly as the older woman turned from the stove to face her.

"It's real nice to meet you, too, child. But don't go bein' all formal," the housekeeper groused, shaking her head. "You call me Betty Lou the same as everybody else, you hear?"

"Yes, ma'am," Summer said, instantly liking the woman. With her dark hair liberally streaked with silver and pulled back into a tight bun at the back of her head, her kind gray eyes and round cheeks flushed from the heat of the stove, Betty Lou looked more like someone's grandmother than a rancher's housekeeper.

Wiping her hands on her gingham apron, she waved toward the trestle table where Ryder had been seated when Summer entered the room. "You find yourself a place to sit and I'll get you fixed up with a plate of eggs, bacon, hash browns and some biscuits and gravy."

"I don't eat much for breakfast," Summer confessed, hoping she didn't offend the woman. She seated herself in one of the tall ladder-back chairs at the honey oak table. "Normally all I have is a bagel or toast and a cup of coffee."

"Well, you'd better eat a hearty meal this mornin' if you're goin' horseback ridin' down to the canyon with Ryder," Betty Lou said, filling a plate and bringing it over to set on the table in front of her.

"We're going for a ride?" Summer asked, crestfallen. She thought they were supposed to discuss her request.

"I thought I'd show you around the ranch," Ryder said, nodding as he brought her coffee over to the table. When Betty Lou went into the pantry, he lowered his voice and leaned close to Summer. "We'll have plenty of time to talk and no one around to overhear the conversation."

"We could have done that in my hotel room," she reminded him.

He raised one dark eyebrow as he sat back down at the head of the table. "For someone who is so concerned with appearances, you haven't thought of the obvious, darlin'."

Ryder's intimate tone and the scent of his clean, masculine skin caused her pulse to beat double time. "Wh-what would that be?" she asked, confused and not at all comfortable with the way she was reacting to him.

"How do you think it would look with us being alone in your room for several hours?" He shrugged. "I doubt anyone would be convinced we were just talking or watching television."

"Oh." She hadn't thought of that. "I suppose you're right."

"Now eat," he said, pointing to her plate.

"Aren't you going to have breakfast?" she asked, taking a bite of the fluffy scrambled eggs.

He took a sip of his coffee and shook his head. "I ate about an hour ago."

When she finished the last of the delicious food, Summer smiled at Betty Lou when she walked over to pick up the plate. "That was wonderful. Thank you."

The woman gave her an approving nod. "That should

tide you over until you eat the sandwiches I packed for the two of you."

"We won't be back in time for lunch?" Summer asked, turning to Ryder. "How far away is the canyon?"

"It's not that far." He gave her a smile that made her radiate from within. "But there's a creek lined with cottonwoods that runs through the canyon, and I thought you might like to have a picnic along the bank."

"I haven't done something like that in years," she said, happy that he had thought of the idea. Going on an outing like the one Ryder suggested was one of the many things she had enjoyed doing with her parents.

"You do know how to ride a horse, don't you?" he asked. When she nodded, he unclipped his cell phone from his belt. "Good. I'll call the barn and have my foreman get the horses saddled and ready for us."

A half hour later as he and Summer rode across the pasture behind the barns, Ryder watched her pat the buckskin mare she was riding. With the autumn sun shining down on her long blond hair, she looked like an angel. A very desirable angel.

He frowned at the thought. They had never been more than friends, and until his brothers started ribbing him about taking her to Sam and Bria's wedding vows renewal celebration, he had purposely avoided thinking of her in that way. So why was it all he could think about now? Of course, her making her plea last night for him to be her baby's daddy sure wasn't helping matters.

"I'm glad you thought of this, Ryder," she said, distracting him from his confusing inner thoughts. "I love going horseback riding. I used to do it all the time. But after I took the job with the rodeo association, I sold my parents' farm and all of the horses and I don't get to ride much anymore."

"Was there a reason you couldn't keep it?" he asked. She said she had plenty of money, so that couldn't be the cause of her selling everything.

She stared off into the distance like the decision might not have been an easy one to make. "With all the travel required for my job, it just didn't seem practical to hang on to it."

"I realize you have to arrive in a town a few days before a rodeo in order to get things set up for the media and schedule interviews for some of the riders, but couldn't you have boarded one of the horses and ridden on the days that you do make it home?" he asked, knowing that was what he would have done.

He could understand her not wanting to hold on to her parents' home without them being there. It would most likely be a painful reminder of all that she had lost when they were killed. But he didn't understand her not keeping at least one of the horses if she liked to ride that much.

"I don't go home," she answered, shrugging one slender shoulder. "I just go on to the next town on the schedule."

"You don't go back to your place on the few days we have off between rodeos?" They normally met up in the next town for the next rodeo and had never traveled together before. It appeared that although they were close friends, there was a lot that they hadn't shared with each other.

But he still couldn't imagine going for weeks without coming back to the ranch. Besides Hank Calvert's Last Chance Ranch, the Blue Canyon was the only place he had ever been able to truly call home. And a home of his own was something he never intended to be without again.

"I...don't have a place," she admitted, looking a little sheepish. "I know it sounds bad, but I couldn't see any sense in paying for the upkeep on my parents' home or rent on an apartment when I'd only be there a few days out of the month."

Reaching out, he took hold of the mare's reins as he stopped both horses. "Let me get this straight. You live out of hotel rooms and you don't have a place to call your own?" When she nodded, he asked, "Where do you keep your things?"

"What I can't pack into the two suitcases I take on the road with me, like furniture and family keepsakes, I keep in a storage unit in Topanga, California, not far from where my parents lived." When he turned loose of the buckskin's reins and they continued on toward the trail leading down into the canyon, she added, "It's much cheaper than paying to keep them in an apartment I'd never use."

Shocked by her revelation, he shook his head. "So for all intents and purposes, you're homeless."

"I guess it could be construed that way." She nibbled on her lower lip a moment as if she might be bothered by it more than she was letting on. "But as long as I'm traveling like I do, I don't mind."

"How long have you lived this way?" he asked, still trying to wrap his mind around what she had told him.

"About three years."

He had been friends with her all that time and not once had he suspected that she lived the life of a nomad. What else was there about her that he didn't know? And how the hell did she plan on taking care of a baby with that kind of lifestyle?

When they reached the canyon's rim, they fell silent as Ryder rode the bay ahead of her to lead the way to the meadow below. But he couldn't stop thinking about her lack of roots. Why did she want a baby when she didn't even have a home? What was she going to do with the poor little thing, raise it in a series of hotel rooms while they traveled from one rodeo to the next for her job? That wasn't any kind of a life for a little kid.

Ryder didn't know what her reasoning was, but he had every intention of finding out. He knew from personal experience that it was important to a kid to have a place to call home.

Leading the way to the spot along the bank that he had in mind for their picnic, he reined in the gelding. "How does this look?"

"It's great," she said, stopping the buckskin mare beside his horse. "There's plenty of shade." She pointed toward one of the cottonwoods. "And under that tree looks like the perfect place to put the blanket."

Dismounting the bay, he dropped the reins to ground-tie the horse, then moved to retrieve the rolled blanket he had tied to the back of the gelding's saddle, along with the insulated saddlebags holding their lunch. From the corner of his eye, he watched Summer jump down from the mare's back and start doing some stretches to loosen up after the ride.

He briefly wondered if she was having muscle cramps, but he quickly forgot all about her possible discomfort as he watched her stretch from side to side, then bend over to touch her toes. Her jeans pulled tight over her perfect little bottom caused his mouth to go as dry as a desert in a drought. When she straightened, then placed her hands on her hips to lean back and relieve pressure on her lower back, he sucked in a sharp breath. Her motions caused her chest to stick out and for the first time since he had known her, he noticed how full and perfect her breasts were.

Ryder muttered a curse under his breath and forced himself to look away. This was Summer. She was his best friend and he'd never thought of her in a romantic light. So why now was he suddenly taking notice of her delightful backside and enticing breasts?

Disgusted with himself, he shook his head and tucking the picnic blanket under his arm, finished unfastening the insulated saddlebags from the bay's saddle and carted everything over to the spot beneath the cottonwood that Summer had pointed out. His fascination with her feminine attributes was probably due to the fact that he hadn't been with a woman in longer than he cared to remember—and he'd have to be blind not to notice that Summer was a damned good-looking woman with a set of curves that could tempt a eunuch. He wasn't at all comfortable thinking of her in that way, but there was no denying it either.

As he set the saddlebags down and unfolded the blanket to spread it out on the ground, he gave some thought to his dilemma. He was a normal, healthy adult male who, like any other man, needed to occasionally get lost in a woman's softness. Once he got back out on the rodeo circuit, he needed to take a trip to one of the local watering holes in whatever town he was in and strike up a cozy little acquaintance with a woman who wasn't looking for anything more than a real good time. Maybe then he would stop having inappropriate thoughts about his best friend.

Three

Sitting beside the lazy little creek after finishing their lunch, Summer glanced over at Ryder's handsome profile. He really was one of the best-looking men she had ever known and she had a hard time believing it took her this long to realize it. Studying his features, she found herself hoping that if he agreed to help her, their child would look like him. But neither of them had brought up the subject of her request and the longer it took for them to start the discussion, the more uncertain she became. What if he refused to be the sperm donor?

He had all the attributes she wanted for her child and asking any of the other men she knew wasn't even a consideration. She didn't know them well enough to determine if they had the traits she was looking for, and truthfully, she didn't want to get that well acquainted with them. She didn't trust any man the way she trusted

Ryder and couldn't imagine anyone else as her baby's father.

"Have you given any more thought to helping me?" she finally asked.

"I really haven't thought about much of anything else," he admitted, turning to face her. "It's not every day that out of the clear blue sky a woman asks me to help her get pregnant." His expression gave nothing away and she had no indication of what he might be thinking.

"As I told you last night, you wouldn't be obligated in any way," she said, hoping to reassure him. "I'll be responsible for everything. You wouldn't even have to acknowledge that you were the donor."

"In other words, you don't want me to be involved at all in my own kid's life," he said flatly. Shaking his head, he added, "You of all people should know that's not the way I roll, darlin'."

The steely determination she heard in his voice surprised her. "I…well…I hadn't thought you would want—"

He held up his hand. "Let's back up. We can cover what would happen after you became pregnant a little later on. Right now, I have a few things I'd like to know."

"Of course," she said pleasantly. She was confident she could answer all of his questions. "What would you like to ask first?"

Ryder's piercing green gaze held her captive. "Why me?"

"You have all the qualities that I would want passed

on to my child," she said, not having to think about her answer. "You're healthy, physically fit, as well as physically appealing. You're also honest, loyal and other than my late father, you're the most trustworthy man I've ever known."

"You make me sound like a prize stud someone would want to cover their herd of mares," he said, shaking his head in obvious disbelief. "How long have you been thinking about this?"

"About six months," she admitted. Things weren't going the way she had hoped. He didn't sound as if he was all that receptive to the idea. "But I didn't seriously think of approaching you until a couple of weeks ago."

Nodding as if he accepted her answer, Ryder stared off into space for a moment before he asked, "Last night you told me you didn't want to wait to see if you change your mind about meeting a man you might want to settle down with."

"That's right." She shook her head. "I don't have any intention of ever getting married."

"Why?"

"As you know, I'm pretty independent," she said, reciting the answer she had rehearsed. "I don't want to lose that. I don't want to be dependent on a man or give anyone that kind of control over me."

He frowned. "Where did you get the idea that whoever you met would want to control you?" Shaking his head, he propped his forearms on his bent knees. "Most men I know admire independence in a woman. Me included."

"Maybe I should rephrase that," she said, thinking

quickly. "I don't want to give that kind of emotional control to anyone."

Staring at her for several long moments, Ryder asked, "Who was the bastard?"

His question startled her. "I...don't know what you mean."

"Someone had to have hurt you pretty bad to make you feel this way," he insisted. "Who was he?"

Ryder's assessment was hitting too close to the truth and she had to force herself to remain calm. "There wasn't anyone," she lied. "I've just never believed that I need a man in my life to validate my worth as a woman nor do I want to depend on him for my happiness."

"Okay," he said slowly. She could tell he wasn't buying her explanation, but before she had the chance to say more, he asked, "Why now? You're only twenty-five. It's not like your biological clock is ticking or the alarm is about to go off."

She took a deep breath. Her answer this time wasn't a lie or a half-truth. "I want to be part of a family again, Ryder. I want someone to love and be loved by in return."

"Ah, darlin'," he said, moving to wrap his strong arms around her. Pulling her to him, he gave her a comforting hug. "I know how alone you've been since your parents passed away, but do you really think having a baby will be the cure for your loneliness?"

"I really do," she said, feeling a bit confused by the fact that Ryder's embrace wasn't the least bit intimidating. Any other man giving her a hug would have sent her into a panic attack.

"What would you do about a home for you and the baby?" he asked, his tone gentle. "You can't raise a kid living in hotel rooms and moving from town to town every week."

His questions had her wondering if he might be seriously considering her request. "I intend to quit my job and buy a house. As I told you before, my parents left me quite well-off. Between their life insurance policies and the sale of the horses and ranch, I never have to work another day in my life if I don't want to." She exhaled slowly. "I'd like to be a stay-at-home mom until my baby is old enough for preschool. Then after my child starts school, I'll decide whether I want to find something to do part-time or continue being a stay-at-home mom." When Ryder remained silent, she leaned back to look at him. He appeared to be in deep thought and she hoped that was a positive sign he was going to help her.

"This is a big decision," he finally said, meeting her questioning gaze. "Let me think about it for a while."

"Of course," she said slowly. "But let me assure you, I don't expect you to do anything past being the donor. Like I said last night...you won't be obligated in any way for anything."

He continued to stare at her for what seemed like an eternity, then he rose to his feet and held out his hand to help her to hers. "I think it's about time we head back to the house."

When she placed her hand in his, a jolt of electric current streaked up her arm and spread throughout her insides. Summer frowned at the lingering sensation as she turned to pick up the blanket. What was going on with her? She wasn't interested in any man and especially not Ryder. He was her best friend and even if she had wanted to have a man in her life—which she didn't—she wasn't willing to jeopardize their friendship by starting something romantic. Sperm donation was one thing, involving emotions was another.

But as they rode back toward the ranch house, she couldn't stop thinking about the unsettling feeling that had coursed through her. Why was she suddenly more aware of Ryder as a man than ever before? And why, when he took her hand in his, did it feel as if something extremely significant had shifted in the universe?

While Summer helped Betty Lou finish up supper in the kitchen, Ryder stood by the window in his office, staring out at the sun sinking low in the western sky. He couldn't stop thinking about Summer's misguided idea that a baby was the solution to her loneliness.

It wasn't that he couldn't understand her wanting a family connection and the sense of belonging that came with it. He could. For the first fourteen years of his life, he had longed for the same thing as he was shuffled from one foster home to another. It wasn't until he was placed in the care of Hank Calvert and taken to live at the Last Chance Ranch that he learned what it felt like to have a home and be part of a family. But he was doubtful that her having a baby would make her feel like she was part of something like that again.

Normally, having a family meant having a built-in support system. But Summer wouldn't have that.

She would be the support system for the baby, but she wouldn't have anyone to help her. Who would be there to lend a hand with a fussy newborn when she got so tired she was about to drop in her tracks? Who would she lean on if, God forbid, the baby came down with a serious illness? That role was usually filled by a husband, a woman's mother or even her sister. Summer wouldn't have any of the three.

He wasn't buying into her claim that fearing the loss of her independence was the reason behind her not wanting to have a man in her life either. She had to know that in this day and time, most men were fine with a woman being strong and self-assured. And that wasn't the only thing that bothered him about their conversation.

Why did she believe that he wouldn't want to be part of his own kid's life? What made her think that if he lost what little sense he had and agreed to father her baby that he could just walk away?

He knew firsthand the effect a parent's abandonment had on a kid. He might have only been four years old when his mother left him in a hospital waiting room for the authorities to find, but her poor choice had a huge impact on his life. Aside from being raised by people who didn't care anything about him past the monthly check they received for housing him, the fallout of being shuffled from one unsuitable family to another had eventually landed him in enough trouble to be sent to the Last Chance Ranch. And although becoming one of Hank's boys had been the best thing that ever happened to him, the way he got there was something nobody would want for a kid.

Of course, Summer wasn't asking him to bond with the child and then leave to let her finish raising him or her. She didn't want him to be part of the baby's life at all. And that bothered the hell out of him.

Until Summer made her request, he had never given a lot of thought to having a child of his own. For one thing, he hadn't ever expected to get married. Finding a woman who understood his painful past and could overlook all that would be a tall order to fill. And for another, thanks to Hank's Cowboy Code, Ryder was old-fashioned enough to believe that you weren't supposed to put the cart before the horse. Getting married was what a man was supposed to do first, then start having kids. Not the other way around.

He couldn't help but smile fondly at the memory of his foster father sitting Ryder and the rest of his brothers down for lessons in manners and morality. Whether it was out of gratitude or they all wanted to emulate the man who had been there for them through thick and thin, Ryder and his brothers had learned their lessons well. A man always treated a woman like a lady, showed her respect and if he fathered a child, he owned up to his responsibility and helped the mother raise it.

He and his brothers all adhered to the Cowboy Code to this day—even Nate. He might be a ladies' man, but he was always respectful of women and limited his amorous activities to one woman at a time.

A knock on the door interrupted his thoughts. "Dinner is almost ready, Ryder," Summer called out to him.

Walking over to open the door, his heart stalled at the sight of her. With strands of her honey-blond hair escaping the confines of her ponytail and her cheeks colored a pretty pink from the heat of cooking, he didn't think he had ever seen her look lovelier.

"Lead the way," he said, wondering if he'd lost his mind. Why did he feel as if he had just run a footrace? Hell, he didn't get this out of breath when he played chicken with a ton of pissed-off beef.

As he watched her walk down the hall ahead of him, Ryder couldn't seem to stop watching the enticing sway of her hips. He gritted his teeth and forced himself to focus on the back of her head. Why, in the past couple of days, had he suddenly become so fascinated with her body?

He wouldn't even begin to entertain the idea of having something develop between them. For that matter, he wasn't willing to become romantically involved with *any* woman. He just couldn't bear the thought of falling for someone special and then seeing the revulsion and fear on her face once she learned the truth about him.

Entering the kitchen, he started toward his place at the head of the table, but Lucifer chose that moment to walk out from behind the kitchen island. As was his usual practice whenever he saw Ryder, the cat arched its back and let loose with a nasty hiss.

"Well, good evening to you, too, Lucifer," Ryder said cheerfully. He would have never believed he would be glad to cross paths with the disagreeable feline, but it had been just the distraction he needed to get his mind off Summer's shapely bottom.

"There's something about you that cat doesn't like," Summer said, crinkling her brow. "Maybe he's sensitive to your cologne."

Ryder shrugged as he sat down at the table. "He might be if I wore cologne. But since I don't, it can't be that."

"Do you have any idea why Lucifer reacts to Ryder the way he does, Betty Lou?" she asked, picking up a bowl of mashed potatoes from the island to set it on the table.

The older woman shook her head. "No, but he's been this way about Ryder ever since I started housekeepin' here four years ago." She walked over to place a platter of country fried steaks in the middle of the table. "I personally think Lucifer is bein' defensive because he's intimidated by Ryder's size." She grinned. "You gotta admit, Ryder's a long, tall drink of water."

"You might be right." Summer smiled as she poured them all glasses of iced tea. "Maybe Lucifer is just warning Ryder to look down and not step on him."

While the two women continued to speculate on why the cat found him so offensive, Ryder's thoughts turned to what he needed to say to change Summer's mind about pursuing her quest to get pregnant. Knowing her the way he did, he needed to be careful not to argue too strongly against her plans. If he did that, she just might end up more determined than ever to proceed with or without his help.

As an idea began to take shape, he waited until Betty Lou turned her attention to getting a pie out of the oven before he motioned Summer over to the table. "I've come to a decision," he said, careful to keep his tone low. "If you aren't too tired, we'll talk about it in my office after we eat."

An hour after Ryder told her he was ready to give her his answer, Summer followed him down the hall to his office. She didn't think she had ever been more nervous than she was at that moment. What if his answer was "no"? What would she do then?

When they walked into the thoroughly masculine room, he motioned toward the big leather armchair in front of his desk as he closed the door behind them. "Have a seat."

Lowering himself into the plush executive chair behind his big walnut desk, Ryder's smile gave her more hope than she'd had since making her request. "Before I agree, I think there are a few details that we need to discuss further."

"You're going to help me?" Her heart soared and unable to sit still she leaned forward. "Thank you, Ryder. You have no idea how much this means to me!"

He held up his hand as he shook his head. "I didn't say that, Summer. I said there would be things we would need to talk over before I agreed to anything."

"I thought I was pretty clear about my plans and your role in them." She had gone over everything so many times in her head, she couldn't think of anything she might have left out.

"You were very clear," he concurred. "But there are a few things that I would want in return for my donation to this cause of yours."

"What would that be?" she asked cautiously.

"You know all about my mother abandoning me when I was four years old and that I spent the rest of my childhood in the foster care system." When she nodded, he went on, "But I don't think I ever told you that I never knew who my father was." He shrugged. "For that matter, I doubt my mother did, either."

"What makes you think she didn't know your father?" Summer asked. "You were so little, maybe you just forgot her mentioning him."

"I don't think so." Shaking his head, Ryder sat back in his chair. "From what one of my caseworkers said just before I was sent to the Last Chance Ranch, my mother had been on their radar practically from the time I was born. Apparently at some point in their investigations, she had told the authorities she wasn't sure who had made her pregnant."

"I'm sorry, Ryder," she said softly. Having had a wonderful childhood with two loving parents, she couldn't imagine not having that security or the sense of identity that came with it. "But what does that have to do with you helping me?"

"I spent the first fourteen years of my life wondering who my father was and wishing that I had a dad to do things with like the other kids I went to school with. It wasn't until Hank Calvert became my foster father that I learned what it was like to have a real dad." He sat forward and placing his forearms on the desk, loosely clasped his hands in front of him. "If I agreed to father your child, I wouldn't want my kid going through that. I don't want him growing up wondering who's responsible for his existence and why his dad isn't around to take him places and do things with him."

"Are you telling me you want to be part of the baby's life?" She had been so busy assuring him that he wouldn't be obligated in any way that she hadn't considered Ryder might actually want the responsibility of helping her raise the child.

"Who knows? This might be the only kid I ever have," he answered. "But whether it is or not, I would want to be there for him or her like my biological father never was for me."

As Summer thought about what he said, she remembered the relationship she had with her father and how much it had meant to both of them. She had so many wonderful memories of things they had done together that she realized she wanted that for her child, as well.

"I would really like for you to be a part of the baby's life," she said, meaning it. She knew Ryder well enough to know that he would be a great father. "I just hadn't considered that you might want to be."

"Would you be agreeable to joint custody?" he asked, looking as if he thought his request might be a deal breaker.

"I haven't given it any thought," she answered truthfully. "But as long as we talk and agree on how to raise the baby, I don't think I would have a problem with it."

He raised one dark eyebrow. "You do realize that I would want equal time with him or her, don't you?"

"I'm sure we could work out something that we both find acceptable." They were best friends and got along quite well, so it shouldn't be that hard to arrange a suitable schedule. "Is that all?"

"No." He met her questioning gaze. "Where were you thinking about buying that house you mentioned?"

"I hadn't thought that far ahead, but I suppose I could buy a home anywhere," she said. With her parents gone and their property sold, there was no longer anything for her in California. "Why?"

Instead of answering her, he asked, "Would you be open to staying here at the ranch while you're pregnant and up until the baby is a year old, then finding a place close by?"

"I'm not sure that's a good idea, Ryder," she said, wondering how her simple request had suddenly become so complex. The longer they talked, the more complicated things became and the more concessions she was having to make.

"Actually, it's the perfect solution," he persisted. "If you stayed here at the ranch, I could experience the pregnancy with you, as well as go to your doctor appointments and whatever prenatal classes we need to take to get ready to become parents. Then once the baby is born, I could help out with its care during the first year. And when the time comes for you to find a house, being close by would make sharing custody a lot easier."

What he said made sense, but she wasn't ready to agree without giving it more thought. They might be best friends, but she wasn't sure she wanted to live with him for the better part of two years.

"Could I think about all of this for a little while?" she finally asked.

He smiled. "Sure. Take your time."

"Is there anything else?" Surely they had covered everything.

Ryder paused for a moment, then continued, "There's just one more thing…"

"I'm listening," she said, wondering what on earth there was left for him to ask of her before he agreed to help her.

"I don't think my making a donation in a cup is the route we should take for the conception." He shook his head. "I've got all the right equipment and trust me, darlin', everything is completely operational," he said, grinning. "Besides, I'd like to be able to tell our kid that we purposely got together because we both wanted him or her."

A knot started to form in the pit of her stomach. "Wh-what are you trying to say, Ryder?"

"If I'm going to help you, the conception would have to be natural."

"You mean, we would—"

"Make love," he finished for her.

"No!" Even she was startled by the vehemence in her one word answer. But there was absolutely no way she was going to bed with any man and especially not Ryder. He was her friend and she didn't want to lose their relationship.

"Then I guess the deal is off," he said, leaning back in his chair.

"Is there anything I can say to change your mind?"

she asked, knowing from his expression that it was unlikely she could convince him to see reason.

"No." He shook his head. "As far as I'm concerned, the means of conception is nonnegotiable."

She stood up to leave. "Then please forget that I asked for your help."

"I can't do that, darlin'." He shook his head as he rose to his feet. "That horse is already out of the barn and there's no way to get it back."

Staring at him a moment, Summer shook her head and hurried out of Ryder's office. As she marched up the stairs to the bedroom she had used since her arrival the night before, several emotions coursed through her. Naturally, she was disappointed. She wanted a baby and she wanted Ryder to father him or her. She was also a bit embarrassed that she'd had such a strong reaction to the idea of their having sex. He had no way of knowing that the very idea of having sex with any man came close to sending her into a panic attack. But more than that, she was angry.

As she'd stood in his office, staring at him as she tried to think of something to make him change his mind, it had occurred to her that she was the one having to make all of the concessions. It was true that most of what he had asked of her made sense. Given that he had never known his father, she could understand why he didn't want that for his child and even admired him for his willingness to be committed to being there for the baby.

But couldn't he at least consider her feelings on the matter? Why wasn't he willing to compromise on how the baby was conceived? Didn't he realize how far over the line that would be taking their friendship? Hadn't he considered that their relationship might not survive their being intimate?

A shiver ran through her and to her dismay it wasn't one of apprehension or panic. She frowned. Surely the unfamiliar sensation wasn't anticipation.

Shaking her head at the foolish thought, she grabbed her pajamas and headed into the bathroom for a quick shower. She needed to think of a way to get him to see reason. Unfortunately, all that kept running through her mind was the idea that Ryder was the only man she would even come close to considering making a baby with the old-fashioned way.

After Summer left his office like the hounds of hell chased her, Ryder sighed heavily and sank back down in his chair behind the desk as he thought about what had taken place. He had accomplished what he set out to do. He had successfully discouraged her from wanting him to father her child. So why didn't he feel good about it?

He hadn't wanted to crush her dream, but he honestly believed she wanted to have a child for the wrong reason. Having a baby simply because she wanted a connection with family again would be putting a lot of expectations on a kid that might prove hard for him or her to live up to.

Of course Summer would love the baby and the kid would love her. Ryder had no doubt about that. But he was of the opinion that a child should be wanted because of a desire to nurture and cherish it, not to be a remedy for loneliness.

But as much as her misguided reason for wanting a baby bothered him, something else bothered him more. What had caused her reaction when he mentioned conceiving a child the old-fashioned way?

Over the course of their friendship, he had seen her in several stressful situations and one of the many things he admired about Summer was her ability to remain calm and self-assured. She could handle a pressroom full of demanding reporters as easily as she applied her makeup. And last year, when one of the young bull riders had died from injuries sustained at one of the rodeos, she had immediately taken charge and somehow managed to keep the media satisfied without them hounding the family while they mourned the loss of their only son.

But he didn't think he had ever seen her thrown off balance the way she had been when he mentioned conceiving a baby by making love. Her confidence seemed to disappear before his eyes and a hesitancy that he would have never expected came over her.

Ryder scowled. Was the thought of making love with him that unpleasant? Or was she afraid of losing the comfortable friendship they had shared for the past several years?

Although he wasn't overly proud of himself for feeling the way he did, a small part of him had actually hoped she would agree to his terms. He had originally thought of his plan as a deterrent—a way to get her to give up on her idea that she wanted him to be her baby daddy. But just the thought of holding Summer's delightful body against his, of burying himself deep inside of her, caused the region south of his belt buckle to harden so fast it made him feel light-headed.

"McClain, you're one miserable son of a bitch," he muttered, rising from his chair and starting toward the office door.

Summer was his best friend, and for the life of him, he couldn't figure out what had changed between them over the past twenty-four hours that kept him in a state of semiarousal. He would like to blame his sudden unwarranted lust on her proposing the idea of him fathering her child. But he couldn't. Her hands on his biceps when they danced at the party had charged him up like the toy rabbit in one of those battery commercials—and that had been hours before she had asked him to help her become pregnant. And he had given up on blaming his brothers' teasing him about her as having any bearing on the situation at all. Hell, they had ribbed him countless times over the past several years about his relationship with her and not once had he started wondering what it would be like to sink himself so deep inside of her that he lost track of where he ended and she began.

His traitorous body tightened further and he made a beeline for the master bathroom and a cold shower. Maybe if he stood beneath the icy spray until he was colder than a penguin's tail feathers on an arctic ice floe, he would once again start thinking of Summer as his friend and stop thinking of her as the desirable woman who wanted him to help her make a baby.

Long after she heard Ryder walk past her room on his way to the master suite, Summer lay in bed staring at the ceiling. She couldn't stop thinking about what he said and how she had reacted to it.

She had been fine with almost all of his requirements. In fact, she decided that she liked the idea of sharing the responsibilities of raising their child with him. As protective as he was of those he cared for and as patient as she knew him to be, he would have been a great father. And she could understand him wanting her to live at the ranch with him during her pregnancy and for the baby's first year, too. He intended to be an involved father—going to doctor appointments and attending childbirth classes, as well as taking his turn at caring for the baby once it was born. She could even appreciate him wanting her to buy a home close to the ranch so that he could be with their child as often as possible. But his idea that they needed to conceive their child naturally was completely out of her comfort zone.

Shivering, she turned to her side and scrunching her eyes shut, she tried to block out the ugly memory behind her intimacy issues. She didn't like thinking about that night and the man who had violated her body and destroyed her trust in men. It gave him and the incident too much importance—too much power over her. Unfortunately, it had become a significant detail of her past and one that had shaped her future, as well as all of her future relationships with other men. At least all of them, that is, but her friendship with Ryder.

From the moment she met him, she had trusted Ryder. She wasn't sure why, but for some reason she had known he was everything he appeared to be—open,

honest and respectful of women. The type of man her
father had been. The type of man all men should be.

But as much as she wanted a baby, having sex with
Ryder—a man she trusted more than any other—was
something she just wasn't certain she could do. For one
thing, she had avoided putting herself in a vulnerable
situation with a man for so long that she wasn't sure she
could do it again. And for another, up until the night she
was raped, she had only been with one other man. That
had been her freshman year in college, and although
having sex with her boyfriend had been all right, their
few times together certainly hadn't lived up to her expectations or sounded anything like the passionate en-
counters her roommate had talked about having with
her boyfriend.

Turning to her back again, Summer opened her eyes
to stare at the ceiling. She still wanted a child and it
looked as if a sperm bank would be her only option.
But did she really want to visit one in order to get the
baby she wanted?

The thought still turned her off big-time. What if she
couldn't find a donor that would be an acceptable substitute for Ryder? Or worse yet, what if she did and the
guy lied about his medical history or his characteristics?

She knew there was a screening process that men
went through before they were allowed to donate and
that did give her some small amount of comfort. But
the bottom line was—her baby would be fathered by
a total stranger and that was something that made her
extremely uneasy.

Upset by the idea of having to visit a sperm bank

and unable to sleep, Summer threw back the covers and got out of bed to walk over to the window seat. Sinking down onto the plush cushion, she drew her legs up to her chest and wrapped her arms around them as she stared out the window at the star-studded night sky. There was only one man she wanted to father her child and that was Ryder McClain.

Now that she knew that no other man would be an acceptable substitute, she had to decide if she could work up the courage to go through with his condition that the conception be natural. It would mean having sex with him, and even though it would only be for the purpose of becoming pregnant, she just wasn't sure she would be able to do it.

The thought caused an empty ache to begin to pool in her lower belly and she quickly stood up to pace the room. It had been so long since she experienced the sensation, she had almost forgotten what it felt like. But there was no mistaking it. Her mind might not be able to come to terms with his demand, but her body was more than ready.

Walking into the bathroom, she bent over the sink, turned on the cold water and splashed some on her face. Ryder was her friend, the only male she felt completely at ease spending time with. As she patted her face dry with a towel, she raised her eyes to meet the gaze of her image in the mirror. And although she wasn't the least bit comfortable with it, he was the only man who had made her feel the stirrings of desire in several years.

Four

The next morning as he brushed the shiny coat of his bay gelding, Ryder couldn't help but wonder if he had done irreparable damage to his friendship with Summer. He hoped with all his heart that wasn't the case.

When he suggested they make love in order for her to conceive, he had only meant to discourage her, not have her running for the hills. But he hadn't seen her since their conversation in his study yesterday evening and she hadn't even bothered coming downstairs for breakfast this morning. But for the life of him, he couldn't think of any other explanation for her absence.

He hadn't expected her to accept his terms and thanks to the ice-cold shower he had taken, his perspective had been restored. Although he realized her refusal had been for the best, he hadn't counted on his demands alienating her. The fact that she was avoiding him was testament to the fact that they probably had and it bothered him. A lot.

"Betty Lou said I'd probably find you here," Summer said, surprising him when she walked into the barn.

"I wasn't entirely sure you would ever talk to me again after our discussion last night," he said honestly. "You didn't join me for breakfast and I figured you were still pretty upset with me over our talk."

He continued brushing the bay to keep from giving in to the overwhelming urge to take her into his arms. That made no sense at all and he couldn't figure out why the feeling was so strong. Theirs had never been that kind of friendship.

She shook her head. "I'm not upset, but you did give me a lot to think about and I had a hard time going to sleep."

"So you overslept this morning?" he asked, relieved she wasn't mad at him, but wondering where the conversation was going.

Nodding, a frown wrinkled her forehead. "I haven't slept that late in years."

"You probably needed the rest." He unsnapped the lead rope he had used to tie his horse to the grooming post and taking hold of the halter, walked the bay gelding back into the stall. Closing the half door, he added, "I've seen you work some pretty crazy hours lately." A slight breeze blew a strand of her blond hair across her cheek and it took monumental effort on his part not to reach out and brush it aside.

"If you aren't too busy, do you mind if we talk a bit

more about last night?" she asked, sounding a little unsure.

His heart slammed against his ribs and the back of his neck tingled with apprehension. What could she want to talk about that they hadn't covered last night? And why did he suddenly want to wrap his arms around her and kiss away the uncertain expression on her pretty face?

Instead, he swallowed around the cotton coating his throat and nodded. "Sure. Would you like to go back up to the house or do you want to talk here?" When she looked around as if checking to see if they were alone, he added, "Don't worry. There's no one around to overhear what we say. My foreman took the men out to check the fences in the far pastures to make sure they're ready for winter."

"Here will be fine," she said as she walked over to sit down on a bale of straw.

He was happy that she was at least still speaking to him, but mystified about what she thought they needed to discuss further. As far as he was concerned, his stipulations had been quite clear and set in stone. She wasn't going to convince him to change his mind.

"What do you think we need to discuss?" he asked, crossing his arms and leaning back against the bay's stall across the wide barn aisle from her.

She took a deep breath. "I spent the majority of last night lying awake, thinking about your requirements and your reasoning behind them."

"And?"

"I agree with most of them." She picked up a piece

of straw and staring down at it began to shred it with her fingers. "I like the idea of the baby having two parents who will love and be there for it. And I also think it would be nice to have you go with me to doctor appointments and help with the baby's care once it's born."

He wondered when she was going to stop beating around the bush and get to the sticking point—the part about them making love in order for her to conceive. He didn't have long to wait.

"The only problem I had with your requests was the part about us having sex to make me pregnant," she said, her voice almost a whisper.

"I understand your refusal and I'm not in the least bit offended, darlin'," he answered. "You don't want to risk our friendship and I'm fine with that. I don't want to lose it either."

His breath lodged in his lungs when she shook her head. "That isn't what I was about to tell you."

Clearing his suddenly rusty throat, he asked, "What were you going to say?"

"I've thought a lot about it…and I believe our friendship is solid enough to withstand our having sexual intercourse for the purpose of conceiving a child."

It was the last thing he'd expected her to say, and he wasn't at all comfortable with his body's reaction at her mention of them making love. Just the thought sent a shaft of longing coursing through him at the speed of light and caused his body to tighten predictably. Removing his hat, he lowered it in front of him with one hand as he ran his other hand through his hair in an effort to hide his reaction to what she had just said.

Hell's bells! He thought he had a handle on things and the matter had been settled. Last night, he'd told her what he wanted in return for helping her get pregnant and she had found his demands unacceptable. That should have been the end of it. When had he lost control of the situation? And what the hell was he going to do about it now?

"You want a baby so much that you're willing to take that step?" he asked, still unable to believe what she had told him. "You're willing to make love with me until you become pregnant?"

She closed her eyes a moment, then nodding, she met his gaze head-on. "Yes. I'm willing to do whatever I have to do in order to have the baby I want."

"Okay," he said slowly. "Can I ask why you changed your mind?"

There was no hesitation when she nodded. "You have all the traits and characteristics—"

"Yeah, I'm the prize stud," he interrupted. "I got that before. What I want to know is what happened to change your mind between last night and now?"

"I realized that you're the only man I want to father my baby." She shrugged one slender shoulder. "You're my best friend and I know you well enough to safely say that you'll be there for the baby no matter what. You'll love the child as much as I will and protect him or her from all harm."

He couldn't argue with her assessment of how he would feel about a kid. There wasn't a doubt in his mind that he would willingly lay down his life if that's what it took to keep it safe. For that matter, he would do the same for Summer.

"And you're completely comfortable with all this?" he asked, feeling like he might be lost somewhere in a parallel universe.

"Yes."

Ryder nodded as he stared off into space. Now what was he supposed to do? His plan had been to discourage her and it had been successful—last night. But now that Summer had changed her mind, he was trapped. He had given her his word that he would help her if she agreed to his terms and short of going back on it, he didn't see any other option but to honor his end of the bargain.

"I guess now all there is left to do is decide when you want to start trying to become pregnant," he finally said, clenching his fist into a tight ball in an effort to control his rapidly hardening body. Unfortunately, it wasn't working.

Squaring her shoulders, she rose to her feet. "I've given that some thought as well and I'd like to get started as soon as possible." Her cheeks colored a pretty pink. "We could start trying sometime today if that's all right with you."

It was all he could do not to groan aloud. A beautiful woman was standing in front of him, telling him that she wanted him to make love to her, and he was going to turn her down? His nobility only went so far and he was man enough to admit that he had reached the end of his.

"Sure," he said thickly as he pushed away from the bay's stall. Just the thought that they were going to make love sent a wave of heat straight to his groin, and he was glad she was too distracted to notice he was still holding his hat in front of jeans that were becoming way too snug at the fly. "I have some chores I have to take care of today, but this evening will be fine."

She nodded as she started to leave. "Now that things are settled, I'll go see if Betty Lou needs help with lunch." Stopping suddenly, she turned back. "By the way, do you wear boxers or briefs?"

"Boxer briefs." He frowned. "Why?"

"I'm not sure about those," she said, nibbling on her lower lip. "Until we're successful, you might want to start wearing boxers."

"Why?" Ryder knew he sounded like a damned parrot, but he couldn't figure out why she was so fixated on the type of underwear he preferred.

"Boxer shorts are less confining and enable more sperm production," she explained.

He laughed, releasing some of the tension that gripped him. "Don't worry about me, darlin'. Everything is in working order and since I sleep in the buff, I have no reason to believe that I won't have more than enough swimmers to get the job done."

"All right," she said as she turned to leave. "I'll trust that detail to you."

When she walked out of the barn, his smile faded and the reality of the situation set in. He and Summer were going to cross a line in their friendship and make love to have a baby. Un-freaking-believable!

If someone had told him three days ago that he would be consciously planning to make any woman pregnant, he would have laughed them right into the next county. But if they had told him that woman would be Summer Patterson, he would have readily told them that they were a few beers shy of a six-pack in the brains department.

A sudden thought had him cussing a blue streak as he jammed his hat back on his head. What were his brothers going to say when they found out about his arrangement with Summer?

He had no doubt that he would have their full support in whatever he did. But it would come with a pretty hefty price tag. Ryder knew as surely as the sun rose in the east each morning that he would have to endure endless ribbing and enough *I told you so's* to last a lifetime.

Picking up the brush he had used on the bay, he headed down the aisle toward the stalls at the end of the barn. His brothers' comments and jokes were just something he would have to cowboy up and deal with. As Hank always told him and his brothers, a man is only as good as his word and it should be as binding as any written contract.

Ryder tied the buckskin mare to the side of the stall and began brushing her dark golden coat. He felt like he was about to jump off a cliff into an unknown abyss, but he had made a promise to Summer and he would climb a barbed-wire fence buck naked before he reneged on it now.

After dinner, Summer helped Betty Lou clean up the kitchen, then slowly walked down the hall to join Ryder in the family room. She was as jittery as she could ever remember being, but she was determined to carry through with her plan. It meant too much to her to let anything stand in her way of having the family she wanted.

"Would you like to see a movie before we head upstairs to bed?" he asked, looking up from the show he had been watching when she entered the room. "There's a comedy you might like on one of the movie channels."

"I…um, no, I don't think so," she said, shaking her head. She'd had the entire day to think about what they were going to do and delaying it further would only increase her anxiety and could very well cause her to lose her nerve. She looked over her shoulder toward the kitchen to make sure Betty Lou had gone to her room. "If you don't mind, I'd just as soon go ahead and get started on our…little project."

He gave a short nod, then picking up the remote control, turned off the television and rose to his feet. "I went ahead and turned down the bed," he said, walking over to her. He paused for a moment before he reached up to touch her cheek with his forefinger. "Darlin', are you 100 percent sure this is what you really want to do?"

"Yes," she said as she fixed her attention on one of the snap closures on his chambray shirt. "Why do you ask?"

"Because you look like you're about to face a firing squad instead of going upstairs to make love with me," he said, frowning. He used his index finger to lift her chin until their gazes met. "You know it's okay if you've changed your mind. I'll understand and we'll go along like nothing ever happened."

The sincerity in his dark green eyes indicated that he really meant every word he said.

"No, I haven't changed my mind," she said decisively. "I just want to get this part over with so I can concentrate on looking forward to when the baby arrives."

His frown deepened as he placed his hand to her back and they walked over to the stairs. "You make it sound like you think making love with me is going to be about as pleasant as getting a tooth pulled."

"Not at all," she lied. "I'm just a little nervous. That's all." That was an understatement, she thought when they reached the top of the stairs and started down the hall. He might stir long dormant desires, but the thought of being intimate with any man was still extremely intimidating.

When she stopped to open the door to the bedroom she had been using, he shook his head. "I think it would be better if we go to my room."

A chilling trepidation streaked up her spine. "Why?"

He smiled encouragingly. "Betty Lou's room downstairs is on this side of the house, and I thought that you might not be overly comfortable with that."

"You're probably right," she said, forcing herself to continue on to the master suite at the end of the hall.

When they entered his bedroom and he turned on a lamp, she tried not to focus on the king-size bed and looked around at the Western decor. A blend of Native American artwork and Western wildlife prints graced the sage-colored walls, while colorful Navajo rugs brightened up the dark hardwood floor. The room was beautiful and perfect for Ryder. He was a Texas cowboy from the top of his dark brown hair to the soles of his big, booted feet and the room reflected that.

"Relax," he said, turning to face her. He reached out and put his arms loosely around her waist. "Just because we're doing this to make a baby doesn't mean it can't be fun, too."

This is Ryder. He's your friend. You can do this.

"I'm not sure about that," she said before she could stop herself. She wasn't certain if she was responding to his statement or answering herself.

"Don't worry," he said with a confident smile. "I'll make sure our lovemaking is enjoyable for both of us."

When Ryder lowered his head to lightly graze her lips with his, a jolt of awareness stronger than anything she had ever experienced instantly coursed through her. She told herself to take a step back, but when his mouth settled over hers to taste and tease, a delicious warmth began to pool in the pit of her stomach.

Lost in all the wonderful sensations swirling through her and unable to comprehend why she was experiencing them, it took a moment for her to realize that he had moved his hand to cover her breast. "Wh-what are you doing?" she asked, breaking the kiss.

"It's called foreplay, Summer." He kissed his way along her jaw to the side of her neck, then whispered in her ear, "Everything will be a lot easier and there's a better chance of success if we're both relaxed and ready to make love."

His warm breath feathering over her ear sent another wave of tingling heat crashing through her and caused her knees to wobble. "I hadn't thought it would be necessary," she said, wondering how she could feel excitement and apprehension at the same time.

Leaning back to look down at her, his dark green eyes held hers. "Are you a virgin, Summer?"

It was the last thing she expected him to ask. "No. Why?"

"Because I've never seen you this nervous," he said, pulling her to his wide chest. "How long has it been since you've been with a man?"

"I don't think that's relevant," she said, curious why her sexual experience, or lack thereof, mattered. "But if you have to know, I've only had sex a few times and that was my freshman year in college."

He nodded. "That explains why you're so tense. I'm betting the poor kid didn't have a clue what he was doing any more than you did. It wasn't all that good for you, was it?"

"No."

She decided to go along with his assumption. It was easier than admitting that her stress stemmed from the reprehensible act by one of the worst examples of his gender.

"I promise that it will be different for you this time," he said, bringing his hand up to thread his fingers through her hair. "I give you my word that I'll ensure your pleasure before I find my own."

Her heart beat double time. "D-don't worry about me. It's not necessary for me to—"

He shook his head as he started to tug the tail of her T-shirt from the waistband of her jeans. "I'm not a self-

ish man, Summer. Part of my satisfaction will be knowing that I've helped you find yours."

She closed her eyes. *You can do this. Just focus on
your goal and you can do this.*

But when Ryder moved to lift the hem of her shirt to
take it off her, she felt the hard evidence straining at his
jeans and her nerves got the better of her. "I—I...can't,"
she said, beginning to tremble as she pushed away from
him. "I can't do this. I thought I could...because I really
want a baby. But I was wrong. I'm sorry. I just can't."

"Whoa! Slow down, darlin'," he said, releasing her
shirt to place his hands on her shoulders. He stared at
her for several long seconds. "Calm down and tell me
what's wrong."

She tried to blink back a wave of tears as she stared
into his concerned eyes. "I...just can't. I...want to. But
I...can't."

Leading her over to the bed, he sat down and pulled
her onto his lap. Cradling her to him as if she were a
child, he held her close. "Talk to me, Summer. Tell me
what's going on."

"I want a baby...but I just can't...do this, Ryder," she
sobbed against his shoulder.

"It's okay, darlin'," he said, his tone gentle. "I give
you my word nothing is going to happen that you don't
want happening. Now, tell me what caused you to be
so afraid."

"I was... I mean, I told him no," she stammered.
"But he wouldn't stop."

She felt Ryder's body go completely still a moment

before he spoke in a voice so deadly quiet that it caused a cold chill to travel the length of her. "You were raped."

Unable to answer, she nodded.

"Was it your first experience?" he asked in the same cold tone.

"N-no. It was someone else." She took a shuddering breath. "I told him no, but we...were on a date. I'm not sure—"

"It doesn't matter if you were on a date or not," Ryder ground out, shaking his head. "No means no. If a man ignores that, then it's rape." His arms tightened around her. "When did it happen, darlin'?"

She hadn't talked about it with anyone. Not when the incident happened and not since. But apparently having suppressed it for so long, once she started talking about it, she couldn't seem to stop herself.

"It was at the end of my sophomore year in college. We were in a communication class together and he seemed nice enough. When he asked me out, I accepted." She shivered uncontrollably. "He turned out to be the worst mistake I've ever made."

"That's why you don't date and why you aren't interested in getting married, isn't it?" he asked, continuing to hold her protectively against him. "You're afraid of being intimate with a man."

"I've tried to get past my issues, but I'm not comfortable being alone with men," she said, swallowing hard. "I don't trust them."

"I'm a man and you've never had a problem being alone with me," he said, gently running his hand up and down her arm in a soothing manner.

"You're different," she said without hesitation.

He leaned back to look at her and she could tell his mock frown was meant to lighten the mood and make her feel a little better. "What do you think I am, darlin', a sexless old gelding?"

"No." For the first time since she'd agreed to his requirements, she smiled. "But you're my friend. I trust you."

His expression became serious. "And I promise that I'll never betray that trust, Summer."

Staring at each other for several long seconds, she finally said, "I still want a baby."

He nodded. "I figured you would."

"Where do we go from here? Will you still help me?" she asked, praying that he would.

"We'll talk more about this in the morning," he said evasively. "I just remembered that I promised my foreman the night off and I forgot to feed the horses."

"Do you need help?" she asked, disheartened that he had avoided answering her question.

"No." After setting her on her feet, he rose from the side of the bed, took her hand in his and led her out of the master suite. Then he walked her down to the room she had been using. "Sleep well, darlin'," he said, brushing her lips with his. "I'll see you in the morning."

Anger stronger than he had experienced in almost twenty years coursed through Ryder as he descended the stairs, grabbed a couple of cold beers from the refrigerator as he passed through the kitchen and stormed out of the house. He had done his best not to let Summer see the effect her telling him about the sexual assault had on him. For one thing, he didn't want to frighten her. And for another, the degree of fury that he felt toward the unnamed man had scared the living daylights out of him.

Entering the barn, he sat down on a bale of straw by the tack room and, popping the top on one of the cans, downed the contents. He knew the incident had taken place a couple of years before he and Summer had even met, but that didn't keep him from wanting to find the sorry son of a bitch and teach him a lesson he would never forget.

Ryder shook his head as he crushed the empty can, then tossing it aside, pulled the tab on the second can to take another swig of cold beer. Real men never took what a woman wasn't ready and willing to give. Period. When a woman told a man no, then he headed for a shower cold enough to cause frostbite, jogged until his shoes fell apart or bench-pressed a bulldozer if he had to in order to work off the adrenaline. And as far as Ryder was concerned, there were no excuses for doing anything else.

Feeling a little more in control, he leaned back against the barn wall. He hadn't liked lying to Summer about needing to feed the horses, but it couldn't be helped. He had needed the time and space to calm down and regain his equilibrium.

He couldn't help but remember another time when he had been filled with the same degree of anger and the consequences that he'd had to suffer through because of it. He had just turned fourteen and had been

sent to live with a foster couple in Fort Worth. His foster mother had been real nice, but his foster dad had
been a real piece of work. A functioning alcoholic, Pete
Ledbetter held a job and to the outward eye everything
was fine. But it hadn't taken Ryder long to realize that
things weren't always as they seemed.

Pete usually stayed stone-cold sober during the day,
but as soon as he got off work he started drinking and
didn't stop until he passed out. Then he would sleep it
off overnight, get up the next morning and the cycle
would start all over again. But there were times before
he passed out that Pete would turn into a mean drunk
and made life a living hell around the Ledbetter home.
Usually his wrath was directed at his wife and he left
Ryder alone. Probably because even at the age of fourteen, Ryder was taller and more muscular than he was.

But the cycle was broken for good one fateful evening when Ryder came home after football practice and
found Ellen Ledbetter sitting at the kitchen table nursing a black eye and a busted lip. She had told him that
Pete was in a particularly nasty mood and that Ryder
should make himself scarce until his foster father drank
himself into oblivion.

Maybe his life would have turned out differently if
he had listened to Ellen. But even at that young age,
he had felt the need to protect those who were unable
to defend themselves and when Pete walked in to take
another swing at his wife, Ryder had stepped between
them. The next thing he knew, Pete Ledbetter lay dead
in a pool of blood on the kitchen floor, and Ryder was

being handcuffed and hauled off to a juvenile detention center.

He took a deep breath and finished his beer. He had eventually been cleared of the involuntary manslaughter charge and sent to the Last Chance Ranch, but the incident had changed his life forever. From that moment forward, he had never raised his fists in anger at any time, for any reason.

He'd had no trouble keeping that promise to himself. Hell, he hadn't even been tempted to go back on it. At least, not until Summer told him about the man who raped her. Ryder knew beyond a shadow of doubt that if he could have gotten hold of the bastard, he would have torn him apart with his bare hands. And that bothered him.

But what scared him more was Summer finding out that he wasn't the person she thought him to be. How would she react if she discovered that the man she trusted above all others had caused another man's death?

Just the thought of watching the revulsion cloud her pretty blue eyes caused a knot the size of his fist to twist his gut. That's why he never intended for her to know about the incident. He couldn't stand the thought of losing her. And he had no doubt that's exactly what would happen if she learned the truth about him.

Five

When Summer finished helping Betty Lou make sandwiches for a picnic lunch, she walked down the hall to Ryder's study. He had been busy making a list of things he wanted his foreman to take care of over the next week while he was working the rodeo with her up in Oklahoma. They hadn't had the opportunity to discuss what had happened last night, but after telling him about the assault she'd done a lot of thinking and had a few things she wanted to talk over with him before they left the Blue Canyon Ranch.

The study door was open and, knocking on the door frame, she stepped into the room. "Ryder, I just finished helping Betty Lou make lunch for us. Do you have time to ride down to the canyon for another picnic?"

When he looked up and smiled, she caught her

breath. He was without a doubt one of the best-looking men she'd ever seen.

"That sounds like a great idea," he said, rising to his feet. He picked up a paper from the desk and walked over to her. "I need to drop this repair list off with my foreman anyway and while I'm down at the barn I'll saddle the horses." His expression turned serious. "I didn't want to ask this morning in front of Betty Lou, but are you feeling better?"

His concern touched her. "I'm fine," she said. "It seems that finally telling someone about what happened was a bit cathartic for me."

He frowned. "You hadn't told anyone? Why didn't you report the assault to the authorities?"

"Besides just wanting to forget that night ever happened, I wasn't sure they would believe me since I was on a date with him," she said, shaking her head.

Wrapping his strong arms around her, Ryder pulled her to his wide chest for a comforting hug. "That's a lot to have to carry by yourself for all these years. You should have told someone, darlin'."

"I guess I was…ashamed that I had been so naive," she said, hugging him back.

When he released her, he shook his head. "You didn't do anything to be ashamed of, Summer. It wasn't your fault and I don't want you thinking that is was."

Shrugging, she fell into step with him as they walked down the hall to the kitchen. "I suppose you're right."

"I know I am," he said vehemently. "Now, while I'm getting the horses ready, you pack the saddlebags and I'll meet you down at the barn."

An hour later as they dismounted the horses beside the lazy little creek on the canyon floor, Summer felt as if she had turned a corner in her life. She only hoped that Ryder would support her decision and still agree to help her.

"This seemed like a nice place the last time," he said, spreading the blanket in the same spot they had picnicked a couple of days before.

"I love that the trees are just beginning to change colors," she murmured, looking around at a few golden leaves on the cottonwood trees. "I think autumn is the prettiest time of year."

"We'll have to come back in a couple of weeks," he said as he lowered himself onto the blanket. "Just about every tree in this canyon will be a bright gold."

"I'll look forward to it." She couldn't help but feel heartened by the fact that he was making plans for them to come back together in the future. "I'm sure it will be beautiful."

While they ate, they exchanged small talk about the upcoming rodeo they would both be working and some of the plans Ryder had for the ranch. Summer enjoyed hearing about the projects he wanted to undertake, but couldn't seem to get her mind off what she needed to discuss with him.

Deciding that there was no easy way to start the conversation, she took a deep breath. "Last night after you left the house to feed the horses, I did a lot of soul-searching," she admitted as she gathered the remnants of their lunch. "And I still want a baby."

He planted his feet at the edge of the blanket and

rested his arms on his bent knees. "That's what you said last night."

"Are you still willing to father my child?" she asked, mentally holding her breath as she awaited his answer.

"I gave you my word and that hasn't changed," he said. "But I won't hold you to our having to make love for you to become pregnant. If you'll make the appointment with your doctor, I'll go get cozy with a specimen cup." She could tell it wasn't in the least bit appealing to him, but he was willing to do it in order to keep her from feeling uncomfortable, as well as honor his commitment to her.

She nibbled on her lower lip a moment before finding the nerve to tell him what she had decided the night before. "Actually, that isn't what I want you to do."

One dark eyebrow rose in question as he slowly turned his head to stare at her. "What are you saying?"

"I'm tired of being afraid, Ryder," she said, knowing it was true. "I'm not sure how this is going to sound, but I want to be a whole woman again. If you're willing, I'd like for you to help me get over my fear of intimacy." She could tell from the look on his face that he was thoroughly shocked by her proclamation. "I think that can be accomplished if we have sex in order to conceive."

"Darlin', I can understand you wanting to go through with having a baby," he said quietly. "And I get that you don't want to be afraid anymore. But are you really sure about this?"

"Yes."

He remained silent for several long moments before he spoke again. "You do realize that it's probably going to take more than one lovemaking session for you to become pregnant?"

She nodded. "I'm aware of that, but I started thinking about something you said when you first agreed to help me...and I realize artificial insemination isn't what I want."

"I say a lot of things, but that doesn't mean I'm always right," he admitted.

"But in this case, you were," she insisted. "You told me that you would like to be able to tell our child that we purposely came together because we wanted him or her, not because a doctor intervened with a clinical procedure." She smiled. "I think it will mean more to our child when he or she is old enough to understand."

He hesitated for a moment before he asked, "Do you still want to get started right away?"

She didn't have to think about her answer. "Yes."

"Then I think instead of you staying in a hotel room, from now on you should stay with me in my camper," he said, meeting her startled gaze. Ryder was one of the many cowboys and rodeo personnel who preferred to travel with their own accommodations, rather than rent a hotel room.

"There's only one drawback to that," she countered. "Everyone will think that we've taken our friendship to the next level."

It took her by surprise when he laughed out loud. "What the hell do you think they'll say when they find out we're having a baby together?"

"I really hadn't thought much about that," she admitted.

"You know how close rodeo people are," he said pointedly. "Word will get around. It's not something we can hide, nor do I intend to try. When your pregnancy starts to show, I'm going to proudly tell people that I'm the daddy, not make it seem like it's an accident from our sneaking around."

What he said made sense. But she had avoided rumors of anything going on between them for so long that old habits were hard to break.

"All right," she said, realizing he was probably right. She didn't want people to think their child was the mistake of a clandestine affair, either. "I guess that settles everything."

Ryder surprised her when he shook his head. "Nope. There's one more thing that we haven't covered."

"What would that be?" For the life of her, she couldn't imagine what there was left to be decided after their countless conversations on the subject.

"We're going to start acting like we're a couple," he stated.

"You mean as if we've fallen in love?" Things just kept getting more and more complicated by the moment.

"It's easier to go with that, than it is to try and explain everything." He leaned over and briefly pressed his lips to hers. "Besides, that's what people are going to think anyway. We might as well go along with it."

"Does that mean we'll be openly affectionate toward each other?" she asked, liking the way his kiss made her tingle all over.

"Yup. That's what people do when they're...involved."

She furrowed her brow. "Do you think we can be convincing?"

"Let's see," he said, lowering his head.

He kissed her again, but this time it wasn't a chaste brushing of the lips between two friends. This time it was the kiss of a man asking a woman to trust him, asking her to let him show her that intimacy didn't have to be feared.

Closing her eyes, Summer forced herself to relax and experience his gentle caress. She knew without question that if she asked him to stop, he would do so in a heartbeat. But that wasn't what she wanted. She wasn't entirely certain why, but for the first time in years, she needed to feel like a real woman again, instead of the frightened female she had become after the assault.

Ryder teased her with his tongue until she parted her lips on a sigh, then slipping inside, he gently explored her tender inner recesses. She didn't even try to stop herself from melting against him. She had avoided men for so long that she had forgotten how nice it was to feel safe in a man's arms, to feel cherished.

"I don't think we'll have any problems convincing anyone that we've taken our friendship to the next level," he said, easing away from the kiss.

"There isn't anyone around right now for us to impress," she said breathlessly. "Why—"

"I thought we could use the practice." His wide grin sent a wave of goose bumps shimmering over her skin. "Besides, I decided you needed to be reminded that kissing is just plain fun."

He rose to his feet, then held his hand out to help her

to hers. Summer didn't even think to hesitate before she placed her hand, as well as her complete trust, in his. They had crossed a line in their friendship, and there was no going back now. The only thing left to do was move forward and see where this latest twist in their relationship took them.

When he and Summer rode the horses back into the ranch yard, Ryder groaned inwardly at the sight of his brother's truck parked beside his own. What was Lane doing here?

"It looks like one of my brother's is going to be the first one to learn about the new development in our friendship," he said as they dismounted and led the horses into the barn.

"Do you think he'll be convinced?" she asked, un-saddling the buckskin mare.

Ryder laughed, releasing some of the tension building across his shoulders. "The other night at Sam and Bria's party, I couldn't convince any of my brothers otherwise. So, no. I don't think we'll have a problem getting him to believe there's something more going on between us." As an afterthought, he added, "But it wouldn't hurt to test-drive our show of affection toward each other."

"In other words, you don't want me freaking out when you put your arm around me?" she asked.

"Or when I kiss you in front of him," he said, nodding.

Summer looked thoughtful for a moment. "That's

why you were irritated with your brothers at the party, wasn't it? They were speculating on our relationship."

"Yup." He led the horses back into their stalls, then draping his arm across her shoulders, started walking them toward the house. "And you can bet by supper tonight, Lane will have reported back to every one of them and let them know that their speculations were right on the money."

She grinned. "Wouldn't you do the same if you discovered something about one of them?"

He laughed as they climbed the steps to the back porch. "Darlin', I wouldn't be able to dial the phone fast enough."

When they entered the kitchen, Lane was seated at the table having a cup of coffee with Betty Lou. "Hey you two, I was beginning to think I was going to miss seeing you," he said, rising to his feet. Nodding at Summer, he added, "It's nice seeing you again, Ms. Patterson."

"Please, call me Summer. And it's nice seeing you again, too, Lane." She smiled at Ryder. "While you visit with your brother, I think I'm going upstairs to take advantage of the Jacuzzi before I help Betty Lou with dinner."

Ryder pulled her to him and covered her mouth with his. He told himself the kiss was for his brother's benefit, but as Summer's lips clung to his, he knew that was a bald-faced lie. The kiss they had shared under the cottonwood tree had left him aching to kiss her again and he couldn't resist seizing the opportunity now.

"I'll see you in a little while, darlin'," he said against her soft lips.

As Summer left the room, he turned back to Lane and almost laughed out loud. For a professional poker player who prided himself on his ability not to show any emotion, Lane was failing miserably. He looked like he had just been treated to the business end of an electric cattle prod. For that matter, so did Betty Lou.

"What?" Ryder asked, feigning ignorance.

The first to recover, his housekeeper got up from the table and walking up to him, patted his cheek. "I'm glad to see you finally woke up," she said, grinning from ear to ear. "You and that little girl are gonna make a real fine couple. The way you always talked about her whenever you came home from a rodeo, I knew it was just a matter of time before you realized there was more going on between the two of you than just being good friends."

When Betty Lou walked on past him to enter the pantry, Ryder turned to see his brother grinning at him like a damned fool. "What's up, bro?" he asked, already knowing he was about to face an inquisition.

"Why don't we grab a couple of beers and go into your office for that visit?" Lane asked, pointing toward the hall. "You can tell me once again that you and Summer are just good friends and I can tell you that you're full of bullroar and buffalo chips."

"I can already tell you're going to be a jerk about this, aren't you?" Ryder groused as he got them both a cold beer and they headed toward his office.

"Oh yeah. But you wouldn't expect anything less from me," Lane shot back. He lowered his lanky frame into the armchair in front of Ryder's desk. "If you had the chance, you'd do the same thing to me or any of the other guys."

Grinning, Ryder nodded. "You bet your sweet ass I would."

Lane took a swallow from his beer bottle. "So what's the story with you and Summer?" He gave Ryder a knowing look. "Since Betty Lou was just as surprised as I was, I take it that you two just started dating?"

Ryder propped his booted feet on the edge of the desk, then crossing his legs at the ankles, leaned back in his desk chair. "We just started thinking of each other as more than friends in the past couple of days." Frowning, he added, "Apparently you guys saw something that night at the party that I didn't because we didn't start talking about taking things up a notch until we were on the way back here."

His brother nodded. "I watched her watching you and I could tell friendship was the last thing on her mind."

"Okay," Ryder said, holding up both hands in surrender. He wasn't about to tell Lane that she'd had something on her mind all right. She had been sizing him up as a prize stud, instead of the romantic encounter his brothers all thought. "I was wrong and you all were right. Does that make you happy?"

"You have no idea how much," Lane answered glibly. "The next time Bria has a family dinner for all of us, you can expect to be the one in the hot seat."

"When you leave here, you won't even make it to the main road before you tell the rest of the guys about this, will you?" Ryder asked, knowing it was already as good as a done deal.

Lane laughed out loud as he shook his head. "You know good and well that finding out something like this has got to be shared. And the sooner, the better."

Ryder knew that if he asked Lane not to tell their brothers, he would keep the confidence. Being a licensed psychologist, Lane knew how to listen and keep his mouth shut. But as much as he dreaded the ribbing he would take from his brothers, Ryder realized it was the best way to get the word out that he and Summer had taken their friendship to the next level and would set the stage for her becoming pregnant.

"Enough about me, what are you up to?" Ryder asked, realizing it was time to change the subject.

"After you two left the party the other night, Bria decided that we all needed to take some cake home with us and I volunteered to bring yours by on my way to Shreveport," Lane replied, checking his gold Rolex. "And that reminds me, I need to get on the road so I can get to the casino and get checked in."

"Are you playing in another big tournament this week?" Ryder asked.

"Not this time." Frowning, Lane set his half-empty beer bottle on the desk. "It's the damnedest thing. Last week, I got a written invitation to a private game with Ben Cunningham."

Ryder recognized the name of one of the most famous players in the world of professional poker. "I thought Cunningham retired."

"So did I." Lane rose to his feet. "But I'm not going

to turn down the chance to play a game with arguably the best player in the history of poker."

"I don't blame you," Ryder said, following his brother down the hall to the kitchen. "It's not every day you're invited to play with a legend. Good luck."

"Thanks, but you know I don't rely on Lady Luck. She's too fickle. I'd much rather use my skills. At least that way I have a fighting chance of winning." Turning to Betty Lou standing at the counter cutting up vegetables, Lane touched the wide brim of his black Resistol. "Betty Lou, you take care and if you have any problems with this big lug, just give me a call. I'll line him out in short order."

"You and whose army?" Ryder laughed, following Lane out to the porch.

"You're working a rodeo at one of the county fairs up in Oklahoma this weekend, aren't you?" Lane asked, his easy expression turning serious.

Ryder nodded. "Why?"

"Nate and Jaron are planning on competing in the bull and bareback riding events. You might want to keep an eye on Nate," he said, starting down the steps. "He's not quite up to par these days."

"What's up with him?" Of all his brothers, Nate was the last one to take life too seriously and Ryder couldn't imagine anything bringing him down for very long.

"That little nurse he's been seeing down in Waco broke things off with him the day after the party and he's not taking it very well," Lane explained.

"Wounded pride?" Ryder asked, a little surprised by the news. To his knowledge, it was the first time that

Nate had been dumped. Normally, he was the one initiating a breakup when things looked like they might be getting too serious.

"I'm not so sure," Lane answered. "There was something about the way Nate looked when he talked about her that led me to believe he had started feeling more for her than he had any other woman."

"I'll be sure to keep an extra close eye on him," Ryder promised as Lane walked to his truck.

Watching his brother's truck disappear down the driveway as Lane headed toward the main road, Ryder felt his protective instincts come to full alert and made a mental vow to be extra vigilant during the bull riding event. Being around the rough stock while nursing a broken heart wasn't a good mix. They had all learned that firsthand a few months back when Sam had been run down by one of the meanest bulls his rodeo stock contracting company had to offer. The accident had ultimately led to his brother and Bria working out their marital problems, but Ryder would just as soon not see another one of his brothers sustain a life-threatening injury as a result of a romantic breakup.

"I'm getting too old for this," he muttered as he turned to go back inside the house.

But as long as he had breath in his body, he knew he would do whatever it took to keep his family safe from harm. And that included Summer and their as-yet-to-be-conceived child.

Summer had just finished packing her luggage for the trip with Ryder when the sound of him bellowing like an outraged bull came from somewhere down-stairs. As she rushed out into the hall the sound of glass breaking, accompanied by his guttural curse, sent her running to see what had happened. Her heart thumped inside her chest as fear began to course through her veins. What on earth could have happened? Was he hurt?

"Will somebody get this damned cat off me?" Ryder shouted when she found him at the bottom of the stair-case.

He was twisting around like a whirling dervish as he tried to reach behind him where Lucifer clung to the middle of his back. The cat screeched and hissed almost as loudly as the rapid-fire curse words Ryder continued to spew out.

"Hold still," Betty Lou commanded, hurrying in from the kitchen. Stepping around the shards of a shat-tered vase that Ryder and Lucifer had knocked off a console table, she carefully tried to disentangle the cat's claws from the fabric of Ryder's shirt. When she finally lifted the cat from his back, she motioned for Summer to step in. "While I get Lucifer calmed down and clean up this glass, see what you can do about smoothing Ry-der's ruffled feathers."

"Are you all right?" Summer asked. "Did you get cut by the glass when the vase broke?"

"No, I'm fine." He scowled. "I swear that cat hates me. And I'm beginning to return the feeling."

"Take off your shirt," she said, noticing some drops of blood dotting the back of it. "Your back is bleeding."

"I'm okay," he insisted, rotating his shoulders. "It's just a few scratches."

"I'm not going to argue with you, Ryder." Why did men have to be so darned stubborn about these things?

"Really, darlin', it's no big deal," he said.

Losing patience, she took him by the hand to lead him up the stairs. "Any time there's a break in the skin, it could become infected. We need to put antibiotic ointment on those scratches."

"I don't see what all the fuss is about," he complained as they entered the master suite and he turned on the bedside lamp. "But if you insist, there should be something in the medicine cabinet in the bathroom."

"Take off your shirt while I go get the ointment," she commanded.

When she found the tube and returned to the bedroom, she stopped short at the sight of Ryder with his shirt off, sitting on the end of the bed. In all of her twenty-five years, she didn't think she had ever seen a more beautiful specimen of a man in his prime. She'd felt the rock hard strength he had been hiding behind his chambray shirts when he held her, but nothing could have prepared her for the perfection of his well-defined chest and finely sculpted abdominal muscles.

She'd known he was in excellent physical condition. He had to be, considering the agility and athleticism required for his job as a bullfighter. But she had never given a thought to how all that would translate to his physique. With his broad shoulders, rippling abs and bulging biceps, he had a body most men envied and women wished their significant other had.

"Summer, are you all right?"

Embarrassed that he had caught her staring, she nodded. "I was wondering if I should go back for bandages."

"No." He shook his head as he turned for her to put the ointment on his back. "I really don't think I need the salve either, but if it makes you feel better, go ahead and put some on the scratches."

"I thought you said you always look up to see where Lucifer is before you walk past the stairs," she said to distract herself. The feel of his warm, firm skin beneath her fingertips caused a pleasant tingling in the pit of her belly and she could swear the temperature in the room had gone up by several degrees.

"Normally, I do make sure I know where he is." Ryder shrugged. "I guess I was distracted about getting things ready so we can take off early tomorrow morning."

"How early is early?" she asked, capping the tube of ointment.

"It's a good six hours' drive up to the fairgrounds where the rodeo is being held, so I'd say we better leave around four or five in the morning." Turning to face her, he smiled as he reached to pull her down onto his lap. "Don't you have to be there by noon?"

"I have to…set up interviews with the local newspaper and…radio stations." With all that bare masculine skin pressed against her side, she was having a little trouble catching her breath. "But that seems awfully… early to be leaving."

"You normally fly when you leave one town to go to

the next one on the rodeo schedule." He grinned. "Road trips take a little longer."

It had been so long since she had traveled by car between the many cities and towns on the circuit, she had forgotten they would need extra time. "I'll be sure to set my alarm," she said, starting to get up from his lap.

He tightened his arms around her to hold her in place. "Don't worry about it. I'll just roll over and wake you."

Her breath lodged in her lungs as she stared at him. She had thought they were going to wait until she stayed with him in his camper before they started trying for her to conceive. But as his green gaze held hers, she realized it was probably for the best that she hadn't had time to anticipate their first time together. There was a very real possibility that if she knew too far in advance her anxiety level would go sky-high and she would lose her nerve again.

Taking a deep breath, she nodded. "I'll go get my pajamas."

"I've been thinking about how to go about getting you past some of your fear," he said slowly. "And I think a compromise is in order."

She wasn't entirely certain she was going to like what he had to say next. But before she could ask what he had in mind, he told her.

"I mentioned that I like to sleep in the buff and you apparently like to be covered up from neck to ankles." He gave her a smile that curled her toes inside her cross trainers. "I'll wear underwear to bed and you can wear your panties and one of my undershirts."

Her heart fluttered wildly. "How is that going to accomplish getting me past the fear of having sex?"

"Before we go any further with this, let's get one thing straight, darlin'." He shook his head. "We aren't going to be having sex. We're going to make love."

"It's the same thing, isn't it?" she asked, frowning.

He hugged her close. "Sex is nothing but mechanics." His tone was so low and intimate it sent shivers of anticipation up her spine. "Making love is two people coming together to bring each other pleasure and to enjoy the shared experience."

She doubted that would be the case for her, but she wasn't going to argue with him. She was still trying to get past the idea of both of them sleeping in the same bed with so little on.

"You still haven't answered my question," she said, finally finding her voice. "How is sleeping in the same bed and wearing so little going to get me past my fear?"

Kissing the top of her head, his deep chuckle seemed to vibrate all the way to her soul. "What do people normally wear when they're making love?"

"Nothing," she said automatically.

He nodded. "And I'm betting that thought bothers you. A lot."

"I…um…well, it does make me a little uncomfortable thinking about it," she admitted.

"Don't you think that us wearing at least a few things to bed would be easier for you in the beginning than if we wore nothing at all?" he asked.

Being naked together wasn't something she had allowed herself to think about before and she wasn't sure she wanted to now. "You're probably right."

When he used his index finger to lift her chin until their eyes met, he asked huskily, "Do you still trust me, Summer?"

She didn't have to think twice about her answer. "Yes."

"Then let's try this." He smiled. "If it doesn't work, then we can always make that appointment with your doctor."

Setting her on her feet, he stood up and, walking over to the dresser, opened one of the drawers. "Here," he said, handing her one of his white cotton undershirts. "While you change and get into bed, I'll go downstairs and turn off the lights."

As she watched Ryder leave the room, she knew he was giving her the time to come to terms with his reasoning. And she had to admit his idea made sense. But as she went into the master bathroom to put the ointment back into the medicine cabinet and change into his undershirt, she wasn't overly confident that it would work.

Hurrying to take off her clothes and put on his shirt, she had just crawled into bed and pulled the comforter up to her chin when Ryder walked into the bedroom and closed the door. "Did Betty Lou get the pieces of the vase cleaned up?" she asked. "I should have helped her with that."

He nodded. "She had everything cleared away and was giving Lucifer a cat treat when I got down there." He shook his head as he sat on the side of the bed to take off his boots. "Can you believe it? He uses me as a scratching post and then gets some kind of reward for doing it."

She appreciated Ryder talking as if they were holding a conversation over coffee instead of getting ready to sleep together. It helped keep her mind off what was about to happen.

"Did you want Betty Lou to give you a cat treat?" she asked, unable to stop a nervous giggle.

Looking over his shoulder at her, he grimaced. "I'm glad to hear you're having a good laugh at my expense." He stood up to remove his jeans. "But you forgot one thing, darlin'."

"Wh-what's that?" she managed to get out as she watched him shove the denim down to his ankles.

"There's this thing called retribution," he said, kicking the garment aside, then turning to stretch out on the bed beside her. Grinning, he reached for her as he added, "And I happen to know just how to even the score."

Apprehension coursed through her a moment before Ryder moved his fingers over her ribs and she dissolved into a fit of laughter. "St-stop," she shrieked as she tried to get away. No match for his strength, she gasped for breath. "Why did I ever…tell you…I'm…ticklish?"

"I don't know, but I'm glad you did." His grin faded as his fingers stilled and his green eyes darkened to a forest-green. "I'm going to kiss you, Summer."

Her pulse sped up as he slowly lowered his head. But the moment their lips met, she eyes drifted shut and she lost herself in the kiss. Moving his mouth over hers, the tenderness and care that he took exploring her brought tears to her eyes. Every time he kissed her it was as if he reaffirmed his commitment to help her get over the assault that had held her prisoner for the past several years.

Using his tongue, he coaxed her to open for him and when she did, the touch of his tongue to hers sent tiny charges of electric current skipping over every nerve ending in her body. But instead of stroking her inner recesses as she expected, he engaged her in a game of advance and retreat as if daring her to do some exploring of her own. As she tentatively followed his lead, she felt his big body shudder when her tongue entered his mouth to taste and tease.

Lost in the heady feeling of being in charge, it took a moment for her to realize that his hand was moving along her side. When he paused at the underside of her breast before cupping its weight in his palm, she caught her breath. The cotton undershirt he had given her to put on was the only barrier between her hardened nipple and his calloused hand, but instead of causing the panicked feeling she expected, a delicious heat began to pool in the pit of her stomach.

The delightful sensations might have continued had she not moved her leg and come into contact with the hard evidence of his arousal straining at his boxer briefs. Her heart skipped a beat and breaking the kiss, she waited to see what happened next.

To her surprise, instead of taking things further, Ryder continued to chafe the tip of her breast as he gave her a brief kiss. Then, removing his hand, he whispered close to her ear, "Don't worry, darlin'. I'm in complete control."

"Are you… I mean, are we going to—"

He held her close as he rolled to his back. "Not tonight."

She couldn't understand the sudden tangle of emotions coursing through her. On one hand, she was relieved that they weren't going to make love. And on the other, she was slightly disappointed. It was the disappointment that she found so confusing.

"Why not?" she asked before she could stop herself.

"Because you're not ready," he said, reaching over to turn off the bedside lamp.

"But you are."

"It doesn't matter." His low chuckle as he pulled the comforter over them caused warmth to spread throughout her chest. "We won't be making love until we're both ready." He pressed a kiss to the top of her head, pillowed on his shoulder. "Now, I suggest you get some sleep because morning will be here before you know it."

Long after she heard Ryder's soft snores, Summer lay awake thinking about his plan to help her overcome her fears. He wasn't going to rush her. He was giving her the time she needed to get used to the idea of sleeping in the same bed with him, used to having him hold and touch her. She knew it had to cost him some measure of physical discomfort, but he was willing to suffer through whatever it took to help her. An unfamiliar emotion began to spread throughout her chest at the thought. How many men would take that kind of care with a woman? Be that understanding?

Feeling more safe and secure than she had in years, she snuggled closer to him. He was her best friend and if she hadn't known that before, she certainly did after his honorable gesture.

But as she started to drift off into a peaceful sleep, her last thought was that she and Ryder had passed a turning point in their relationship—one that neither of them had seen coming and there was no way of reversing now.

Six

"Nate, you look like you don't know whether you lost a horse or just found a halter," Ryder said, spotting his brother leaning against the outside of the arena fence. Normally the most carefree of his brothers, Nate didn't appear to have his head in the game and that could spell disaster for a bull rider. "What's up?"

"Nothing," Nate answered, looking up. He replaced his serious expression with a smile. "I've just been mentally reviewing what I know about the bull I drew for today's round. That's all."

To the outward eye, most anyone would think Nate was shooting straight with them. Ryder knew better. There was a shadow in his brother's eyes that he had never seen before, and Nate's easy expression looked forced.

Lane had been right. There was more going on with

Nate than a case of wounded pride over being dumped for the first time in his life.

Ryder claimed a space along the fence next to his brother and, leaning back against it, folded his arms across his chest. "You want to talk about it?"

"Nope." To his brother's credit, Nate didn't try to deny there was more going on with him than thinking about the bull he'd drawn.

He hadn't expected his brother to open up to him and it wasn't Ryder's style to push the issue. "You know I'll have your back out there. But just in case, keep your mind on business or turn out and call it a day. There's no sense in either one of us getting hurt if you're not up for this."

His suggestion that Nate have the bull released into the arena without riding him when it came his turn, produced the result Ryder had been looking for. Determination had replaced the shadow in Nate's gaze.

"Like hell I will," Nate retorted, shoving away from the fence. "I've never turned out and I'm not about to start now." Squaring his shoulders, he gave Ryder his familiar cocky grin. "You better take your own advice and be a little more careful, brother. You're the one with the sexy lady waiting on you when the round is over."

"Talked to Lane, did you?" Ryder asked. He had expected Nate to mention the new development between himself and Summer at some point.

Nodding, Nate reached behind his thigh to buckle his leather chaps, then did the same with the other leg. "Yeah, Lane was in charge of holding the money for the pool."

"So what was the bet and which one of you won?"

Ryder wasn't the least bit surprised that his brothers had been making wagers on his relationship with Summer. They all made bets with each other on just about everything. Always had and probably always would.

"The bet was a hundred bucks each on how long it would take for you to wake up," Nate answered, laughing. "Jaron won."

"What did I win?" Jaron asked, walking over to join them.

"The pool where you all bet on when I'd wake up and realize Summer is more than my best friend," Ryder said, shaking his head. "So what's the next bet?"

"When the two of you tie the knot," Nate and Jaron both said in unison.

"I've got Thanksgiving," Jaron said, grinning.

Nate nodded. "If you could just hold out until Christmas, I'd appreciate it. I could use the money for Christmas presents."

"I hope you aren't holding your breath for either one of those dates," Ryder grumbled as he turned toward his camper to change into his bullfighting gear. "You'll both turn blue and pass out before that happens."

As he walked the distance to the designated camping area where he'd parked his trailer, he hoped that his talk with Nate helped his brother regain his focus. Otherwise, Nate would end up in a heap on the ground about two jumps into his eight-second ride, and Ryder would be responsible for saving his tail end from being run down by a ton of ornery beef.

Quickly changing into his protective undergear and

the uniform supplied by one of the rodeo association's sponsors, Ryder tied his running cleats, then grabbing his black Resistol, headed back to the arena. That's when he spotted Summer with her electronic tablet, directing photographers where they could safely stand for their action shots.

Watching her, he would be the first to admit she was pretty damned awesome. Every rodeo she coordinated ran like a well-oiled machine and there wasn't a doubt in anyone's mind who was in charge. She was the epitome of self-confidence and had no trouble ordering around men twice her size. That's why it had come as a shock to learn that her strength and self-assuredness didn't extend to her personal life, as well.

He couldn't help but wince when he thought about his role in helping her regain her courage in that particular area. For the past few nights, he had lain awake with his arms around her and his body urging him to sink himself into her softness. But he had promised they would both be ready before they took things to the next level. And he wasn't about to betray that trust, no matter how much his body ached.

Fortunately, he didn't think it would be much longer before she was comfortable enough with him to make love. If her snuggling against him at night was any indication, she trusted him without hesitation. And as far as he was concerned, a woman placing her complete trust in a man was what made the difference between making love and just having sex.

"Hey, cowboy," she said when she looked up to find him watching her. "Are you ready to dance?"

He nodded. "Yup. Dances With Bulls at your service, ma'am."

She reached up to brush a piece of lint from his black shirt. "I'm glad the rodeo association opted to have bullfighters wear these jerseys and athletic shorts. The job you do is too important for you to dress like a clown."

"Yeah, I guess it's hard to take a guy's job all that serious when he's wearing more makeup than most women," he said, grinning.

"Well, now that you mention it, that is a factor," she chuckled. Then her expression turned serious. "Please be careful, Ryder."

When the announcement came across the PA system that bull riding would be the next event, he leaned down and pressed his lips to hers. "Don't worry, darlin'. I understand those old bulls better than I do most people."

Turning, he jogged into the arena and, taking his position beside the chute gates, focused on the task at hand. He could give more thought to Summer's uncharacteristic plea for him to be careful after he'd done his job. Right now, he had over two dozen cowboys, including two of his brothers, counting on him to protect them from animals that had nothing more on their minds than making roadkill out of the person who had the audacity to try to ride them.

"Good luck," he called when he noticed Jaron was in the first group of riders.

"Thanks," his brother answered with a wave of his hand. "I'm going to need it with this one."

With his adrenaline level at its peak, Ryder stepped in when Jaron successfully rode his bull for the full eight seconds. Deftly dodging the animal's sharp horns, he ensured that his brother had time to sprint to the fence and out of danger before he lured the bull to the open gate leading out of the arena.

"Thanks, bro," Jaron said, jumping from his perch on the fence to gather his bull rope and wait for his score to be posted.

"All in a day's work," Ryder replied, grinning as he exchanged a high five with his brother.

As the afternoon wore on, he and the other bull-fighter working the event managed to distract one angry bull after another and keep the riders protected from getting stomped or gored. With only one bull rider left to ride in the day round, Ryder watched Nate climb on the back of Freight Train, a big, black bull known for running over whoever had the misfortune to get in his way.

He hoped Nate's mind was on taking care of business, but when his brother nodded that he was ready and the gate swung open, Ryder knew immediately that Nate was in serious trouble. His balance was off and when the bull went into a flat spin, Ryder's gut clenched as he watched Nate slide down into the well. Being on the inside of the spin was one of the most dangerous places a bull rider could find himself, and to make matters worse, Nate's hand was hung up in the bull rope.

Without a thought to his own safety, Ryder jumped into action, and while the other bullfighter tried to divert the angry animal out of the spin, he ran alongside the bull and worked on the rope to dislodge Nate's hand. Thankfully, Nate had managed to regain his footing when the bull stopped spinning and switched directions to chase the other bullfighter. But when Ryder finally managed to free his brother from the rope, Nate dropped to his knees, making him completely helpless if the bull decided to turn his attention back to the man who had tried to ride him.

"Get up and haul ass, Nate!" Ryder shouted as the bull turned toward him.

Slapping the bull's nose to keep its attention on him, Ryder continued to taunt the animal until he was certain Nate had made it to safety. Only then did he and the other bullfighter maneuver the bull toward the open gate leading out of the arena and back to the holding pens.

Angry with Nate for even attempting the ride when his mind was elsewhere, Ryder was glad that the events were over for the day. Jogging out of the arena, he had every intention of finding his brother and giving him a good tongue-lashing for putting them both in more danger than was necessary.

"Thank goodness you made it out of there without getting injured!" Summer cried, running up to him.

Ryder stopped when he noticed that she was trembling. His problem with Nate's carelessness forgotten, he took her into his arms and hugged her close.

"I'm fine, darlin'." Leaning back to look down at her, he brushed a lock of her honey-blond hair from her creamy cheek. "You've seen me in a lot worse situations than that one. What was there about this time that scared you?"

"I'm not sure, but..." Frowning, she paused for a moment like she might be as surprised by her reaction as he was. "…it seemed to take forever for you to free Nate and for all of you to make it to safety."

"But we made it just fine," Ryder assured her. He looked around as he searched for his brother. "Although, when I get the chance, I've got some choice things to say to Nate that he's not going to be all that fine with."

"I think he and Jaron are already on their way to the training room to gather their things," she said. "Will he be competing tomorrow?"

Ryder nodded. "I'll catch him then." He gave her a kiss, then stepped back. "Right now, I'd better go get a quick shower and change before the barbecue and dance."

"I'll be waiting." Her sweet smile and the promise in her cornflower-blue eyes caused heat to coil low in his belly.

As he turned toward the camping area, one thought kept running through his mind. He was in real trouble if all it took to rev up his libido was one little smile. He had another endless evening ahead of him, holding and kissing her without being able to make love to her.

Ryder shook his head as he entered the camper and went straight to the small shower to turn on the cold water. "It's going to be a long night," he muttered as he stripped out of his uniform and stepped under the stinging spray. He sucked in a sharp breath. "One hell of a long night."

One of the many things Summer liked about her job was the fact that nearly every rodeo had a barbecue and dance after the Saturday events. It didn't matter what town they were in, tables were always piled high with all kinds of food, the scent of burning mesquite hung on the crisp night air, and the live band, although not always the best, played with enough enthusiasm no one cared. Tonight was no different, except for one little detail. Tonight she wasn't with Ryder as just his friend. They were acting like a couple.

Amazingly, no one had appeared to be all that surprised by the change in their relationship status. Not even when they arrived together hand in hand or when they chose a table off to themselves.

After dining on some of the most delicious food she could ever remember, she and Ryder watched the band tune their guitars and adjust their microphones in preparation for the dance to begin. When she glanced up, he was smiling at her.

"Do you have any idea how pretty you are?" he asked, covering her hand with his where it rested on the table.

Her heart skipped a beat at his compliment and the feel of his warm, calloused palm against her much smoother skin. It caused a pleasant tingling to spread throughout her body. "Thank you." She smiled. "You clean up real nice yourself, cowboy."

Her breath caught when she realized they were actually flirting with each other. Was this part of Ryder's plan? Were they role-playing for the benefit of one of their coworkers?

Looking around, she didn't think so. There wasn't anyone they knew close enough to overhear their conversation. Frowning, she realized that for her, their flirting had felt very real.

Before she could speculate further on the matter, he stood up when the band started playing a slow number and held out his hand. "Can I have this dance, darlin'?"

As she stared up at him, her pulse began to race. Like a lot of Texas men, Ryder called all females "darlin'," whether they were one or one hundred. He had called her that from the first time they met and she had never given it a second thought. But this time there was something about the tone of his voice and the look in his eyes that made his use of the word extremely personal. This time, he actually meant it as an endearment. And instead of upsetting her as it might have a week ago, it made her feel incredibly special.

Confused, she placed her hand in his while she tried to process what might be happening between them. He helped her to her feet, then leading her out onto the dance floor, took her in his arms and pulled her to him. Without thinking twice, she wrapped her arms around his waist and it felt like the most natural thing in the world to rest her head against his broad chest.

When they had danced at Sam and Bria's party, they had both been mindful to keep a respectable space between them, to keep things companionable. But tonight there wasn't anything platonic about the way Ryder held her or the way she leaned against him.

As they swayed in time to the music, it felt as if the world was reduced to just the two of them and she had never felt as content as she did at that moment. For the first time in longer than she cared to remember, she felt

as if she was where she belonged. That in itself should
have scared her as little else could. But it didn't. She
knew without question that Ryder would never do anything to harm her, either emotionally or physically. He
was her safe haven.

Not even the feel of his hardening body pressed snug-
gly to her stomach frightened her. Instead, it made her
feel as if the blood in her veins had been turned to warm
honey and created an aching feeling in the most feminine part of her.

"Are you doing okay?" Ryder whispered close to her
ear. "I'm not scaring you, am I?"

For the past several nights as she lay in his arms,
she'd felt his body harden with desire and not once had
he tried to press for them to make love. Leaning back
to look up at him, she shook her head. "I trust you more
than I've ever trusted anyone...and I doubt there's anything about you that would frighten me."

When the song ended, he stared at her for endless
seconds. "Do you want to stay and dance some more?
Or do you think you're ready to go back to my camper?"

There was a spark of need in his eyes that stole her
breath. If she hadn't already felt the evidence of his desire, the look in his dark green gaze would have been
enough to let her know that he wanted her. And with
sudden clarity, she realized he was asking if she was
ready for more than just returning to his trailer for the
night. He was asking if she was ready to make love
with him.

She took a deep breath, then another as she searched
his face. With Ryder she was safe and there wasn't a

doubt in her mind that if she said she wasn't ready, he would accept her decision. But was that what she wanted?

"I think I am ready to leave," she finally said, nodding.

Ryder closed his eyes a moment, then giving her a kiss that caused her head to spin, he took her by the hand and led her through the crowd. "There's Nate with Jaron over there," she said, pointing toward the dessert table. "Didn't you say you wanted to talk to him?"

"Yeah, but taking Nate to task in front of a bunch of people isn't my style," Ryder replied, as they walked across the rodeo grounds toward the camping area. "I'll wait until I can get him alone tomorrow before I chew on his sorry hide." He raised her hand to his mouth to kiss it. "Besides, I have other things on my mind right now."

When they reached his fifth wheel trailer, he unlocked the door, then helped her up the steps. The deluxe camper had more amenities than any hotel room and she could understand why Ryder preferred taking his accommodations with him. It truly was a home away from home. And a very luxurious one at that.

When he closed the door and secured the lock, he turned and immediately reached for her. "You do know I was asking if you felt ready to try making love again?" he asked, raining tiny kisses along the side of her neck.

His warm breath feathering over her skin sent shivers of excitement coursing the length of her and caused her knees to feel as if they were made of rubber. "Y-yes."

"I don't want you to feel rushed, Summer." He reached up to cup her face in his hands. "Are you sure?"

She nodded. "Yes."

His smile sent her temperature soaring. "If at any time you need to slow down or want to call a halt to things, tell me."

"I will."

Lowering his head, he gave her a kiss that sent tiny electric charges skipping over her nerve endings and caused heat to gather in her lower belly. Then, without a word, he took her by the hand and led her up the steps to the bedroom at the front of the camper.

"Aren't you going to turn on the light?" she asked when he knelt to remove her boots, then pulled off his.

"Not unless you want me to." His low, sexy tone caused her insides to feel as if they had been turned to warm pudding. "I want whatever makes you the most at ease with what we're doing."

She nodded as he wrapped his arms around her and hugged her close. "I think I'm good with the light off... for now."

"That's fine, darlin'." He kissed his way from her cheek, down her neck to the fluttering pulse at the base of her throat. "I'm going to take my clothes off first," he murmured against her skin. "Then I'll take off yours."

She briefly wondered why he was telling her everything he was about to do. Then it dawned on her that Ryder was making sure there were no surprises, as well as giving her the opportunity to stop him if her insecurities got the better of her. Her chest tightened with emotion at the lengths he was going to in order to help her overcome her fears.

Neither of them spoke as he removed his shirt and jeans, then reached for the pearl buttons on the front of her pink silk blouse. When his fingers brushed her collarbone as he worked the tiny disks free, she shivered. No other man's touch had ever caused her to feel the excitement or anticipation that Ryder's did. And she knew as surely as she knew her own name that no other man's touch ever would.

Her heart skipped several beats and she struggled to take a breath. Was she beginning to fall for him?

It went without saying that for the past few years she had been closer to him than she had been with any other man. And there was no doubt that she was extremely fond of him. But what she felt now was different and went beyond mere friendship.

"Darlin', I'm going to take off your blouse and unfasten your bra," he whispered, causing her to abandon her unsettling speculation.

When he slowly brushed the pink silk from her shoulders, then released the front clasp of her bra to slide the straps down her arms, he gently pulled her to him. The slight abrasion of his hair-roughened flesh against her overly sensitive nipples sent a need like nothing she had ever known coursing through her.

"O-oh…m-my," she stammered, wrapping her arms around his waist when her knees threatened to give way.

"Are you still doing okay?" he asked, kissing her bare shoulder as he reached between them to unsnap her jeans and slowly slide them down her thighs.

"Mmm…yes," she managed as she kicked the denim aside.

Waves of heat coursed from the top of her head to the tips of her toes when he wrapped his arms around her and covered her mouth with his. His firm lips moved over hers with such tenderness she thought she just might melt into a puddle at his feet. But when he coaxed her to open for him, the feel of his tongue as he stroked hers, the tender care he took as he explored her thoroughly, caused the heat inside of her to tighten into a deep coil of need.

The feeling intensified when he ran his hands down her back to cup her bottom and pull her into the cradle of his hips. The only barriers separating them were his cotton underwear and her lace panties.

"You feel so…good, darlin'." His tone was raspy and it sounded as if he had as much trouble drawing in oxygen as she was having. "Do you need for me to slow down?"

"N-no. I'm fine."

"I'm going to take the rest of our clothes off," he said, raining tiny kisses from her forehead to her chin.

Unable to make her vocal cords work, she simply nodded.

Ryder quickly pushed his boxer briefs down his long legs and kicked them aside, then reaching out, placed his hands at her waist and slowly slid his fingers under the elastic at her waist. Her breath caught at the slight abrasion of his calloused palms skimming over her hips and down her thighs as he lowered her panties.

Stepping out of them, she could hear the beating

of her own heart when he drew her to him. The sudden heat of his hard masculine flesh against her softer feminine skin sent a shock wave of desire all the way through her.

She had expected a moment of panic, but it never came. There was nothing frightening about feeling Ryder's body aligned with hers. Having her breasts crushed against his chest, feeling his hard, hot arousal snug against her lower stomach only caused the need inside of her to intensify.

"Why don't we lie down?" he suggested, swinging her up in his arms to carry her over to the bed. He placed her in the middle of the mattress as if she was a precious gift, then stretched out beside her. "I want you to be completely comfortable with everything we do, Summer." When she started to tell him that she was, he placed his index finger to her lips. "That's why I'm only going to take things so far. I'll make sure we're both ready to make love, then I'm going to let you take control."

"What do you mean?" she asked, confused.

Giving her a kiss hot enough to melt metal, he lightly touched her cheek. "I've seen you flinch a couple of times when I lean over you to kiss you good-night. I think you'll feel more at ease if you're the one on top of me instead of the other way around."

What he said was true. She still felt extremely vulnerable lying flat on her back.

"You don't mind?"

His low chuckle sent a wave of goose bumps over her entire body. "Darlin', you know I'm not an insecure man." She could just make out his wide grin in the darkened room. "Lovin' is lovin' whether I'm on bottom, on top or standing on my head."

Summer smiled. "That last position might be a little difficult."

Shrugging, he brushed her lips with his. "If that's what it takes to make you happy, then I'd give it my best shot."

Her heart swelled with emotion. "Ryder McClain, you're a very special man," she whispered, touching his lean cheek with her fingertips.

"Nah, I'm just a guy trying to help out his best friend," he said, running is hands over her bare back.

His calloused palms felt absolutely wonderful on her sensitized skin, but having him mention their friendship bothered her. And she wasn't entirely certain why. But as he continued to touch her, she gave up trying to pin down the reason she found it unsettling. At the moment, having Ryder's hands on her bare skin was creating far too many delicious sensations within her to concentrate on anything but the way he was making her feel.

When he lowered his lips to hers, she gave herself up to the mastery of his kiss and forgot about anything but the man holding her to him. As his mouth moved over hers, he slid his hand from her back to the underside of her breast, then cupping her, used his thumb to gently chafe the hardened tip. Tiny electric sparks skipped over every part of her and she couldn't have stopped her moan of pleasure if she'd tried.

"Does that feel good, Summer?" he asked, raining

kisses down her neck to her collarbone, then the valley between her breasts.

"Y-yes."

He continued to tease her with his thumb for a moment before kissing his way down the slope of her breast to take her into his mouth. His tongue against her tight flesh caused stars to burst behind her closed eyes and she was certain that if he continued much longer she would surely burn to a cinder.

"Y-you're driving me...crazy," she gasped.

"Darlin', it's only going to get better," he murmured as he moved to take her hand in his. Guiding her to him, he whispered, "I want you to touch me. I want you to see that there's nothing threatening about a man's body."

Doing as he commanded, she tentatively ran her palm over his hard flesh, then the softness below. She felt him shudder with need, but he didn't stop her exploration and made no demands of her.

"Now I'm going to touch you," he said, his tone tight, but nonthreatening.

When he found her, the coil inside her lower body tightened to an almost unbearable ache. "P-please, Ryder."

"What do you want, Summer?"

"You."

Giving her a quick kiss, he rolled to his back and pulled her on top of him. "I'm all yours, darlin'."

True to his word, he was handing her control and making sure she wasn't threatened by his much larger body hovering over hers, pinning her down, trapping her. His concessions caused a deep emotion she didn't dare identify to fill her chest as she straddled his lean hips.

When he helped her guide him to her, she closed her eyes as she slowly took him in. She didn't think she had ever felt more complete as she did at that moment. It was as if she had finally found a part of herself that she hadn't even realized was missing.

Placing his hands at her hips, he helped her set an easy pace as she began to rock against him. Her body quickly responded to being at one with him and all too soon she felt herself reaching for the completion they both sought.

"I'm going to touch you again, darlin'," Ryder said, sliding his hand between them.

The moment he stroked the tiny nub of sensation, the tight coil inside of her set her free and wave after wave of intense pleasure flowed through her. A moment later she felt Ryder go completely still, then with a low, raspy groan he wrapped his arms around her and released his sperm deep inside of her.

Collapsing on top of him, Summer felt as if their souls had touched and she knew in that moment why his calling her his friend bothered her. Ryder was more than her friend, he was the man she was falling for.

Seven

The following morning, Ryder watched Summer from across the pressroom as she sat in on an interview a reporter from a national magazine was doing with Nate. A top contender for the Champion All-Around Cowboy title, his brother's outgoing personality and quick wit were exactly what the rodeo association was looking for to promote their upcoming national finals.

But as proud as Ryder was of his brother and his accomplishments, his main focus was on Summer. She was amazing and without a doubt the most captivating, desirable woman he had ever met. What he couldn't get over was why he had been immune to her charms before. How could he have been so blind?

When they had returned to his camper from the dance last night, he'd half expected for her to decide that she wasn't yet ready to make love. And although he hadn't looked forward to it, he had been fully prepared to endure a shower cold enough to freeze the balls off a pool table.

But Summer had surprised him and they had shared the most mind-blowing night of lovemaking he had ever experienced. He had done everything he could think of to make her feel as comfortable as possible, and with the exception of wanting the light off, she had been fine. She had even seemed to forget that they were making love for the purpose of conceiving a baby. For that matter so had he. All he'd been able to think about was the woman in his bed and how she excited him in ways he could have never imagined.

He frowned as he mulled that over. When had he lost sight of wanting to help Summer with her request of having a baby and simply started wanting her?

He had come to terms with the notion that their friendship had been permanently altered. That had happened the first time he had kissed her. In all of his thirty-three years, he'd never tasted lips so sweet or as soft as Summer's.

But what bothered him the most about the whole damn thing was that he could very well be helping her get over her fears of intimacy only to have her meet another man she decided she could settle down with. Then where would he be? He would not only lose his best friend, he would forfeit the right to make love to the most exhilarating woman he had ever known.

He tried to tell himself that it didn't matter since they really had no future together. Besides the fact that he didn't want to saddle any woman with his past, how could he tell Summer that the man she thought had such a high degree of integrity was a miserable fraud?

The thought had Ryder getting up from the chair he had been sitting in to amble out of the pressroom into the hallway. What the hell was wrong with him?

He wasn't interested in taking their relationship any further than they already had. So why did he have a knot the size of a football twisting his gut at the thought of Summer finding out about his past or moving on with her life in the arms of another man?

"Bro, you look like you got hold of a persimmon that wasn't quite ripe," Nate said, striding up to him as he walked out of the pressroom. "Are you all right?"

"Yeah, but you're not going to be if you pull another stunt like the one you did yesterday," Ryder shot back. It was easier to focus on his brother's lack of concentration yesterday in the bull riding event than it was to think about what he could never have with Summer. "If your head isn't in the game, don't climb on the back of another bull and risk getting into a wreck that might get you hurt real bad or worse."

Nate had the good sense not to argue. "I'm sorry about yesterday. But don't worry, bro. I've got things under control now." He grinned. "You know it's hard to keep me down for very long."

"Already turning on the charm with another unsuspecting woman, are you?" Ryder asked, relieved to see that Nate was more himself than he had been the day before.

"Nope." Nate shrugged. "I've decided to take a break

from the ladies for a while and focus on winning the All-Around."

Ryder frowned. Lane had been right; there was a lot more going on with Nate than a case of wounded pride. He must have fallen pretty hard for that nurse he'd been seeing if he was willingly giving up female companionship in favor of a rodeo title.

Before he could caution his brother further, Summer's hand on his arm stopped him. "Ryder, when you get time, I need to talk with you before the events start," she said, giving him a smile that caused his jeans to feel like they were a couple of sizes too small in the stride.

"Sure thing, darlin'." He turned back to Nate. "You know I'll have your back out there this afternoon. But remember what I said and pay attention to what you're doing."

"Will do," Nate said before he walked down the hall toward the training room.

"Is he all right?" Summer asked.

"I think so." Ryder put his arm around her shoulders and started back toward the pressroom. "Now what do you need to talk to me about?"

When they entered the empty room, she closed the door behind them. "I just wanted to tell you to be safe out there this afternoon," she said, wrapping her arms around his waist.

Hugging her close, he nodded. "I'll make sure of it. I have plans for tonight."

"Really?"

He lowered his head to brush her perfect coral lips

with his. "Oh yeah. I think we should skip the dance this evening and go to bed early."

"You're already sleepy?" The twinkle in her blue eyes indicated that she knew better.

"Darlin', when we go to bed tonight, I seriously doubt that sleeping will be on either of our minds," he murmured, kissing her until they both gasped for breath. "Are you doing all right? You should have woke me when you got up this morning."

"I couldn't be better," she said, rising on tiptoes to kiss his chin. "And you were sleeping so peacefully, I couldn't bring myself to wake you. Your job is so much more physically demanding than mine, I wanted you to rest."

"So now you're taking care of me?" Other than his brothers and his foster father, Hank, no one had ever bothered to look after his well-being.

She looked thoughtful for a moment, then nodded. "You're so busy watching out for everyone else, you need someone to take care of you."

Before he could respond, a knock on the pressroom door caused Summer to pull from his arms. When the door opened, a man holding a microphone like it was some kind of trophy walked in. "Excuse me, but would either of you know where I could find the PR guy?"

The man inquiring looked to be somewhere around his own age and a little too slick and sure of himself. "Who wants to know?" Ryder asked, taking an instant dislike to the man.

"I'm Chip Marx from Live Eye News," the fellow answered, managing to look down his nose at Ryder even though he was a good six inches shorter than Ryder's six-foot-two-inch frame.

He acted like they should immediately recognize him and his name. Besides finding the guy irritating as hell, it didn't mean squat to Ryder.

"I'm Summer Patterson, the regional rodeo association's public relations director," she said, extending her hand. "What can I do for you, Mr. Marx?"

The little weasel's demeanor changed immediately. "Well, now, this is a pleasant surprise," Marx said, flashing a bleach-toothed grin as he took her hand. He didn't shake it, but continued to hold on to it. "I can tell I'm going to enjoy doing this story after all."

Ryder watched Summer tug her hand free before reaching for a copy of the press release she had prepared. "Here's the information you'll need. If you have any questions, let me know. Since this is the last day and most of the cowboys are already getting ready to compete, I doubt that I'd be able to arrange an interview with one of them." She nodded cordially at him. "They usually take off to make the trip to the next rodeo as soon as the events are over with on the last day."

"Oh, this isn't for this week's dog and pony show," he said, laughing as he shook his head. "I'm here to do an advance story on the rodeo next week down in New Mexico. I'd also like for my cameraman to get some footage of the cowboys doing whatever it is they do."

"All right," Summer said, sounding reluctant. Ryder could tell she didn't like the guy any more than he did. "I'll arrange for a couple of seats in the VIP area. It's closer to the arena action. You should get some pretty good footage of the events from there."

"We would rather follow you around and get some of the behind-the-scenes stories." Marx pointed to his cameraman just outside the door. "He can get some video of the animals as well as the cowboys preparing for their rides."

"That isn't going to happen, Mr. Marx." Ryder had seen that look of determination on Summer's face before. She was the one calling the shots and wasn't about to let the guy dictate to her what he was going to do. "For one thing, this is a rodeo. It's not a 'dog and pony show.' And for another, you don't tell me what you're going to do. I tell you. The reason for that is to ensure your safety as well as that of the crew behind the chutes. Now if you can accept those terms, I'll be more than happy to arrange for you to get your story. If you can't, then our business here is finished."

Ryder had never been more proud of her. He had seen her deal with pushy reporters before, and he could have told Marx his dictatorial tactics wouldn't work. But watching her tell the man in no uncertain terms that she was in charge was a lot more enjoyable.

The guy didn't look the least bit happy, but apparently realizing Summer wasn't going to budge, he shrugged. "Well, I suppose we could get whatever footage we need from the VIP section." He flashed his practiced grin. "Would it be possible to get an interview with you after the events are over?"

"That could probably be arranged," she answered slowly. "But it will have to be brief."

"That's fine," Marx said. "I'll get what I can today and then set up something with you for next week's rodeo."

"I'll call the VIP attendant and have your seats waiting for you," Summer said, dismissing the man.

Marx looked like he would like to say more, but instead turned and walked out without so much as a thank-you. "Someone needs to teach that jerk some manners," Ryder said darkly.

"I've dealt with his type before," she replied, shrugging as she reached for her cell phone.

Ryder checked his watch. "While you make that call, I'll go get changed." He gave her a quick kiss. "I'll see you in a little while, darlin'."

"Be careful," she said, looking a little worried.

"Always am," he assured her.

During the bull riding event, Summer was too nervous to watch Ryder play tag with a ton of bovine fury. It was completely ridiculous, considering she had seen him do it almost every weekend for the past three years. But that was before he'd held her, kissed her, made love to her.

Busying herself with clearing out the pressroom to keep her mind off what was happening between them, an ominous announcement over the loud speaker caused a chill to snake up her spine and sent her running toward the area behind the chutes. The medical trainers were calling for an ambulance to enter the arena. That meant someone had been injured. And it was serious if they weren't bringing the rider back to the training room for evaluation before sending him on to the hospital.

Searching for Ryder, her heart felt as if it stopped beating completely until she spotted him kneeling beside a rider lying facedown in the loose dirt on the arena floor. Weak with relief, she looked around to make sure the fallen rider wasn't one of his brothers.

"Who is it?" she asked the chute boss.

He named one of the younger cowboys, then added, "The kid fell forward on Sidewinder's first jump out of the gate and knocked himself out. If it hadn't been for Ryder, that boy would have been a goner for sure. As soon as he hit the dirt, Ryder fell on top of him to protect him from getting kicked or stomped."

"Is Ryder okay?" she asked, holding her breath. On several different occasions she had seen him put himself in jeopardy to protect a cowboy who had no chance of protecting himself.

"I think he might have been shook-up when Sidewinder butted him in the side, but that's about it," the man answered. "He might be a little sore in the morning, but his Kevlar vest should have kept him from getting a couple of cracked ribs."

Once she learned that the young cowboy had regained consciousness and would be transported to the hospital for a CT scan and observation, the bull riding resumed and Summer had to wait until the rest of the event was concluded before she could approach Ryder. It felt like an eternity. She needed to talk to him and see for herself that he was all right.

As she impatiently paced the area behind the chutes,

she tried to figure out why she was so anxious…why she was more upset by his bravery than she had ever been before. She had always known it was his job to put himself between the cowboys and the dangerous bulls. He was one of the best and hundreds of men had Ryder to thank for saving them from serious injury and, in some cases, for saving their lives.

But the stakes had been raised and she had a feeling she knew why. She had always been fond of him, but this time she was seeing his acts of heroism through the eyes of a woman who was falling harder for him than she had any other man.

Summer took a bolstering breath as she acknowledged her feelings. She had suspected her feelings for him had developed into something much deeper than mere friendship after they made love last night, but she had refused to think about it. She had told herself not to jump to conclusions—that it was probably just the afterglow of their lovemaking she was experiencing. She knew now that her feelings went far deeper than that.

"Darlin', if you don't stop pacing, you're going to wear the dirt down to bedrock," Ryder said from behind her.

Turning, she hurried over to him and threw her arms around his neck. "Are you all right?"

His arms immediately closed around her. "I'm fine. Old Sidewinder just gave me a couple of nudges to tell me hello."

Suddenly angered by his casual dismissal of what had been a very serious situation, she stepped away from him. "Don't you dare say it was nothing, Ryder

McClain! You could have been hurt or worse. What if that stupid bull had stepped on you?"

"Whoa! Where's this coming from?" He looked confused. "You know it's my job to save riders. Hell, you've seen me do it at least a hundred times over the past few years."

"That was before," she protested, knowing she was overreacting but unable to stop herself.

He frowned. "Before what?"

She couldn't tell him that she had fallen for him. "We'll talk about this tonight," she said before turning to walk back to the pressroom. "I have to get things packed up and ready for next weekend."

"I'll help you," he said, falling into step beside her.

Out of the corner of her eye, she saw him glance at her several times as if trying to figure out what had gotten into her. She knew beyond a shadow of doubt what the problem was, but how was she supposed to explain that for the first time, instead of seeing him as a friend and coworker putting himself in danger, she had been watching through the eyes of a woman who was on the verge of falling head over heels in love with him? She hadn't fully come to terms with it herself and he probably wasn't expecting to hear it anyway.

"Did you get the interview with that little weasel over with?" he asked.

"Oh rats! I forgot all about that." How could a day start out to be so good, then turn into a royal headache so fast?

When they entered the pressroom, she sighed. Chip Marx was waiting for her.

"I was beginning to wonder if you were going to stand me up," he said, his smile barely hiding his impatience.

"I'm sure you can understand that when we have a rider taken away by ambulance it's a serious matter," she said, doing her best not to lose her temper with the man. "My first priority is to get accurate information about the cowboy's injuries and assess whether I need to notify his family or make a statement to the media."

"Of course." He didn't look at all as if he understood or cared. "Why don't we do a dinner interview? That way I'll have your undivided attention."

When Summer glanced at Ryder, she caught her breath. He looked furious. And she couldn't blame him. She was angered by the man's insensitivity, as well. He hadn't even bothered to ask if the injured rider was going to be all right.

"I'm sorry, but I won't have time to talk with you after all, Mr. Marx."

"Please, call me Chip," he said, his tone suggestive.

He gave her a grin that she was sure he'd stood in front of a mirror practicing—probably for years. If he thought it would win her over, he was sadly mistaken.

"As I told you, I don't have time…Chip." She hadn't meant for his name to come out sounding as if she said a dirty word, but at the moment she really didn't care.

"You have to eat anyway," he insisted. "It might as well be with me."

She'd just as soon dine with a snake. "Thank you, but I meant it when I said I don't have time. Now, if you'll excuse me, I have to get the rest of the pressroom shut down and ready to move on to the venue in New Mexico."

The man didn't seem to grasp the concept that she wanted nothing more to do with him and, stepping forward, took hold of her arm. "Surely you can—"

"The lady says she doesn't have time," Ryder interrupted, moving in to wrap his hand around the man's wrist and remove it from her arm. "Now, I suggest you take Ms. Patterson at her word and find another story."

She had only heard Ryder use that deadly tone one other time. The night she had told him about being raped.

Ryder must have applied pressure to the man's wrist because Chip Marx let out a yelp and winced in pain. "You can't do this." He glared at his cameraman. "Don't just stand there! Get footage of this. I'll need it when I sue this goat roper for assault."

The cameraman glanced from Marx to Ryder, then back to Marx. "You're on your own, Chip," he said, turning to walk out of the room. "I didn't see a thing."

Summer had never seen Ryder look as dangerous as he did at that moment and she couldn't say she blamed the cameraman for bailing on the arrogant reporter. Calling a cowboy a "goat roper" was extremely insulting and not at all wise when the cowboy in question had a vise-grip hold on your arm.

"It's all right, Ryder," she said, hoping to defuse the situation. "He was just leaving, weren't you, Mr. Marx?"

Before the reporter could answer, Ryder nodded toward the door. "You'd better take her advice, Marx. Otherwise, you'll force me to kick your ass. Since I'm still wearing cleats, something tells me that would make the experience doubly painful. And just so we have things straight…I'd better not catch you bothering Ms. Patterson again." Turning the man loose, he finished, "Because if you do, you'll be picking your bleached teeth up off the floor. Are we clear on that?"

His face beet-red, Chip Marx turned to rush from the room. But apparently as stupid as he was arrogant, he turned back for one parting shot. "This isn't over."

"Yes, it is," Ryder said, taking a step forward. The man fled as if he was being chased by the devil.

"Thank you, Ryder, but I'm sure I could have handled that situation myself," she said, reaching for a stack of brochures. She wasn't at all sure, but she didn't want him to know just how vulnerable she had felt.

He shook his head. "I know you're capable of taking care of most things like this, and I'm fine with that. But when that lowlife put his hand on you…" His voice trailed off for a moment before he took a deep breath and cleared his throat. "I'm not going to apologize because I'm not sorry I stepped in." Turning, he walked to the door. "And just so you know. As long as I have breath in my body, no man will ever treat you the way that bastard just tried to do and get away with it."

Long after Ryder left, Summer stared at the empty doorway. For the past several years, she had dealt with pushy reporters who thought they could bully or charm her into doing what they wanted and she'd never had a problem putting them in their place. But until today, none of them had ever crossed the line and put his hands on her.

She shuddered as she finished packing the small container with brochures and picked it up to leave. The only man's touch that didn't make her want to shrink away in revulsion, the only man she ever wanted to touch her, was Ryder.

Her heart skipped a beat as she acknowledged her feelings. She had tried to avoid putting a name to how her relationship with him had evolved. Acting as if they were a couple was only supposed to have been roles they were playing for the benefit of their coworkers and his brothers in preparation for the baby they were going to have together. But there was no sense in evading any longer what she knew in her heart was true. Even if she didn't feel she could reveal to him how she really felt, she could at least admit it to herself. She had fallen in love with Ryder McClain.

Ryder leaned up against the side of the arena, waiting on Summer. After leaving the pressroom, he had decided to make sure that Marx was long gone and wouldn't give her any more trouble. And he had no doubt that if given the chance, the man was stupid enough to try putting the moves on her again. Pushy little weasels like Marx thought they were God's gift to women and couldn't get it through their thick heads that they weren't adored by every female they came in contact with.

He sighed heavily. The last thing he had wanted was for her to see him lose his temper. And he'd been damned close to doing just that. Fortunately, for her sake as well as Marx's, Ryder had been able to keep a tight rein on his control.

He couldn't have cared less that the man had insulted him. As far as he was concerned, Marx's opinion of him didn't matter one way or the other. But when he grabbed Summer's arm, Ryder had damned near come unglued. It had taken every ounce of restraint he had in him to keep from knocking the jerk into the middle of next week. Unfortunately, he couldn't guarantee that the next time he would be able to stop himself. And that bothered him almost as much as Marx putting his hand on Summer.

"I thought you left to go back to the camper to shower and change clothes," Summer said, stopping in front of him as she left the arena.

"Nope." He shoved away from the wall to take the small box she carried. "I thought I'd stick around to carry this for you."

As they walked across the fairgrounds toward his camper, they fell silent. He hated the awkwardness and figured she was still upset that he hadn't let her handle Marx on her own. But he had told her the truth. As long as he was around, no one would ever lay an unwelcomed hand on her.

Stowing the container in the outside cargo area of the fifth wheel, he unlocked the door and helped her up the steps. "As soon as I shower and get changed, we can go to the barbecue if you'd like."

"I thought you wanted to stay in this evening," she said, frowning. "I was going to make some sandwiches for us."

"After that run-in with Marx, I wasn't sure you'd want—" Stopping himself, Ryder shook his head. "Never mind. Whatever you want to do is fine with me."

She stared at him for several seconds, then surprising the hell out of him, moved closer to wrap her arms around him. His arms automatically closed around her to hold her close.

"Today was the first time since I started this job that I felt threatened," she said, her voice trembling. "I didn't want to admit it, but when Chip Marx took hold of my arm, I was actually afraid."

"Summer, I was right there with you." Ryder leaned back to look down at her. "You've got to know there's no way in hell I'd ever let him do anything to you."

She nodded. "I know that. And I wasn't upset with you for stepping in to stop him. I was mad at myself for allowing him to frighten me." She shuddered against him. "But he gives me the creeps."

"Forget about Marx. He's not worth the time and trouble to give him a second thought." He kissed the tip of her nose. "Now, while I go take a shower, why don't you make those sandwiches."

"I can do that," she said, her sweet smile sending his hormones racing around like the steel bearings in a pinball machine.

He swallowed hard and forced himself to climb the steps to the upper level of the camper. "I'll only be a few minutes."

Showering in record time, he wrapped a towel around his waist and walked into the bedroom. He stopped short at the sight of Summer wearing nothing but his T-shirt and her panties.

Her cheeks turned pink as she grabbed her robe and held it in front of her. "I thought your shower would take a little longer."

"Nope."

"Since we aren't going out...I thought I would change into something more comfortable," she said hesitantly. Her gaze drifted to his bare chest and she reached out to lightly touch the small white scar just below his left pectoral muscle. "I didn't notice this the other night when I put ointment on the scratches. What happened?"

Ryder clenched his teeth at the surge of heat caused by her fingertips caressing his skin. "I got hooked by a bull about ten years ago."

"You weren't wearing your Kevlar vest?" she asked, stepping closer. She rested her palm over the scar and he felt like he'd been branded.

The light herbal scent of her hair and her soft touch caused his body to harden and he had to clear his throat before he could answer. "It didn't happen at a rodeo. I was helping Hank move one of his herds and a bull got loose. When it started to charge him, I figured I had a better chance of dodging it than he did because I could move a little faster."

She raised her eyes to meet his and the spark of desire he detected in the blue depths robbed him of breath. "You're a true hero, Ryder McClain."

Taking the robe from her other hand, he tossed it aside then took her in his arms and pulled her close. "Summer, I'm flattered that you think I'm such a nice guy. But I didn't do anything more than any other man would have done in the same situation."

"You're my hero," she insisted, gazing up at him.

As they stared at each other, Ryder felt guilty as hell. He didn't deserve her admiration, but he couldn't tell her that the man she held in such high regard wasn't what she thought he was.

To distract her from saying something else that would only end up making him feel even worse than he already did, he lowered his mouth to hers. The sweet taste of her lips quickly had him forgetting about anything but the woman in his arms and how much he wanted her. Considering that the only things keeping him from having all of her against him was the towel around his waist and the thin cotton T-shirt and panties she had on, it was no wonder his lower body had come to full alert.

When she raised her arms to wrap them around his neck and leaned more fully against him, he half expected her to bolt at the feel of his arousal pressed to her soft stomach. But to his immense satisfaction, instead of pulling away, her lips parted on a sigh. Encouraged by her response, he deepened the kiss to coax and tease.

"Darlin'...I think...we'd better...slow down," he said when he broke the kiss to nibble his way along her jaw to the delicate shell of her ear. "I give you my word that nothing is going to happen unless you want it to, but I'm hotter than a two-dollar pistol on Saturday night and want you more now than I've ever wanted anything in my entire life."

"But it's not...dark yet," she said, looking a little unsure despite the blush of desire coloring her cheeks.

Ryder laughed, releasing some of the tension that gripped him. "Our bodies will fit together just as well in the daylight as they do in the dark."

"I'm well aware of that, cowboy," she retorted, giving him a look that suggested he might be a little simple-minded. "But when it's dark it's not as easy to see..." Her voice trailed off and her cheeks turned a deeper shade of pink.

He could have told her that although his T-shirt covered her from neck to midthigh, it was still thin enough for him to see the silhouette of her delightful curves and the shape and size of her perfect breasts. But he wisely kept that bit of information to himself. Although she had become a little more comfortable with intimacy in the past few days, she still had a couple of lingering issues.

"Do you still want to make a baby with me, Summer?" he said huskily.

"Yes. But—"

"And do you still trust me?" he asked.

She nodded. "Of course."

He gave her a quick kiss. "I give you my word on this, darlin'. I won't see any more of you than what you want me to see."

Eight

Ryder's heated look sent a wave of goose bumps shimmering over her skin as he swung her up into his arms, then placing her in the middle of the bed, reached for the towel at his waist. Scrunching her eyes shut, Summer waited until she felt him stretch out beside her and pull the sheet over them.

Opening her eyes, she turned onto her side to face him. "You certainly aren't shy about your body."

"Nope." He smiled. "Most guys aren't hung up with modesty issues like women are."

"I wonder why?"

He reached out to take her in his arms. "Do you really want to talk about the lack of inhibitions in men right now?"

The hunger in his eyes stole her breath and she suddenly wasn't sure what he had asked her. When he covered her mouth with his, she decided it really didn't matter. All she could think about was the way Ryder was making her feel.

Less than a week ago, she had thought she was immune to desire and passion. But Ryder's kiss, his gentle touch and the concessions he had made for her peace of mind, had not only convinced her that her trust was well placed, it created a need in her stronger than she had ever dreamed possible.

Parting her lips, she welcomed him slipping his tongue inside to explore her with a thoroughness that sent a delicious warmth coursing throughout her body. But when he slowly glided his hand down her thigh to the hem of the T-shirt she was wearing and lifted it as he brought his hand back up to cup her breast, the heat inside of her coiled into a pool of deep need.

"Look at me, Summer," he whispered close to her ear. When her eyes met his, he smiled. "I'm going to take off this shirt and your panties now, darlin'."

A shiver of anticipation made its way up her spine as he swept the T-shirt up and over her head, then reached for the elastic at her waist. Not once did his gaze waver from hers and by the time the scrap of satin and lace was sent to join the shirt over the side of the bed, she realized that Ryder had kept his word. He hadn't so much as glanced at her body. She loved him even more for his integrity and the understanding he had shown for her self-consciousness.

Her heart skipped a beat and she closed her eyes as she felt her love for him blossom. She was no longer making love with her best friend in order to have a baby. She was making love with her soul mate—the man she had fallen hopelessly in love with. She had even forgotten all about their coming together for her to become pregnant.

But apparently he hadn't lost sight of the reason behind the intimacy they had shared last night and were about to share again. Why else would he have mentioned it?

She sighed. If he was still focused on their goal, that meant his feelings for her hadn't developed into anything more than what they had always felt for each other—a deep abiding friendship and a wealth of mutual respect.

Before she could give the matter more thought and come to terms with the fact that Ryder might not ever feel anything more for her, his fingers grazed her cheek. "What's wrong, Summer?"

When she opened her eyes, he was propped up on one elbow, staring down at her, his expression reflecting his concern. Reaching up, she cupped his lean cheek with her palm. "How could anything be wrong?" she asked, evading his question. "My best friend and I are about to make a baby."

He stared at her for endless seconds, as if trying to determine the real reason behind her heartfelt sigh, then lowering his lips to hers, gave her a kiss so tender it caused tears to flood her eyes. Ryder might be a giant compared to her petite frame, but he was the most gentle man she had ever known.

As he deepened the kiss to tease and explore her with feathery flicks of his tongue, his hand moved along her

side and down her thigh. Caressing the back of her knee
for a moment, he skimmed his palm back up to the apex
of her thighs. Parting her, his touch caused her body
to hum with an energy that threatened to consume her.

Lost in the delightful sensations he aroused in the
most feminine part of her, it took a moment for her to
realize that he was lifting her leg to drape it over his
hips. "Ryder?"

"We're going to make love face-to-face, Summer.
You need to see that it's me making love to you, not
some selfish bastard taking what he wants." He kissed
her bare shoulder. "I want to watch the moment I bring
you pleasure…and I want you to see me when you help
me find mine."

Her chest swelled with emotion. Ryder was an incredibly compassionate man. He had vowed to help her
get over her intimacy issues, and he was doing everything he could to reassure her that she was safe in his
arms.

Before she could find her voice to tell him how much
his consideration meant to her, he moved to align their
hips and she felt his blunt tip poised to enter her. His
green eyes darkened as he captured her gaze with his
and he slowly pressed forward. Feeling herself become
one with the man she loved, seeing the tender passion
on his handsome face as he filled her was utterly breathtaking.

With their eyes locked, he slowly began to move
within her. Neither spoke as their bodies communi-
cated in ways no words could ever express and all too
soon, Summer felt the coil of need inside of her begin

to tighten as she moved closer to the pinnacle. Her body ached to hold on, to prolong the moment of being one with Ryder, but he deepened his thrusts and she suddenly felt herself trembling from the pleasure rushing through every part of her. Unable to stop herself, she closed her eyes as she savored the exquisite feelings of unbridled fulfillment.

Ryder suddenly went completely still for a moment. Opening her eyes to focus on the man she loved with all her heart and soul, Summer watched as he found the satisfaction of his own release. A groan rumbled up from deep in Ryder's chest as his big body shuddered against her and he filled her with his essence.

For the next several days when he wasn't in the open-air arena at the fairgrounds just outside of Albuquerque saving some poor rodeo rider's hide from being stomped on by a bull, Ryder found himself hanging around the press tent. He liked watching Summer do her job. She was nothing short of a miracle worker when it came to dealing with schedule changes and any number of other problems that arose at the last minute. He had watched her put together press kits and arrange a goodwill trip for some of the cowboys to a children's wing in one of the hospitals, in addition to coordinating interviews with the media so they could get their stories and photographs without being in harm's way.

Walking up behind her, he wrapped his arms around her waist and pulled her back against him. "Do you have any idea just how incredible you are, Summer Patterson?"

"Incredibly tired is more like it," she sighed, leaning back against him. "I haven't been getting a lot of sleep lately."

He turned her to face him. "Is that a complaint?"

Her sweet smile sent his temperature sky high. "Not at all, cowboy. I've just recently discovered how relaxing nighttime activities can be."

Laughing out loud, Ryder pulled her to him for a quick hug. "We can always skip the barbecue and dance tonight and turn in early."

"I'm actually looking forward to the party," she said, snuggling closer. "After tonight I won't have to worry about the possibility of running into a certain pushy reporter who has a problem taking 'no' for an answer."

"Has old Chip contacted you?" he asked, hoping like hell the man had the good sense to look elsewhere for a story. He didn't like any man who tried to get a woman to bend to his will, but the behavior Chip Marx had displayed bordered on harassment and Ryder wasn't about to tolerate it.

"No, I haven't heard from Mr. Marx and I doubt that I will now. Since everything is drawing to a close today, he's missed his chance to find something to report." She rose up on tiptoe to kiss his lips. "Thanks to you, I'm pretty sure he got the message."

"He'd better," Ryder said, then reluctantly took a step back. "I need to go change and get ready to tango with a bunch of bovines."

"Be careful and save some of those dance moves for tonight," she said, smiling as she turned back to straighten a display of promotional items.

As he left the tent and headed toward the trailer, Ryder couldn't help but grin. Summer had conquered most of her intimacy issues, and although she was still hung up on how much they saw of each other in the bedroom, she seemed completely comfortable making love with him. In fact, she had even initiated their lovemaking last night.

His easy expression faded and he couldn't help but wonder what would happen once she became pregnant. Would he continue to have the privilege of holding her every night, to be able to make love to the most captivating woman he had ever met? Or would they try to return to the easy friendship they had enjoyed before?

He shook his head as he let himself into the trailer and gathered his bullfighting gear. He didn't see any way in hell they could go back. Not when he knew how responsive she was to his touch, how when they made love he felt like he had finally discovered the other half of himself.

Sucking in a sharp breath, he stood as still as a marble statue. Had he fallen in love with Summer? Was that why he couldn't imagine his life going on without the sweet intimacy they shared?

With his heart thumping against his ribs, he cursed his foolishness and finished getting ready to do his job. He wasn't in love with Summer. She was his best friend and the woman he was trying to make a baby with. He had the same needs as any other normal, red-blooded male and after a long dry spell without the softness of a woman, it was only natural that making love to her every night was influencing his emotions.

He stood up to leave the trailer and go back to the arena. And if he kept outlining all the reasons why he was starting to feel the way he did about Summer, he just might start to believe them.

Ryder held her hand as they walked to the pavilion where the after-rodeo barbecue and dance were being held. Truth be told, Summer didn't think she had ever been happier. Since beginning their physical relationship, she had started feeling like a woman again and not the skittish female who shuddered at the thought of being alone with a man. It was empowering and she loved the cowboy walking beside her for the special man he was and for helping her heal the emotional scars she hadn't thought she could ever overcome.

"I don't know what you're thinking, but it must be pretty nice," Ryder murmured, leaning down close to her ear in order to be heard above the live band.

"Why do you say that?" she asked, unwilling to reveal her feelings before she knew for certain he felt the same.

"Because you look like you know something nobody else knows and you can't wait to share it," he said with a wide grin.

"Maybe I do." She loved the intimate teasing and playfulness that had developed between them over the past couple of weeks.

"Want to let me in on the secret?" he asked, looking as if he already knew what she might be thinking.

"Not yet."

She actually had more than one secret, but she wasn't

going to jinx either one of them by talking about them too soon. She was certain that she loved Ryder and she would eventually tell him when the time was right. But her other secret was one that would take a trip to the drugstore and the purchase of an early pregnancy test to confirm. She was only a couple of days late, but due to the fact that her cycle had always been quite regular and she hadn't had any of the premenstrual symptoms she normally experienced, she was almost positive they had already been successful in conceiving.

"Let's dance," she said, tugging him toward the dance floor when the band started playing a slow tune.

When he took her in his arms, Summer leaned against him and realized that she was never more content than when they were holding each other. And knowing him the way she did, she had a feeling Ryder just might be feeling the same way.

"While I go get us a couple of drinks, why don't you find a table, darlin'?" he said when the dance ended.

Kissing his chin, she grinned. "You've got a deal, cowboy."

When she spotted an empty table in a secluded corner of the pavilion, Summer started toward it. She liked the idea of being able to talk with Ryder and not have to worry about being overheard. But as she made her way along the edge of the crowd, she stopped short when an imposing figure stepped out of the shadows and into her path.

"Well, imagine meeting you here," Chip Marx said, his speech slurred. He had obviously had too much to drink and, if the sarcastic expression on his face was any indication, he wasn't a very nice drunk.

"Good evening, Mr. Marx," she responded, attempting to step around him.

He caught her by the wrist to stop her. "Hey, where you going?"

A cold chill slithered up her spine. But she wasn't going to let him see that he was frightening her. Arrogant jerks like Marx fed on fear and intimidation. If she could keep from it, she refused to give him that kind of power over her.

"It's none of your business where I'm going," she said, pulling her arm back in an attempt to break his hold.

He tightened his grip and her hand began to ache from having the circulation cut off. "Where's your friend?" he asked, glancing around. "I'll bet you're not nearly as high-and-mighty when the goat roper isn't around."

"Number one, I don't appreciate you insulting Ryder," she said, stalling for time. Chip Marx was inching them away from the crowd and closer to the shadows where no one could see what he was up to. "And number two, he should be returning with our drinks at any moment. Do you really want him to see you with your hand on me again?"

"Too late," Ryder said from behind her.

A mixture of relief and dread coursed through her. She was relieved that Ryder had arrived before the man had a chance to drag her into the shadows, but if she had thought his voice sounded dangerous the first time

Chip Marx had grabbed her, it was nothing compared to the deadliness in his deep baritone now.

"Ryder, I'm sure Mr. Marx was leaving," she said, hoping to avoid a confrontation.

"No, I wasn't," Marx said, showing that he was every bit as stupid as she suspected. "And I'm not going to let the likes of him keep me from getting to know you better."

Marx suddenly released his hold on her and, shoving her to the side, took a swing at Ryder. Easily dodging the man's doubled fist, Ryder's punch was forceful, accurate and very effective. Chip Marx fell to the dirt like a discarded rag doll and as Ryder had promised the man the first time he grabbed her, two of his once sparkling white teeth, now bloody and broken, lay on the ground beside him.

Ryder immediately took her in his arms. "Are you all right?"

Nodding slowly, she hitched in a breath as she stared down at Chip Marx. She didn't like seeing anyone hurt, but she had no doubt that if Ryder hadn't arrived when he did, Marx would have dragged her off into the shadows and... She didn't even want to think about what he might have done.

"I was frightened, but I didn't want him to see it. I'm glad you showed up when you did." Glancing up, Summer wasn't prepared for the look of abject misery on Ryder's handsome face. "Are you all right?" When he remained silent as he continued to stare down at Marx's limp body, she started to become alarmed. "Ryder?"

It took a moment for him to finally look at her. "I

didn't want to have to do that," he said, his voice rough with emotion.

Summer shook her head. "He really didn't give you a lot of choice."

"We saw the whole thing and Summer's right, bro."

Looking up at the sound of the male voice, Summer was glad to see Nate and Jaron jogging toward them.

"It isn't your fault there's no cure for stupid," Jaron said, kneeling beside Marx. He took off his black Resistol and fanned it over Marx's face to help bring him around. "It was a case of punch or be punched, Ryder."

"I agree," an unfamiliar voice said. As Summer watched, a security guard hurried over to join them. "Are you all right, ma'am?"

"I'm fine," she answered.

"I saw the whole thing and it was self-defense. Plain and simple." The uniformed man shook his head as they watched Marx begin to stir. "When I saw him accost this little lady, I was trying to get over here to intervene, but I couldn't get through the crowd fast enough." The older man looked directly at Ryder. "To tell you the truth, I admire your restraint, son. If the bastard had grabbed my woman the way he did yours, I'd probably still be pounding on his worthless hide."

"We probably need to call the police and make a report," Ryder said, taking a deep breath. Nothing any of the other men had said seemed to be able to ease the morose expression on Ryder's face.

"Don't worry about it," the security guard said, pointing to a camera mounted on one of the pavilion rafters. "I've got the whole thing on tape and you can give me your name and where you can be reached in case the police get involved." He chuckled. "But it's my guess that once this fellow is fully conscious and he sees the video I'm going to show him, he won't be all that eager about getting the police in on this. If he does, he's going to be facing assault charges for man-handling the lady."

Once Ryder had given the guard the information he asked for, he turned to her. "Are you ready to go back to the trailer?"

Summer didn't have to think twice about her answer. "Yes."

Her concern increased when she glanced at Nate and Jaron. They looked just as concerned as she was.

"We'll talk to you when we meet up at the rodeo in Las Cruces a few days from now," Nate said, helping Jaron haul Chip Marx to his feet. "Hang in there, Ryder. You didn't have a choice."

As she and Ryder walked the short distance to the camping area, Summer realized that he was still deeply affected by the incident and didn't seem to be able to shake it off. "Are you all right?" she asked when he unlocked the door and they entered the trailer. "Please talk to me, Ryder."

"I'll be okay," he said, reaching for her after they both had removed their boots and left them in the hall-way. He held her close as if she were a lifeline and it scared her more than his obvious anguish over the in-cident. "I don't want you to be afraid of me, Summer. I swear with everything that's in me that I'd die before I ever hurt you in any way."

Leaning back, she cupped his lean cheeks with her palms. "It never crossed my mind that you would."

Sensing that he wouldn't allow himself to believe her, she tried to think of something that would convince him of her unwavering trust in him. Unable to think of anything she could say to persuade him, she took him by the hand and led him up the steps to the bedroom. Words might not be adequate enough to prove her confidence in him, but actions might.

When they stopped at the side of the bed, Summer turned on the bedside lamp. "Ryder, I need you."

"Summer, I don't think this is a good idea..."

"I do," she said, reaching to unbutton her turquoise blouse. "If you won't believe me when I tell you how much faith I have in you, then I'm going to show you."

All things considered, she was a bit surprised by the strength in her own voice. But as she stared up at Ryder, she realized it was true. She not only needed to show him that there wasn't a single aspect of their relationship that she wasn't completely sure of or comfortable with, she needed to help him restore his faith in himself.

As she removed the silk garment and reached for the front clasp of her bra, she watched a spark of hunger ignite in the depths of his green eyes. "Darlin', I don't want you doing something that you aren't ready for."

"I've never been more ready for anything in my entire life," she said, sliding the straps of the silk and lace down her arms.

Rewarded by his rough groan, she looked up to see that the spark in his eyes had ignited into a flame of deep need. Quickly unzipping her jeans before she lost her nerve, she slid them and her panties down her thighs, then stepping out of them, shoved them in the direction of the rest of her clothes.

Summer had thought she might feel some degree of apprehension, but as she stood before Ryder, an emotion unlike anything she had ever experienced before began to fill her. She wasn't just showing him her trust and faith in him, she was laying herself bare both physically and emotionally. She loved Ryder with all her heart and soul and she needed for him to know it.

"You're beautiful," he said, his voice filled with awe.

Reaching for the snaps on his shirt, she made quick work of the closures, then shoved the chambray off his shoulders and tossed it on top of her clothes. "So are you, cowboy," she said, placing her hands on his warm flesh.

He closed his eyes and took a deep breath. When he opened them, he stepped back to take off the rest of his clothes, then reached over to pull her into his arms. The feel of his hard body pressed intimately to hers caused Summer's knees to give way and she had to hold on to his biceps to keep from melting into a puddle at his feet.

"I don't want to scare you, but I need you more right now than I need my next breath," he said, his voice raw with desire.

Without thinking twice, Summer got into bed and held her arms up in invitation. "Make love to me, Ryder."

When he lay down beside her, he immediately wrapped his arms around her and covered her mouth with his. There was a desperation in his kiss, an urgency that she ached to ease.

Moving his lips over hers, then down to the slope of her breast, his mouth closed over her beaded nipple. Writhing with pleasure, she tangled her fingers in the sheets as the sensations he created inside of her threatened to consume her. She felt as if she might burst into flames from the wave of heat sweeping through her when he slid his calloused palm over her abdomen to the most feminine part of her...and she knew she needed him as desperately as he needed her.

"Please make love...to me...Ryder," she gasped as she reached to find him. Stroking him, she wanted him to feel the same excitement, the same hungry anticipation that swirled within her.

She watched him close his eyes and swallow hard as he struggled for control. But when he started to pull her on top of him, she shook her head as she kissed her way down along his strong jaw to his chest, then the thick pads of his pectoral muscles.

"I want to feel you...surround me," she said, lying back against the pillow.

A groan rumbled up from deep in his chest as he nudged her knees apart and settled himself over her. Without hesitation, Summer guided him to her and as she enveloped him with her warmth, her heart felt as if it might burst from the overwhelming emotion filling her. She loved him with every fiber of her being and knew without question that she always would.

When Ryder began to move against her, she welcomed the feeling of his larger body covering hers, making her feel as if she truly had become part of him. But all too soon the urgency of their passion took control and she found herself poised on the edge. Apparently attuned to her needs, he increased the rhythm and depth of the pace he'd set and she suddenly felt herself released from the tension holding her captive. Pleasure, sweet and pure, flowed from the top of her head to the soles of her feet and when Ryder surged into her one final time, it felt as if their souls united.

When he collapsed on top of her, she held him to her and in that moment, she knew without question that she was forever his.

"Are you all right?" he asked as he levered himself to her side.

"I've never been better," she said truthfully. She wanted to tell him she loved him, but she wasn't sure he was ready for that. Instead, she snuggled against him and sighed with contentment. "That was absolutely incredible."

"You're incredible," he said, kissing her until they both gasped for breath.

He held her tightly to him and they were both silent for some time before he finally released her. Clearing his throat, his gaze didn't quite meet hers when he spoke. "I almost forgot to tell you. I got a call from my foreman this afternoon just before the bull riding event. You're going to have to go on to Las Cruces without me. I have to head home tomorrow."

The finality in his voice had her sitting up to tuck the sheet under her arms to cover her breasts. "Is something wrong at the ranch? Is Betty Lou all right? Do you need me to go back with you?"

"No. Betty Lou is fine. It's just ranch stuff. I can handle it." He sat up on the side of the bed and reached for his clothes. "The first thing in the morning, I'll arrange for a charter flight to take you down to Las Cruces."

Her heart seemed to come to a complete halt. "Do you have any idea when you'll be coming back to work?"

Shaking his head, he got to his feet to pull up his jeans. "No."

"Ryder, what's going on?" she asked, tugging the sheet loose to wrap around her as she got out of bed. She had never seen him so stoic or as unwilling to talk to her.

When he turned to face her, she detected a sadness in his eyes that sent a chill up her spine. He quickly shuttered the emotion, replacing it with a look of determination. "Do I really have to spell it out for you, Summer? It was nice while it lasted, but this is over. We're over."

She stared at him in total shock for a moment before she shook her head. "What brought this on? Surely that run-in with Chip Marx—"

"I've changed my mind," he said, cutting her off. "I won't be able to help you with your plan to have a baby after all."

She couldn't believe what was happening. How could everything have fallen apart so fast? And why?

"Don't I even deserve an explanation?" she asked, fighting to keep her emotions under control.

She needed to keep her wits about her in order to

think. Something was going on with him, but for the life of her she couldn't think of what it might be.

"Let's face facts, darlin'. I'm just not cut out to be a daddy and we were only fooling ourselves thinking that I was." He started toward the door. "But now that you've overcome your fears, I'm sure you'll be able to find someone you can settle down with and have a whole houseful of kids."

"Is that…what you really want?" she asked, following him. She hated that she couldn't keep the anguish out of her voice.

"Sure, darlin'." He smiled, but there was a sadness about it that brought tears to her eyes. "Remember? I'm your friend. All I've ever wanted was for you to be happy."

"Where are you going now?" she prodded, desperately trying to think of some way to get him to open up and tell her what was really wrong. She certainly wasn't buying his story that he had changed his mind. He couldn't have made such tender, exquisite love to her and not have it mean anything.

"I'm going out for a while," he said, descending the steps into the main part of the camper. "I don't know what time I'll be back, so don't bother waiting up."

When she watched the door close behind him, Summer felt as if a band tightened around her chest. Why was Ryder shutting her out? Why wouldn't he talk to her?

Tears streamed down her cheeks as she retraced her steps up to the bedroom and sat on the side of the bed. She had never seen him like this. He wasn't the same man she had known and been best friends with for the past few years, the one she trusted above all others. The cowboy she loved.

The man who had just broken her heart was a complete stranger to her.

Nine

Ryder stopped grooming the bay and propped his forearms on the gelding's back to stare at the brush in his hand like it might hold a solution to his problems. After he dropped Summer off at the airport, he had called the rodeo association office and taken an extended leave from his contract commitment with them in order to regain his perspective. But he had been home for a week and his mood still hadn't changed for the better. He was miserable and apparently, without even trying, he was making those around him just as unhappy as he was.

It wasn't that he was irritable and lashed out at anyone. That wasn't his style. Hell, most of the time he tried to keep to himself, either in his office or by taking a ride down to the canyon. But Betty Lou had been hard to avoid. She'd quit at least three times yesterday and once today because she said he was too depressing to be around. Even Lucifer seemed to sense something was wrong and instead of hissing and spitting at him, the cat had rubbed up against Ryder's leg a couple of times as if trying to console him.

But there was nothing anyone could say or do that was going to change the facts. He was here at the Blue Canyon Ranch and Summer was out somewhere on the rodeo circuit. Without him.

Telling her that things were over between them and that he had changed his mind about having a baby with her had been the hardest thing he'd ever had to do in his entire life. But when he lost his temper with Chip Marx and knocked the guy out, it had scared the living hell out of him. All he had been able to think about was the last time he'd thrown a punch in anger. Pete Ledbetter had died because of it and although Ryder had only meant to defend himself and his foster mother, his actions had ended up killing the man. And even if it had been an accident, there was no excuse for it. No one had the right to take another's life.

He wasn't overly proud of the way he handled things that night with Summer either. After punching out Marx, he had realized that he had to let her go, had to let her find happiness with a man who didn't have the kind of baggage he would carry for the rest of his life. But he'd ended up being selfish. He'd had to make love to her one last time before he stepped aside to let her get on with her life, needed to store up one more memory of making love to the woman who would always own him heart and soul.

When his cell phone rang, Ryder groaned. Summer

hadn't tried calling him, but his brothers had. In fact, all five of them had called him at least once a day and sometimes more than that after they learned he had taken a leave of absence from his bullfighting duties on the rodeo circuit.

He knew Nate and Jaron had spread the word about the unfortunate incident and they were all concerned about him. They knew the hell he'd gone through as a teenager as he came to terms with Pete Ledbetter's death and his fear of something like that ever happening again. But as much as they meant to him and as close as they all had been since their days at the Last Chance Ranch, they were the last people he wanted to talk to. He didn't need to hear them tell him that he was making a mountain out of a molehill—or that he was selling Summer short by not telling her about his past and letting her decide for herself what was best.

The bottom line was, he knew he'd done the right thing. They would do well to respect that and leave him alone.

When the phone chirped again he checked the caller ID. His housekeeper probably wanted to tell him she was quitting again.

"What's up, Betty Lou?"

"I think you better come up to the house," she said, sounding a little shaky.

He immediately tossed the brush aside and started toward the barn's double door. "What's wrong?"

"We've got a bit of a situation that you're going to have to handle," she said evasively. "You'd better get up here to the house, pronto."

He'd never heard Betty Lou sound so distressed. "I'm on my way."

The first thing he did as he sprinted across the barnyard was check to see if there was smoke billowing from the house. There wasn't. At least the house wasn't on fire. Then he wondered if Betty Lou had somehow hurt herself. She might have cut herself with a knife while making supper or fallen off the little step stool she used to reach the top shelves in the pantry.

All sorts of disasters ran through his mind and by the time he reached the house, Ryder took the porch steps two at a time. "Betty Lou, are you okay?" he shouted as he jerked open the kitchen door.

Instead of finding Betty Lou bleeding profusely or cradling a broken arm from taking a fall, all five of his brothers sat at the kitchen table, their coffee cups raised in an obviously staged greeting. "Ah, hell," he muttered, glaring at them. He hadn't seen even one of their trucks. If he had, he would have taken off in the opposite direction. "Where did you park?"

"On the other side of the equipment shed," Nate said, grinning.

"We figured you couldn't ignore us if we used the element of surprise," Sam added.

"That was my idea," T.J. chimed in, looking particularly proud of himself.

"And you went along with it, Betty Lou," Ryder accused. "I should fire you for being a traitor."

Unconcerned, Betty Lou shrugged as she turned to stir a big pot on top of the stove. "You can't. I already quit this morning."

"Why don't we get out of Betty Lou's way and go into your office?" Lane suggested, rising from his chair at the table.

"I'd rather not," Ryder said even as he followed his brothers down the hall.

"You know why we're here don't you?" Jaron asked as they filed into the room.

"Yeah, you've dropped by to give me hell over breaking it off with Summer," he said, lowering himself into the chair behind his desk. "But I didn't expect you all to turn it into an intervention."

"It wouldn't have been if you'd taken any of our calls," Sam said as he took a seat on the leather couch.

Fortunately, the office was big enough that the decorator included a couch, as well as the two armchairs in front of his desk. Or maybe in this case, that was unfortunate. There was more than enough room for all of his brothers to sit comfortably while they pointed out the error of his ways.

Glowering at them, he shook his head. "While I appreciate your concern, there's no reason for it. I'll be okay."

"Can it, bro," Jaron spoke up. "If you'll remember, Nate and I were there. We saw how the incident affected you."

"That arrogant bastard didn't give you a choice," Nate added. "He started it and all you did was end it. You were only defending Summer and yourself."

"Yeah and any one of us would have done the same thing," Sam agreed. "If some son of a bitch tried anything like that with Bria, I'd probably have done a whole lot more than just knock out a couple of his teeth."

"A real man doesn't treat a woman like that." T.J. shook his head adamantly. "The jerk needed to be taught a lesson."

"Yeah, but I'd have given anything not to have to be the one teaching the class," Ryder groused.

"How do you feel about what happened?" Lane asked, looking pensive.

Ryder glared at his brother. "Put your psychology degree away, Donaldson. I don't need analysis. I'll be fine."

"Take it from me, you won't be okay until you've talked about it with Summer," Sam advised. "I had to learn my lesson the hard way. Don't be me, Ryder. Don't wait until it's almost too late and you come close to losing her."

Ryder stared at his brother. Sam's stubborn pride had damned near cost him and Bria their marriage and it wasn't until Sam had been injured in an accident that he woke up and realized how much he had to lose. But he and Summer weren't married and it would be easier for him to do the right thing and walk away from her now than it would be later on. He couldn't bear telling her about his past and then watch disillusionment fill her pretty blue eyes when she realized that he wasn't the man she thought him to be.

Before he could set Sam straight and remind him that their situations were different, Lane looked him square in the eye. "Ask yourself what the outcome would have been if you hadn't intervened—both times. Could you have lived with yourself if you'd stood by and let Led-better beat his wife to death? Could you have watched Marx while he manhandled Summer and done nothing to stop him?" Checking his watch, he rose to his feet. "I hate to cut this short, but I have an appointment." Turning to the others, he added, "And I believe we've given Ryder a few things he needs to think over."

Watching his brothers file out of the office, Ryder grimaced. One thing about it, his brothers didn't pull any punches. No matter how painful the truth was, they were nothing if not honest with each other.

But they didn't know the whole situation. They weren't aware that Summer had an unshakable belief that he was something he wasn't. She was convinced that he was forthright and incapable of doing any real harm to anyone. The thought of having her find out differently made him feel sick to his stomach.

He would give everything he had to be that man for her. But he couldn't and nothing he could say or do was ever going to change that. He couldn't go back and re-write his past any more than he could stop the sun from rising in the east each morning.

Unable to sit still, he stalked out of the office and headed back to the barn to saddle the bay. As he rode out of the ranch yard and across the pasture toward the canyon, he knew in his heart that he'd done what was best for her.

His run-in with Marx had turned out all right and had that been the only time he'd had to raise his fists to defend someone, he might feel differently about things.

But he loved Summer too much to saddle her with his youthful mistakes…and a past that he couldn't erase.

Several hours after his brothers left the ranch, Ryder sat beneath the cottonwood tree and watched the breeze cause ripples in the lazy little stream as he tried to figure out what he was going to do with the rest of his life. He couldn't go back to playing chicken with a ton of pissed-off beef. Eventually his and Summer's paths would cross at some rodeo and it would kill him to see her with another man. And there wasn't a doubt in his mind that's exactly what would happen. She was too pretty, too vivacious and full of life not to have a string of men just waiting for the chance to gain her attention.

Leaning back against the tree, he stared up at the gold-colored leaves. His brothers had meant well when they advised him to tell Summer about his past and leave it up to her to decide what was best. But they didn't understand. They had all been in trouble for one thing or another, but robbing a store or running a con game wasn't the same as being responsible for someone's death.

Lost in his own misery, it took a moment for Ryder to realize that someone was approaching on horseback. It was probably one of his men coming to check on the pasture conditions at the far end of the canyon he decided as he got to his feet.

When he looked up, his heart lurched as he watched Summer ride the buckskin mare over beside his bay gelding. Dismounting, she ground tied the horse, then started walking toward him.

"What are you doing here?" he asked, not entirely sure he wasn't dreaming.

From the determined expression on her pretty face, he could tell she was angry. "You owe me an explanation…and I'm not leaving until I get it."

It was all he could do not to take her in his arms and kiss her senseless when she sauntered up to stand in front of him. But that would only further complicate matters. And God only knew everything was complicated enough.

"I don't know what you think I need to explain." It was a barefaced lie. He knew damned good and well what she wanted to know, but it wasn't something she would want to hear.

"Give me a break, cowboy," she said, propping her hands on her shapely hips. "I thought friends were honest with each other."

He took in some much-needed air, then slowly released it. "I'm sorry, darlin', but I don't think I can be your friend anymore."

Her pretty blue eyes narrowed. "Why not?"

"I think you already know the answer to that," he hedged. Why couldn't she just let it go?

"Don't assume that I know anything for certain." Her stubborn little chin was set and he'd seen that expression on her lovely face one too many times not to know that hell would freeze over before she gave up. "I was confident we were best friends and now it appears that's over. I want to know the reason why you ended our friendship. You owe me that much."

Lowering himself to sit at the base of the tree, he shrugged. "We crossed a line and made love."

"I'm well aware of that," she said, sitting on the grass in front of him. "In fact, we crossed that line several times."

"Dammit, Summer, I know how irresistible you are, how responsive," he said, taking off his hat to run his hand over the tension building at the back of his neck. "I can't go back to seeing you every day and not being able to make love to you."

"Who said you had to?" she pressed.

"The deal was that we would make love until you became pregnant," he stated flatly.

"That's true, but that was before," she said, shrugging.

Good Lord she was driving him nuts and she probably didn't even realize it. Or maybe she did and she was determined to make him pay for his transgressions.

"Before what?"

Her expression softened. "Before we fell in love."

She couldn't have shocked him more if she'd tried. "You think we're in love?"

"No, I don't think we are," she said, shaking her head. "I know we are. And I'm here to find out why you're trying to throw away what we have together."

He closed his eyes against the gut-wrenching pain knifing through him. She loved the man she thought he was, not who he really was. In that moment he knew she'd forced his hand and he was going to have to tell her the one thing that would end things between them for good.

"Summer, I'm no good for you," he said, feeling like he had the weight of the world resting on his shoulders. "I'm no good for any woman."

Her honey-blond ponytail swung back and forth as she shook her head. "That's a bunch of garbage. You're the most honest, trustworthy man I've ever known."

"No, I'm not." He took a deep breath. "I haven't been honest with you. I've got a past and it isn't a pretty one, darlin'. You're better off not knowing what I've done."

She met his gaze head-on. "Why don't you tell me about it and let me be the judge of that?"

A knot formed deep in his gut. He was about to see the confidence in her eyes turn to disillusionment and then revulsion. But it was the only way he could convince her that she would be better off without him in her life.

"You know I was a foster kid and finished growing up at the Last Chance Ranch." When she nodded, he swallowed hard. "Do you really want to know why I was sent there?"

"Yes, if that will explain why you think you're not good enough to be in a relationship with me when we both know we're in love."

"I killed a man." Just saying the words caused the knot to twist painfully. "I didn't mean to, but I did."

Her sharp intake of breath made him feel like a piece of his soul had been ripped apart. "My God, Ryder. What happened?"

Telling her about his drunken foster father and the man's habit of beating his wife, Ryder stared down at his balled fists. "When he started to take another swing at my foster mother, I stepped between them. That just pissed him off even more and he drew back to punch me. Because he was drunk he wasn't as steady on his feet and when my fist landed along his jaw, he fell backward." Ryder took a deep breath as the memory of old Pete lying on the floor in a pool of blood ran through his mind. "He hit his head on the kitchen counter, and the next thing I knew he was dead and I was being hauled off to jail and charged with manslaughter."

"That's why you reacted the way you did after that confrontation with Chip Marx, isn't it?" she guessed.

He nodded. "That brought back a lot of bad memories."

"Oh, Ryder, I'm so sorry you had to go through that," she said, surprising him when she rose to her knees to put her arms around him. "But you're being too hard on yourself. Don't you see that the altercation with Marx wasn't your fault any more than it was with your foster father? Both times you were only defending yourself."

"It doesn't bother you that a man died because of me?" he asked, unable to believe she could accept what he'd done.

"Yes, I'm bothered that it happened, but not for the reason you're thinking," she said, cupping his face with her soft palms. "I'm disturbed by the idea that the man tried to hurt you and because of that you've been left feeling that you've done something terribly wrong." She kissed him lovingly. "Yes, it was tragic that the man died, but it was an accident. It's in the past and there's nothing you can do to change that. Don't you think you've punished yourself long enough?"

Wrapping his arms around her, he held her close as he felt a drop of moisture trickle down his cheek. "I can't forget what happened."

Her arms tightened around him. "I'm not saying you should forget. I'm telling you that you didn't do anything wrong and that it's time to stop blaming yourself for the choices other people made. You need to accept and forgive yourself for an unfortunate accident that was out of your control."

Ryder felt free for the first time in years. He wasn't responsible for the actions of others, and although he regretted what happened all those years ago, Summer was right. He needed to look forward instead of living his life regretting the past.

"Did you mean it, Summer?" he asked suddenly.

She looked confused. "What?"

"You said we fell in love." He looked into her crystalline blue eyes. "Do you really love me, darlin'?"

Her smile caused his chest to swell with emotion. "Absolutely. I love you with all my heart and soul, Ryder McClain. You're my best friend and the love of my life. That's something else that you need to accept that's never going to change."

A lump the size of his fist clogged his throat. "Thank God! I love you more than life itself."

Kissing her until he thought they both might pass out from a lack of oxygen, he asked, "Will you marry me, Summer? I want to be the man you go to bed with every night and wake up with every morning. My family will be yours and we'll start our own with a whole houseful of babies." He smiled. "I give you my word, you'll never be alone again. I'll be with you until the day I die."

To his relief, there wasn't a moment's hesitation in her answer. "Yes." Her smile was the sweetest he had ever seen. "But there's something I need to tell you, cowboy."

Holding her to his chest, he kissed the top of her head then the tip of her nose. "What's that, darlin'?"

"I'm thrilled I'll finally be part of a big family," she said, giving him a watery smile. "And just so you know, you were right about those swimmers."

Ryder frowned. "What are you talking about?"

"We've already started on that houseful of babies," she said, grinning.

He felt his heart come to a complete halt, then start thumping hard against his ribs. "You're pregnant?"

"I haven't seen a doctor yet, but the test I bought at the pharmacy says I am," she said, nodding.

He couldn't stop grinning. "It looks like Bria's sister, Mariah, and Jaron will have two reasons to argue about babies and whether they'll be boys or girls."

When she touched his cheek, he felt like the luckiest man in the entire world. "I love you, cowboy."

"And I love you, darlin'." He rose to his feet, then held out his hand to help her up. When she placed her hand in his, he felt as if he'd been handed a rare and precious gift. "Let's go back to the house. We have a few phone calls to make."

"Your brothers?" she asked.

He laughed. "I can't remember the last time I knew something about myself that they didn't know first."

Epilogue

"I'm telling you, they'll both be girls, Jaron Lambert," Mariah insisted.

Jaron stubbornly shook his head. "And I'm telling *you,* they're going to be boys."

Ryder stood with his brothers, watching Mariah and Jaron debate the gender of the babies Summer and Bria were going to have. "Do you think it's crossed their minds that we might have one of each?"

Sam shrugged as he took a swig of beer from the bottle in his hand. "I doubt it. I don't think it matters to either one of them what sex the babies are. They just like to argue."

"So who's next?" T.J. asked, grinning like a fool.

"Next for what?" Nate asked, distracted. He had his eye on a willowy redhead across the dance floor, and

Ryder was glad to see that his brother had finally gotten over that little nurse up in Waco and was moving on.

"The next to get married, genius," T.J. shot back.

"My money is on you and that neighbor of yours, T.J.," Lane said with a grin.

"I keep telling you, I'd rather go buck naked for eight seconds on a porcupine than to take up with the likes of her," T.J. said, shaking his head. "She's still letting that stud of hers jump the fence and get with my mares."

Ryder blocked out his brother's complaints about his neighbor and the horse she couldn't seem to keep at home as he scanned the crowd, looking for his wife. When he spotted her in that gorgeous white wedding gown, he caught his breath. He doubted there would ever be a time that the sight of her didn't have that effect on him.

"It might be you, Lane," Ryder said, checking his watch. Another hour and it should be socially acceptable for him to take his bride and leave the wedding reception to start their honeymoon.

"Getting married isn't part of my life plan," Lane quipped. "The ranch I won last month in that poker game in Shreveport is as close to settling down as I intend to get."

They all looked at Nate for a moment. His attention had already turned from the redhead to a curvy brunette.

"That's a sucker bet if I ever saw one," Lane said, laughing.

"While you all carry on about who the next will be to take dip in the marital pool with me and Sam, I'm going to dance with my wife," Ryder announced, turning to walk across the dance floor.

When he approached Summer, her smile caused his body to tighten and he wished like hell they were already on that island in the Caribbean where they were spending their honeymoon. "Could I have this dance, darlin'?"

She placed her hand in the crook of his arm as she smiled up at him. "This one and all of the dances for the rest of my life."

"That's sounds like a good idea to me," he murmured, taking her in his arms. When she rested her head against his chest, he kissed her forehead. "Are you happy, Summer?"

"I've never been happier, Ryder." Leaning back to look up at him, the love shining in the depths of her eyes sent his hormones into overdrive. "You've given me every one of my dreams."

"And you've given me every one of mine, darlin'." He grinned. "All except for one."

"Which one is that?" she asked, clearly intrigued.

"As beautiful as you look in your wedding gown, when you were walking down the aisle toward me, all I could do was stand there and daydream about the moment I get to take it off you," he whispered close to her ear.

She shivered against him and he knew she was looking forward to starting their lives together as much as he was. "I've been dreaming about you doing that, too." Smiling, she kissed him tenderly. "I love you, cowboy."

"And I love you, darlin'." Grinning, he took her by

the hand and started toward the door. "Now, let's go somewhere a little more private and I'll see what I can do about making both of our dreams come true."

* * * * *

A sneaky peek at next month...

Desire

PASSIONATE AND DRAMATIC LOVE STORIES

My wish list for next month's titles...

In stores from 19th July 2013:

❏ Deep in a Texan's Heart – Sara Orwig

& Affairs of State – Jennifer Lewis

❏ His for the Taking – Ann Major

& His Instant Heir – Katherine Garbera

❏ Canyon – Brenda Jackson

& The Baby Deal – Kat Cantrell

2 stories in each book - only **£5.49!**

Available at WHSmith, Tesco, Asda, Eason, Amazon and Apple

Just can't wait?

Visit us Online

You can buy our books online a month before they hit the shops! **www.millsandboon.co.uk**

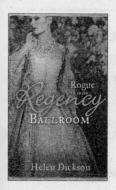

The World of Mills & Boon®

There's a Mills & Boon® series that's perfect for you. We publish ten series and, with new titles every month, you never have to wait long for your favourite to come along.

Blaze®
Scorching hot, sexy reads
4 new stories every month

By Request
Relive the romance with the best of the best
9 new stories every month

Cherish™
Romance to melt the heart every time
12 new stories every month

Desire™
Passionate and dramatic love stories
8 new stories every month